KAZE no HANA

Ushio Mizta Akiyoshi Ohta

1

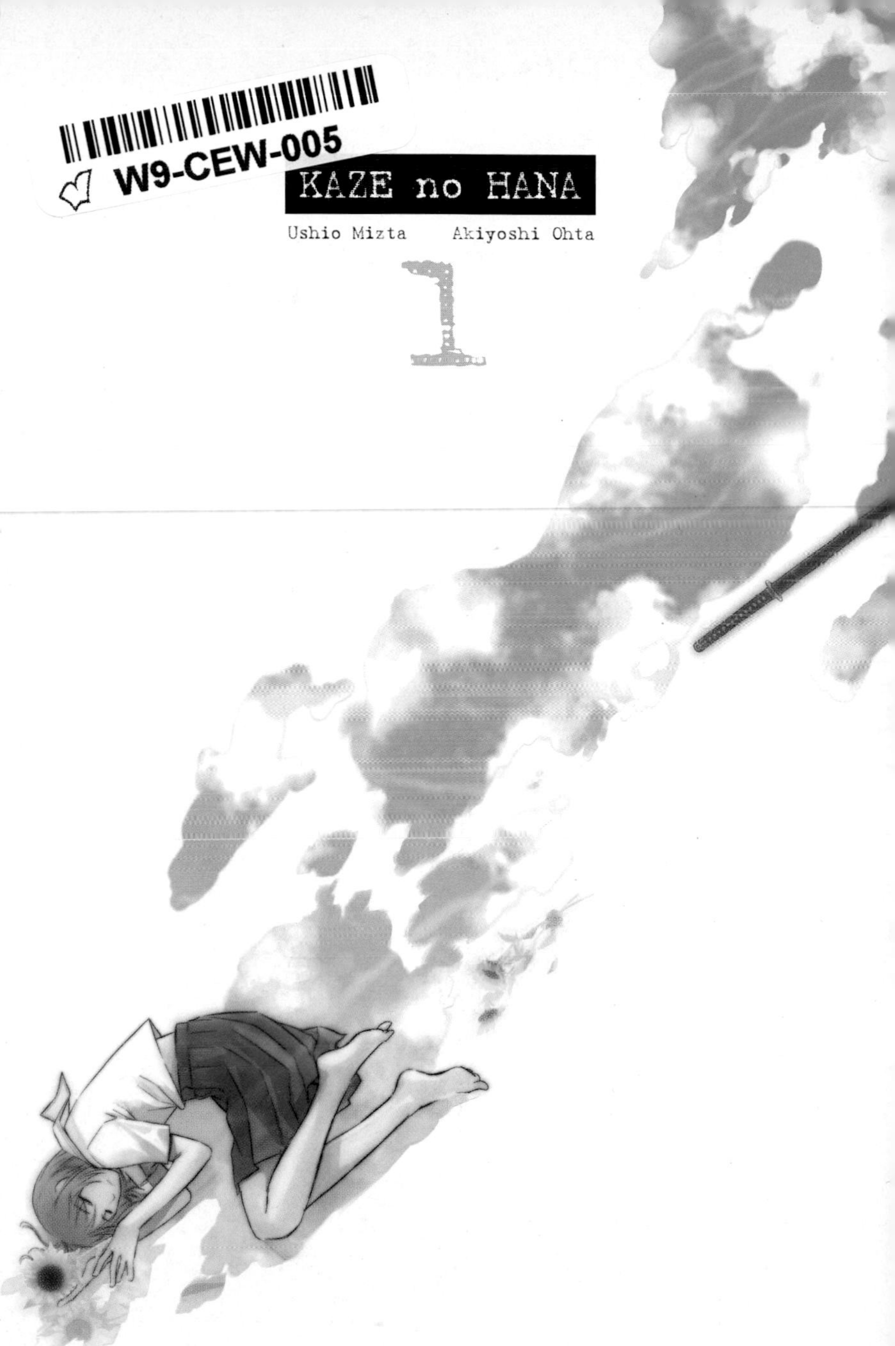

KAZE no HANA

1
Contents

LONG AGO, A FIERCE
DRAGON LIVED DEEP IN THE
MOUNTAINS OF SHINANO.

THAT DRAGON LOVED ITS PEOPLE SO
MUCH THAT IT COULD NOT FORGIVE THE
HEAVENLY GOD FOR PLAYING WITH THEIR
LIVES. THOUGH IT DEFEATED ITS NEMESIS
AFTER AN INTENSE BATTLE, IT PERISHED
AS WELL.

HOWEVER, CONTINUOUS MISFORTUNE LED
THE DRAGON TO DIVIDE ITS POWER INTO
EIGHT SWORDS, WHICH IT ENTRUSTED
TO ITS FOLLOWERS.

Excerpt from *Legends and Folklores of Mitsurugi City*,
Mitsurugi City Board of Education version

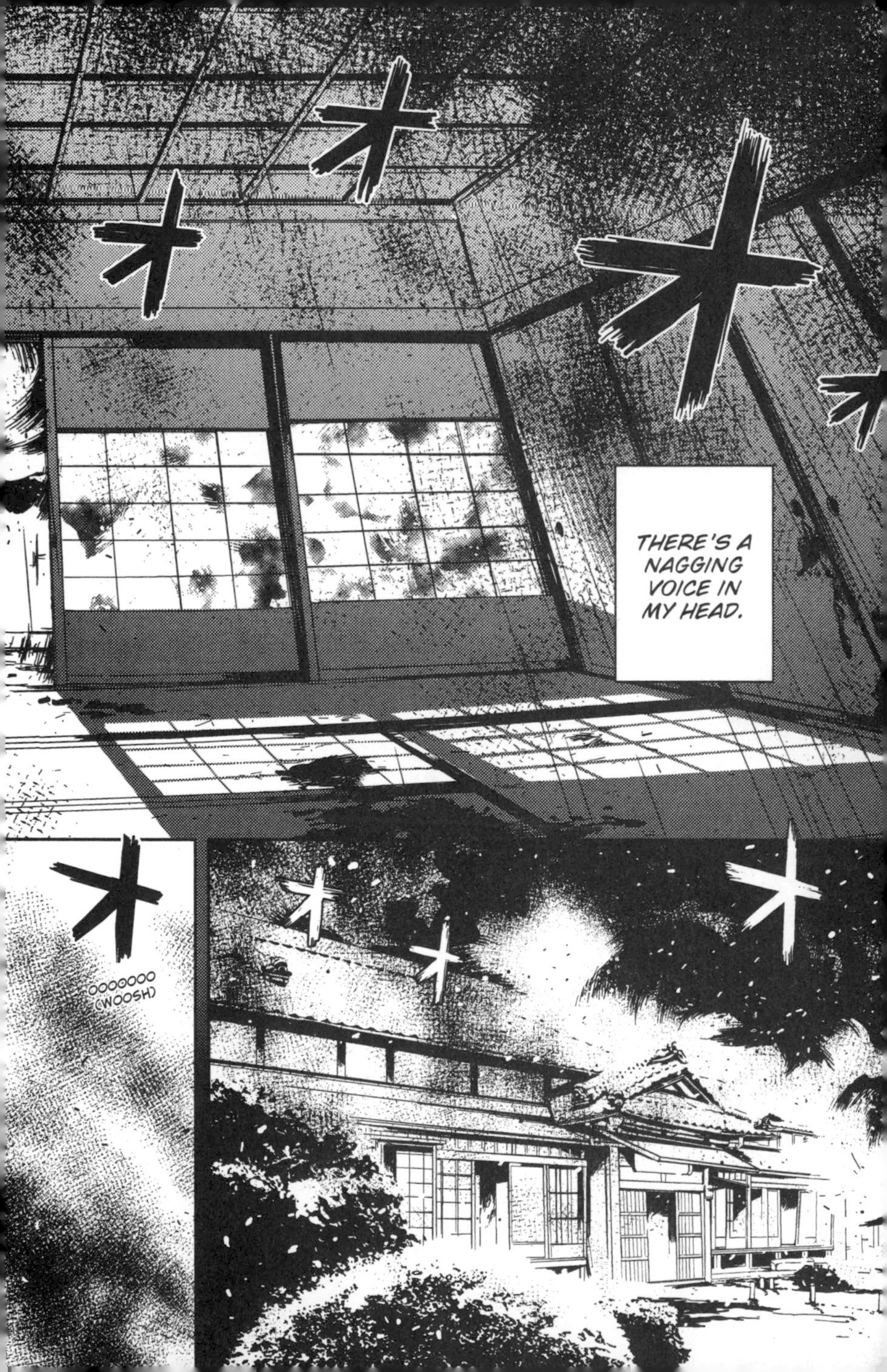
THERE'S A NAGGING VOICE IN MY HEAD.
OOOOOOO (WOOSH)

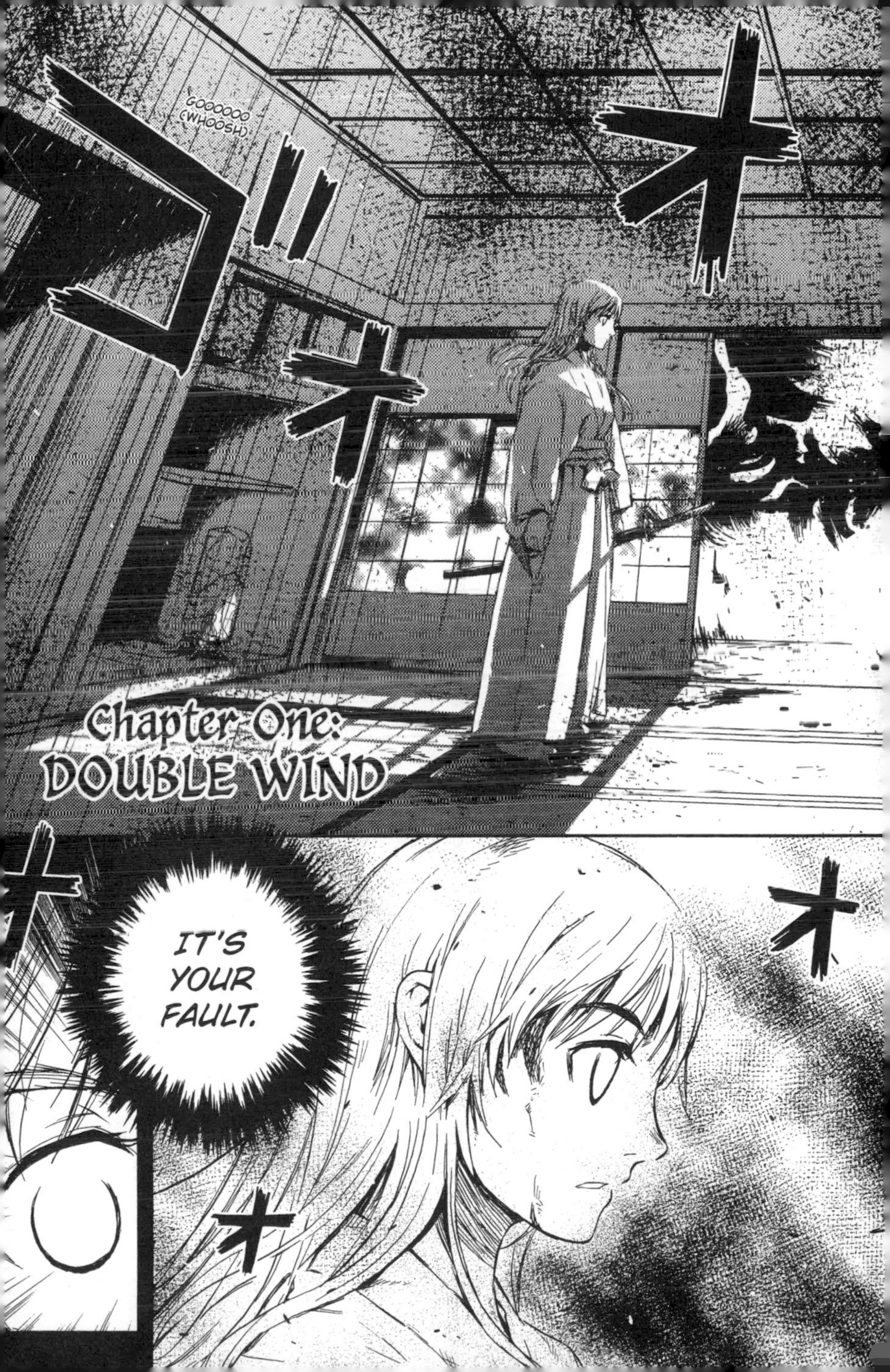
GOOOOOO
(WHOOSH)
Chapter One:
DOUBLE WIND
IT'S YOUR FAULT.

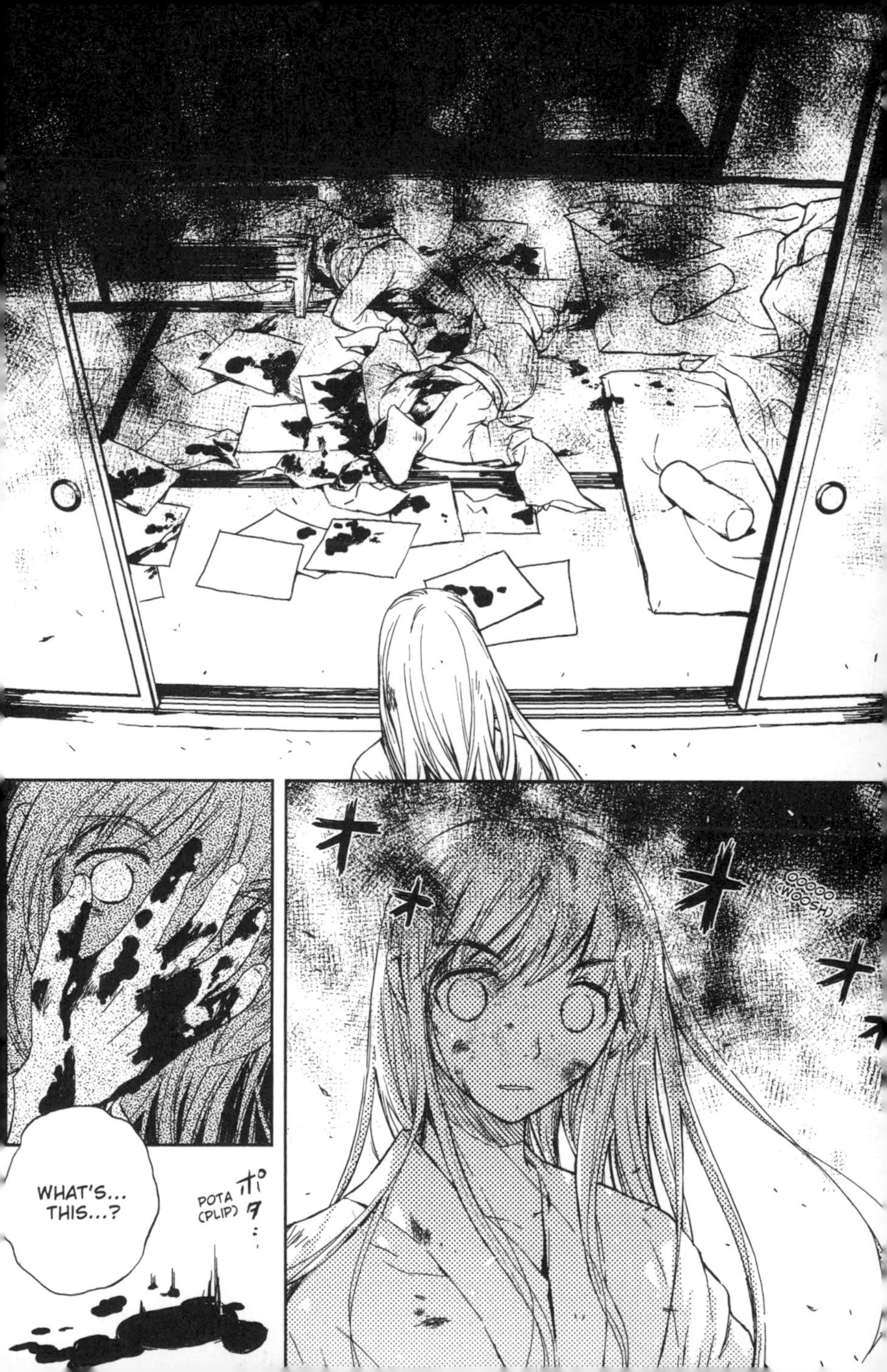
OOOOO
(WOOSH)
WHAT'S... THIS...?
POTA
(PLIP)

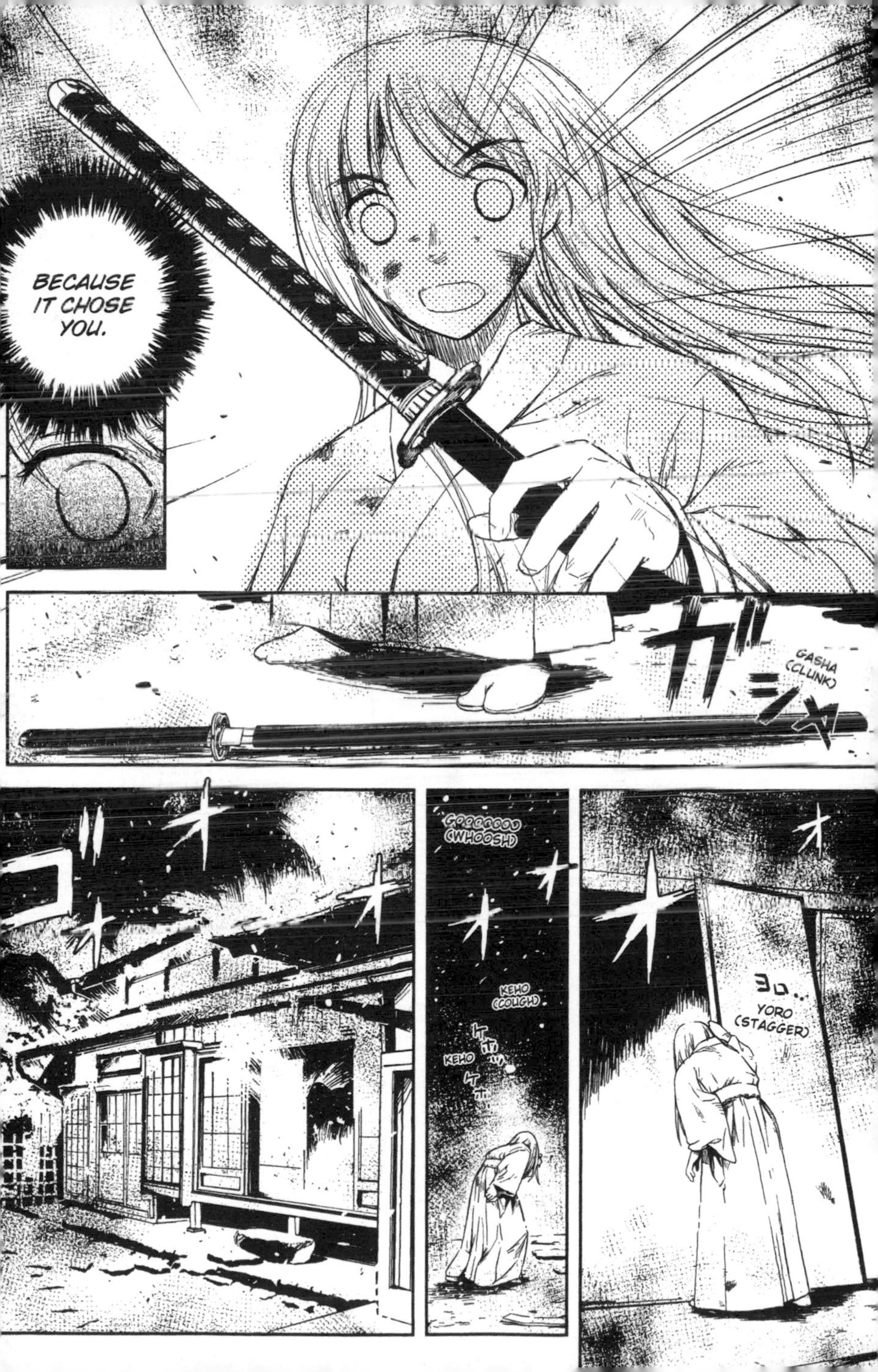
BECAUSE IT CHOSE YOU.
ガシャ
GASHA (CLUNK)
ヨロ…
YORO (STAGGER)
GOOOOOOO (WHOOSH)
KEHO (COUGH)
KEHO

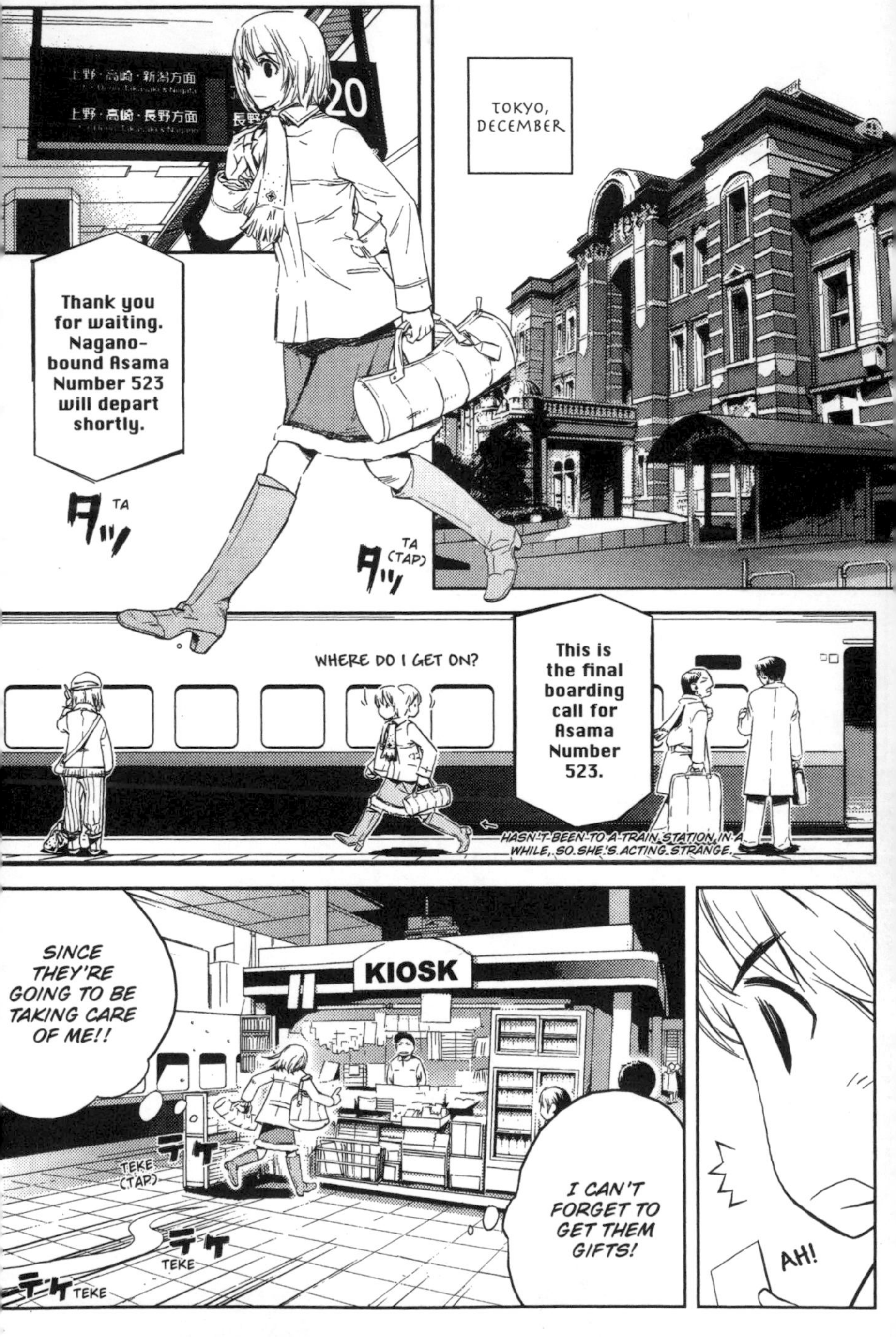
TOKYO, DECEMBER
上野・高崎・新潟方面
上野・高崎・長野方面
20
Thank you for waiting. Nagano-bound Asama Number 523 will depart shortly.
タッ TA
タッ TA (TAP)
This is the final boarding call for Asama Number 523.
WHERE DO I GET ON?
HASN'T BEEN TO A TRAIN STATION IN A WHILE, SO SHE'S ACTING STRANGE.
AH!
KIOSK
SINCE THEY'RE GOING TO BE TAKING CARE OF ME!!
I CAN'T FORGET TO GET THEM GIFTS!
テケ TEKE (TAP)
テケ TEKE
テケ TEKE

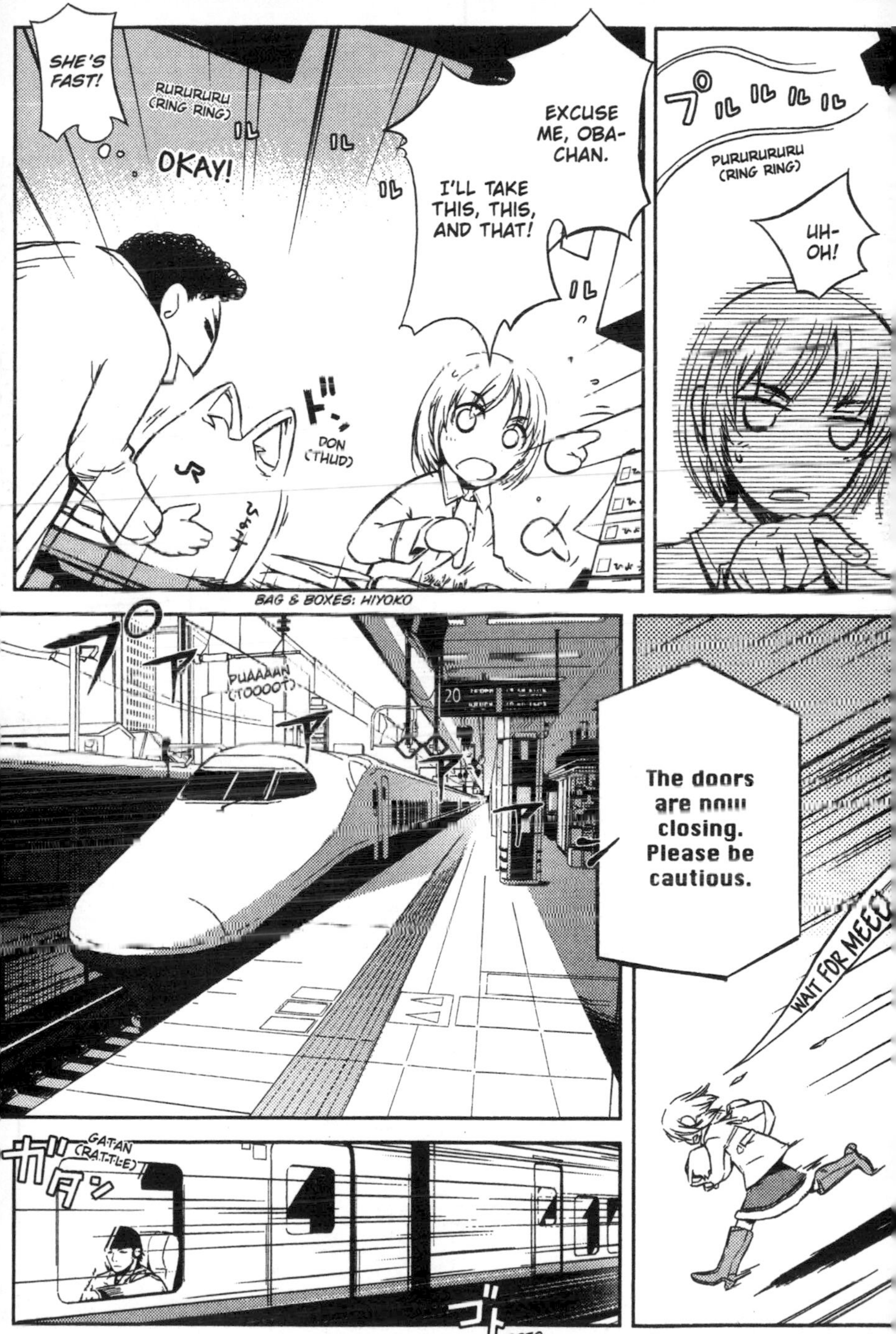
プルルルル
PURURURURU (RING RING)
UH-OH!
EXCUSE ME, OBA-CHAN.
I'LL TAKE THIS, THIS, AND THAT!
SHE'S FAST!
RURURURU (RING RING)
OKAY!
DON (THUD)
BAG & BOXES: HIYOKO
WAIT FOR MEE
The doors are now closing. Please be cautious.
PUAAAAN (TOOOOT)
GATAN (RATTLE)
GOTO (RATTLE)

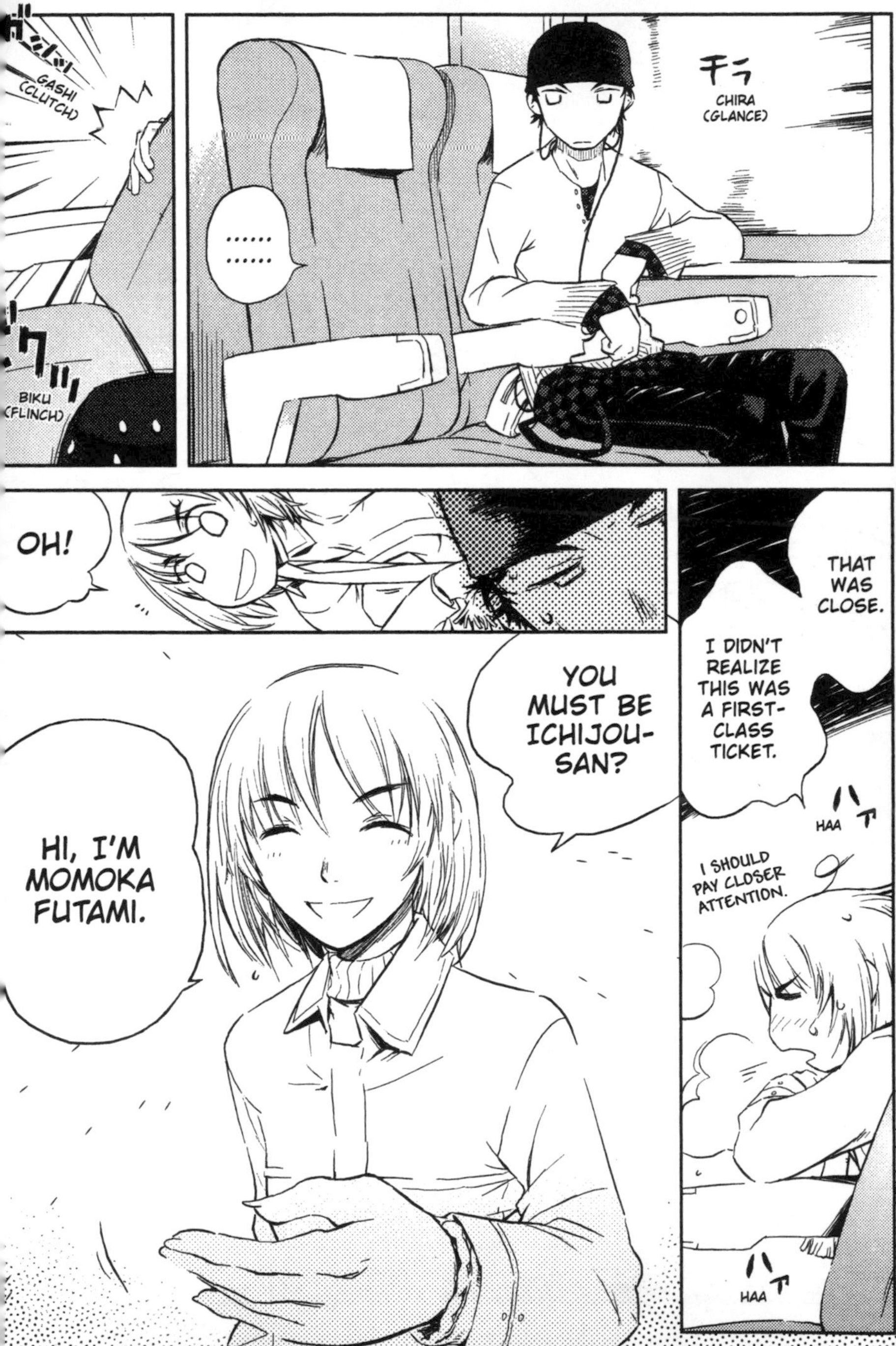

チラ
CHIRA (GLANCE)
....
GASHI (CLUTCH)
BIKU (FLINCH)
THAT WAS CLOSE.
I DIDN'T REALIZE THIS WAS A FIRST-CLASS TICKET.
ハア
HAA
I SHOULD PAY CLOSER ATTENTION.
ハア
HAA
OH!
YOU MUST BE ICHIJOU-SAN?
HI, I'M MOMOKA FUTAMI.

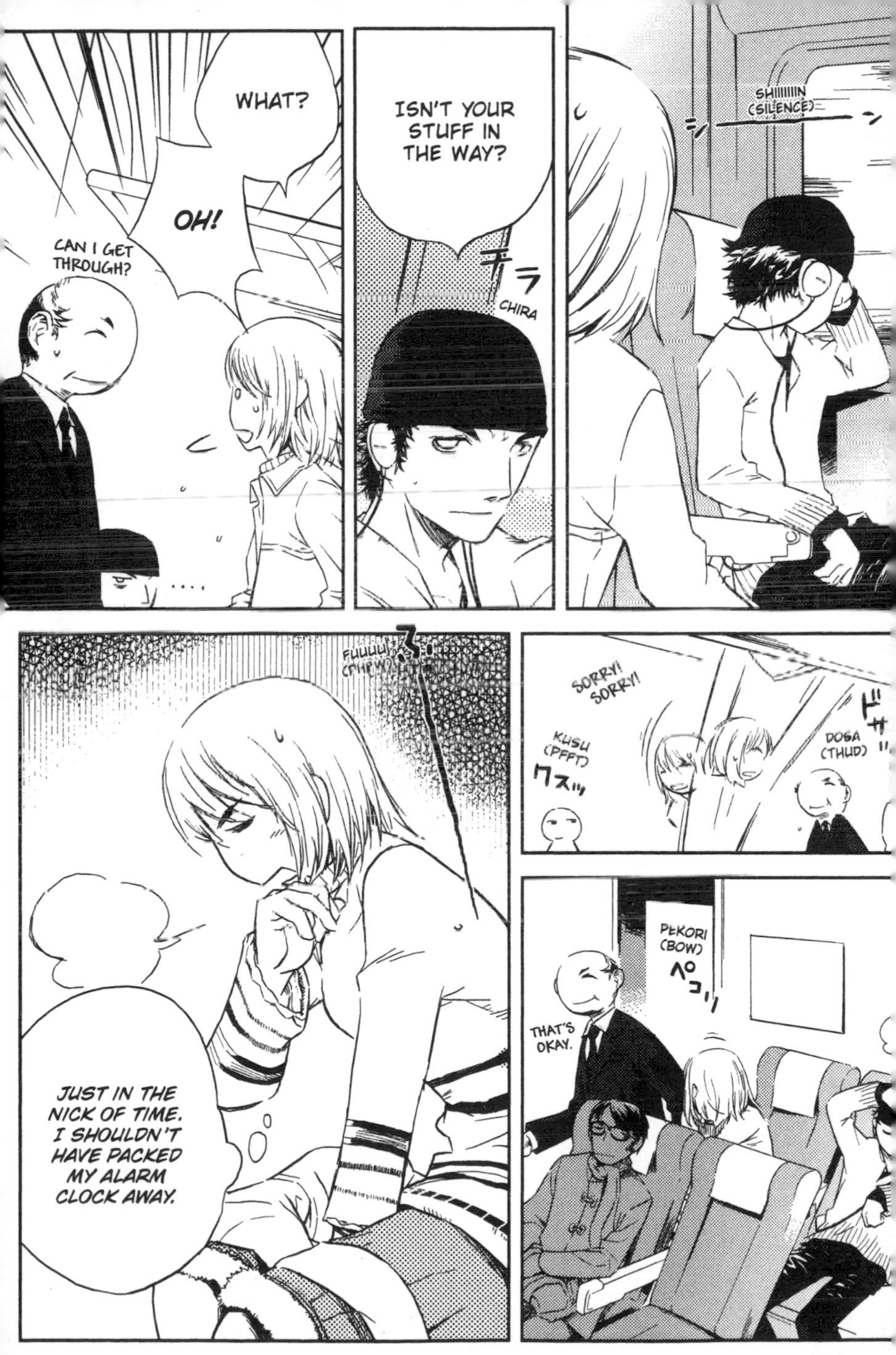
SHIIIIIIIN (SILENCE)
ISN'T YOUR STUFF IN THE WAY?
チラ
CHIRA
WHAT?
OH!
CAN I GET THROUGH?
....
SORRY! SORRY!
KUSU (PFFT)
クスッ
DOSA (THUD)
PEKORI (BOW)
ペコッ
THAT'S OKAY.
FHUUU (PHEW)
JUST IN THE NICK OF TIME. I SHOULDN'T HAVE PACKED MY ALARM CLOCK AWAY.

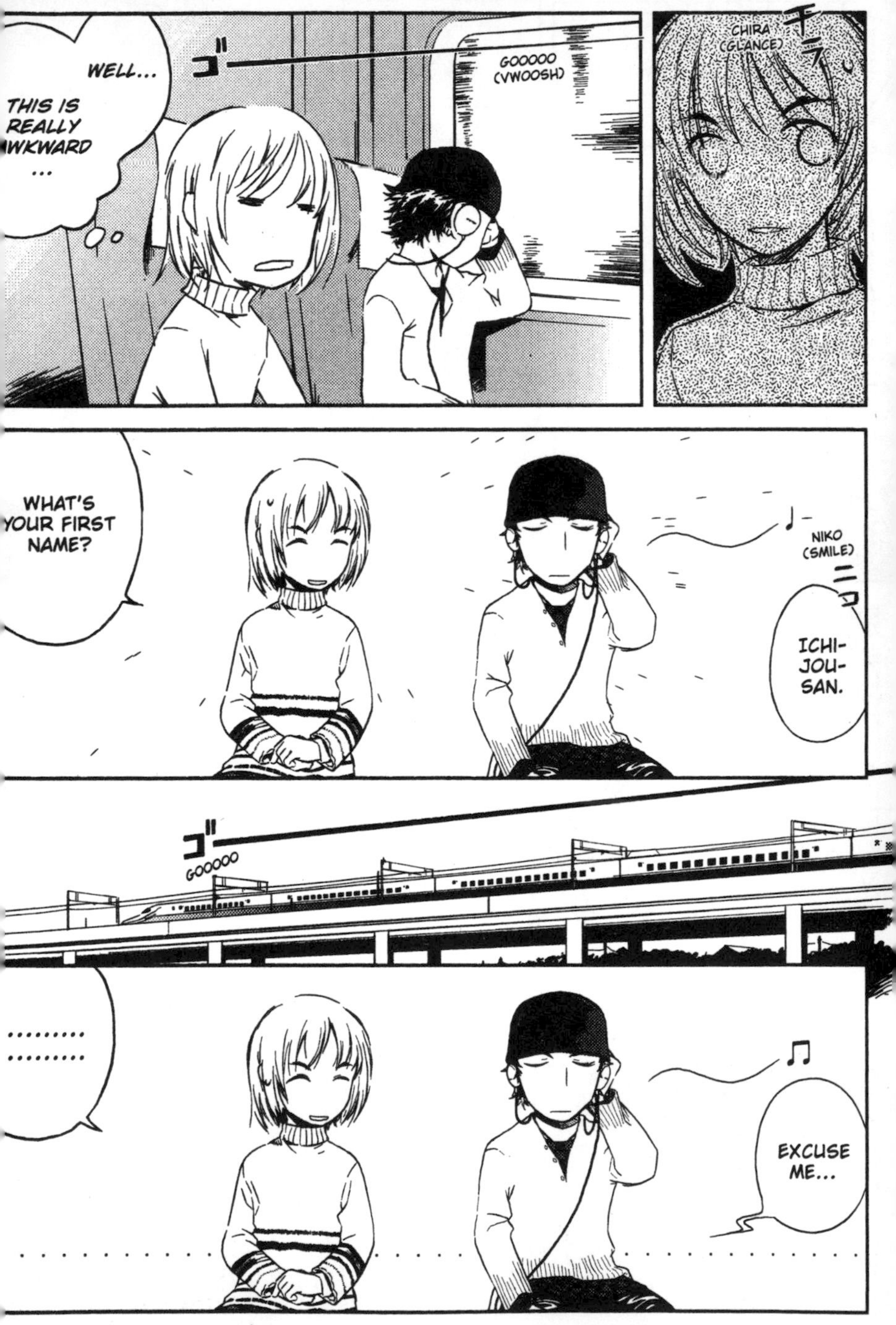
CHIRA (GLANCE)
GOOOOO (VWOOSH)
WELL...
THIS IS REALLY WKWARD ...
NIKO (SMILE)
ICHI-JOU-SAN.
WHAT'S YOUR FIRST NAME?
GOOOOO
EXCUSE ME...
....
....

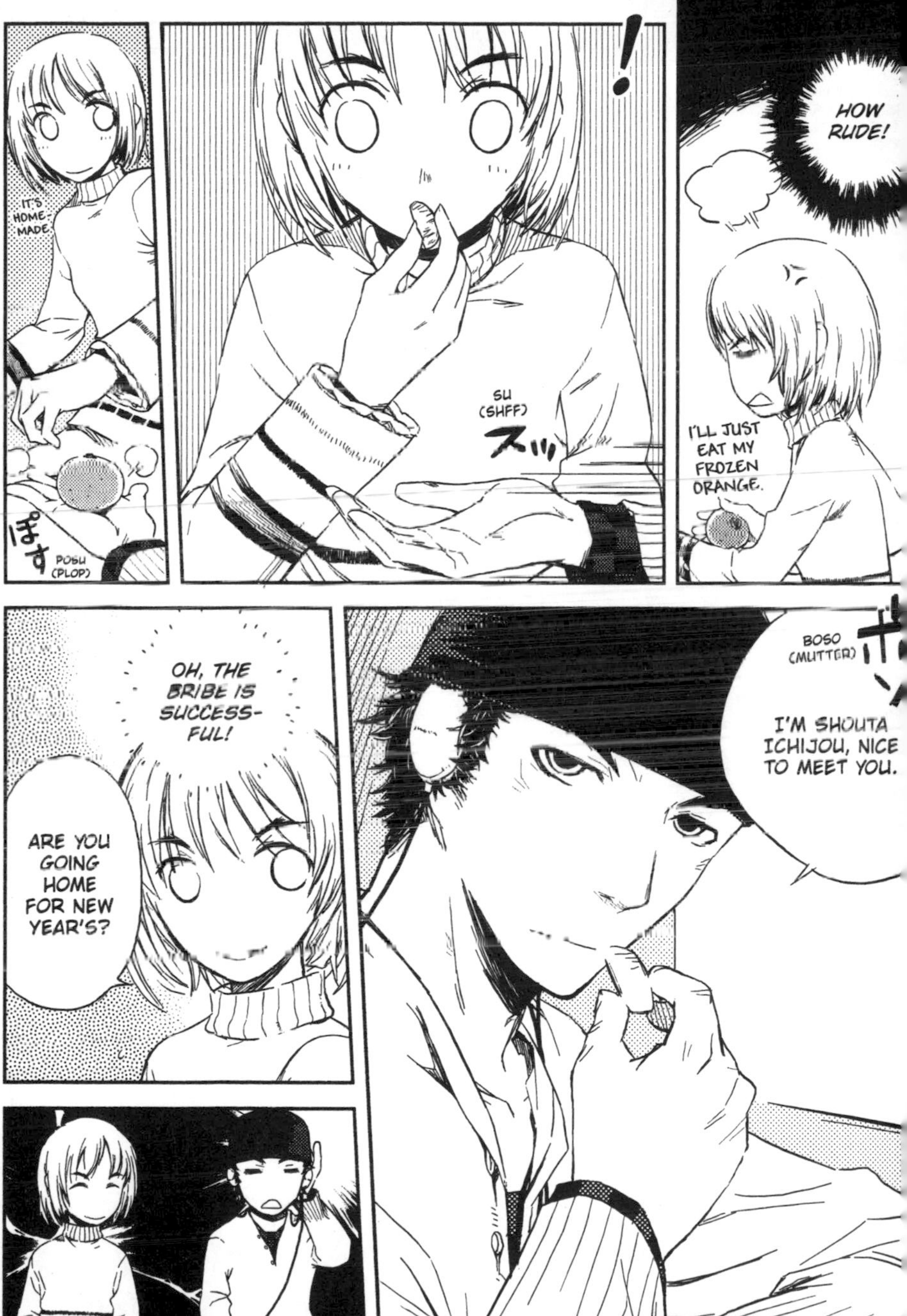
HOW RUDE!
I'LL JUST EAT MY FROZEN ORANGE.
!
SU (SHFF)
スッ
IT'S HOME-MADE
ぽす
POSU (PLOP)
BOSO (MUTTER)
ボソ
I'M SHOUTA ICHIJOU, NICE TO MEET YOU.
OH, THE BRIBE IS SUCCESS-FUL!
ARE YOU GOING HOME FOR NEW YEAR'S?

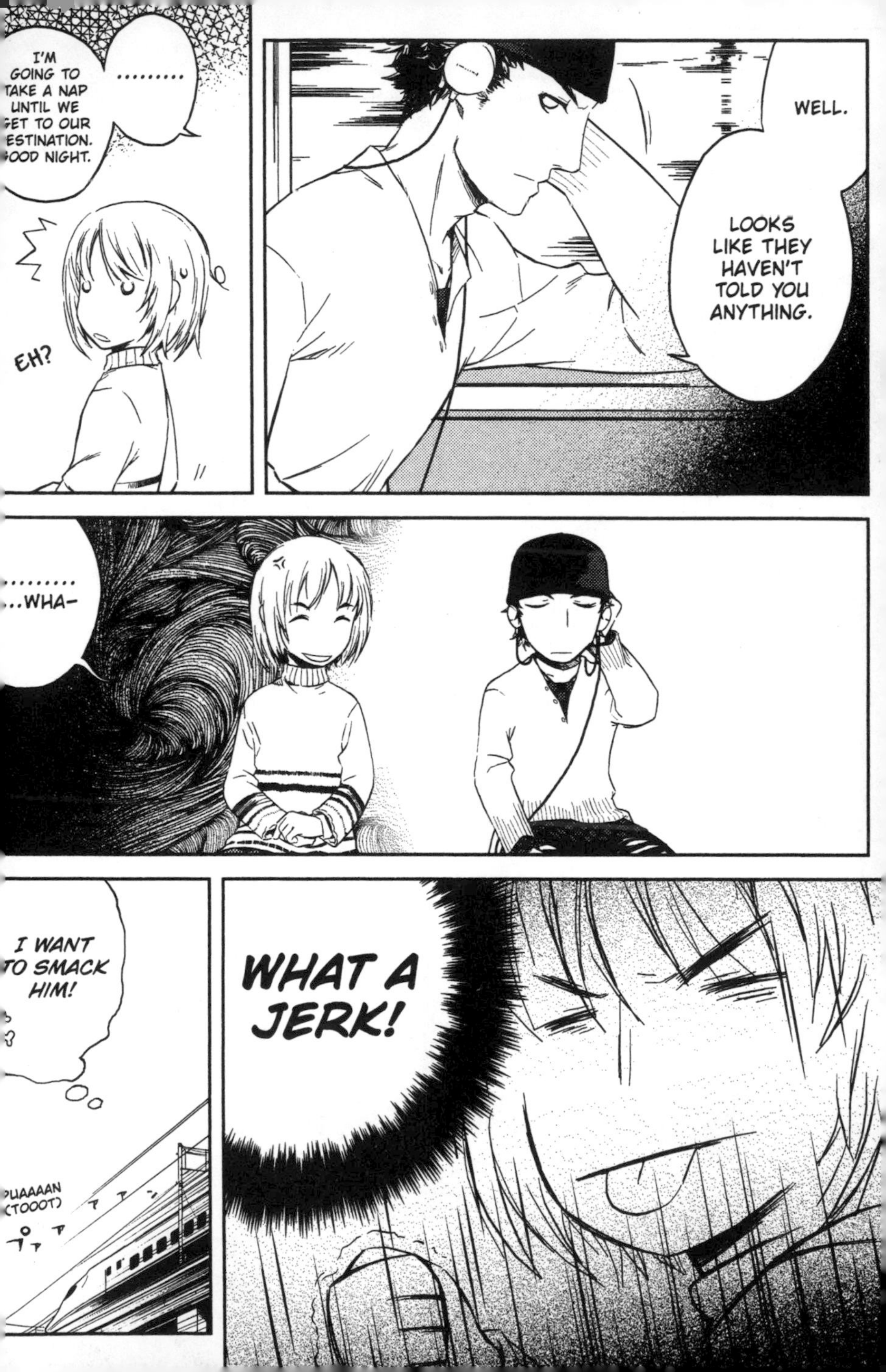
WELL.
LOOKS LIKE THEY HAVEN'T TOLD YOU ANYTHING.
I'M GOING TO TAKE A NAP UNTIL WE ET TO OUR ESTINATION. OOD NIGHT.
....
EH?
....WHA-
WHAT A JERK!
I WANT O SMACK HIM!
UAAAAN (TOOOT)

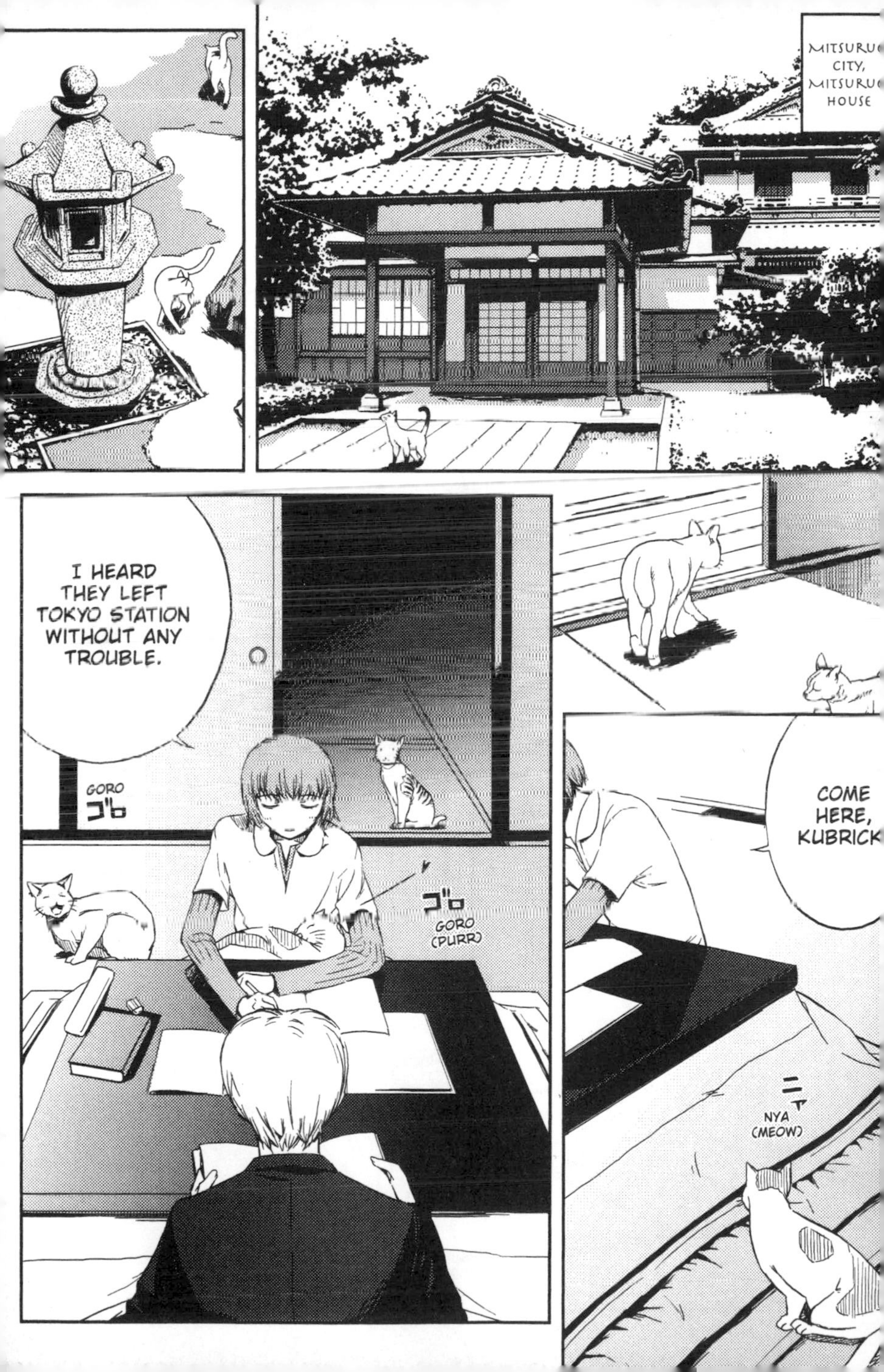
MITSURU
CITY,
MITSURU
HOUSE
COME HERE, KUBRICK
ニャ
NYA (MEOW)
I HEARD THEY LEFT TOKYO STATION WITHOUT ANY TROUBLE.
ゴロ
GORO
ゴロ
GORO (PURR)

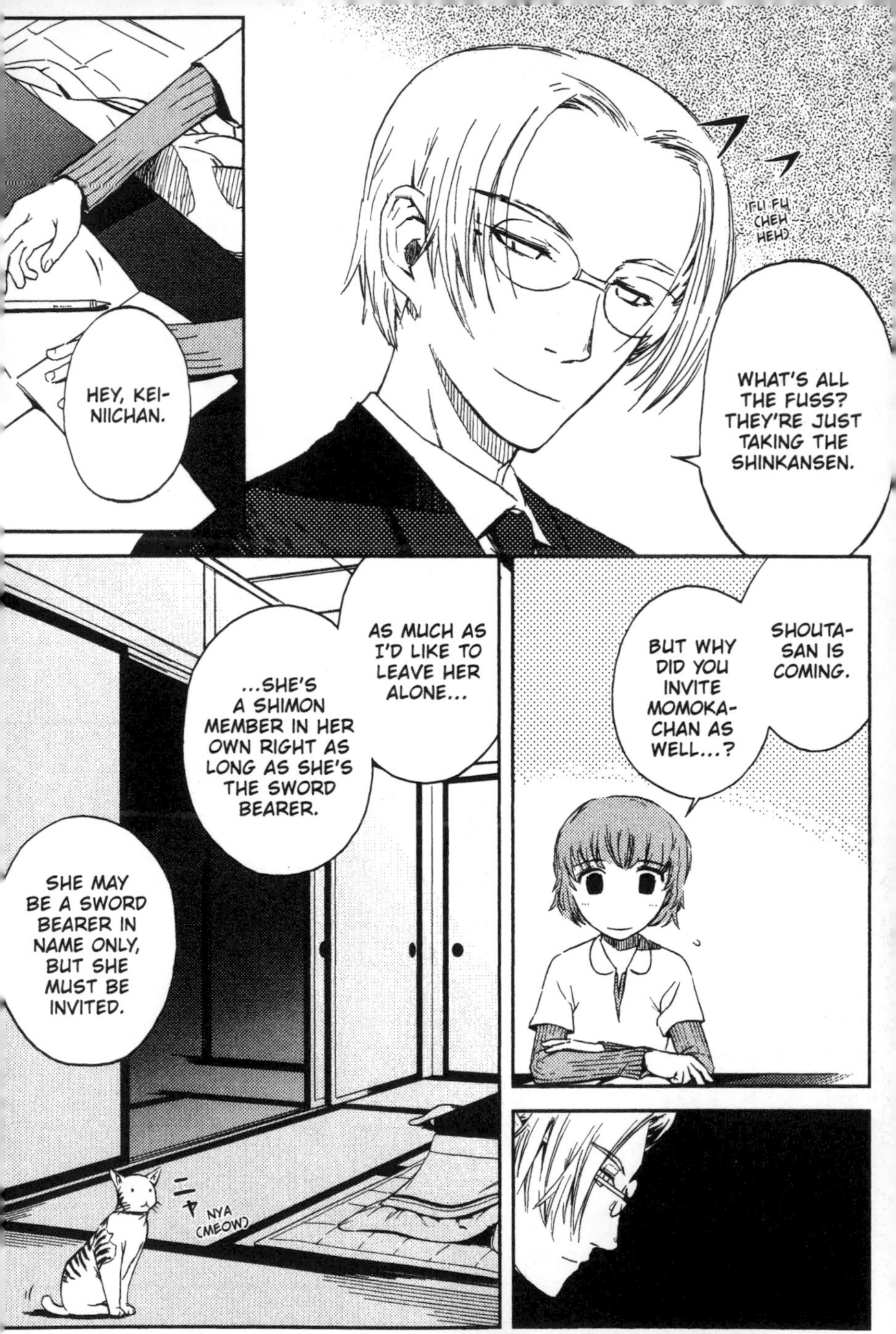
FU FU (HEH HEH)
WHAT'S ALL THE FUSS? THEY'RE JUST TAKING THE SHINKANSEN.
HEY, KEI-NIICHAN.
SHOUTA-SAN IS COMING.
BUT WHY DID YOU INVITE MOMOKA-CHAN AS WELL...?
AS MUCH AS I'D LIKE TO LEAVE HER ALONE...
...SHE'S A SHIMON MEMBER IN HER OWN RIGHT AS LONG AS SHE'S THE SWORD BEARER.
SHE MAY BE A SWORD BEARER IN NAME ONLY, BUT SHE MUST BE INVITED.
NYA (MEOW)

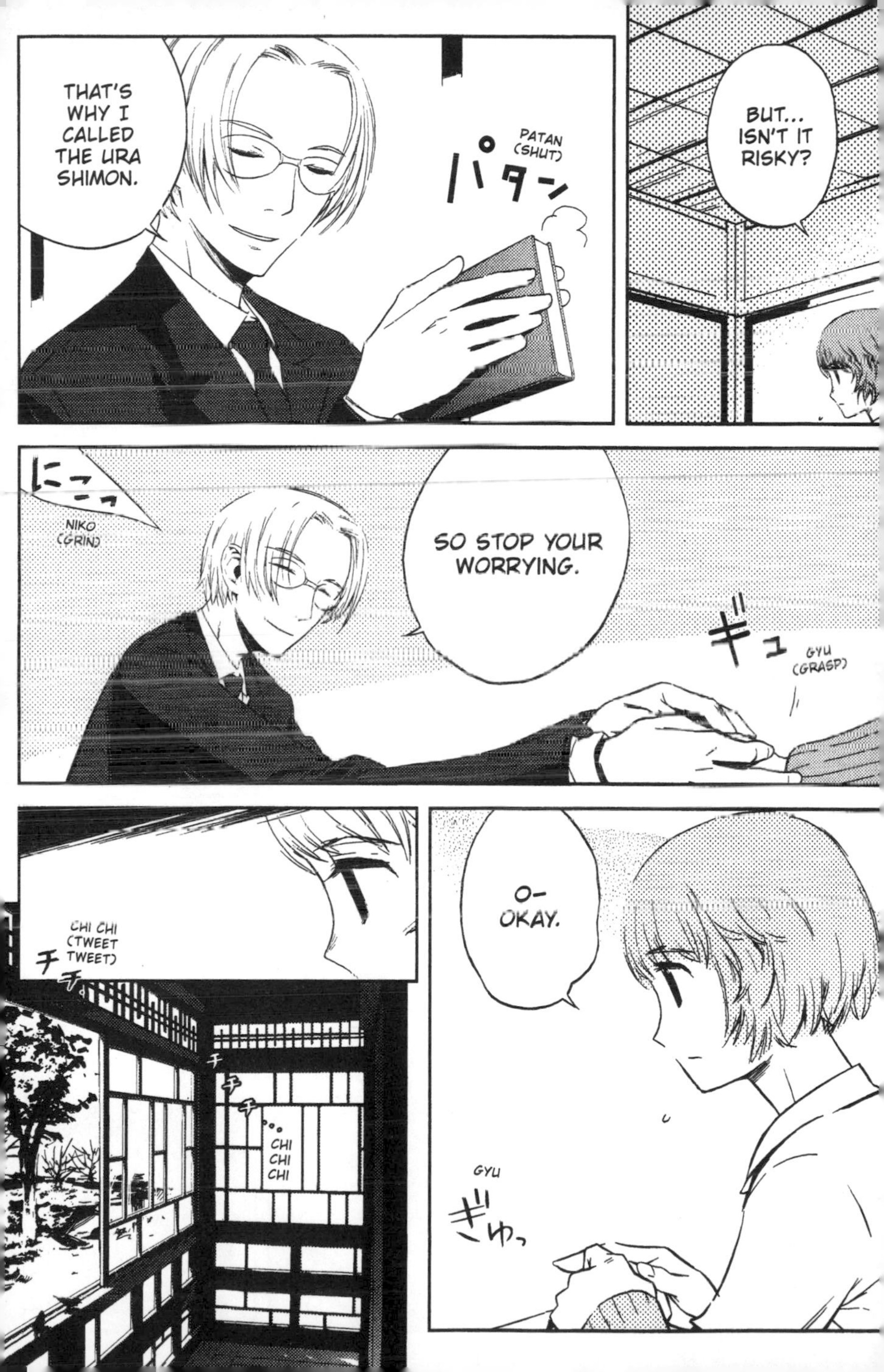
BUT... ISN'T IT RISKY?
THAT'S WHY I CALLED THE URA SHIMON.
パタン
PATAN (SHUT)
SO STOP YOUR WORRYING.
ギュ
GYU (GRASP)
にっ
NIKO (GRIN)
O-OKAY.
ぎゅっ
GYU
チチ
CHI CHI (TWEET TWEET)
チチチ...
CHI CHI CHI

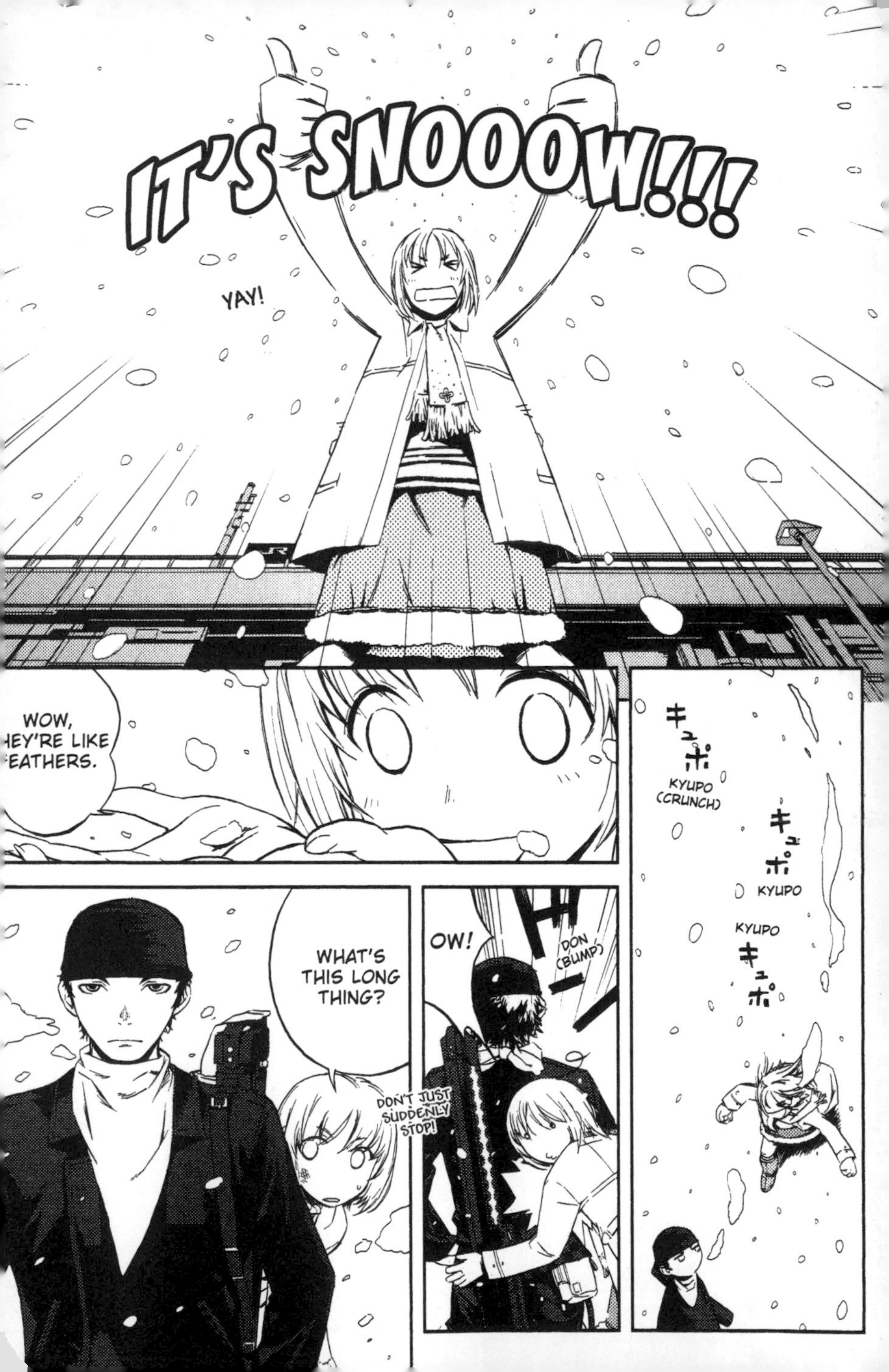

IT'S SNOOOW!!!
YAY!
キュポ
KYUPO (CRUNCH)
キュポ
KYUPO
KYUPO
キュポ
WOW, HEY'RE LIKE EATHERS.
OW!
DON (BUMP)
WHAT'S THIS LONG THING?
DON'T JUST SUDDENLY STOP!

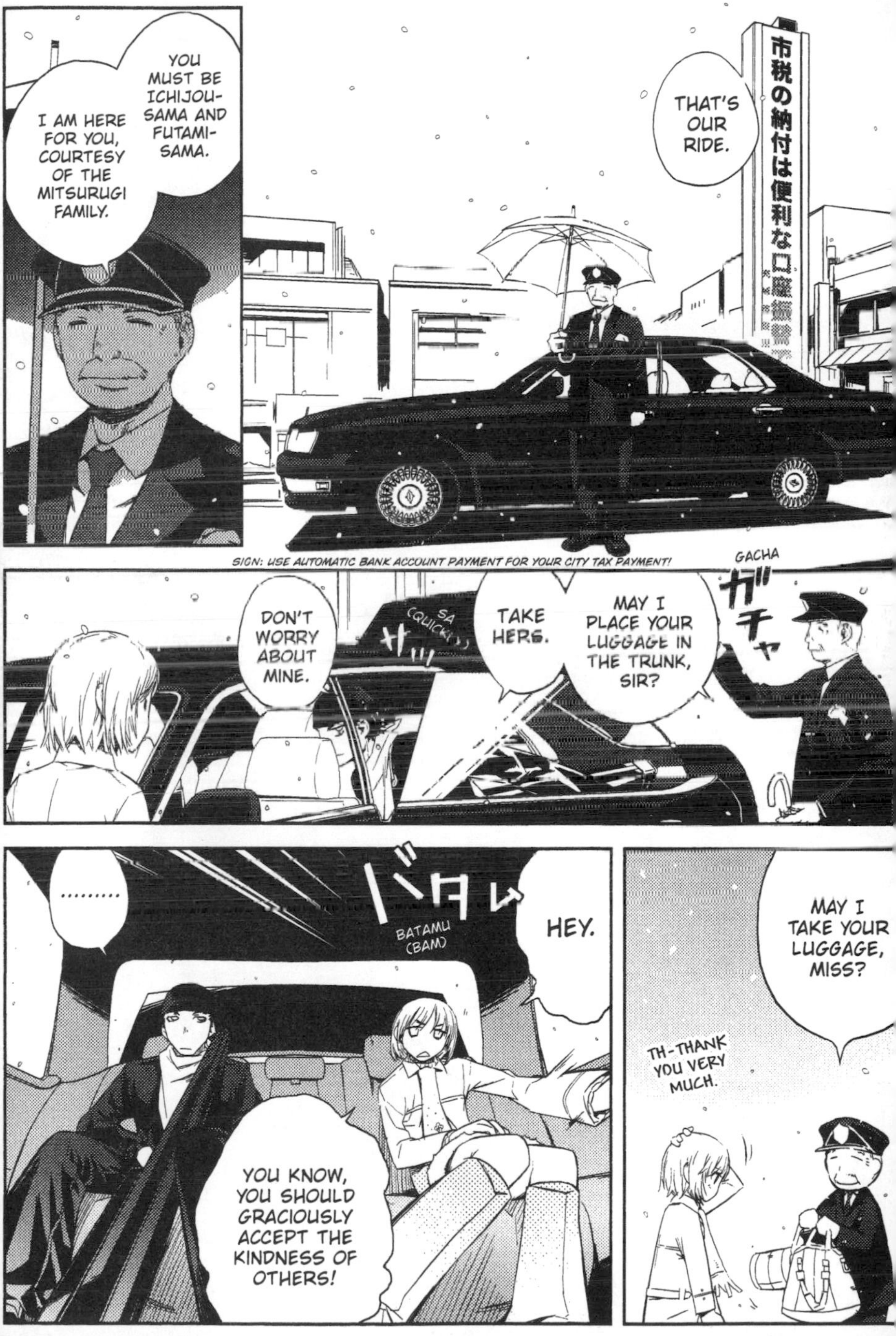
THAT'S OUR RIDE.
市税の納付は便利な口座振替
SIGN: USE AUTOMATIC BANK ACCOUNT PAYMENT FOR YOUR CITY TAX PAYMENT!
YOU MUST BE ICHIJOU-SAMA AND FUTAMI-SAMA.
I AM HERE FOR YOU, COURTESY OF THE MITSURUGI FAMILY.
ガチャ
GACHA
MAY I PLACE YOUR LUGGAGE IN THE TRUNK, SIR?
TAKE HERS.
サッ
SA (QUICK)
DON'T WORRY ABOUT MINE.
MAY I TAKE YOUR LUGGAGE, MISS?
TH-THANK YOU VERY MUCH.
HEY.
バタム
BATAMU (BAM)
....
YOU KNOW, YOU SHOULD GRACIOUSLY ACCEPT THE KINDNESS OF OTHERS!

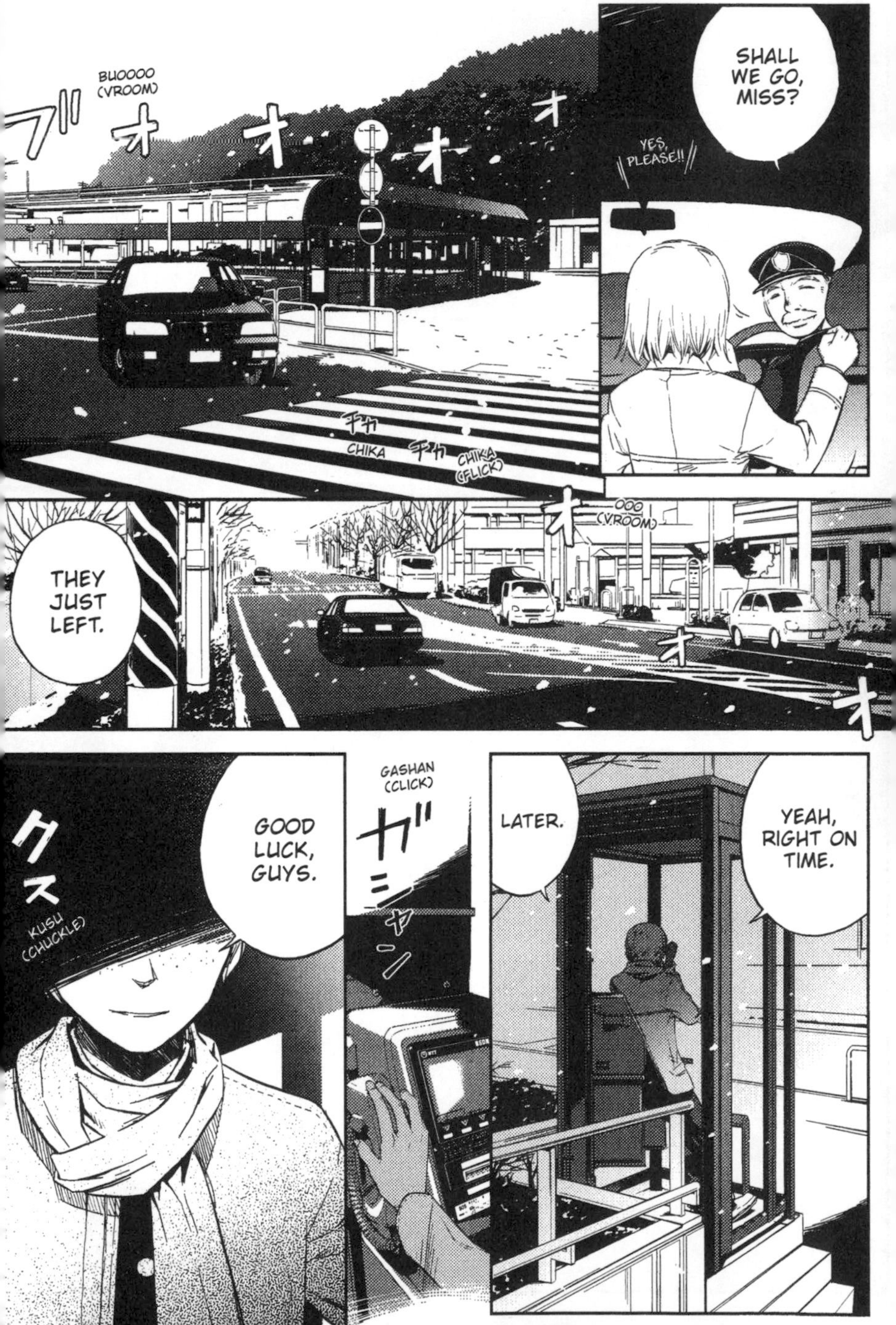
SHALL WE GO, MISS?
YES, PLEASE!!
BUOOOO (VROOM)
CHIKA CHIKA (FLICK)
OOO (VROOM)
THEY JUST LEFT.
YEAH, RIGHT ON TIME.
LATER.
GASHAN (CLICK)
GOOD LUCK, GUYS.
KUSU (CHUCKLE)

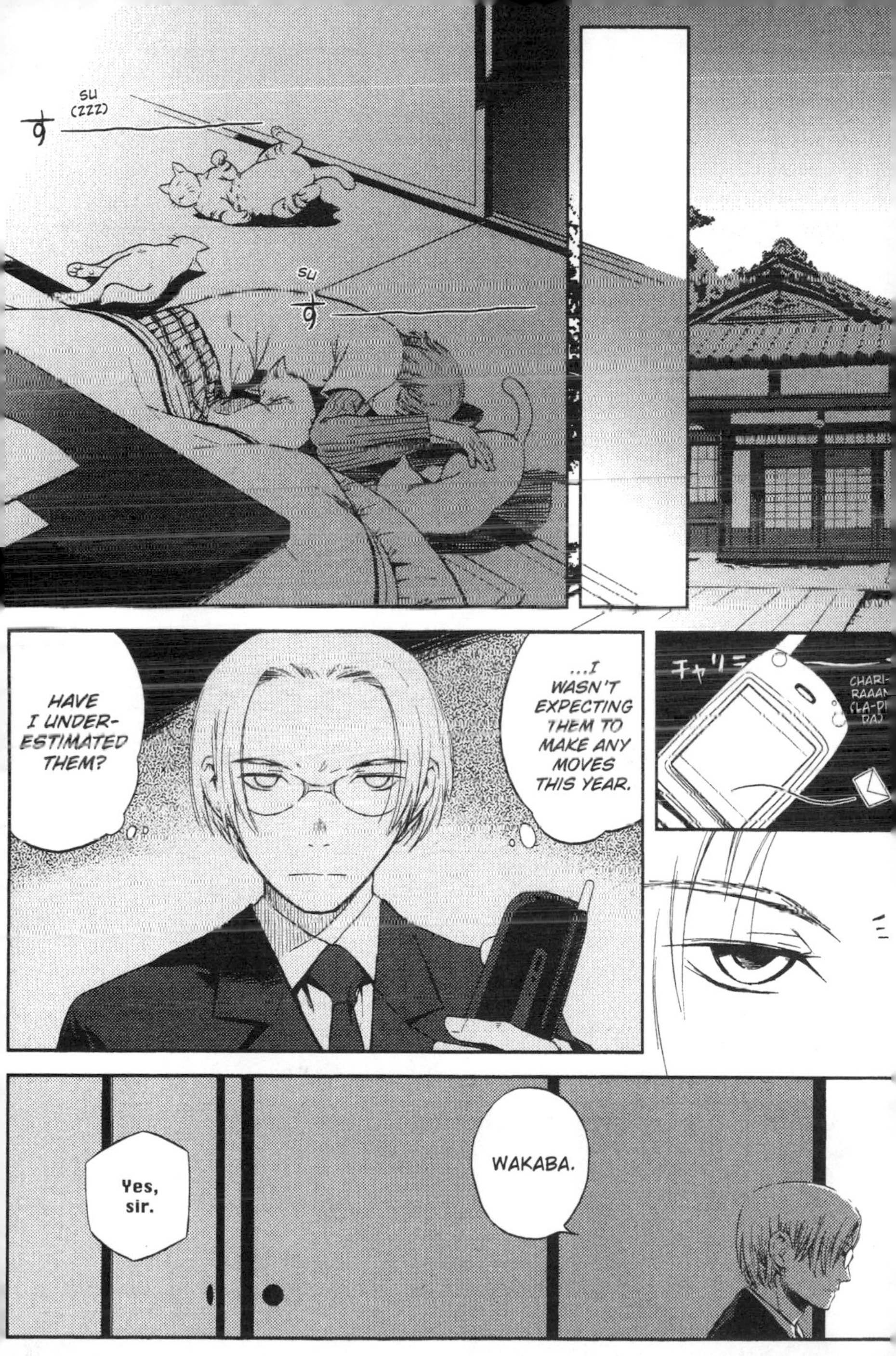す
SU (ZZZ)
す
SU
チャリ
CHARI-RAAAN (LA-PI DA)
...I WASN'T EXPECTING THEM TO MAKE ANY MOVES THIS YEAR.
HAVE I UNDER-ESTIMATED THEM?
WAKABA.
Yes, sir.

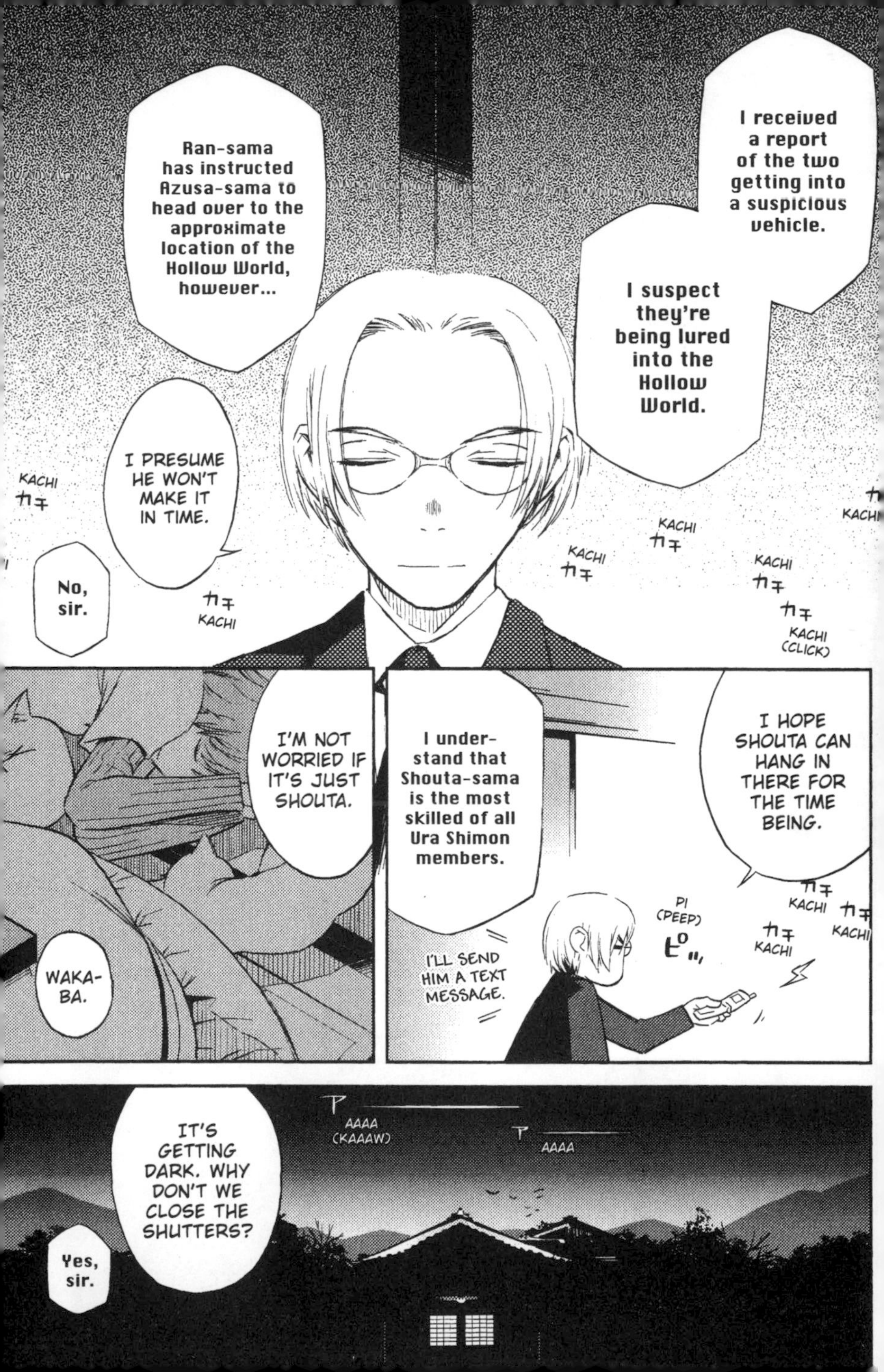
I received a report of the two getting into a suspicious vehicle.
I suspect they're being lured into the Hollow World.
Ran-sama has instructed Azusa-sama to head over to the approximate location of the Hollow World, however...
I PRESUME HE WON'T MAKE IT IN TIME.
No, sir.
KACHI カチ
KACHI カチ
KACHI カチ
KACHI カチ
カチ KACHI (CLICK)
カチ KACHI
KACHI カチ
I HOPE SHOUTA CAN HANG IN THERE FOR THE TIME BEING.
カチ KACHI
カチ KACHI
カチ KACHI
PI (PEEP)
ピ
I under-stand that Shouta-sama is the most skilled of all Ura Shimon members.
I'LL SEND HIM A TEXT MESSAGE.
I'M NOT WORRIED IF IT'S JUST SHOUTA.
WAKA-BA.
AAAA (KAAAW)
AAAA
IT'S GETTING DARK. WHY DON'T WE CLOSE THE SHUTTERS?
Yes, sir.

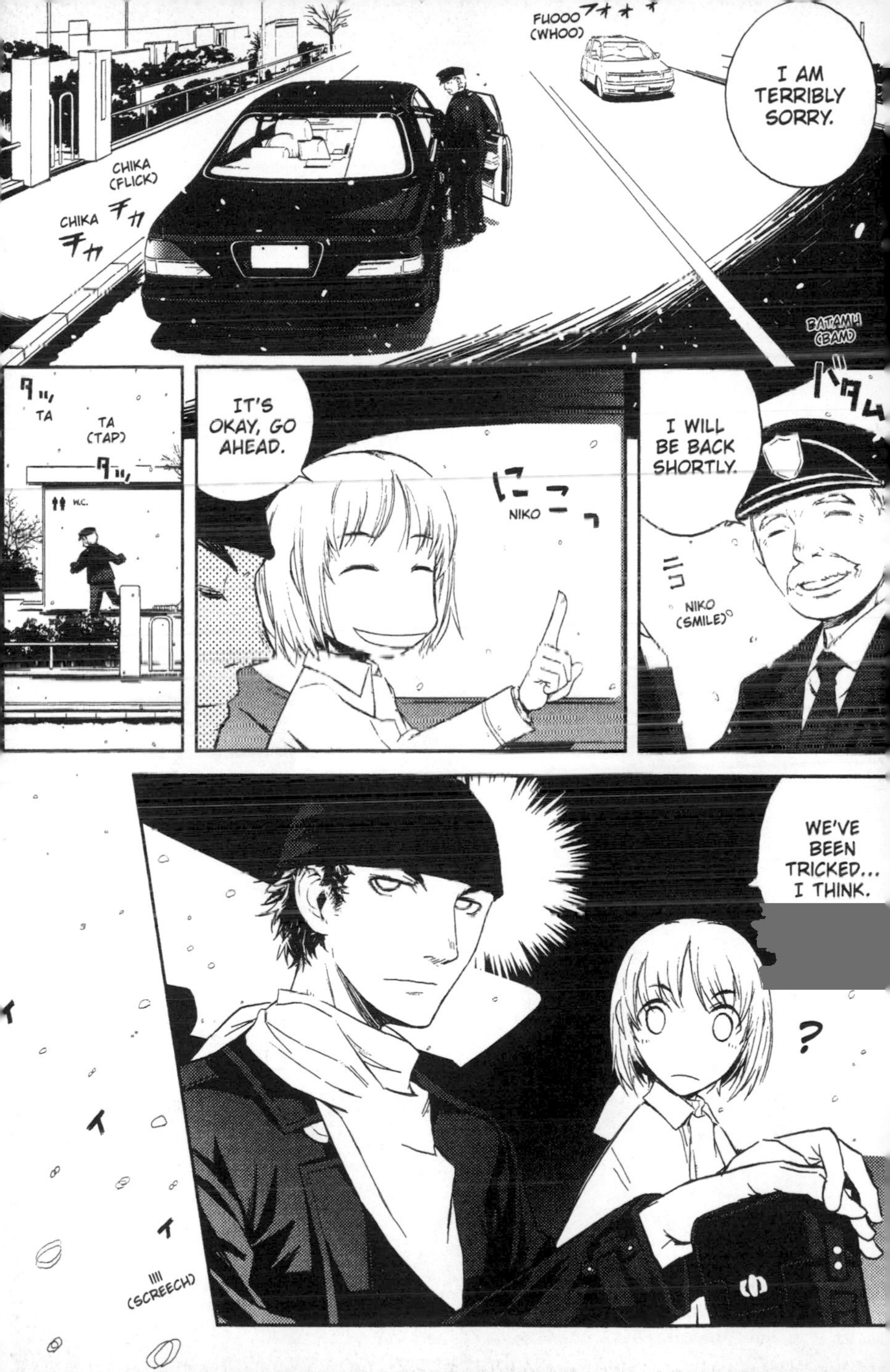
I AM TERRIBLY SORRY.
FUOOO フォオオ
(WHOO)
CHIKA
(FLICK)
CHIKA
BATAMU
(BAM)
I WILL BE BACK SHORTLY.
NIKO
(SMILE)
IT'S OKAY, GO AHEAD.
NIKO
TA
TA
(TAP)
W.C.
WE'VE BEEN TRICKED... I THINK.
?
IIII
(SCREECH)

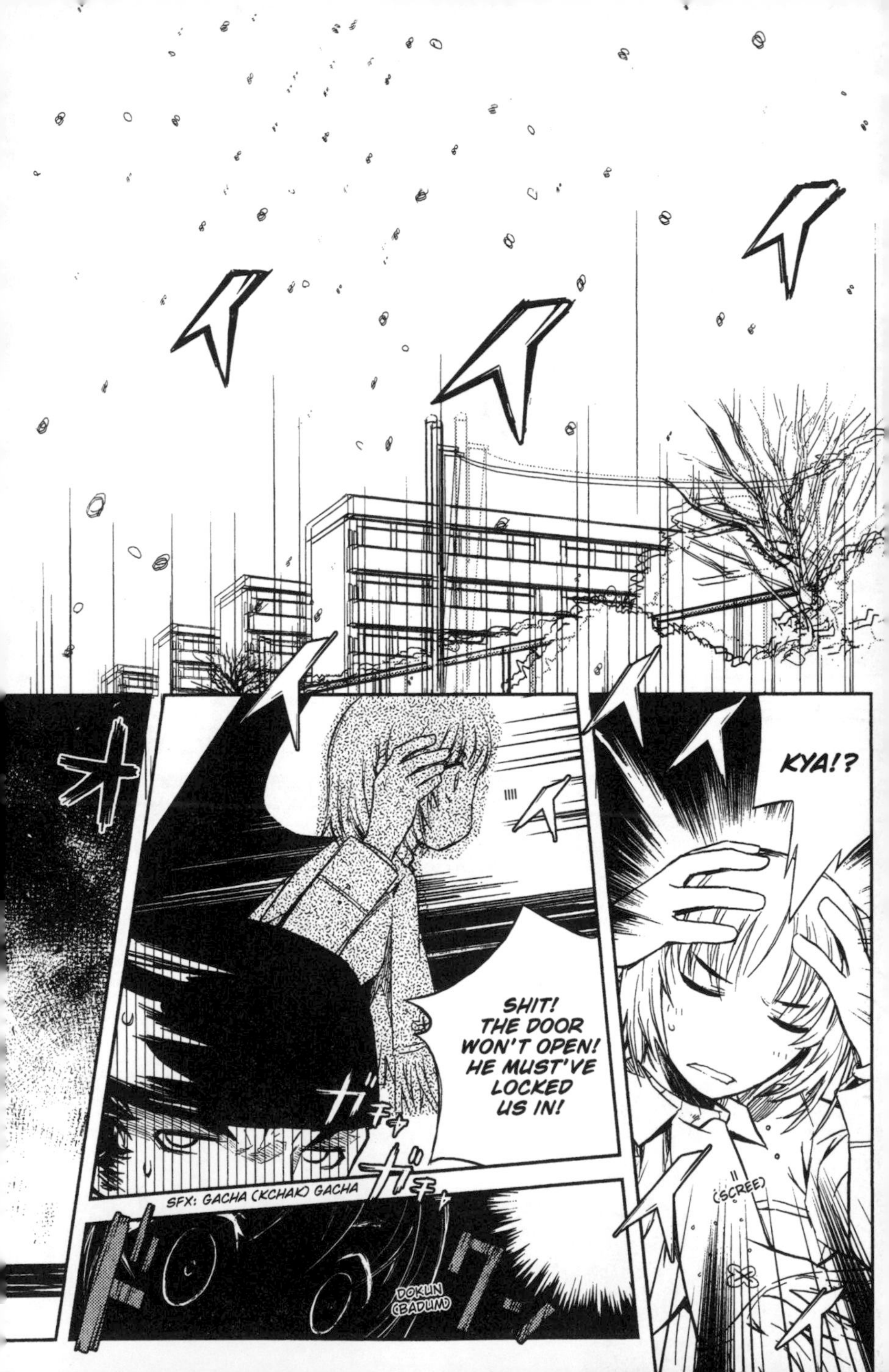
KYA!?
(SCREE)
SHIT! THE DOOR WON'T OPEN! HE MUST'VE LOCKED US IN!
SFX: GACHA (KCHAK) GACHA
DOKUN (BADUM)

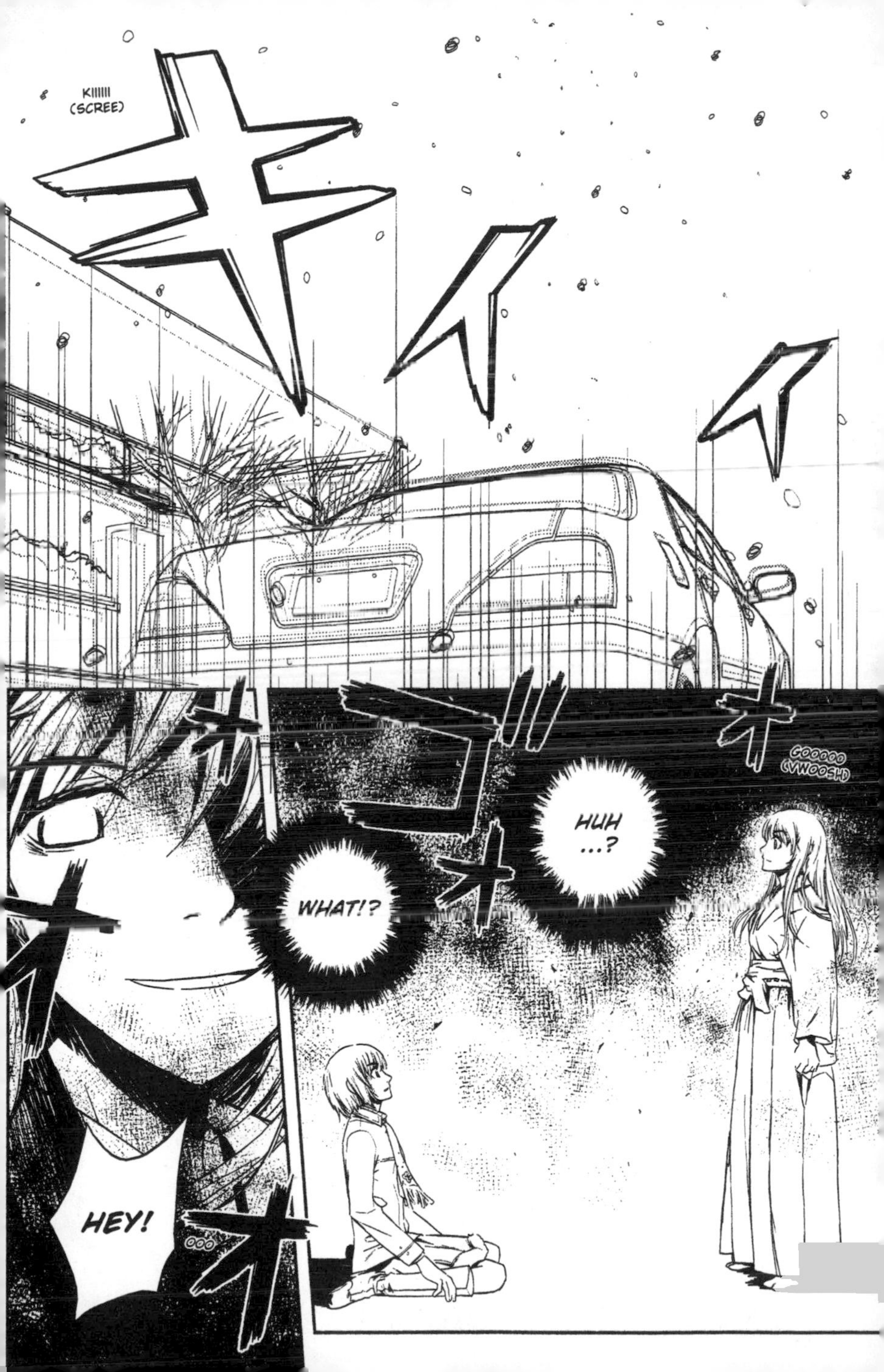
KIIIIII
(SCREE)
GOOOOO
(VWOOSH)
HUH ...?
WHAT!?
HEY!

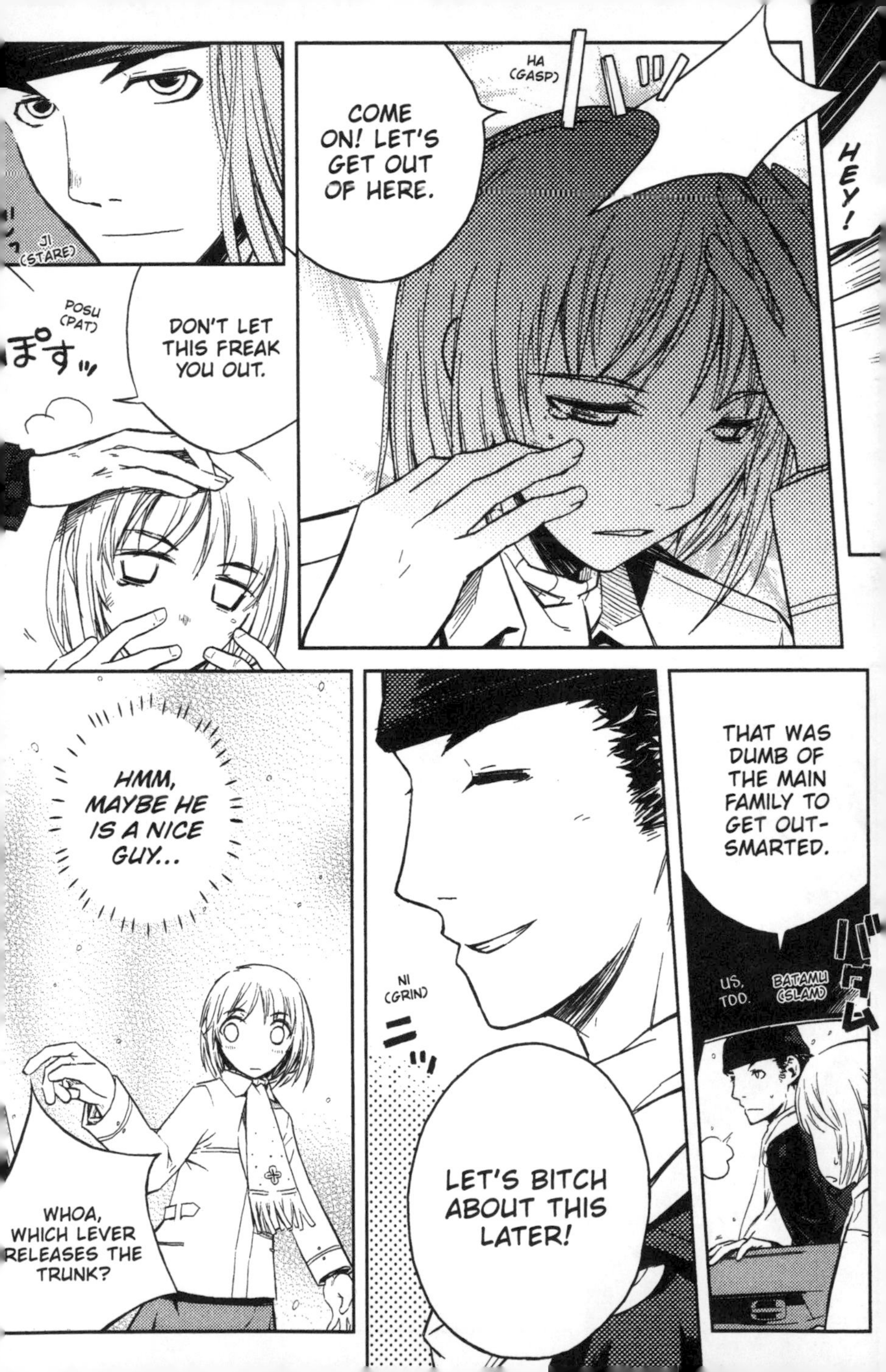
HEY!
HA (GASP)
COME ON! LET'S GET OUT OF HERE.
JI (STARE)
POSU (PAT)
ぽすッ
DON'T LET THIS FREAK YOU OUT.
THAT WAS DUMB OF THE MAIN FAMILY TO GET OUT-SMARTED.
US, TOO.
BATAMU (SLAM)
バタム
NI (GRIN)
ニッ
LET'S BITCH ABOUT THIS LATER!
HMM, MAYBE HE IS A NICE GUY...
WHOA, WHICH LEVER RELEASES THE TRUNK?

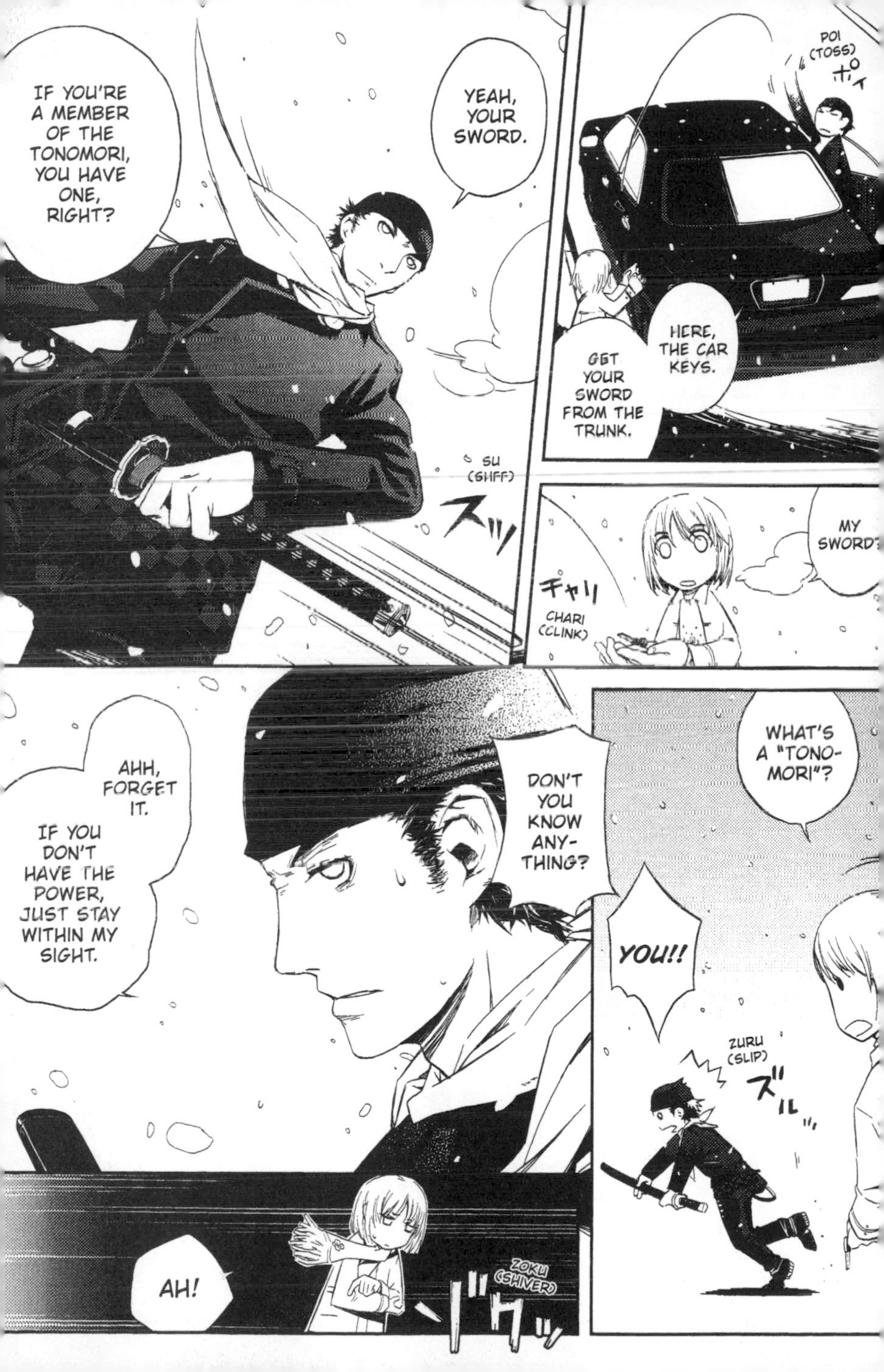
POI (TOSS)
HERE, THE CAR KEYS.
GET YOUR SWORD FROM THE TRUNK.
MY SWORD?
CHARI (CLINK)
YEAH, YOUR SWORD.
IF YOU'RE A MEMBER OF THE TONOMORI, YOU HAVE ONE, RIGHT?
SU (SHFF)
WHAT'S A "TONO-MORI"?
YOU!!
ZURU (SLIP)
DON'T YOU KNOW ANY-THING?
AHH, FORGET IT.
IF YOU DON'T HAVE THE POWER, JUST STAY WITHIN MY SIGHT.
AH!
ZOKU (SHIVER)

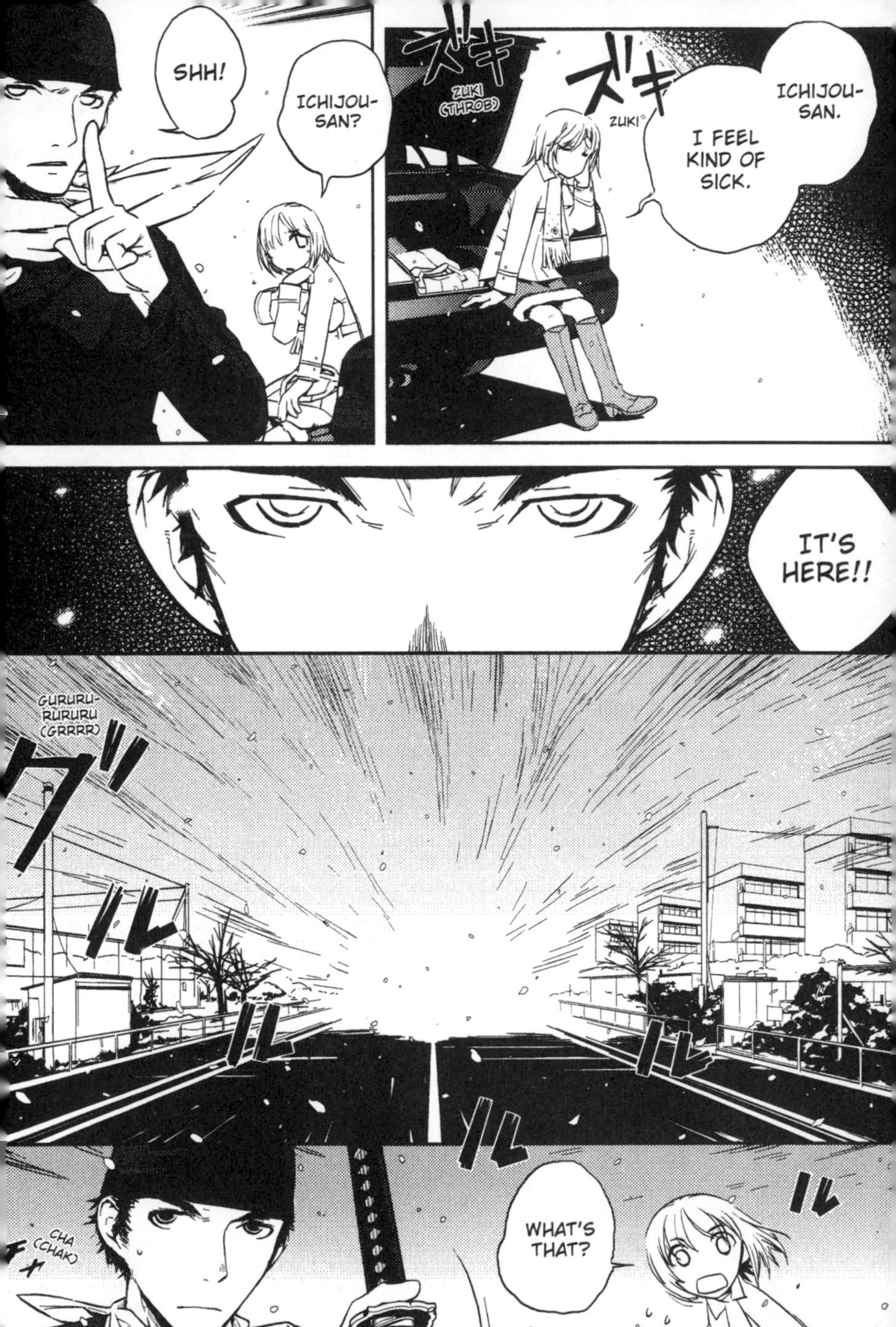
ZUKI (THROB)
ZUKI
ICHIJOU-SAN.
I FEEL KIND OF SICK.
ICHIJOU-SAN?
SHH!
IT'S HERE!!
GURURU-RURURU (GRRRR)
WHAT'S THAT?
CHA (CHAK)

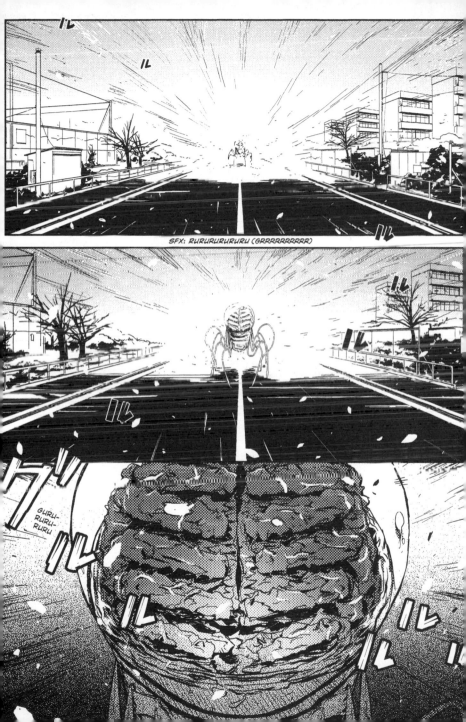

SFX: RURURURURURU (GRRRRRRRRRR)

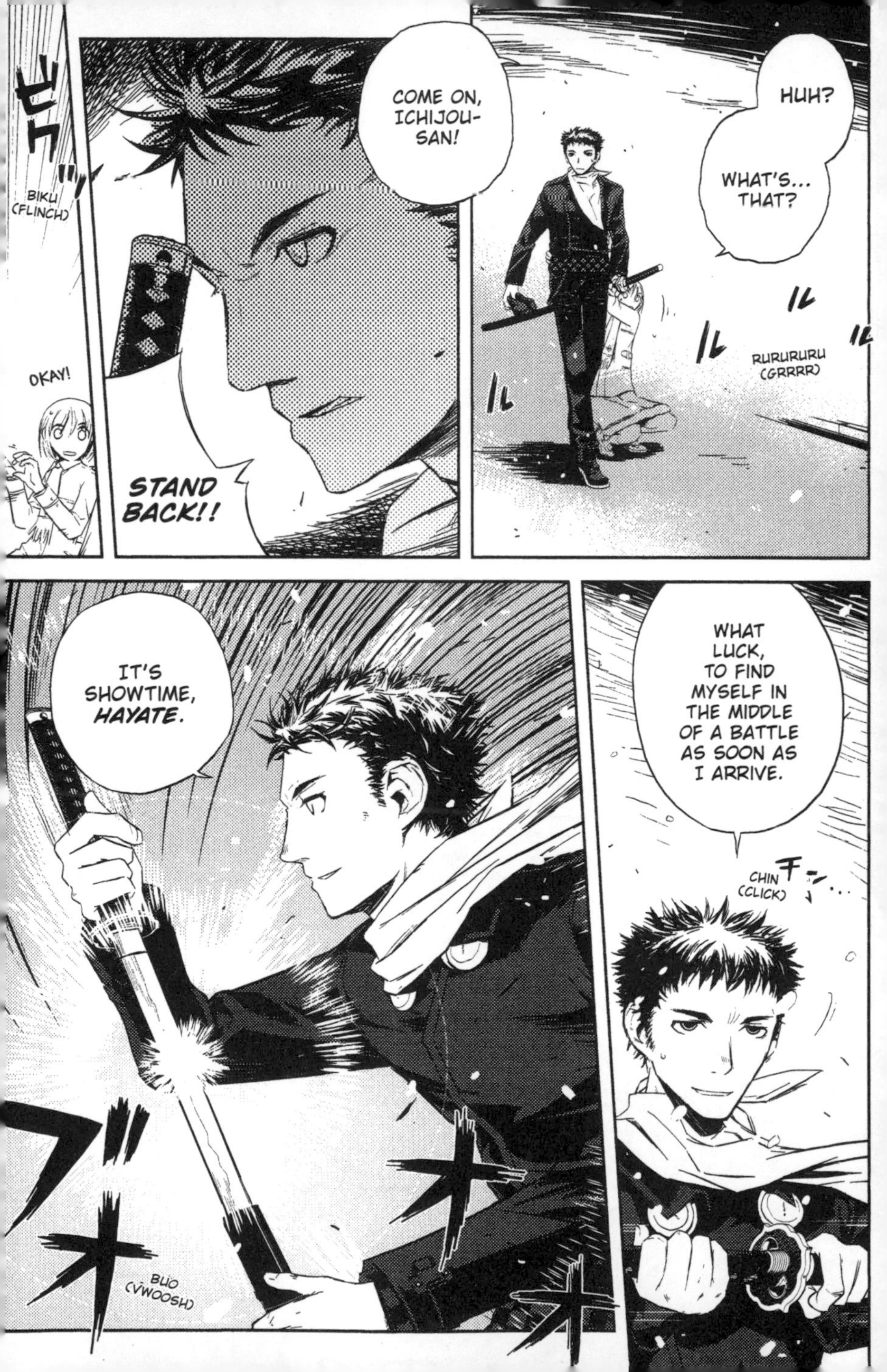
HUH?
WHAT'S... THAT?
RURURURU (GRRRR)
COME ON, ICHIJOU-SAN!
STAND BACK!!
BIKU (FLINCH)
OKAY!
WHAT LUCK, TO FIND MYSELF IN THE MIDDLE OF A BATTLE AS SOON AS I ARRIVE.
CHIN (CLICK)
IT'S SHOWTIME, *HAYATE*.
BUO (VWOOSH)

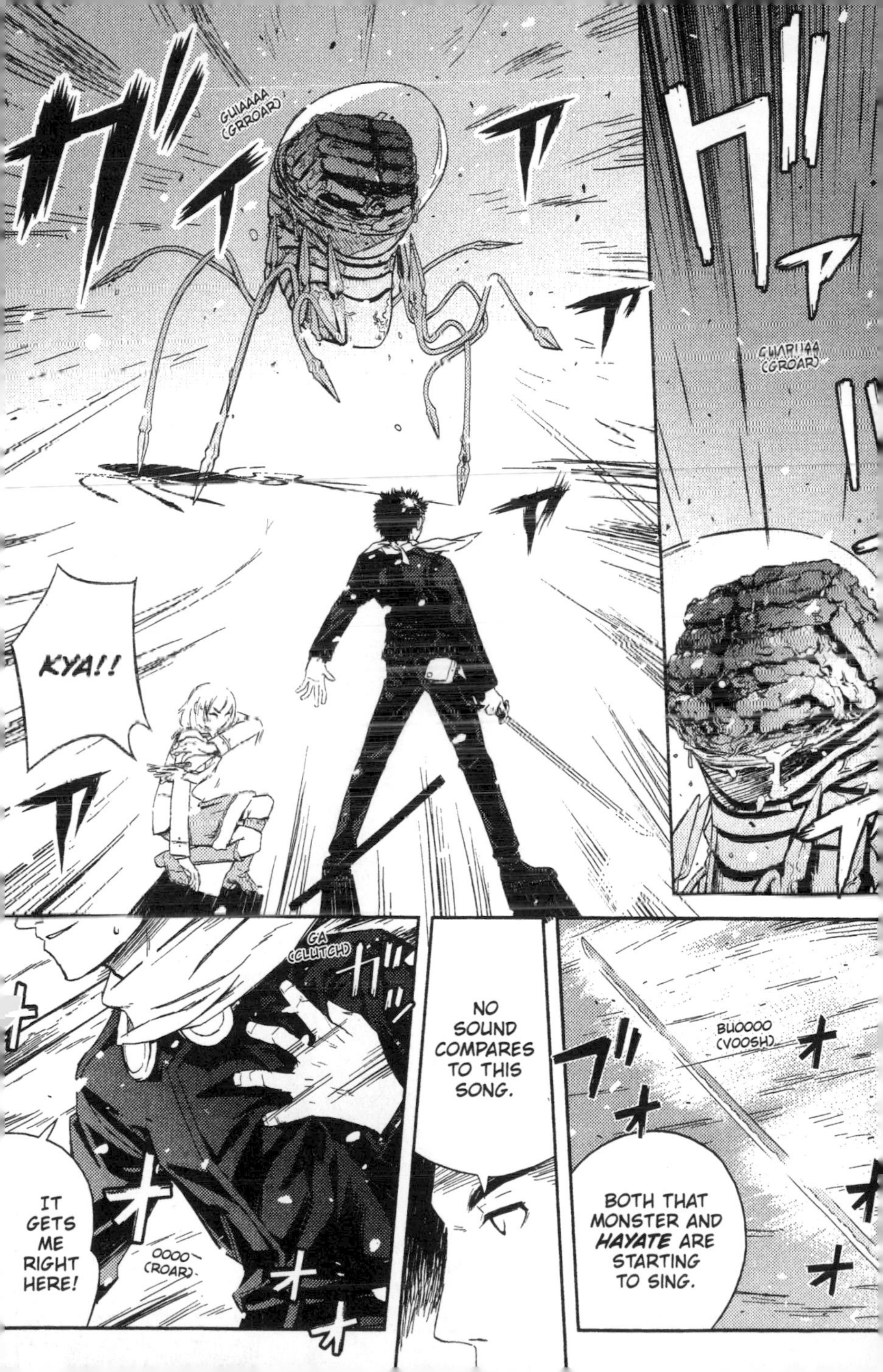
GWARUAA (GROAR)
GUIAAAA (GRROAR)
KYA!!
BUOOOO (VOOSH)
BOTH THAT MONSTER AND *HAYATE* ARE STARTING TO SING.
NO SOUND COMPARES TO THIS SONG.
GA (CLUTCH)
IT GETS ME RIGHT HERE!
OOOO (ROAR)

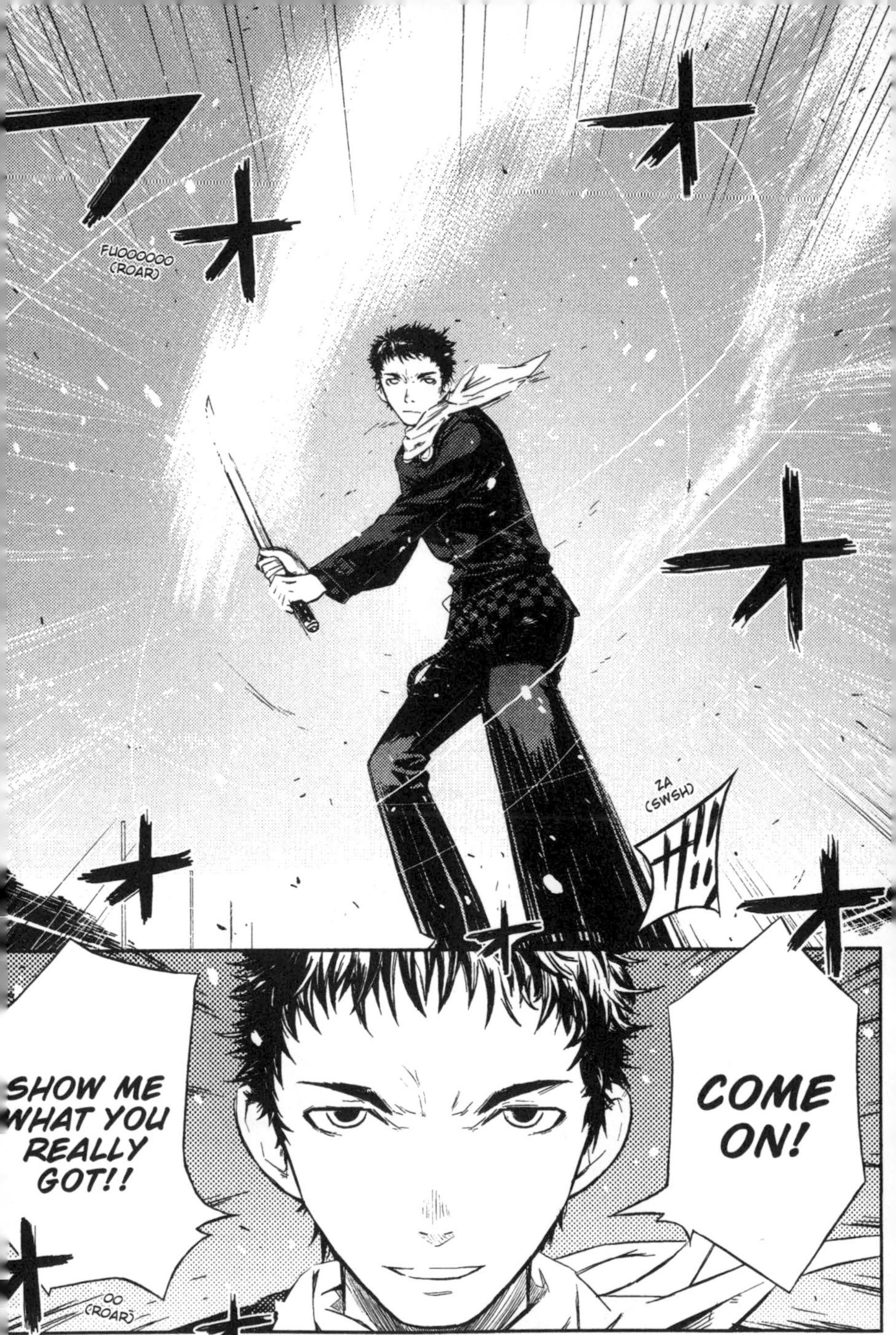
FUOOOOOO (ROAR)
ZA (SWSH)
COME ON!
SHOW ME WHAT YOU REALLY GOT!!
OO (ROAR)

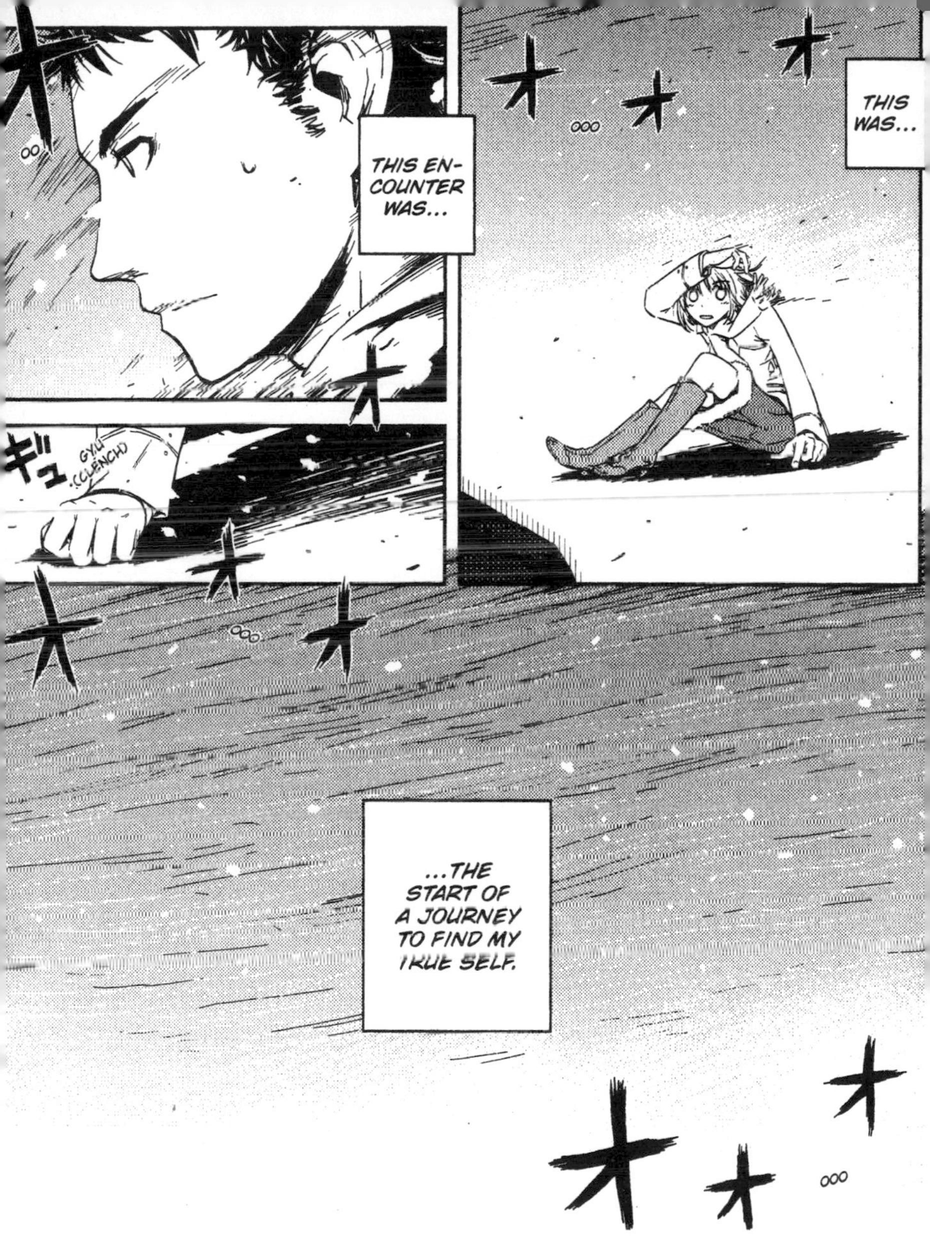
THIS WAS...
THIS EN-COUNTER WAS...
ギュ
GYU (CLENCH)
...THE START OF A JOURNEY TO FIND MY TRUE SELF.

RE: PICKING YOU UP
Too late!
> That car belongs
> to Shichijou Group.
> Try to defend
> Momoka until
> Azusa arrives.
> Keiichirou

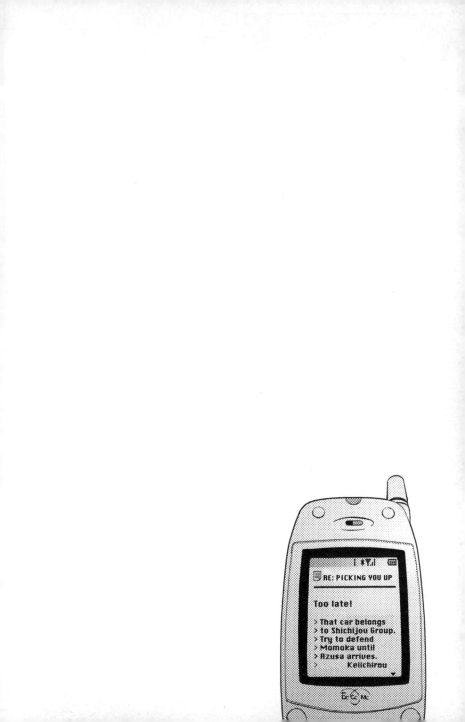

*IT SEEMS
I LOST MY
PARENTS AND
MY MEMORIES
IN AN ACCIDENT
FOUR YEARS
AGO.*

Chapter Two:
WHIRLWIND

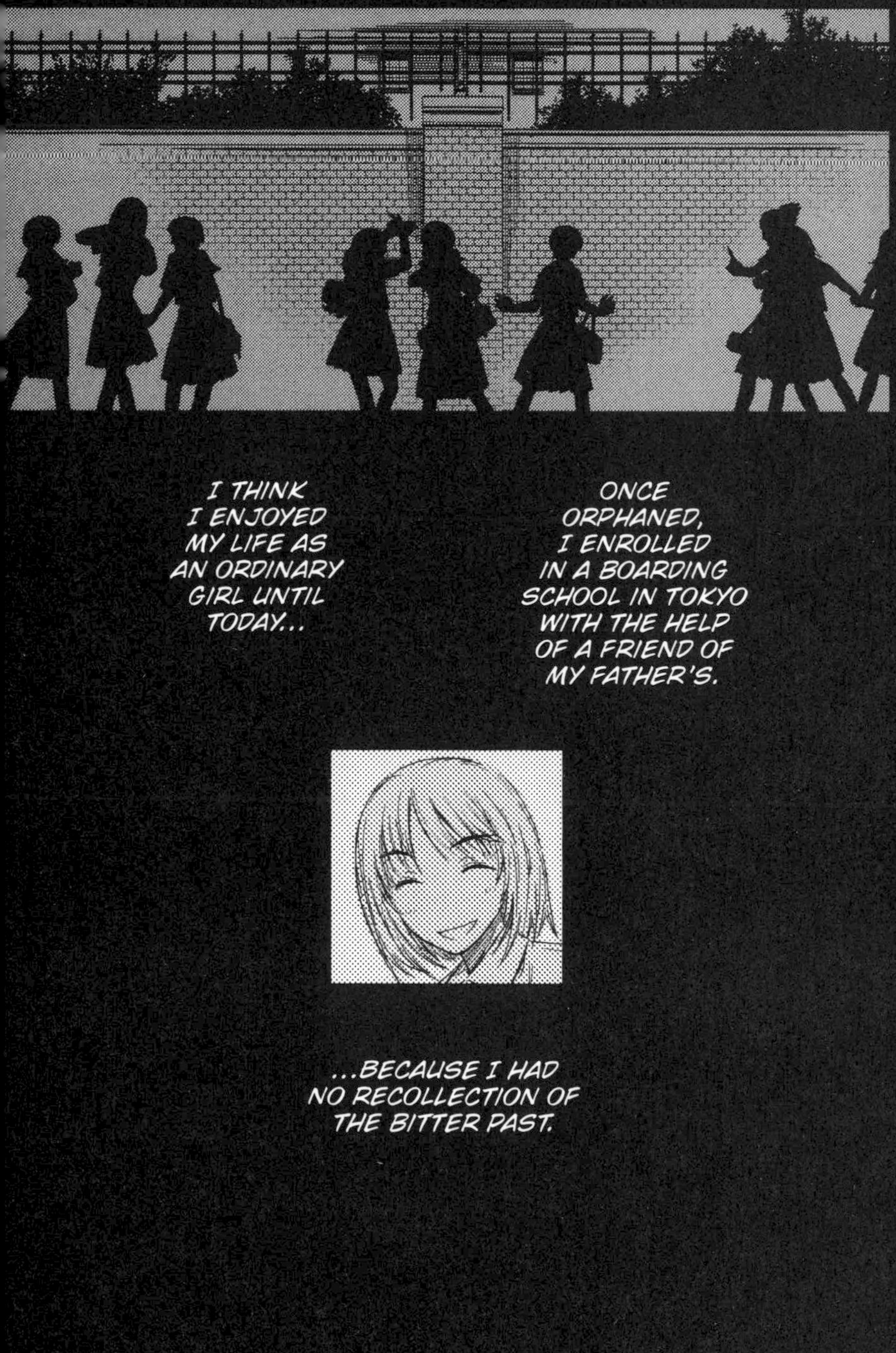
ONCE ORPHANED, I ENROLLED IN A BOARDING SCHOOL IN TOKYO WITH THE HELP OF A FRIEND OF MY FATHER'S.
I THINK I ENJOYED MY LIFE AS AN ORDINARY GIRL UNTIL TODAY...
...BECAUSE I HAD NO RECOLLECTION OF THE BITTER PAST.

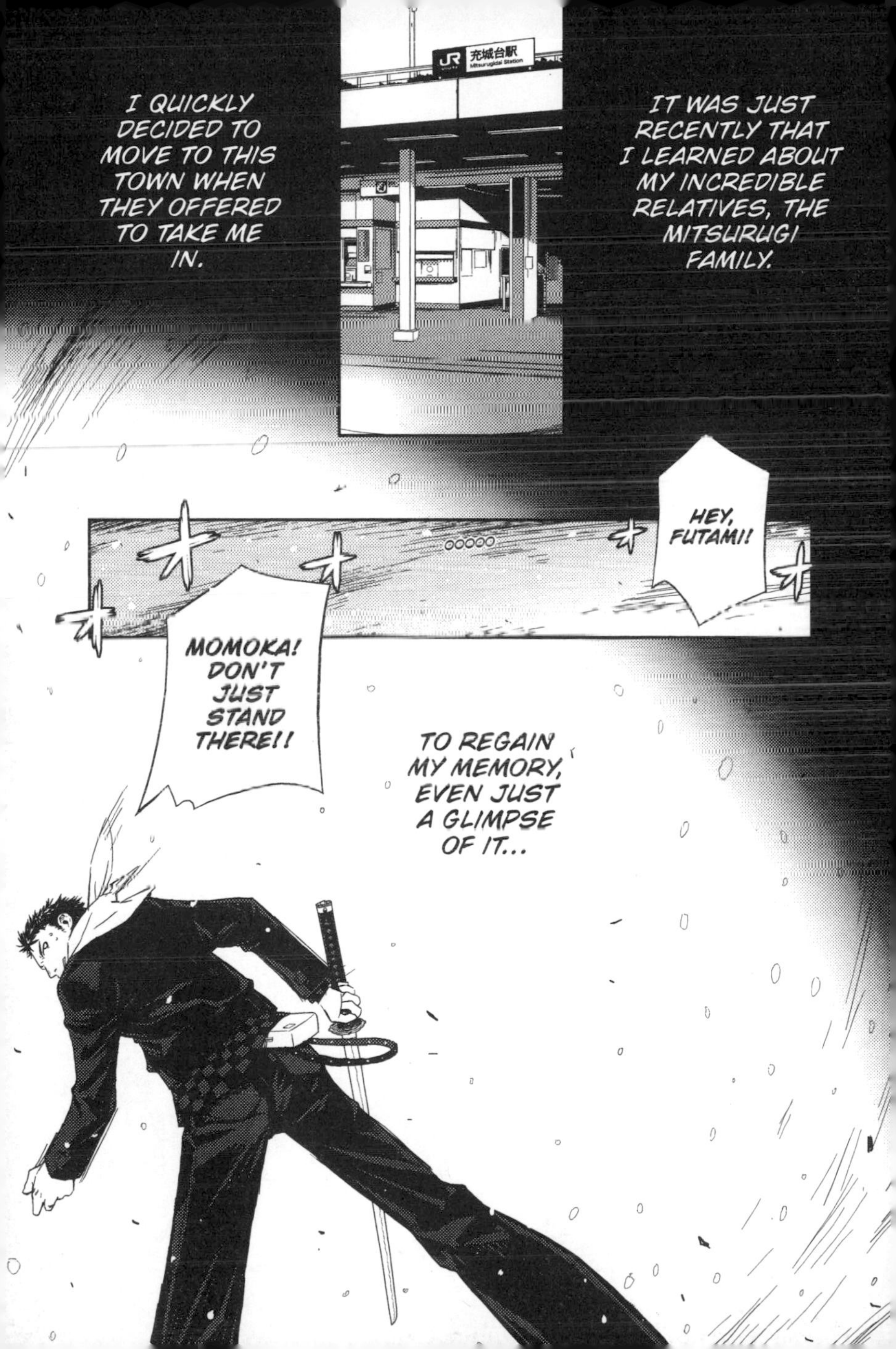
IT WAS JUST RECENTLY THAT I LEARNED ABOUT MY INCREDIBLE RELATIVES, THE MITSURUGI FAMILY.
JR 充城台駅
Mitsurugidai Station
I QUICKLY DECIDED TO MOVE TO THIS TOWN WHEN THEY OFFERED TO TAKE ME IN.
HEY, FUTAMI!!
MOMOKA! DON'T JUST STAND THERE!!
TO REGAIN MY MEMORY, EVEN JUST A GLIMPSE OF IT...

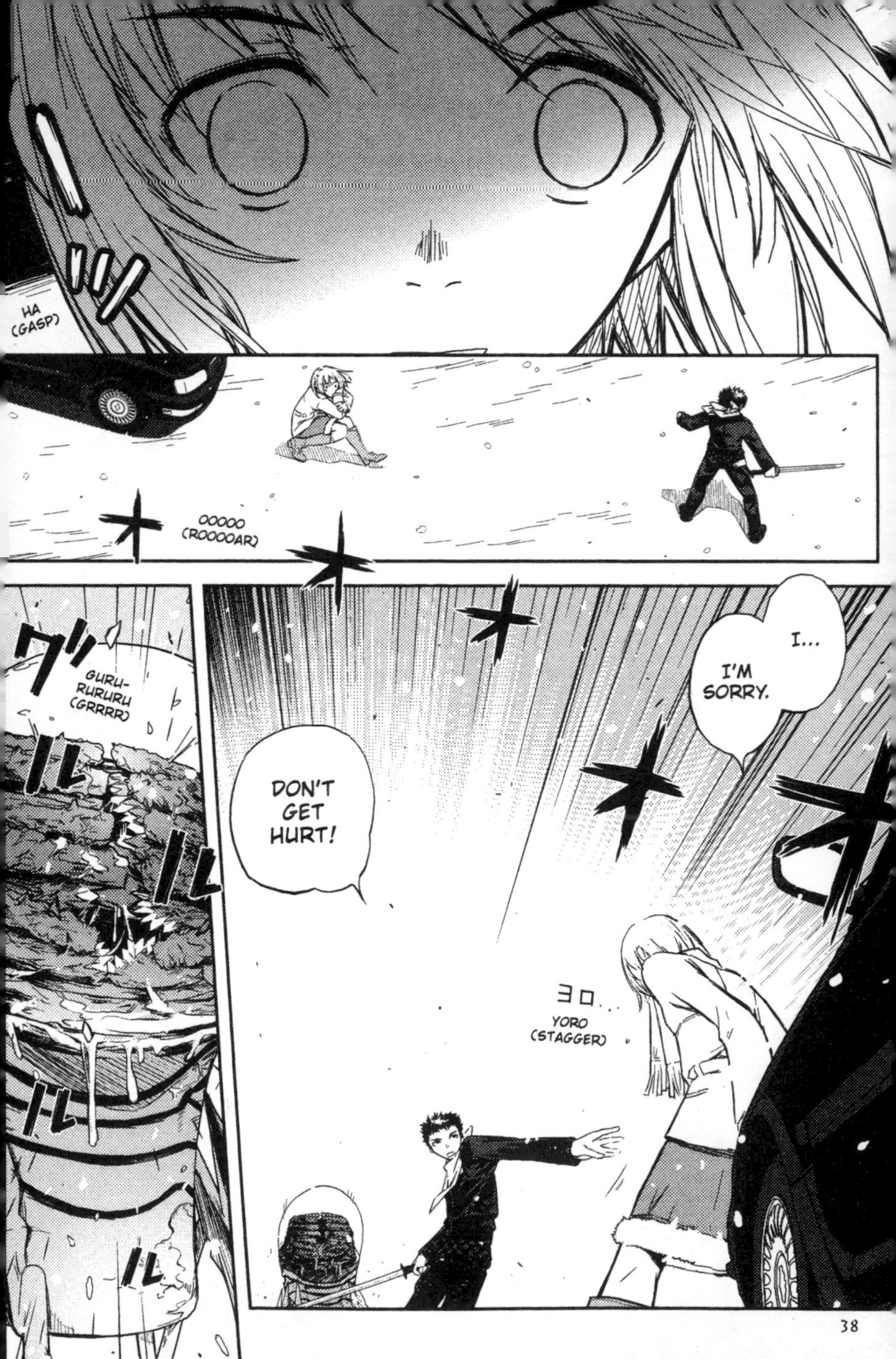
HA (GASP)
OOOOO (ROOOOAR)
I... I'M SORRY.
DON'T GET HURT!
ヨロ...
YORO (STAGGER)
GURU-RURURU (GRRRR)

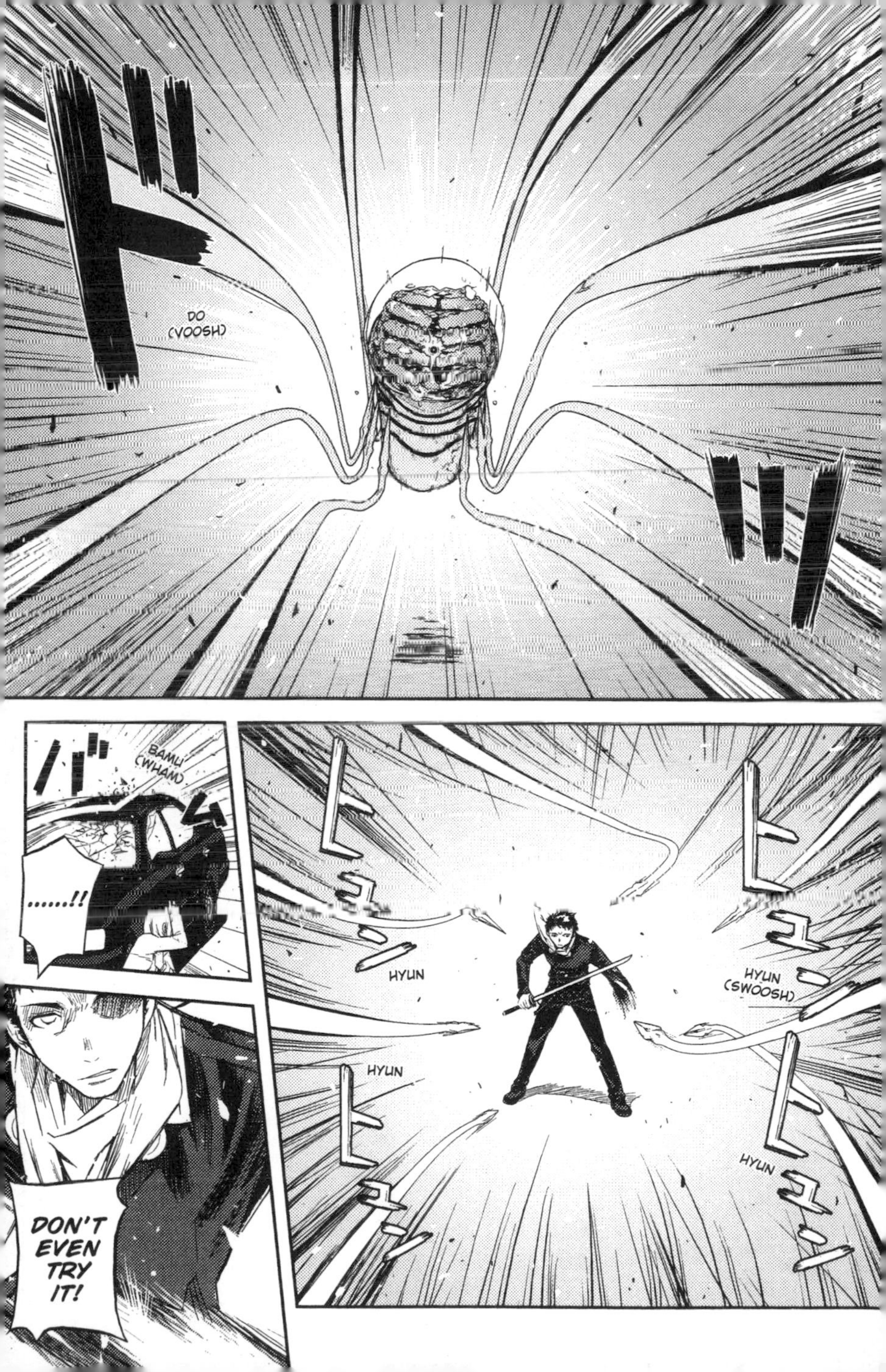
DO
(VOOSH)
HYUN
(SWOOSH)
HYUN
HYUN
HYUN
BAMU
(WHAM)
......!!
DON'T EVEN TRY IT!

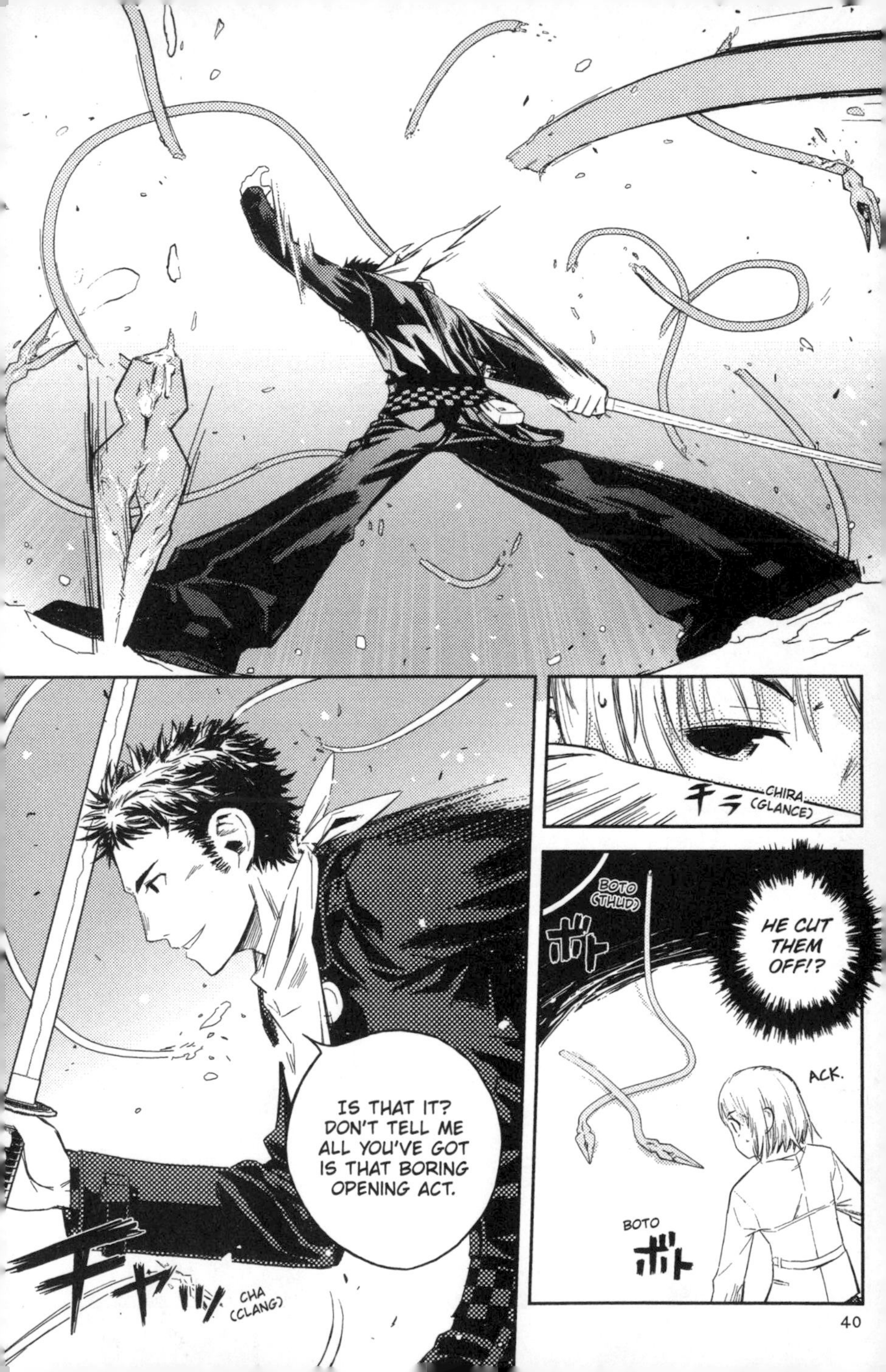
チラ
CHIRA (GLANCE)
BOTO (THUD)
ボト
HE CUT THEM OFF!?
ACK.
BOTO
ボト
IS THAT IT? DON'T TELL ME ALL YOU'VE GOT IS THAT BORING OPENING ACT.
CHA (CLANG)

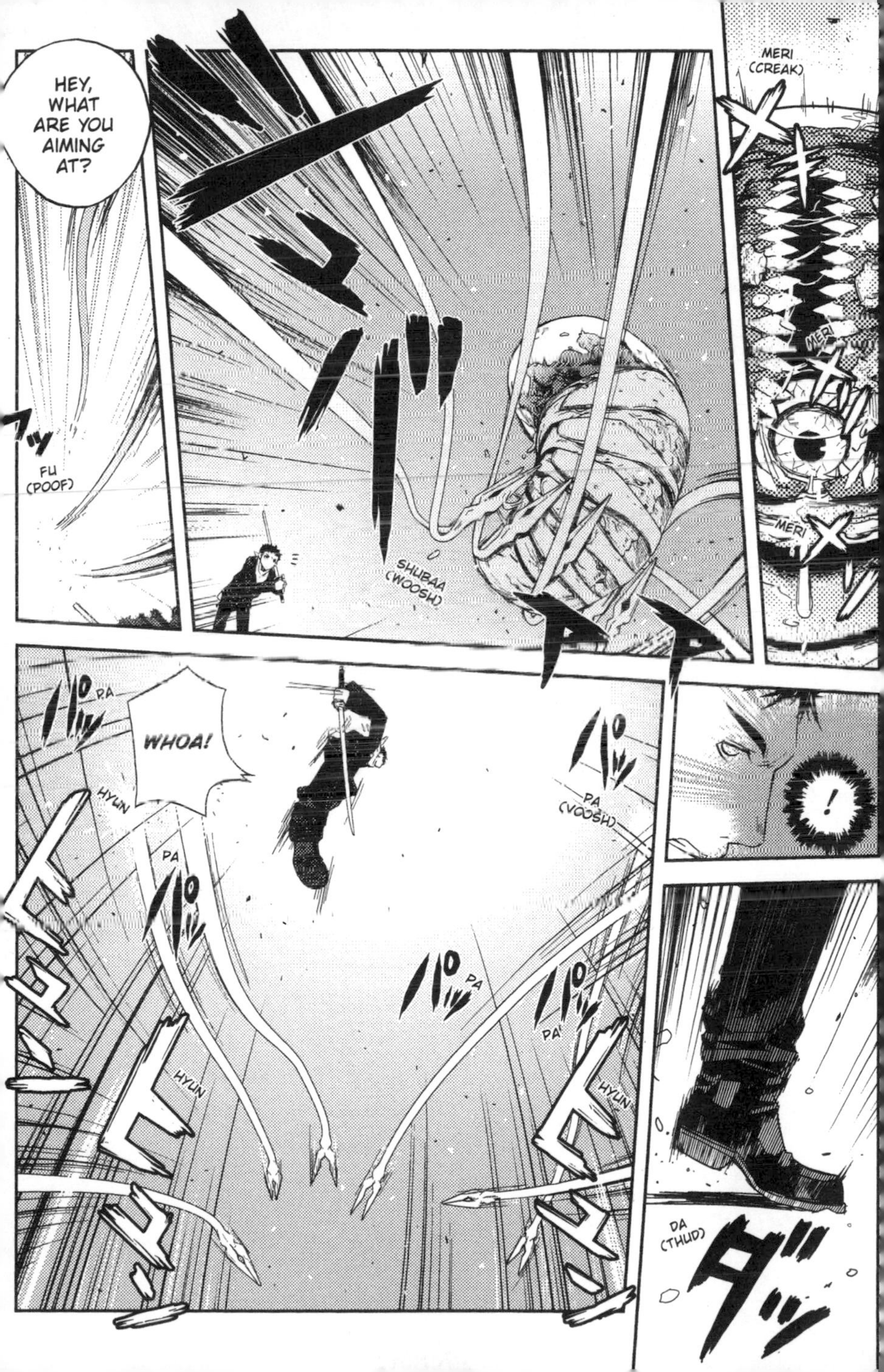
MERI (CREAK)
MERI
MERI
SHUBAA (WOOSH)
HEY, WHAT ARE YOU AIMING AT?
FU (POOF)
!
DA (THUD)
PA (VOOSH)
PA
WHOA!
HYUN
PA
PA
PA
HYUN
HYUN

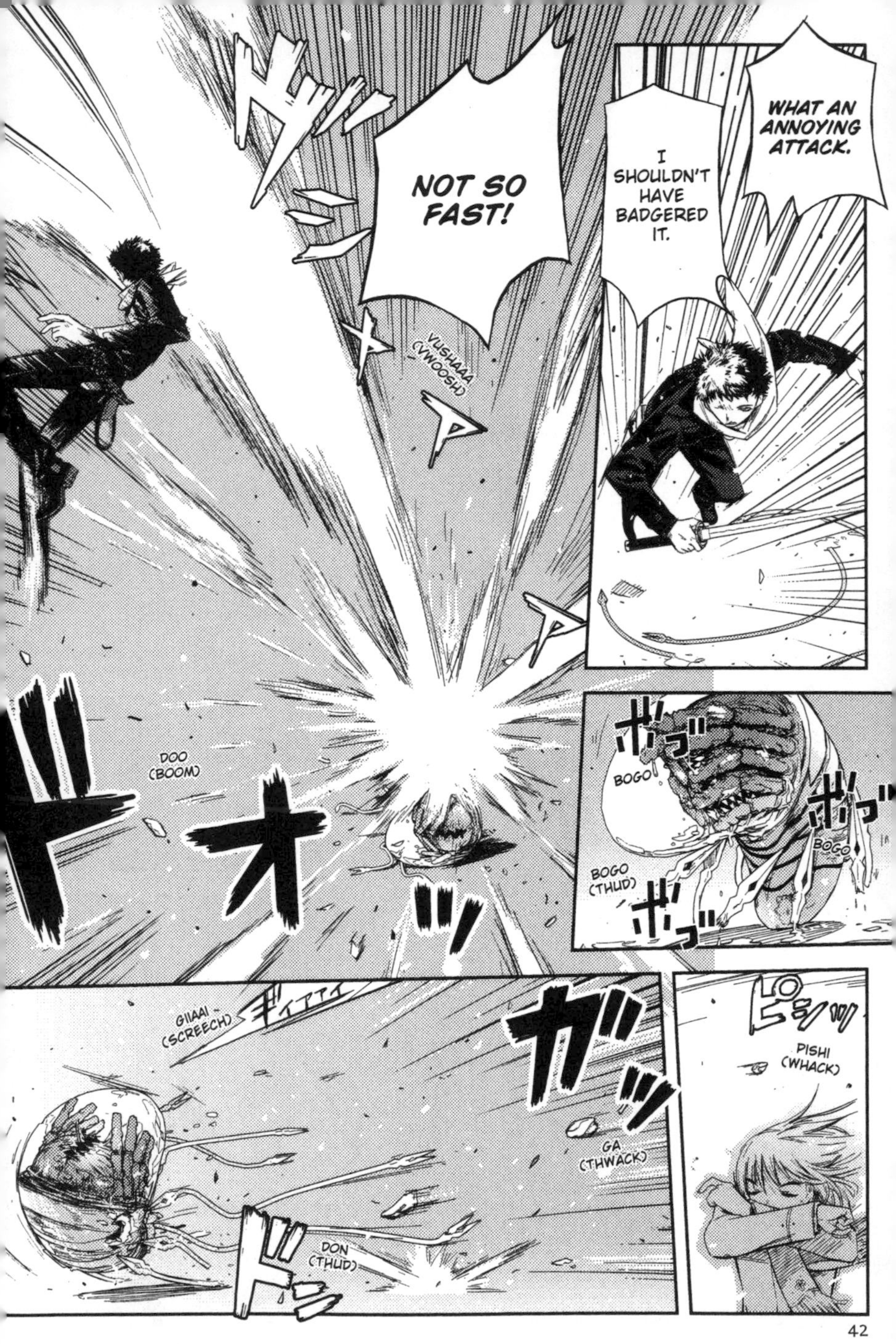

WHAT AN ANNOYING ATTACK.
I SHOULDN'T HAVE BADGERED IT.
BOGO
BOGO
BOGO (THUD)
NOT SO FAST!
VUSHAAA (VWOOSH)
DOO (BOOM)
PISHI (WHACK)
GIIAAI (SCREECH)
GA (THWACK)
DON (THUD)

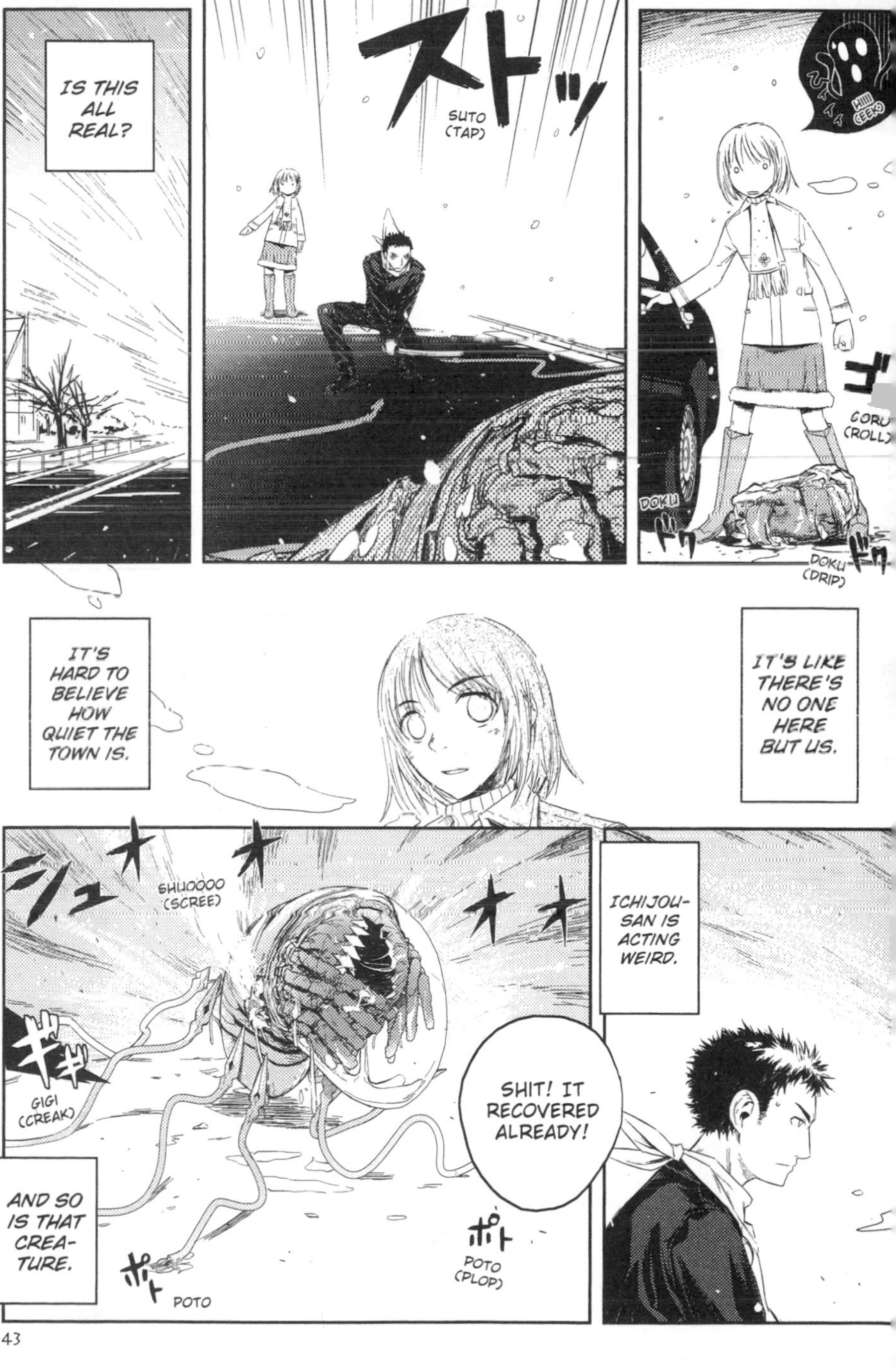
HIII (EEK)
CORU (ROLL)
DOKU
DOKU (DRIP)
SUTO (TAP)
IS THIS ALL REAL?
IT'S LIKE THERE'S NO ONE HERE BUT US.
IT'S HARD TO BELIEVE HOW QUIET THE TOWN IS.
ICHIJOU-SAN IS ACTING WEIRD.
SHIT! IT RECOVERED ALREADY!
SHUOOOO (SCREE)
GIGI (CREAK)
POTO (PLOP)
AND SO IS THAT CREATURE.
POTO

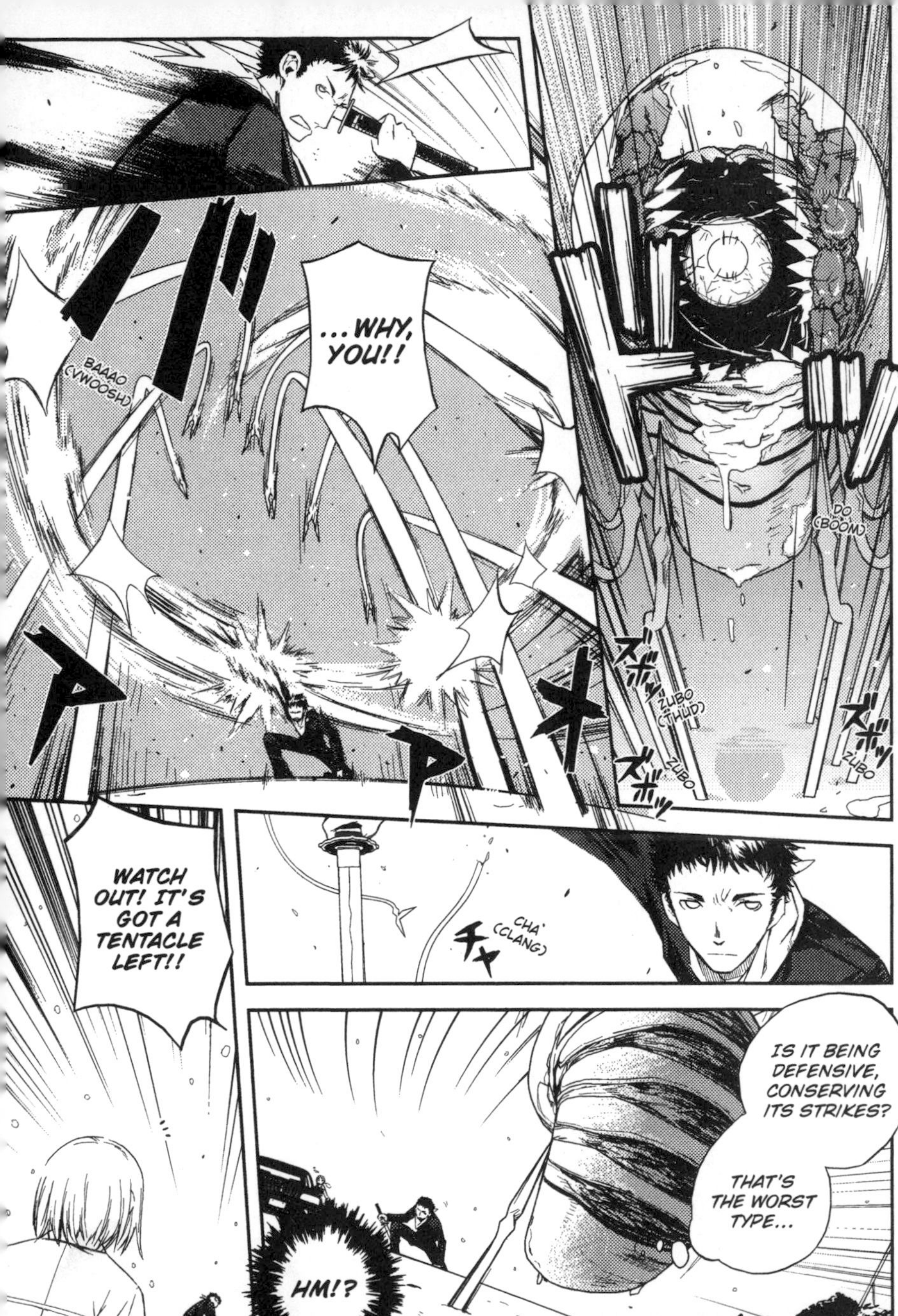
DO (BOOM)
ZUBO (THUD)
ZUBO
ZUBO
BAAAO (VWOOSH)
...WHY, YOU!!
CHA' (CLANG)
IS IT BEING DEFENSIVE, CONSERVING ITS STRIKES?
THAT'S THE WORST TYPE...
HM!?
WATCH OUT! IT'S GOT A TENTACLE LEFT!!

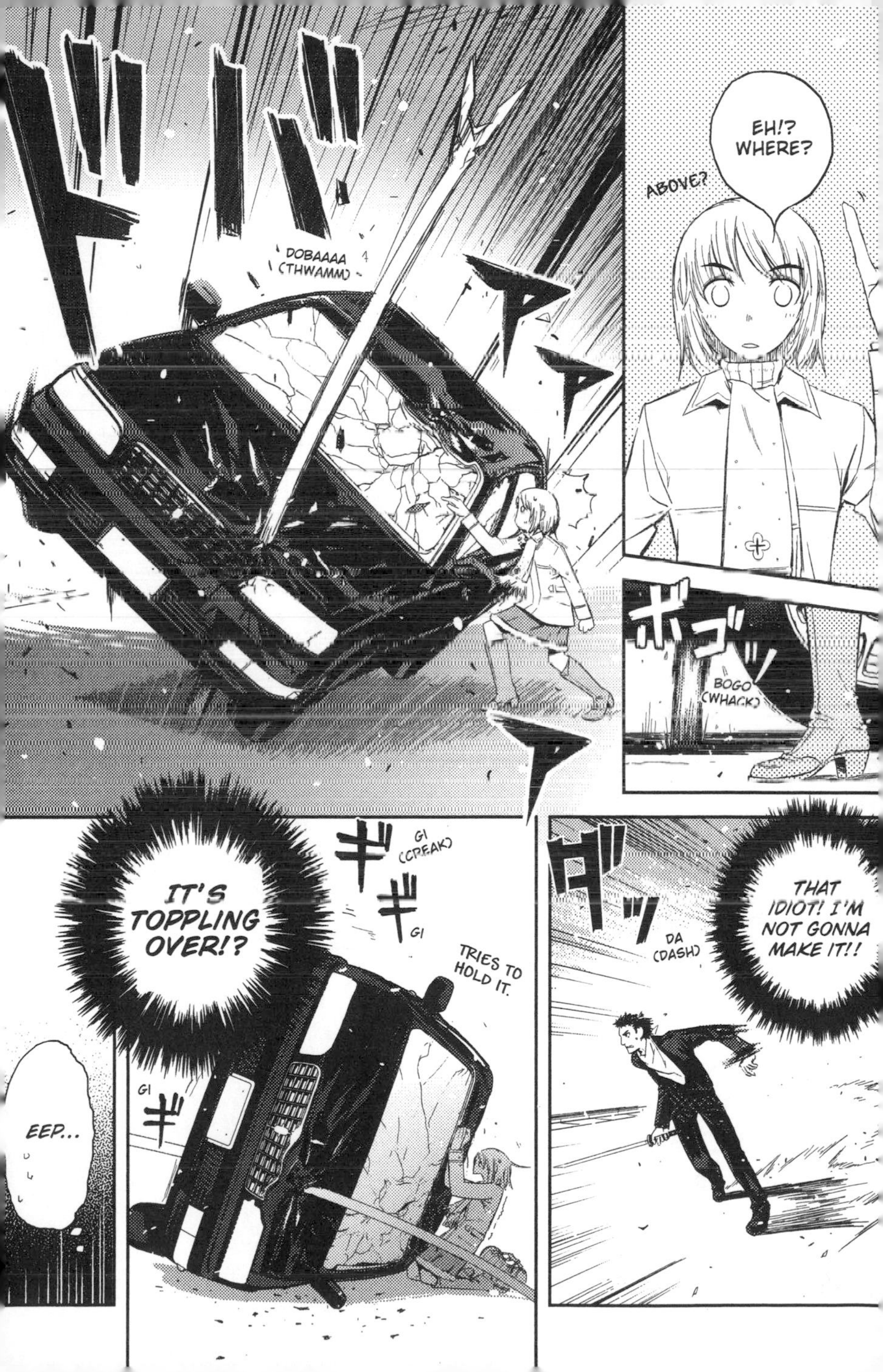
EH!? WHERE?
ABOVE?
BOGO (WHACK)
DOBAAAA (THWAMM)
THAT IDIOT! I'M NOT GONNA MAKE IT!!
DA (DASH)
IT'S TOPPLING OVER!?
GI (CREAK)
GI
TRIES TO HOLD IT.
GI
EEP...

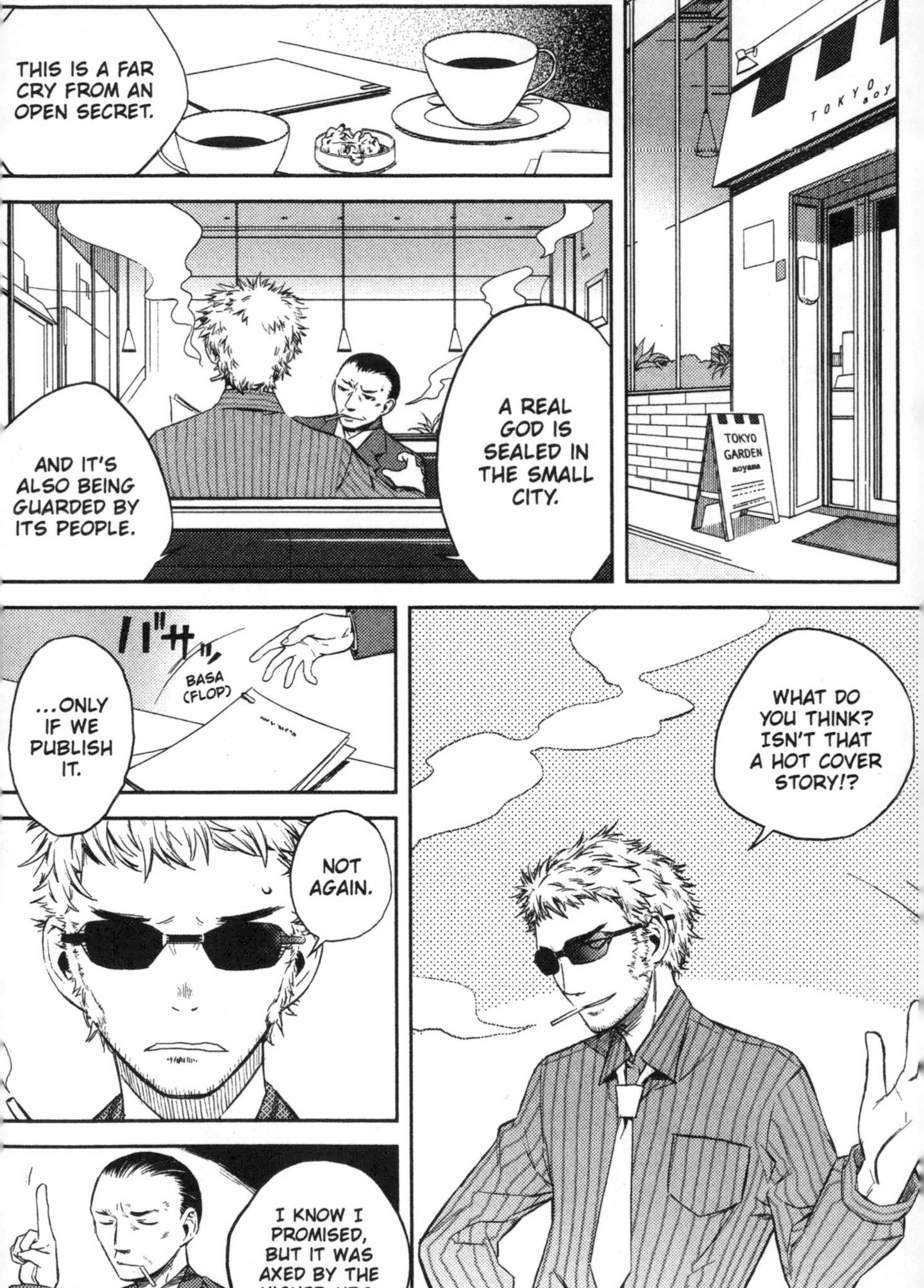
TOKYO aoy
TOKYO GARDEN aoyama
THIS IS A FAR CRY FROM AN OPEN SECRET.
A REAL GOD IS SEALED IN THE SMALL CITY.
AND IT'S ALSO BEING GUARDED BY ITS PEOPLE.
WHAT DO YOU THINK? ISN'T THAT A HOT COVER STORY!?
BASA (FLOP)
...ONLY IF WE PUBLISH IT.
NOT AGAIN.
I KNOW I PROMISED, BUT IT WAS AXED BY THE HIGHER-UPS.

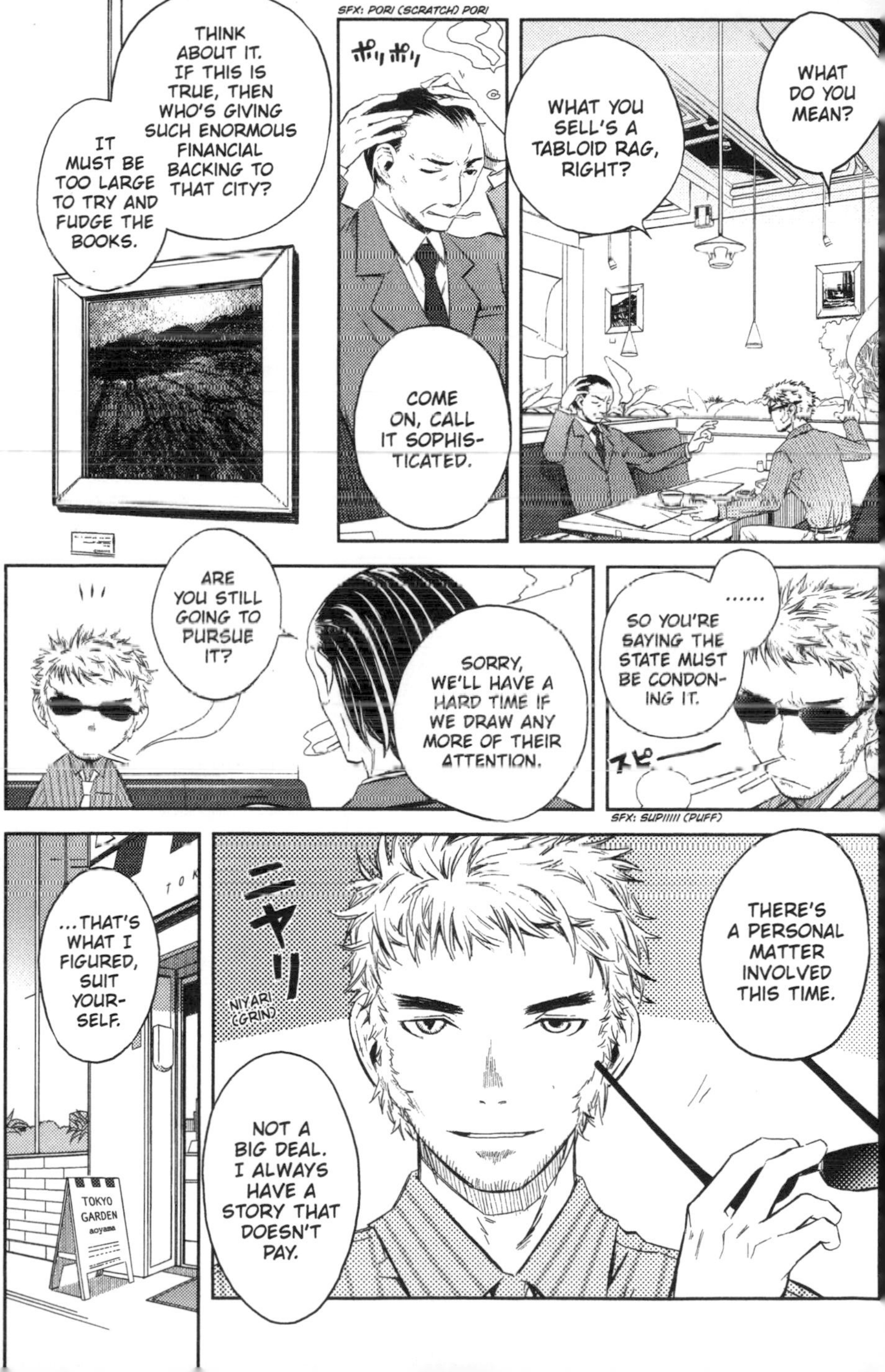
WHAT DO YOU MEAN?
WHAT YOU SELL'S A TABLOID RAG, RIGHT?
SFX: PORI (SCRATCH) PORI
ポリポリ
COME ON, CALL IT SOPHISTICATED.
THINK ABOUT IT. IF THIS IS TRUE, THEN WHO'S GIVING SUCH ENORMOUS FINANCIAL BACKING TO THAT CITY?
IT MUST BE TOO LARGE TO TRY AND FUDGE THE BOOKS.
......
SO YOU'RE SAYING THE STATE MUST BE CONDONING IT.
スピー
SFX: SUPIIIII (PUFF)
SORRY, WE'LL HAVE A HARD TIME IF WE DRAW ANY MORE OF THEIR ATTENTION.
ARE YOU STILL GOING TO PURSUE IT?
THERE'S A PERSONAL MATTER INVOLVED THIS TIME.
ニヤリ
NIYARI (GRIN)
NOT A BIG DEAL. I ALWAYS HAVE A STORY THAT DOESN'T PAY.
...THAT'S WHAT I FIGURED, SUIT YOURSELF.
TOKYO GARDEN aoyama

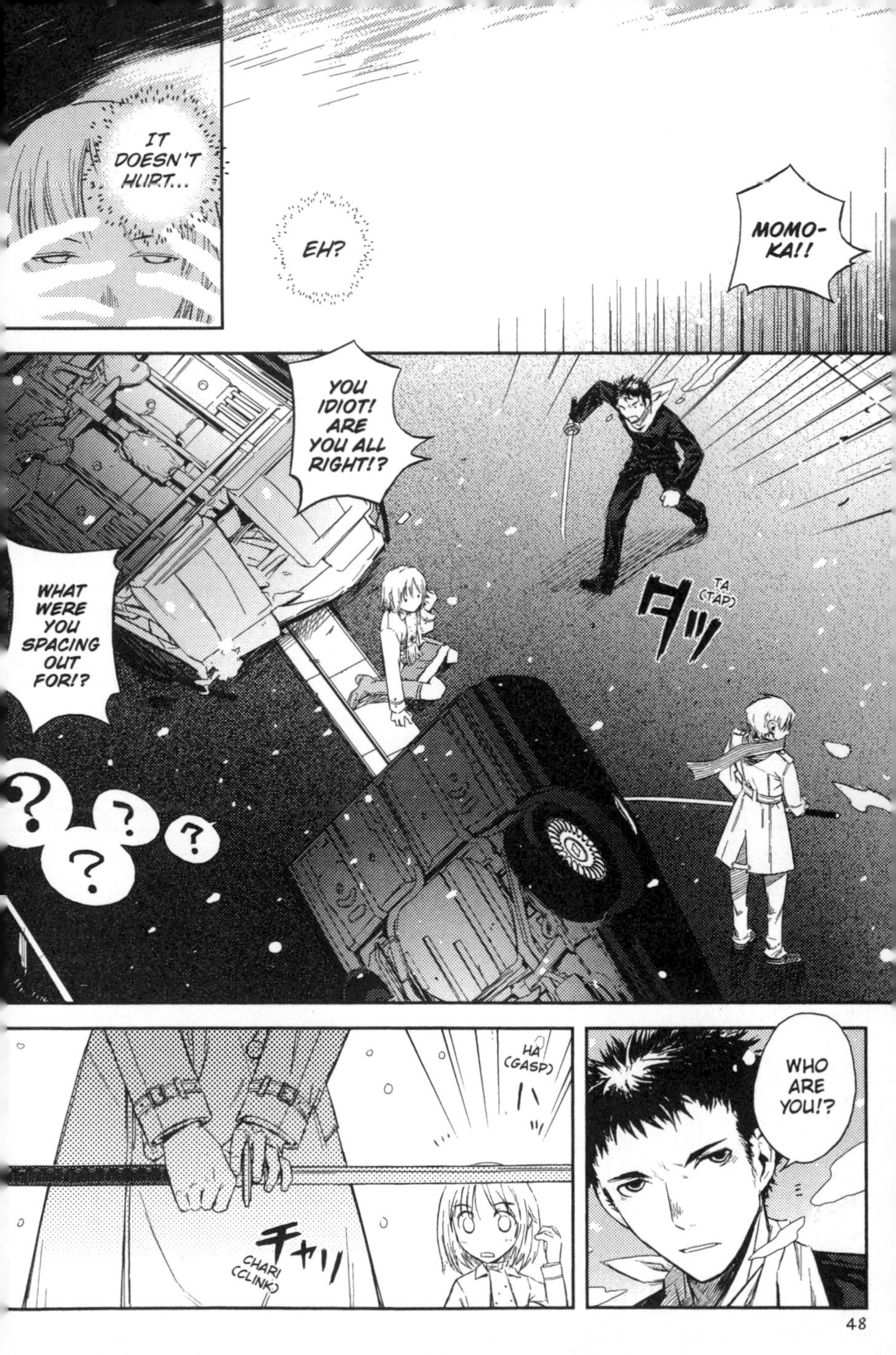
MOMO-KA!!
EH?
IT DOESN'T HURT...
YOU IDIOT! ARE YOU ALL RIGHT!?
ダッ
TA (TAP)
WHAT WERE YOU SPACING OUT FOR!?
? ? ? ?
WHO ARE YOU!?
HA (GASP)
ハ
チャリ
CHARI (CLINK)

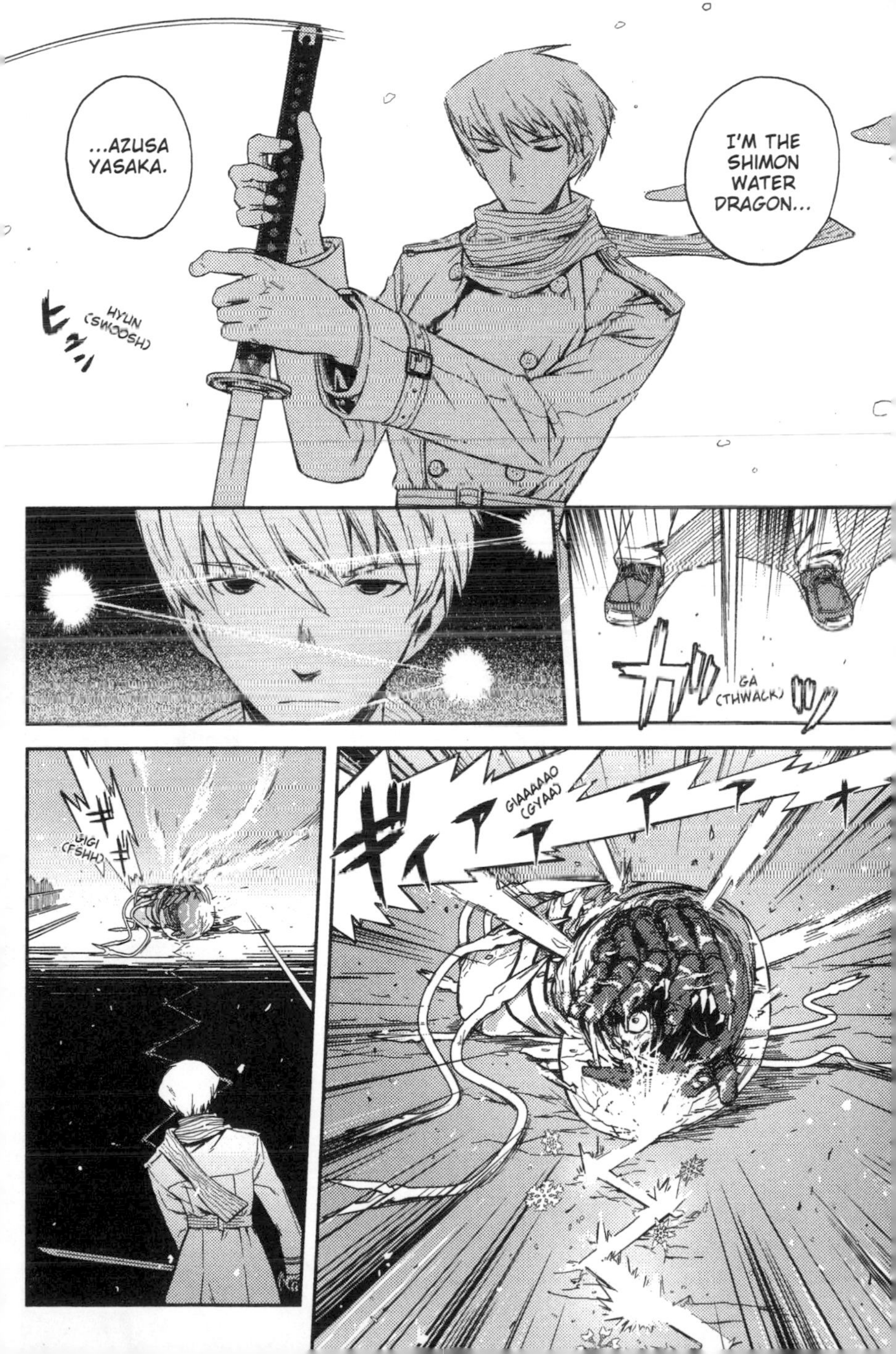
I'M THE SHIMON WATER DRAGON...
...AZUSA YASAKA.
HYUN (SWOOSH)
GA (THWACK)
GIAAAAAO (GYAA)
GIGI (FSHH)

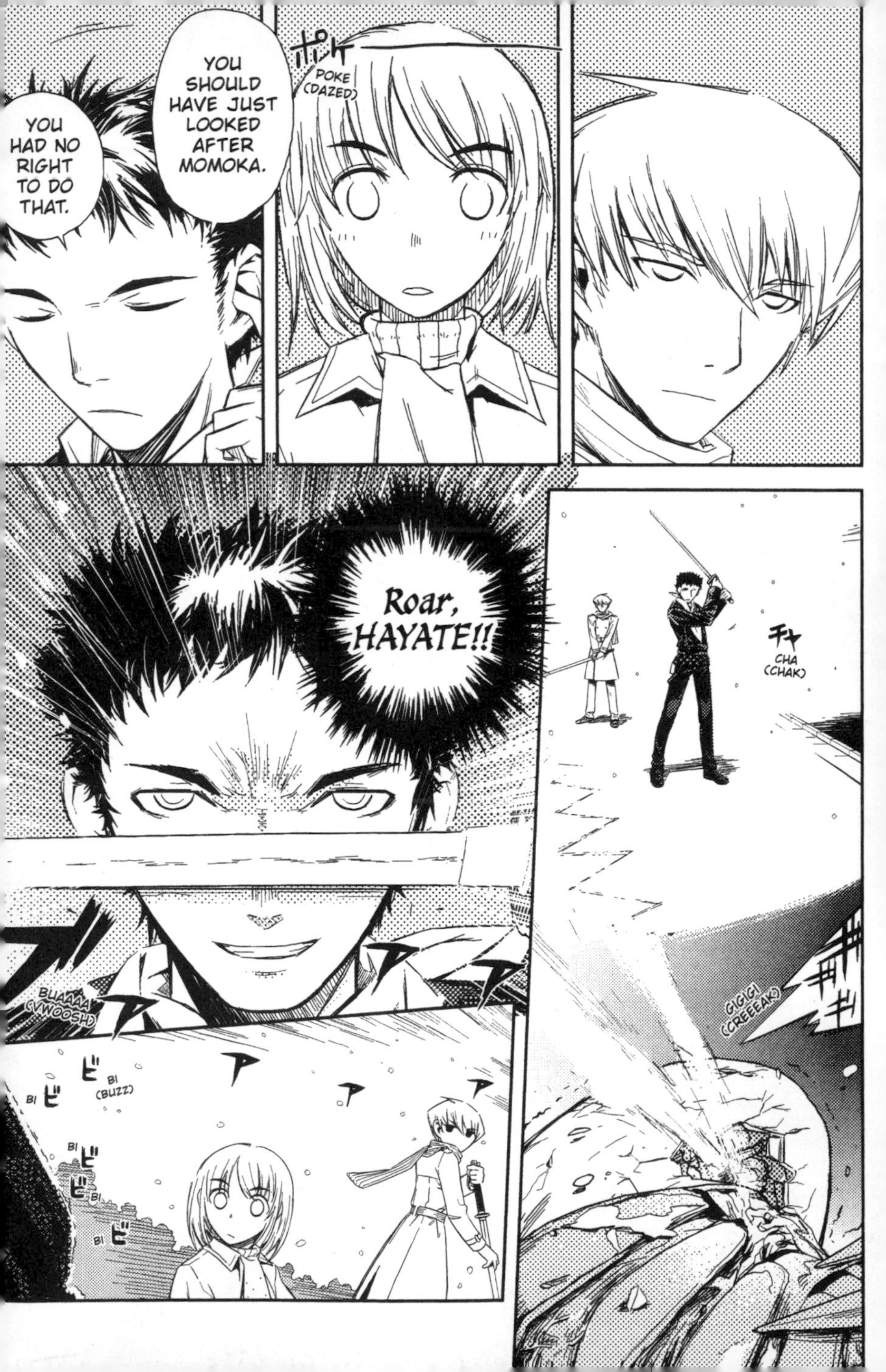

POKE (DAZED)
YOU SHOULD HAVE JUST LOOKED AFTER MOMOKA.
YOU HAD NO RIGHT TO DO THAT.
CHA (CHAK)
GIGIGI (CREEEAK)
Roar, HAYATE!!
BUAAAA (VWOOSH)
BI
BI (BUZZ)
BI
BI
BI

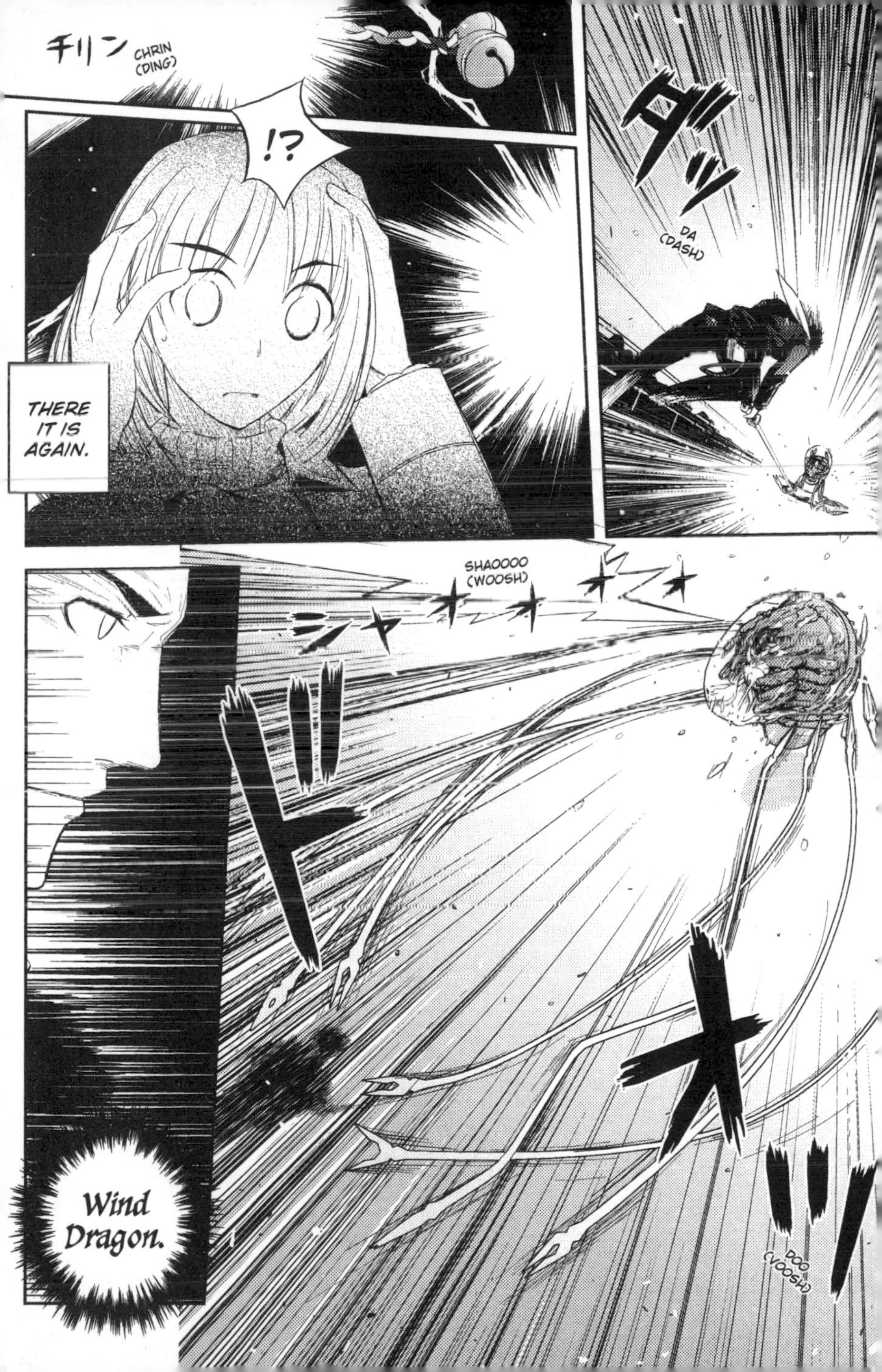
ダッ
DA
(DASH)
チリン
CHRIN
(DING)
!?
THERE IT IS AGAIN.
SHAOOOO
(WOOSH)
DOO
(VOOSH)
Wind Dragon.

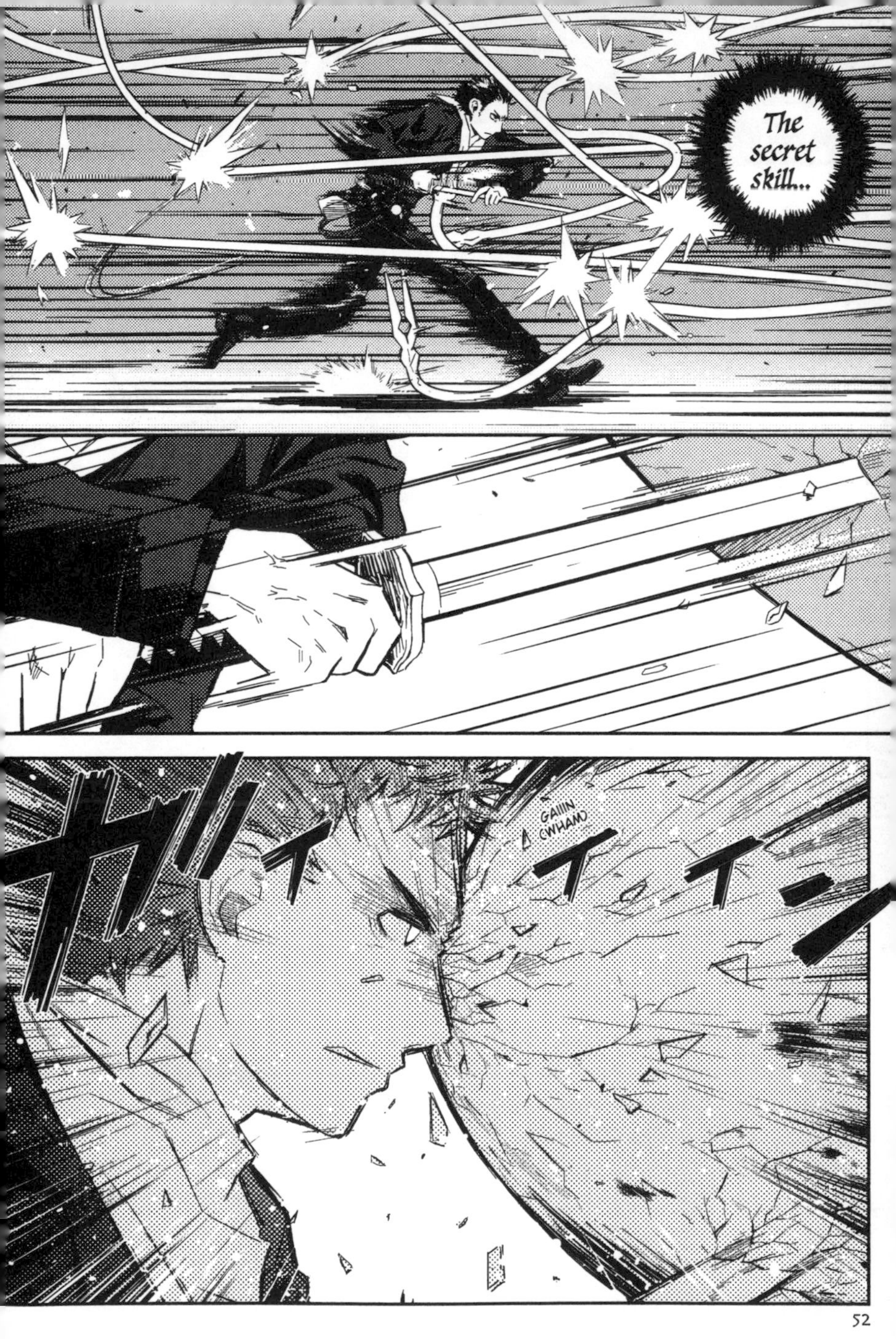
The secret skill...
GAIIN (WHAM)

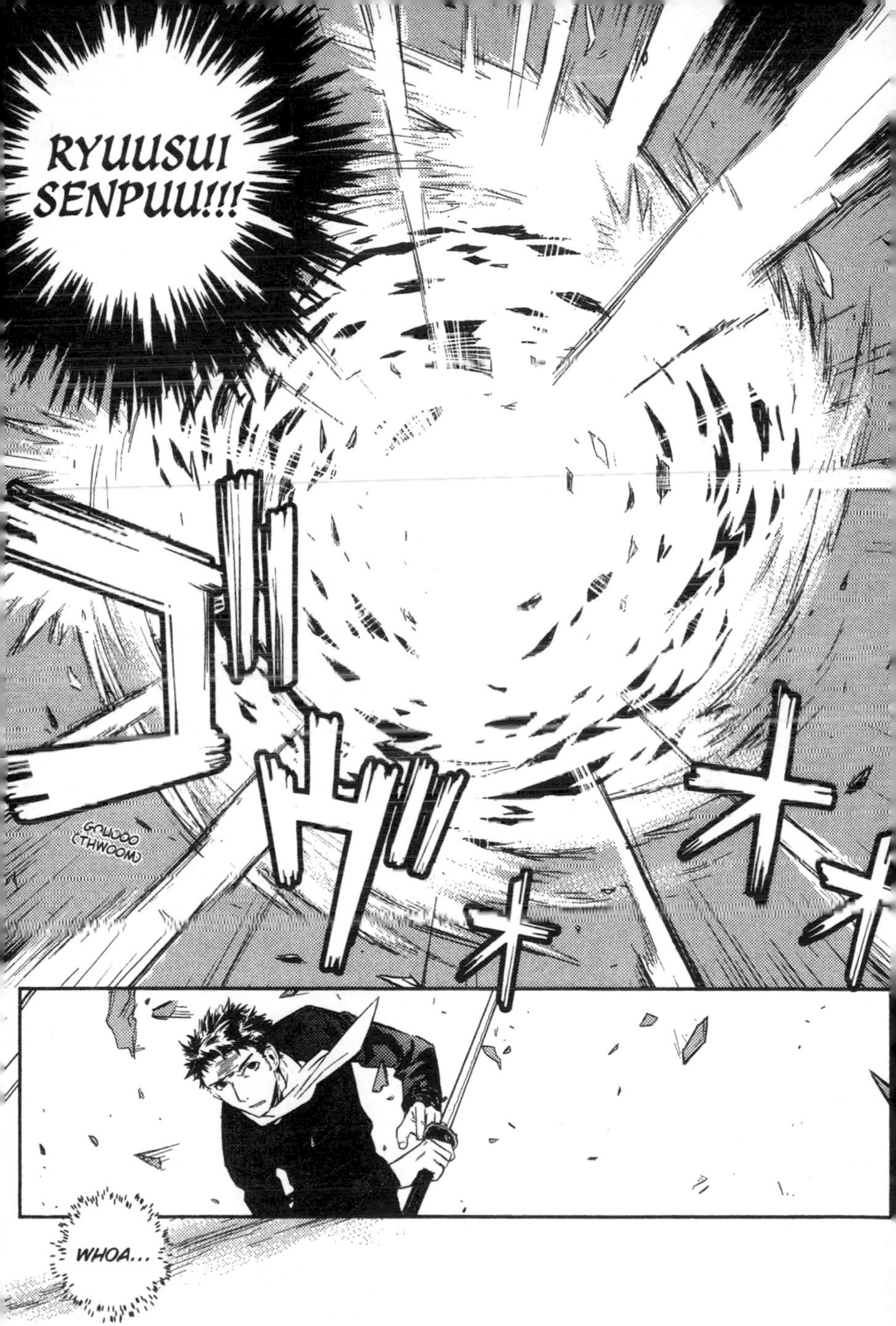
RYUUSUI SENPUU!!!
GOWOOO (THWOOM)
WHOA...

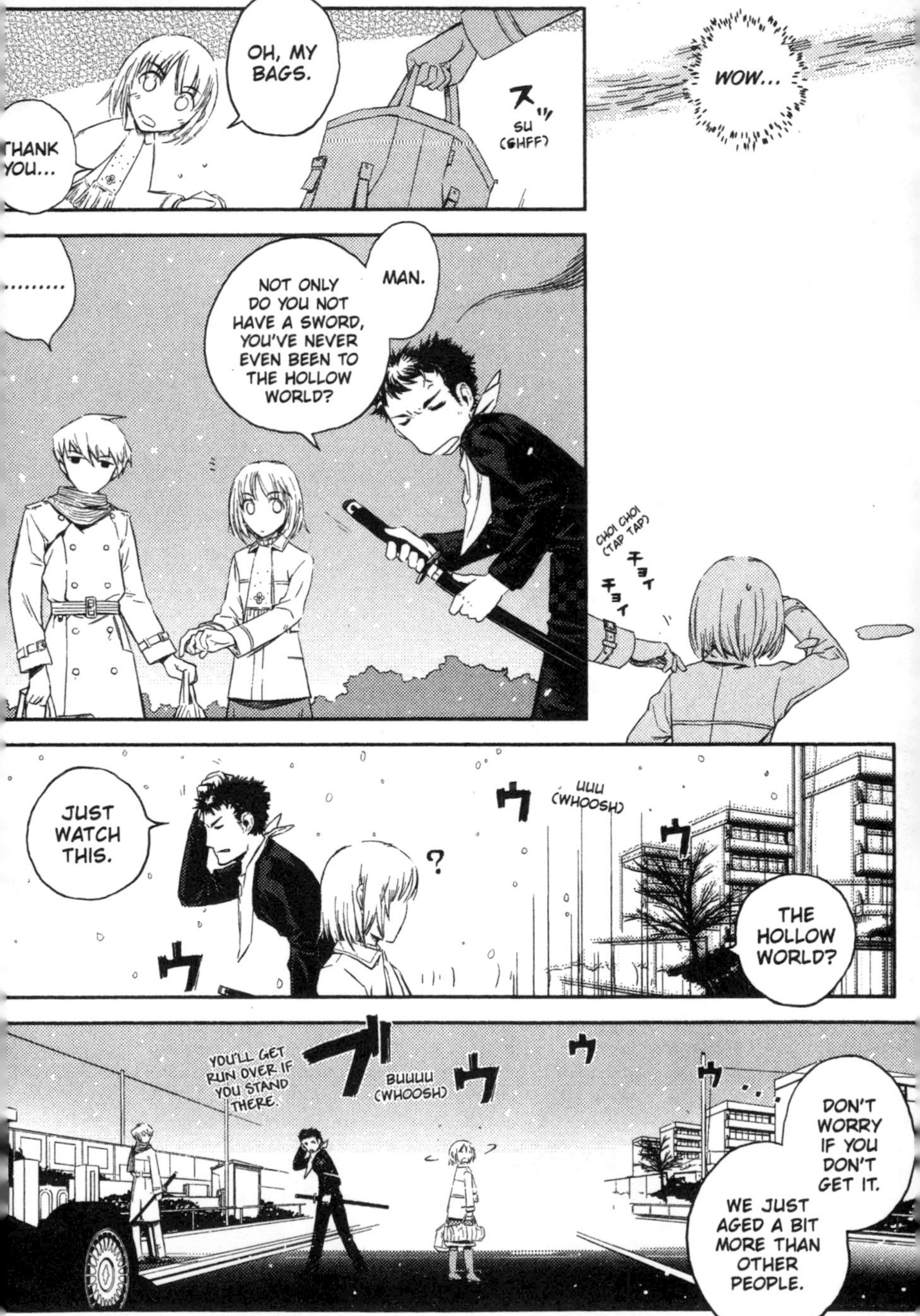
WOW...
OH, MY BAGS.
スッ
SU (SHFF)
THANK YOU...
チョイ チョイ
CHOI CHOI (TAP TAP)
MAN.
NOT ONLY DO YOU NOT HAVE A SWORD, YOU'VE NEVER EVEN BEEN TO THE HOLLOW WORLD?
....
THE HOLLOW WORLD?
ウ
UUU (WHOOSH)
ウ
?
JUST WATCH THIS.
ウ
DON'T WORRY IF YOU DON'T GET IT.
WE JUST AGED A BIT MORE THAN OTHER PEOPLE.
ウ
ウ
ブ
ウ
BUUUU (WHOOSH)
YOU'LL GET RUN OVER IF YOU STAND THERE.

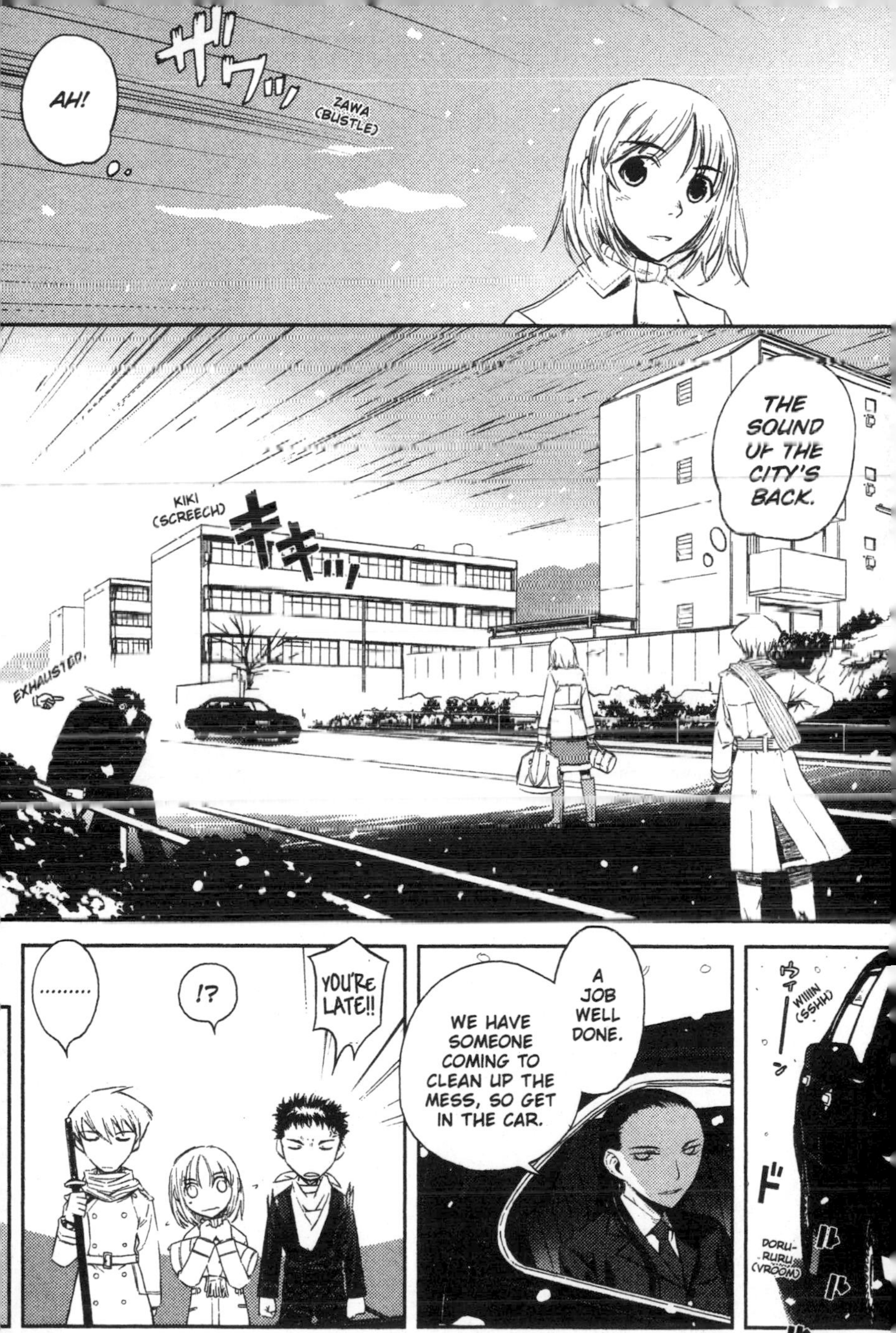
AH!
ZAWA (BUSTLE)
THE SOUND OF THE CITY'S BACK.
KIKI (SCREECH)
EXHAUSTED.
WIIIN (SSHH)
DORU-RURU (VROOM)
A JOB WELL DONE.
WE HAVE SOMEONE COMING TO CLEAN UP THE MESS, SO GET IN THE CAR.
YOU'RE LATE!!
!?
....

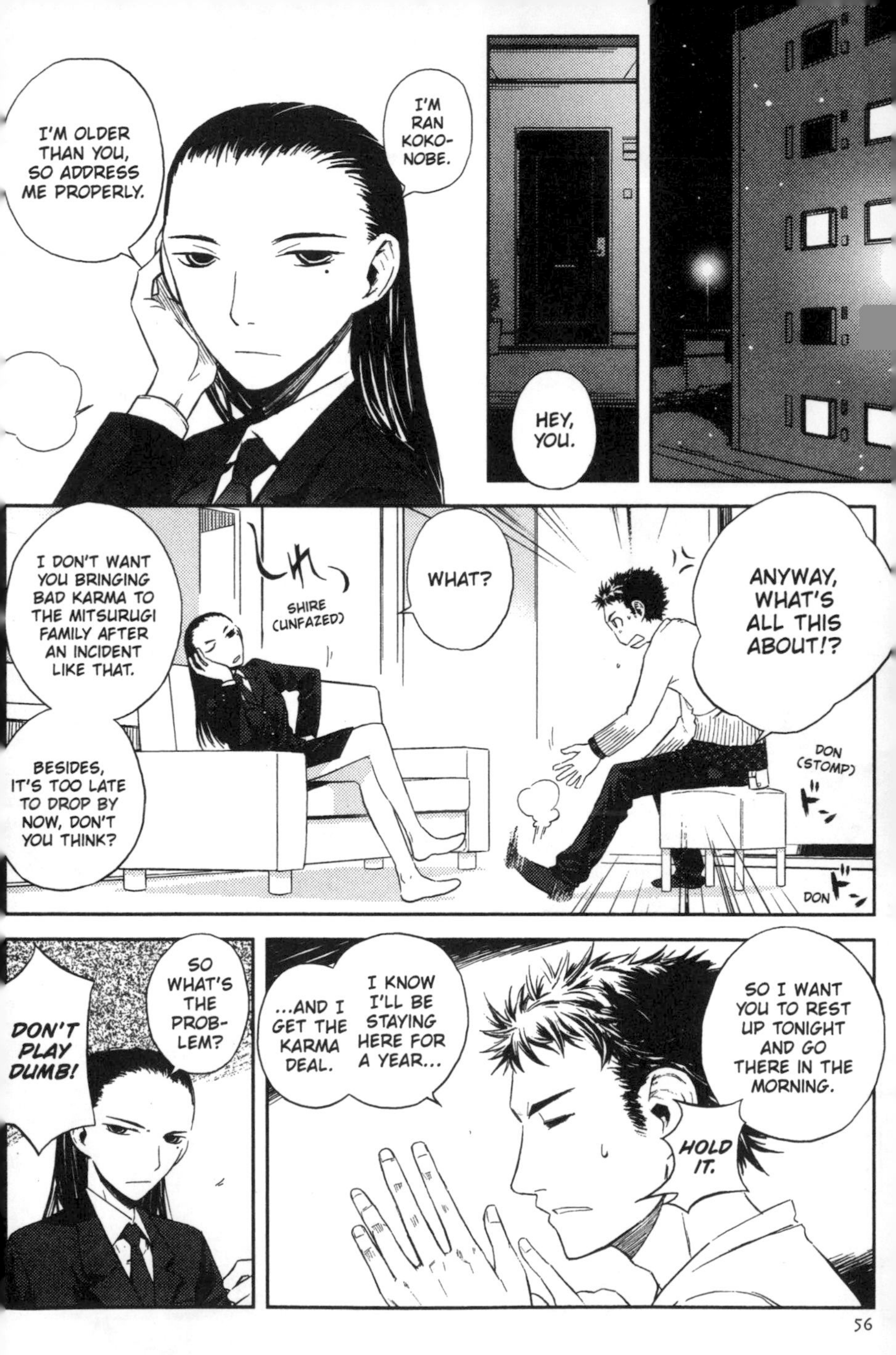
HEY, YOU.
I'M RAN KOKO-NOBE.
I'M OLDER THAN YOU, SO ADDRESS ME PROPERLY.
ANYWAY, WHAT'S ALL THIS ABOUT!?
DON (STOMP)
DON
WHAT?
SHIRE (UNFAZED)
I DON'T WANT YOU BRINGING BAD KARMA TO THE MITSURUGI FAMILY AFTER AN INCIDENT LIKE THAT.
BESIDES, IT'S TOO LATE TO DROP BY NOW, DON'T YOU THINK?
SO I WANT YOU TO REST UP TONIGHT AND GO THERE IN THE MORNING.
HOLD IT.
I KNOW I'LL BE STAYING HERE FOR A YEAR...
...AND I GET THE KARMA DEAL.
SO WHAT'S THE PROB-LEM?
DON'T PLAY DUMB!

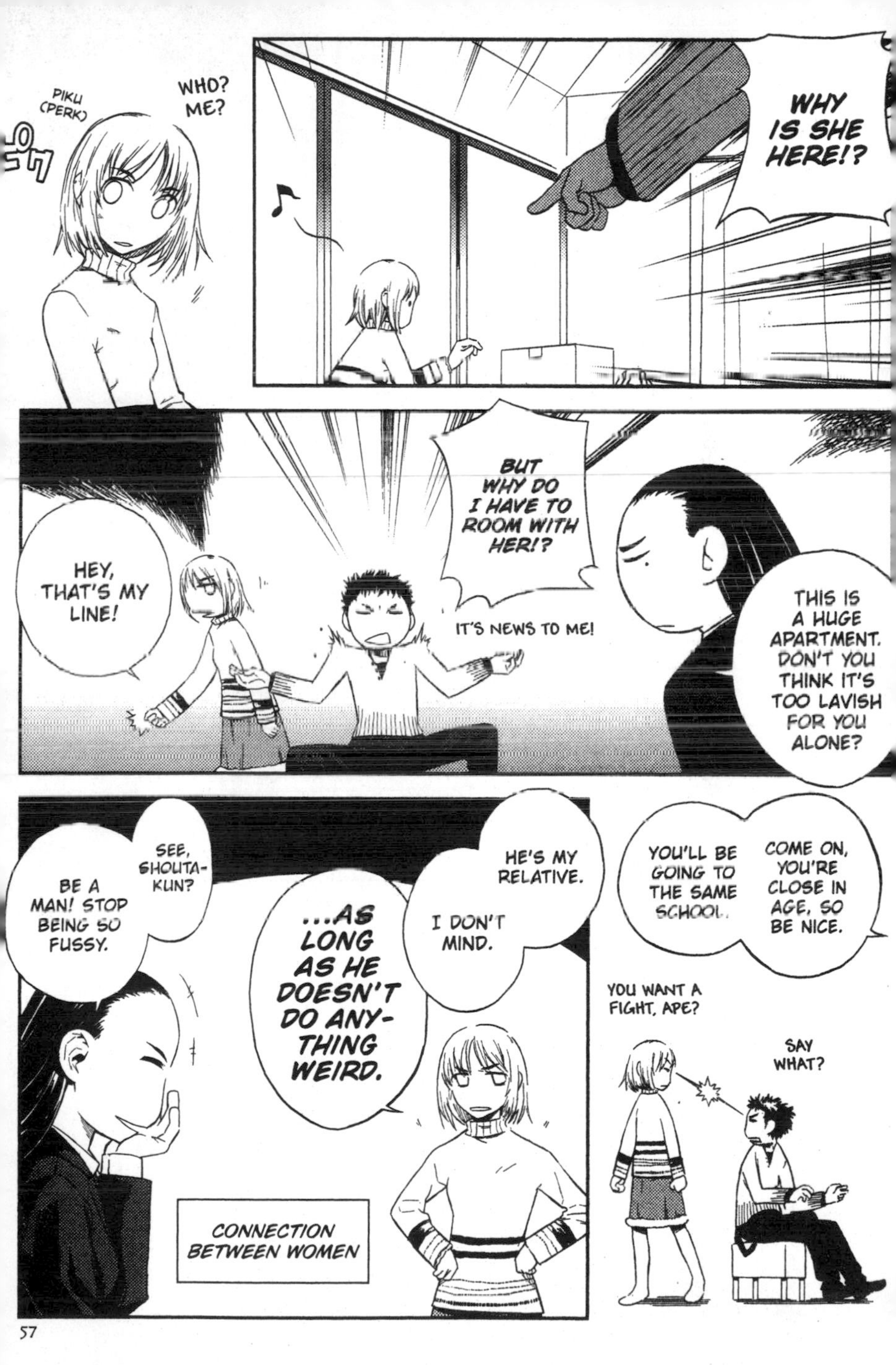
WHY IS SHE HERE!?
PIKU (PERK)
WHO? ME?
THIS IS A HUGE APARTMENT. DON'T YOU THINK IT'S TOO LAVISH FOR YOU ALONE?
BUT WHY DO I HAVE TO ROOM WITH HER!?
IT'S NEWS TO ME!
HEY, THAT'S MY LINE!
COME ON, YOU'RE CLOSE IN AGE, SO BE NICE.
YOU'LL BE GOING TO THE SAME SCHOOL.
SAY WHAT?
YOU WANT A FIGHT, APE?
HE'S MY RELATIVE.
I DON'T MIND.
...AS LONG AS HE DOESN'T DO ANY-THING WEIRD.
SEE, SHOUTA-KUN?
BE A MAN! STOP BEING SO FUSSY.
CONNECTION BETWEEN WOMEN

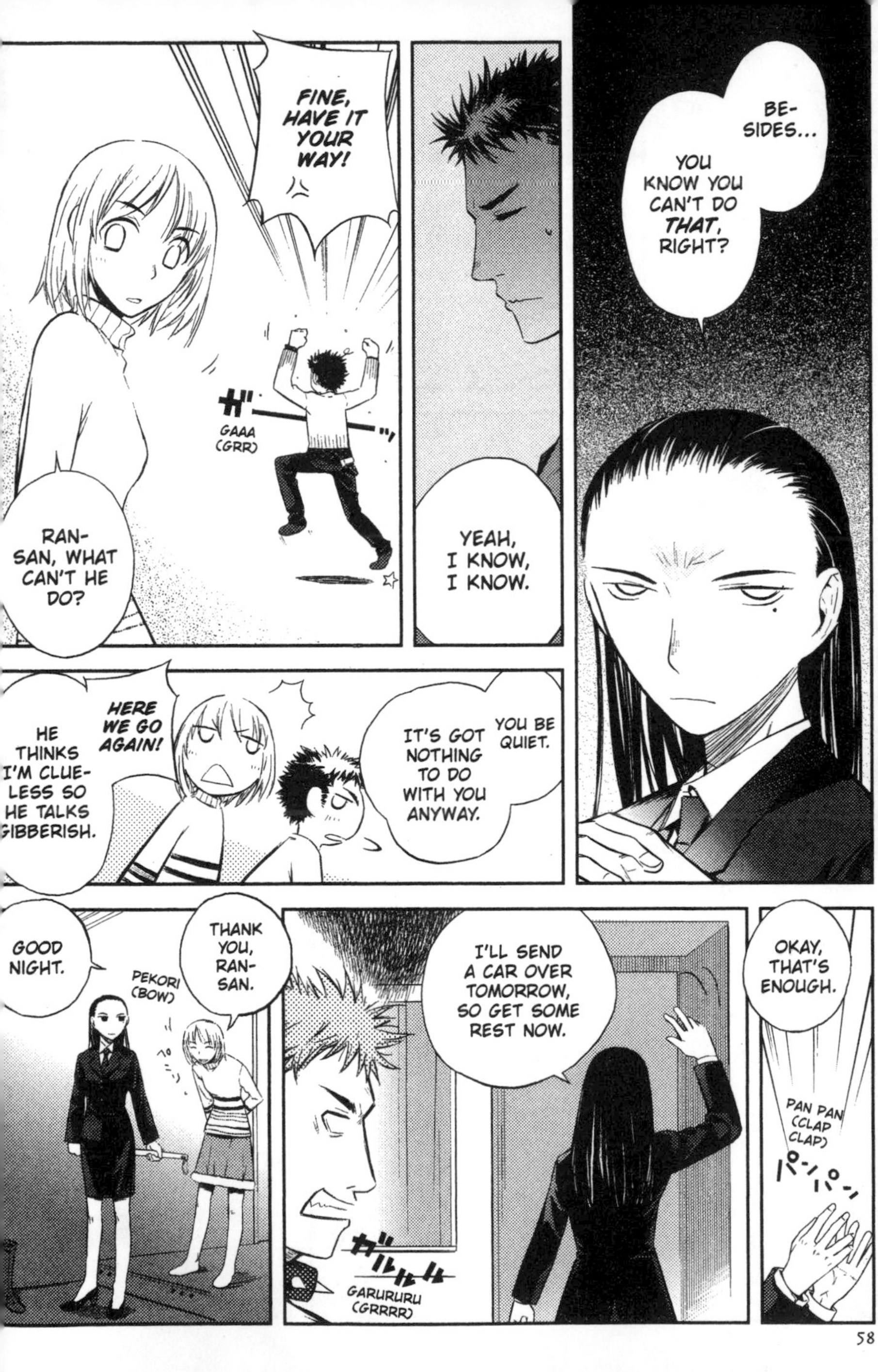
BE-SIDES...
YOU KNOW YOU CAN'T DO *THAT*, RIGHT?
YEAH, I KNOW, I KNOW.
FINE, HAVE IT YOUR WAY!
GAAA (GRR)
RAN-SAN, WHAT CAN'T HE DO?
YOU BE QUIET.
IT'S GOT NOTHING TO DO WITH YOU ANYWAY.
HERE WE GO AGAIN!
HE THINKS I'M CLUELESS SO HE TALKS GIBBERISH.
OKAY, THAT'S ENOUGH.
PAN PAN (CLAP CLAP)
I'LL SEND A CAR OVER TOMORROW, SO GET SOME REST NOW.
GARURURU (GRRRR)
THANK YOU, RAN-SAN.
PEKORI (BOW)
GOOD NIGHT.

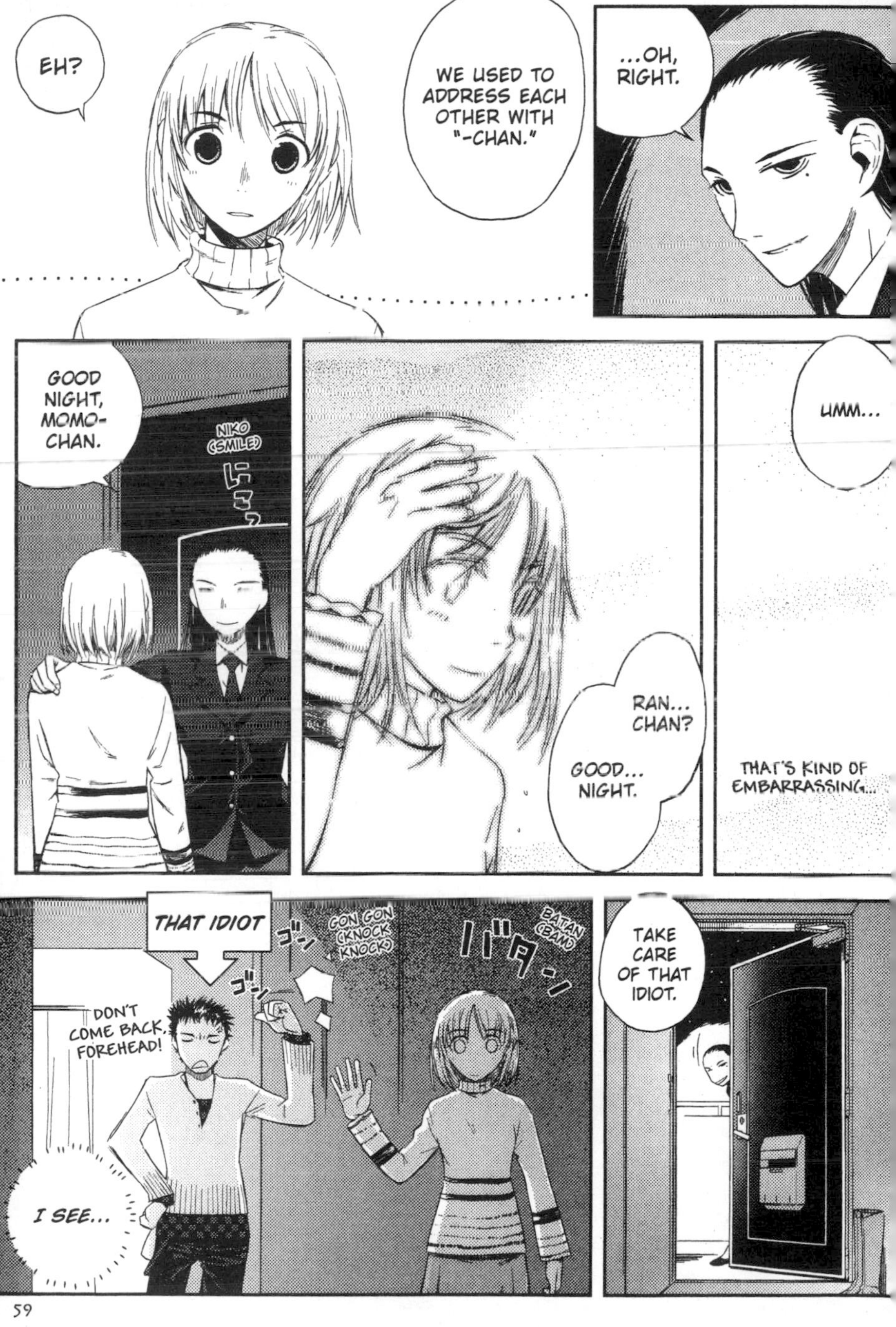
...OH, RIGHT.
WE USED TO ADDRESS EACH OTHER WITH "-CHAN."
EH?
UMM...
THAT'S KIND OF EMBARRASSING...
RAN... CHAN?
GOOD... NIGHT.
GOOD NIGHT, MOMO-CHAN.
NIKO (SMILE)
TAKE CARE OF THAT IDIOT.
BATAN (BAM)
GON GON (KNOCK KNOCK)
THAT IDIOT
DON'T COME BACK, FOREHEAD!
I SEE...

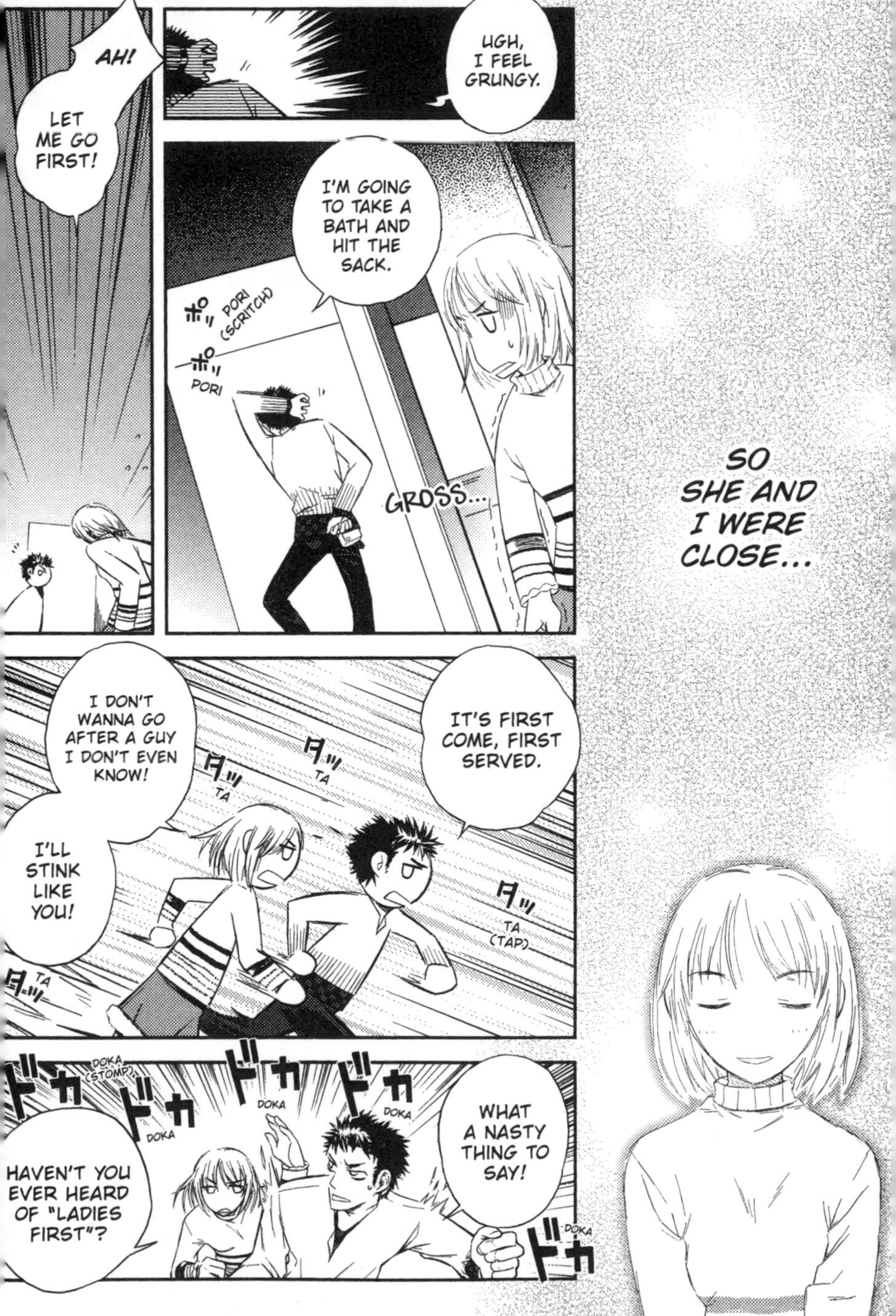
SO SHE AND I WERE CLOSE...
UGH, I FEEL GRUNGY.
I'M GOING TO TAKE A BATH AND HIT THE SACK.
PORI (SCRITCH)
PORI
GROSS...
AH!
LET ME GO FIRST!
IT'S FIRST COME, FIRST SERVED.
TA
TA (TAP)
I DON'T WANNA GO AFTER A GUY I DON'T EVEN KNOW!
TA
I'LL STINK LIKE YOU!
TA
DOKA
DOKA
WHAT A NASTY THING TO SAY!
DOKA
DOKA
DOKA (STOMP)
HAVEN'T YOU EVER HEARD OF "LADIES FIRST"?

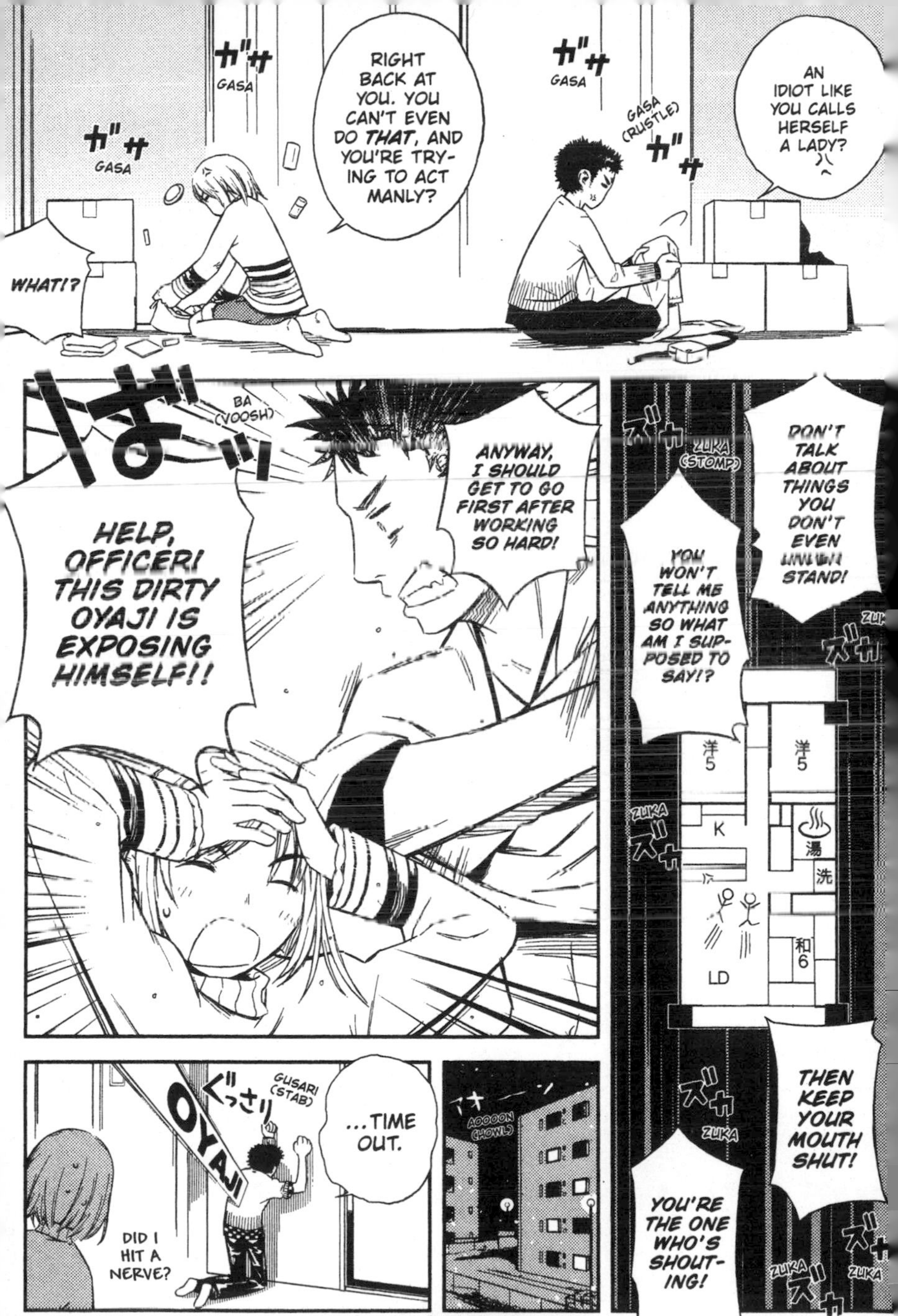
AN IDIOT LIKE YOU CALLS HERSELF A LADY?
GASA (RUSTLE)
GASA
RIGHT BACK AT YOU. YOU CAN'T EVEN DO THAT, AND YOU'RE TRYING TO ACT MANLY?
GASA
GASA
WHAT!?
DON'T TALK ABOUT THINGS YOU DON'T EVEN UNDERSTAND!
ZUKA (STOMP)
YOU WON'T TELL ME ANYTHING SO WHAT AM I SUPPOSED TO SAY!?
ZUKA
洋5
洋5
K
湯
洗
和6
LD
ZUKA
THEN KEEP YOUR MOUTH SHUT!
ZUKA
YOU'RE THE ONE WHO'S SHOUTING!
ZUKA
ZUKA
BA (VOOSH)
ANYWAY, I SHOULD GET TO GO FIRST AFTER WORKING SO HARD!
HELP, OFFICER! THIS DIRTY OYAJI IS EXPOSING HIMSELF!!
AOOOON (HOWL)
...TIME OUT.
GUSARI (STAB)
OYAJI
DID I HIT A NERVE?

FLOOR PLAN: (RIGHT) WESTERN-STYLE, 5 TATAMI / KITCHEN / LIVING, DINING ROOM; (LEFT) WESTERN-STYLE, 5 TATAMI / BATHTUB / WASHROOM / JAPANESE-STYLE, 6 TATAMI

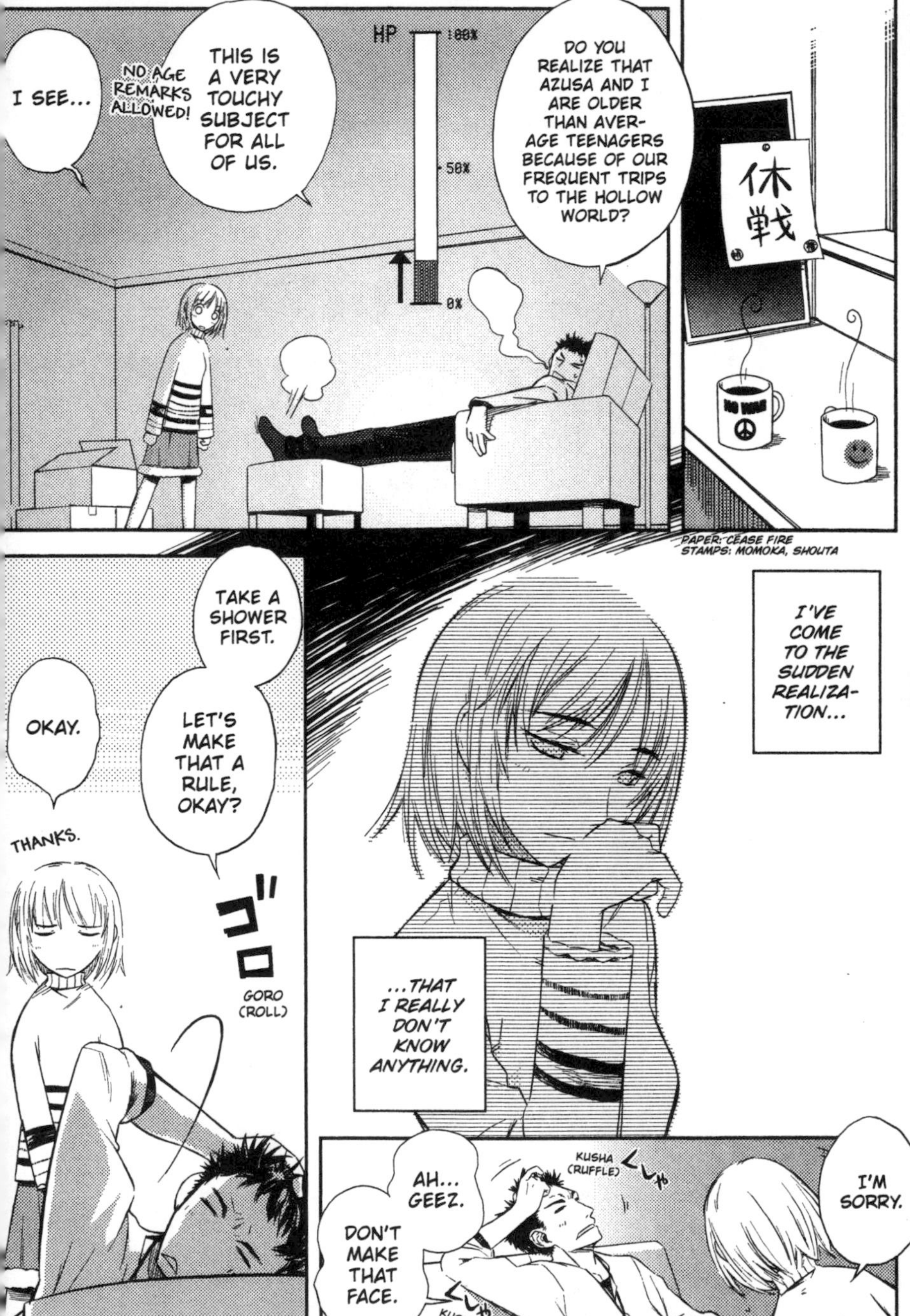
休戦
PAPER: CEASE FIRE
STAMPS: MOMOKA, SHOUTA
DO YOU REALIZE THAT AZUSA AND I ARE OLDER THAN AVER-AGE TEENAGERS BECAUSE OF OUR FREQUENT TRIPS TO THE HOLLOW WORLD?
HP
100%
50%
0%
THIS IS A VERY TOUCHY SUBJECT FOR ALL OF US.
NO AGE REMARKS ALLOWED!
I SEE...
I'VE COME TO THE SUDDEN REALIZA-TION...
...THAT I REALLY DON'T KNOW ANYTHING.
I'M SORRY.
くしゃ
KUSHA (RUFFLE)
AH... GEEZ.
DON'T MAKE THAT FACE.
くしゃ
KUSHA
TAKE A SHOWER FIRST.
OKAY.
LET'S MAKE THAT A RULE, OKAY?
THANKS.
ゴロ
GORO (ROLL)

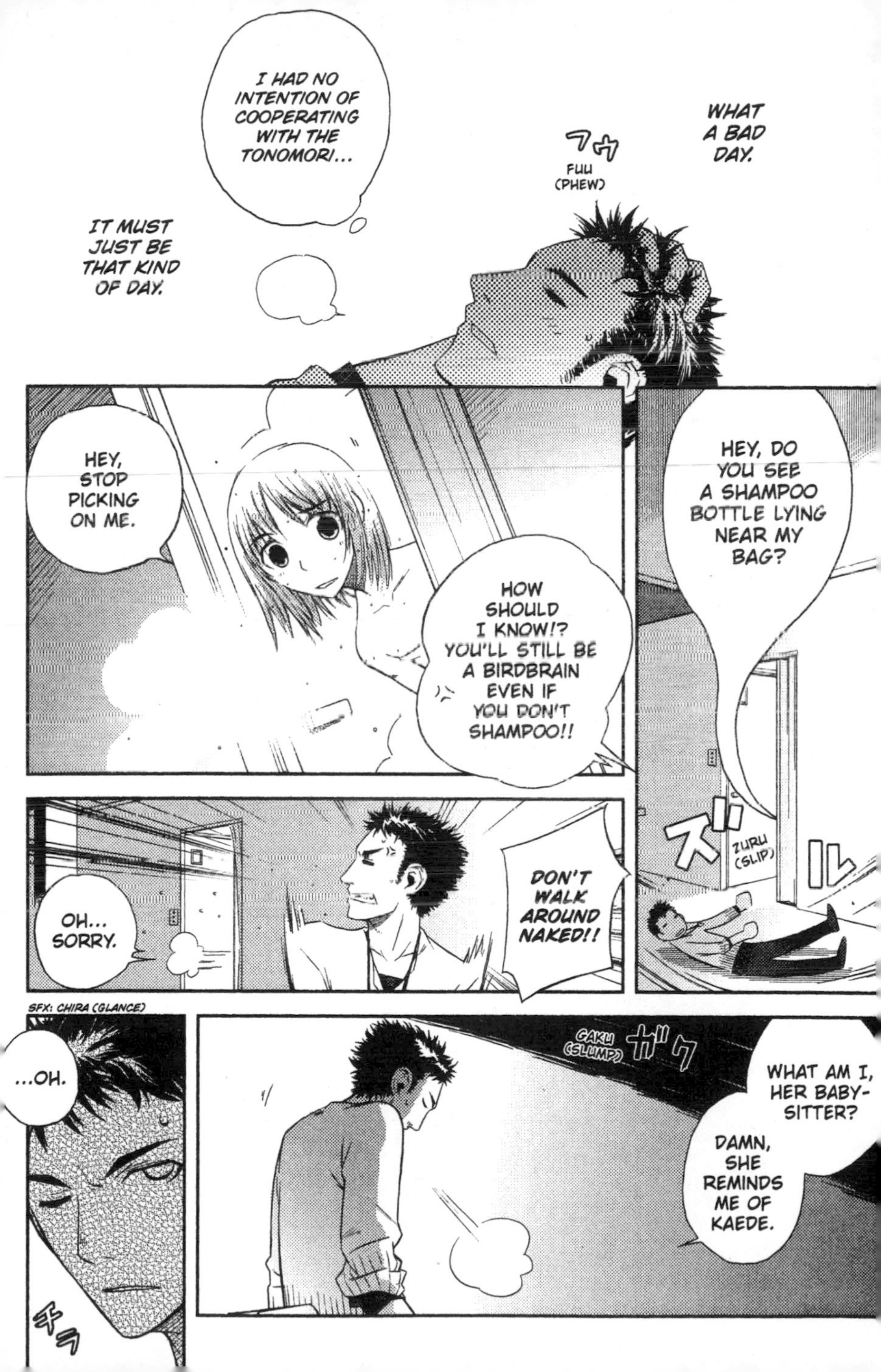
WHAT A BAD DAY.
フウ
FUU (PHEW)
I HAD NO INTENTION OF COOPERATING WITH THE TONOMORI...
IT MUST JUST BE THAT KIND OF DAY.
HEY, DO YOU SEE A SHAMPOO BOTTLE LYING NEAR MY BAG?
ズル
ZURU (SLIP)
HOW SHOULD I KNOW!? YOU'LL STILL BE A BIRDBRAIN EVEN IF YOU DON'T SHAMPOO!!
HEY, STOP PICKING ON ME.
DON'T WALK AROUND NAKED!!
OH... SORRY.
GAKU (SLUMP)
ガク
WHAT AM I, HER BABY-SITTER?
DAMN, SHE REMINDS ME OF KAEDE.
...OH.
チラ
SFX: CHIRA (GLANCE)

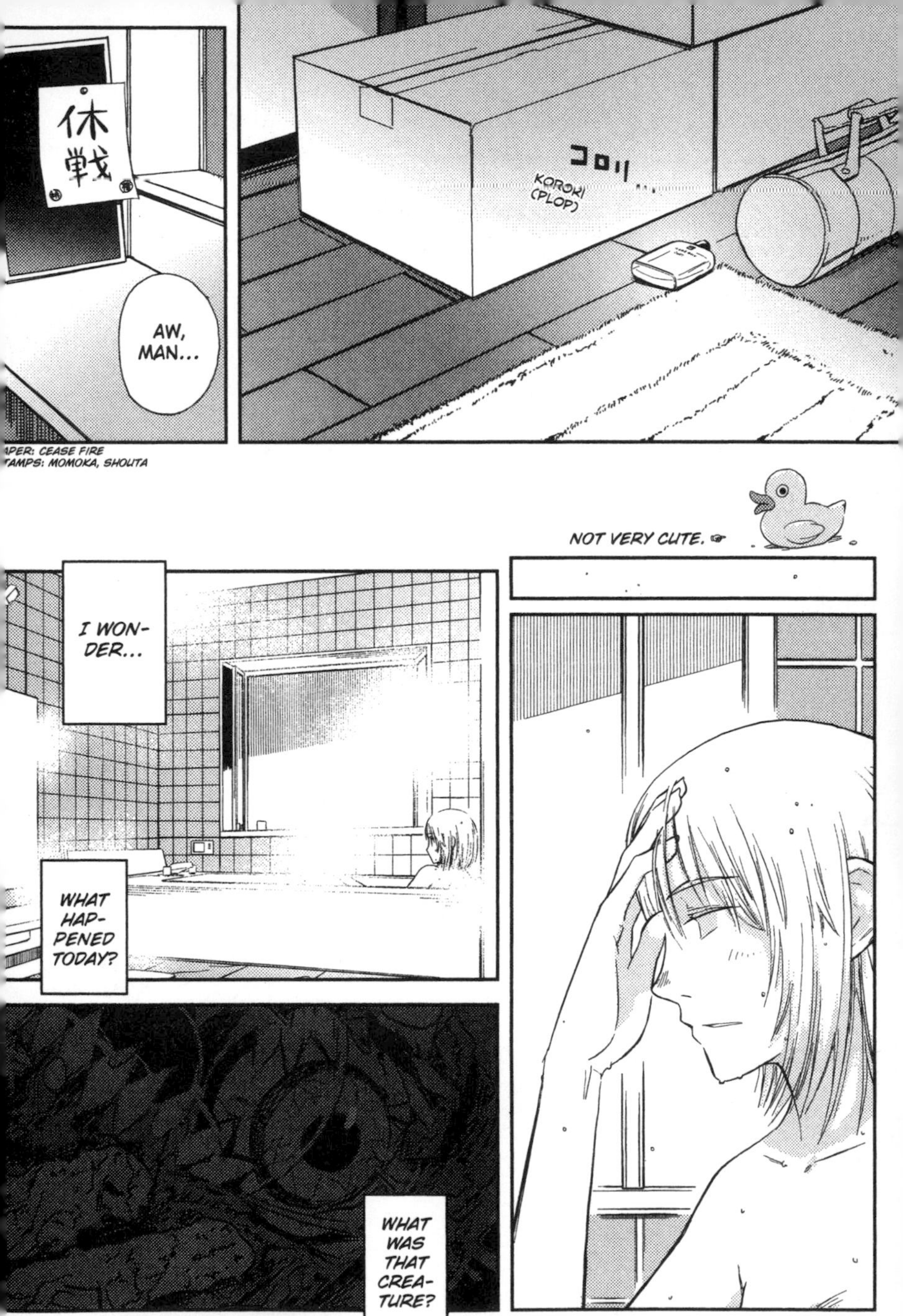

KOROKI (PLOP)
AW, MAN...
PAPER: CEASE FIRE
STAMPS: MOMOKA, SHOUTA
NOT VERY CUTE.
I WON-DER...
WHAT HAP-PENED TODAY?
WHAT WAS THAT CREA-TURE?

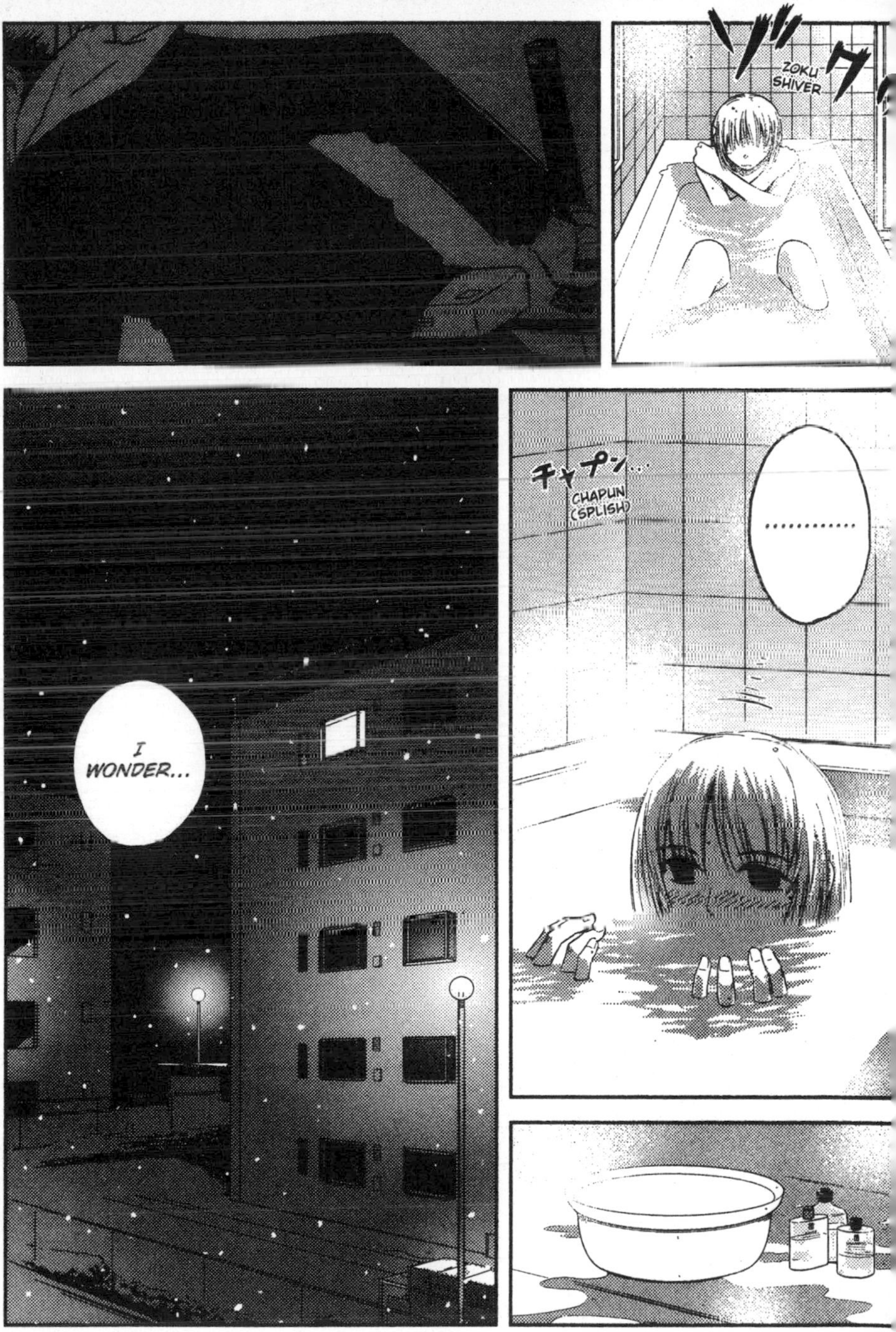
ゾク
ZOKU
SHIVER
チャプン...
CHAPUN
(SPLISH)
....
I WONDER...

BOARD (CLOCKWISE):

TRASH
TUES/SAT: FLAMMABLES - MOMOKA
THURS: PLASTIC - SHOUTA
FRI: GLASS/CANS - SHOUTA

CEASE FIRE
[LEFT] MOMOKA [RIGHT] SHOUTA

APARTMENT ASSOCIATION
[PHONE NUMBER]
YAMAMOTO

MITSURUGIS'
[PHONE NUMBER]

NEIGHBORHOOD NOTICE

BICYCLE KEY -> ON SHOE RACK
COATROOM KEY -> ON KITCHEN SHELF

CUT DOWN ELECTRIC BILL!
CONSERVE! NO LIGHTS IN HALLWAYS!

BATH
MOMOKA GOES FIRST
CLEAN IN TURNS

DUE ON THE 1ST!
-OO YEN
FRIGERA-
KEEP IN LEFT SIDE

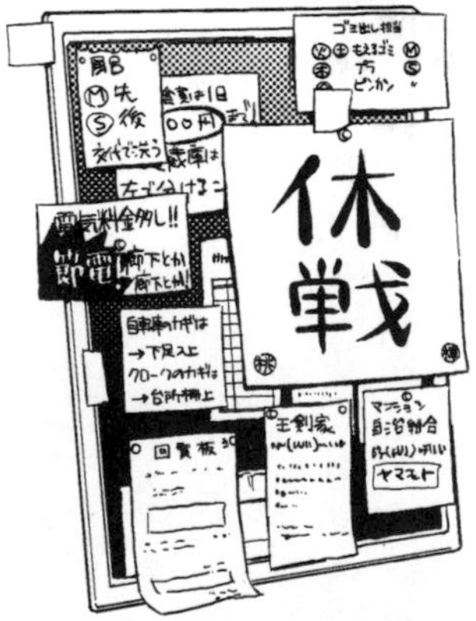
休戦
節電

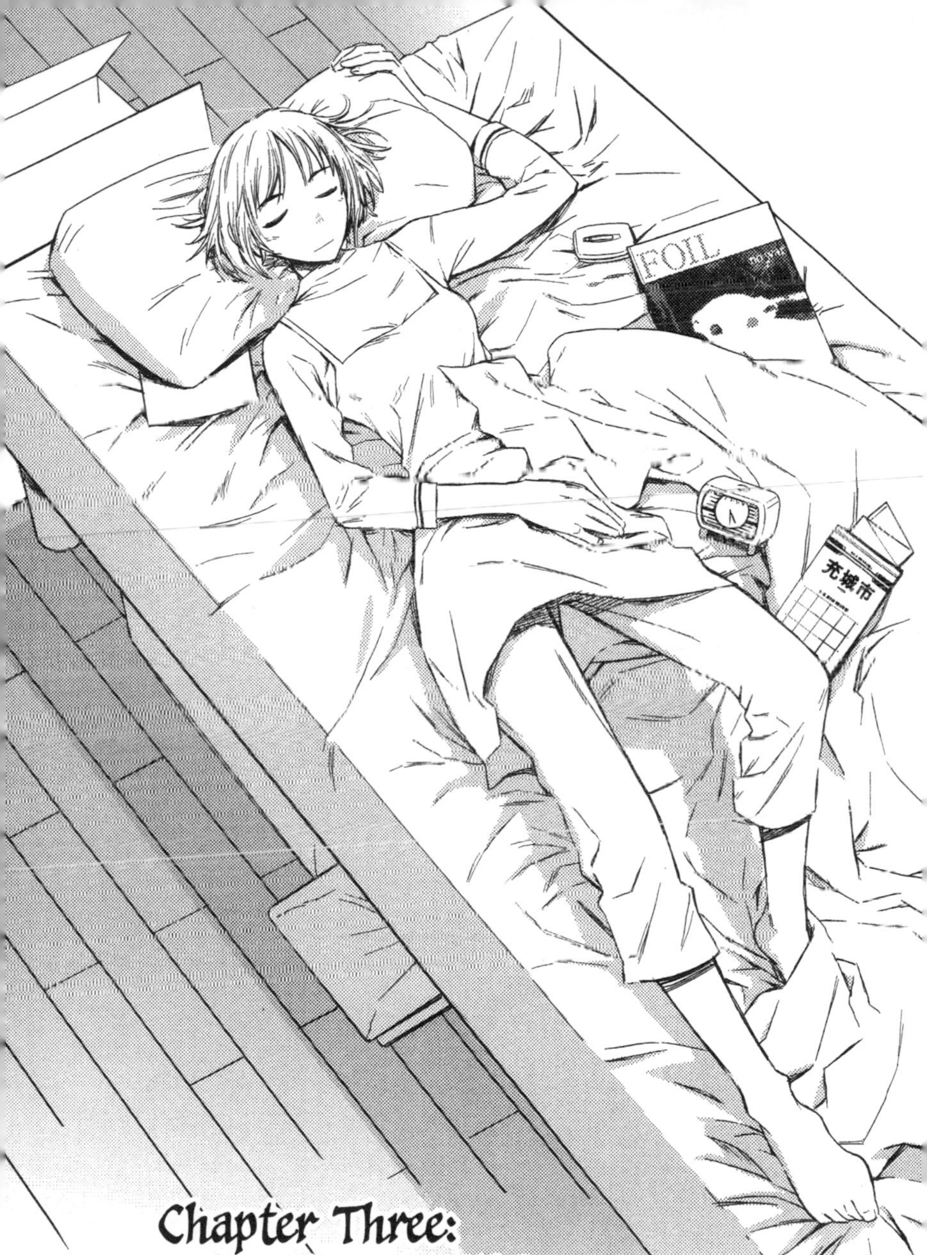
FOIL
充城市

Chapter Three: BLOOD RELATIVES

BOOK: MITSURUGI CITY

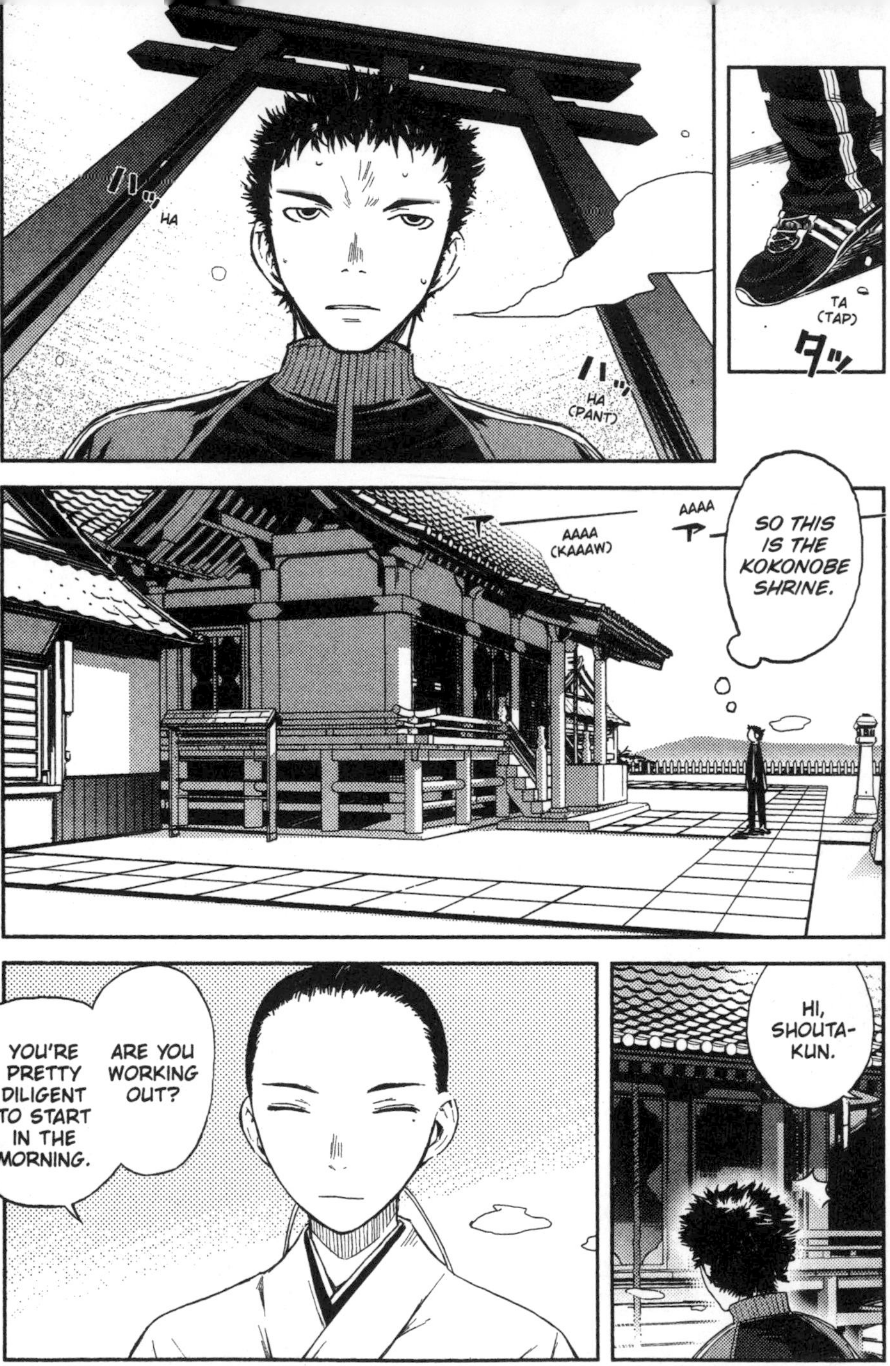

タッ
TA (TAP)
ハッ
HA
ハッ
HA (PANT)
SO THIS IS THE KOKONOBE SHRINE.
ア
AAAA
ア
AAAA (KAAAW)
HI, SHOUTA-KUN.
ARE YOU WORKING OUT?
YOU'RE PRETTY DILIGENT TO START IN THE MORNING.

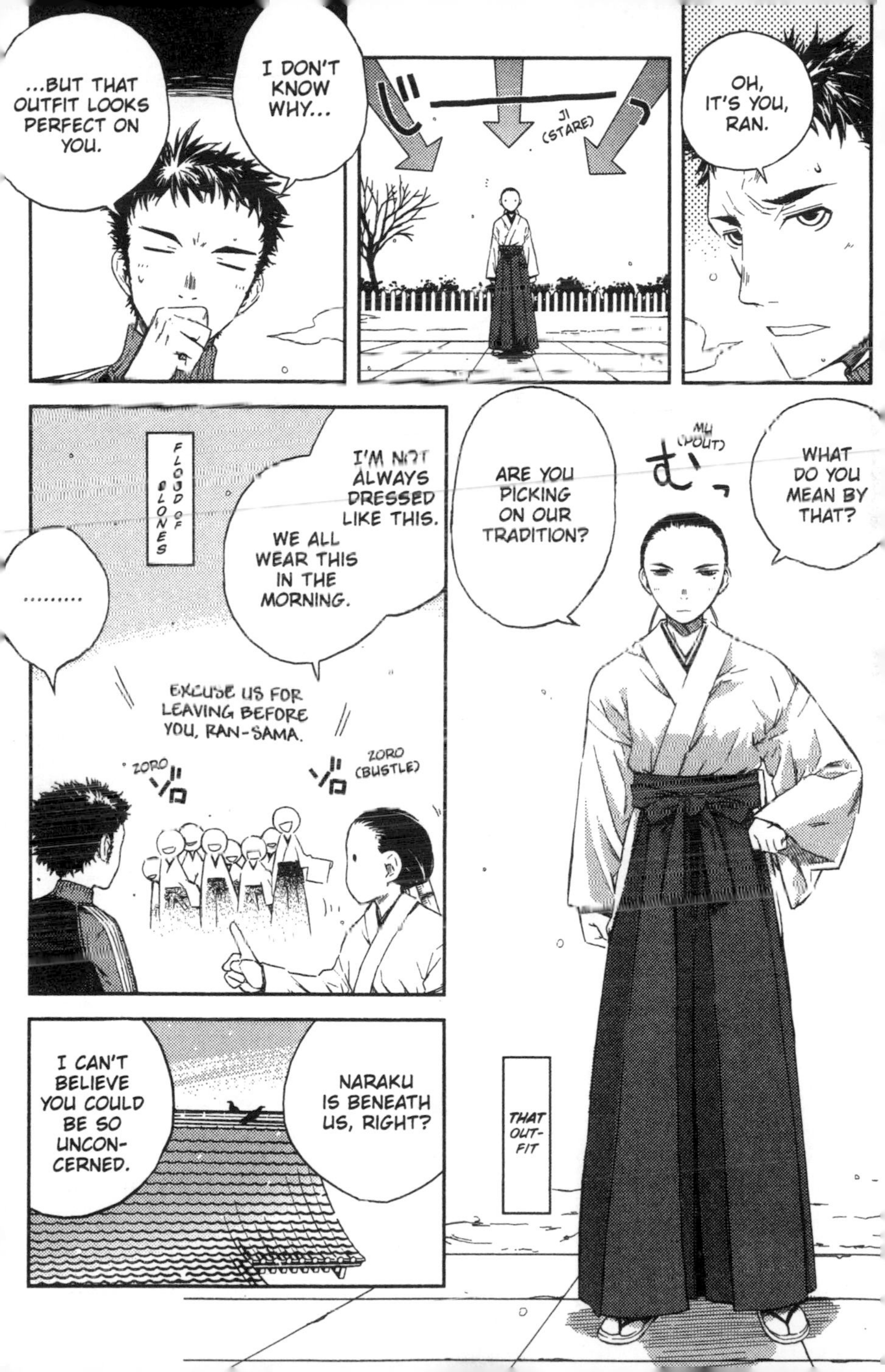
OH, IT'S YOU, RAN.
JI (STARE)
I DON'T KNOW WHY...
...BUT THAT OUTFIT LOOKS PERFECT ON YOU.
MU (POUT)
WHAT DO YOU MEAN BY THAT?
ARE YOU PICKING ON OUR TRADITION?
THAT OUT-FIT
I'M NOT ALWAYS DRESSED LIKE THIS.
WE ALL WEAR THIS IN THE MORNING.
FLOOD OF CLONES
....
EXCUSE US FOR LEAVING BEFORE YOU, RAN-SAMA.
ZORO (BUSTLE)
ZORO
NARAKU IS BENEATH US, RIGHT?
I CAN'T BELIEVE YOU COULD BE SO UNCON-CERNED.

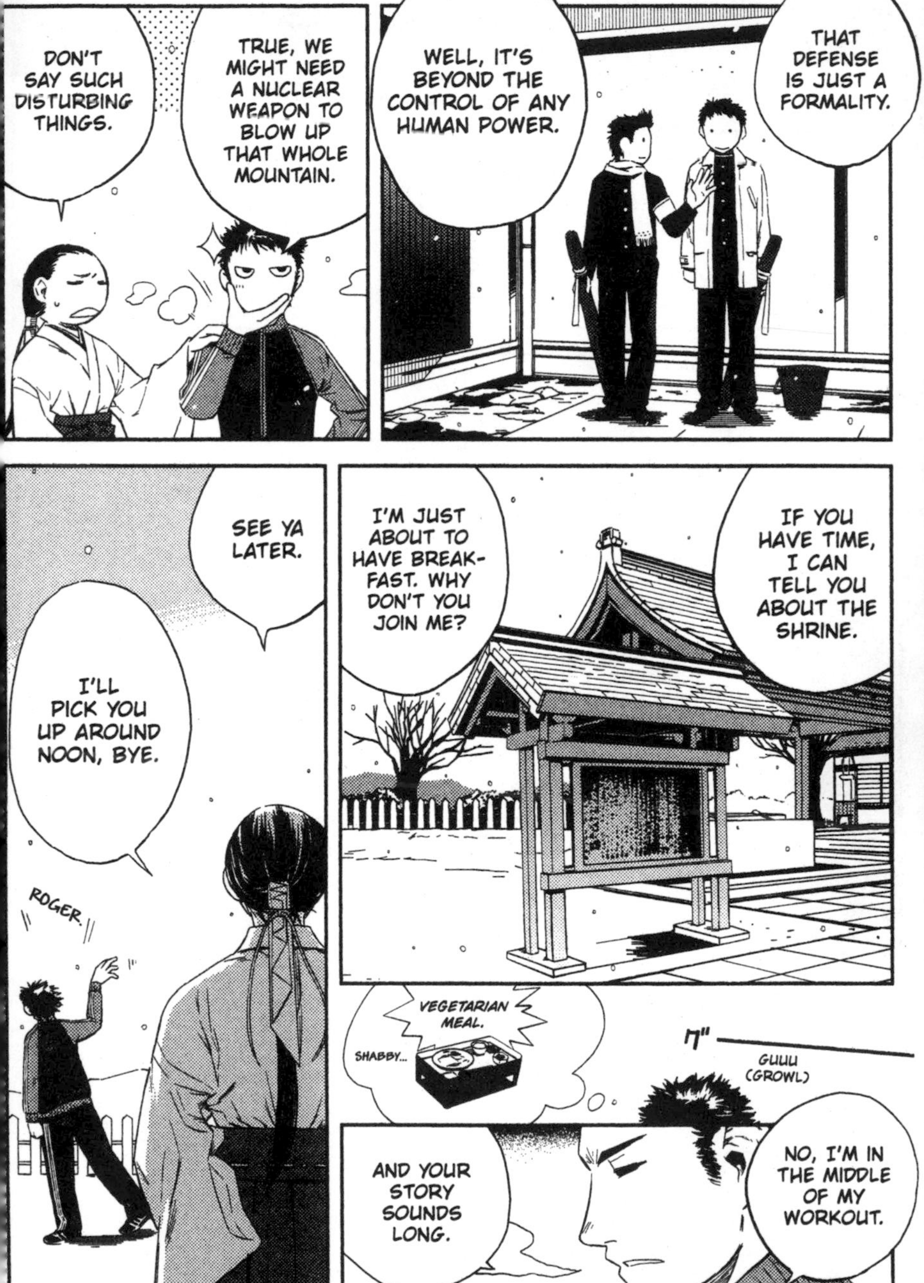
THAT DEFENSE IS JUST A FORMALITY.
WELL, IT'S BEYOND THE CONTROL OF ANY HUMAN POWER.
TRUE, WE MIGHT NEED A NUCLEAR WEAPON TO BLOW UP THAT WHOLE MOUNTAIN.
DON'T SAY SUCH DISTURBING THINGS.
IF YOU HAVE TIME, I CAN TELL YOU ABOUT THE SHRINE.
I'M JUST ABOUT TO HAVE BREAK-FAST. WHY DON'T YOU JOIN ME?
VEGETARIAN MEAL.
SHABBY...
GUUU (GROWL)
NO, I'M IN THE MIDDLE OF MY WORKOUT.
AND YOUR STORY SOUNDS LONG.
SEE YA LATER.
I'LL PICK YOU UP AROUND NOON, BYE.
ROGER.

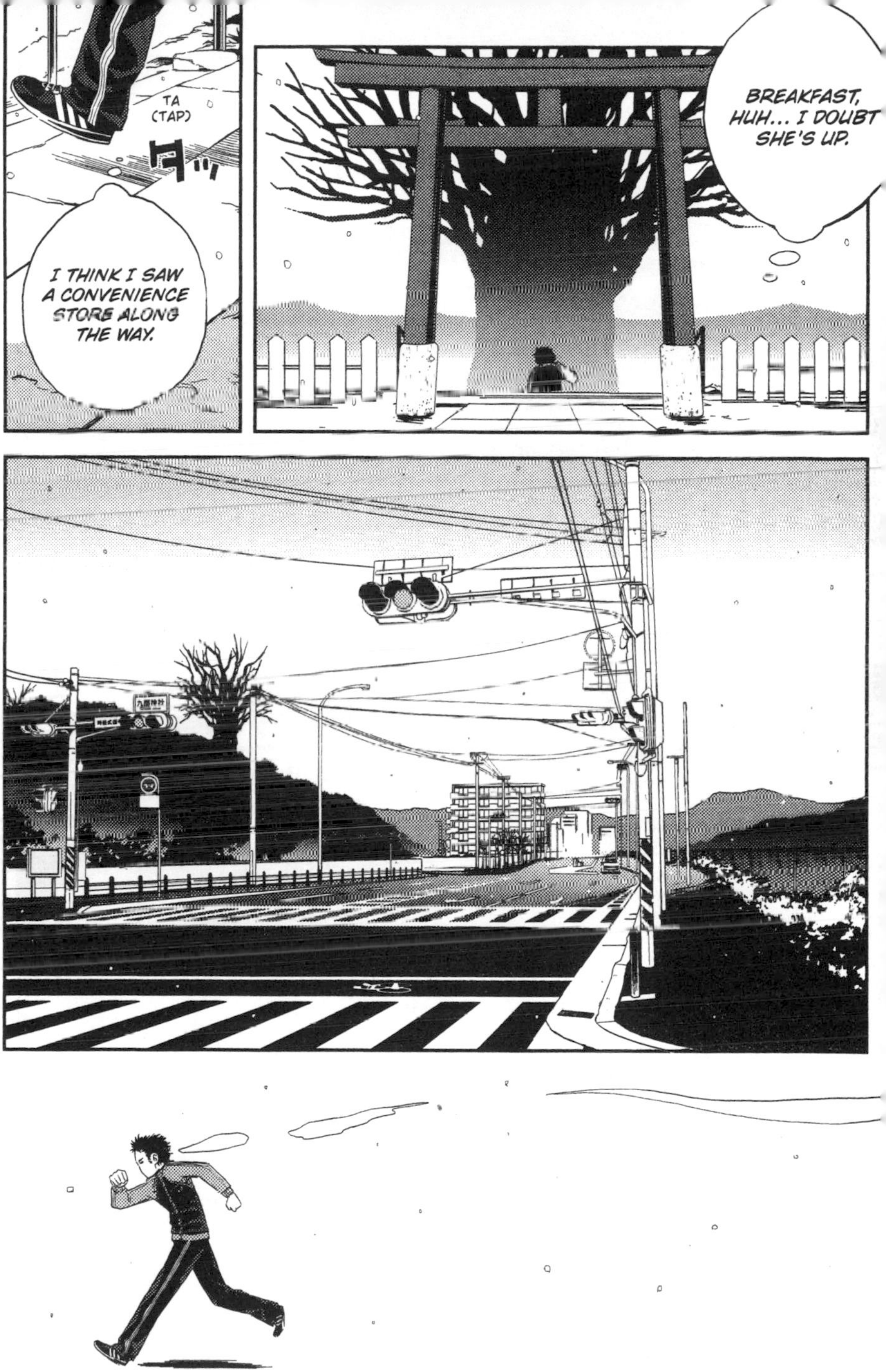
BREAKFAST, HUH... I DOUBT SHE'S UP.
TA (TAP)
I THINK I SAW A CONVENIENCE STORE ALONG THE WAY.

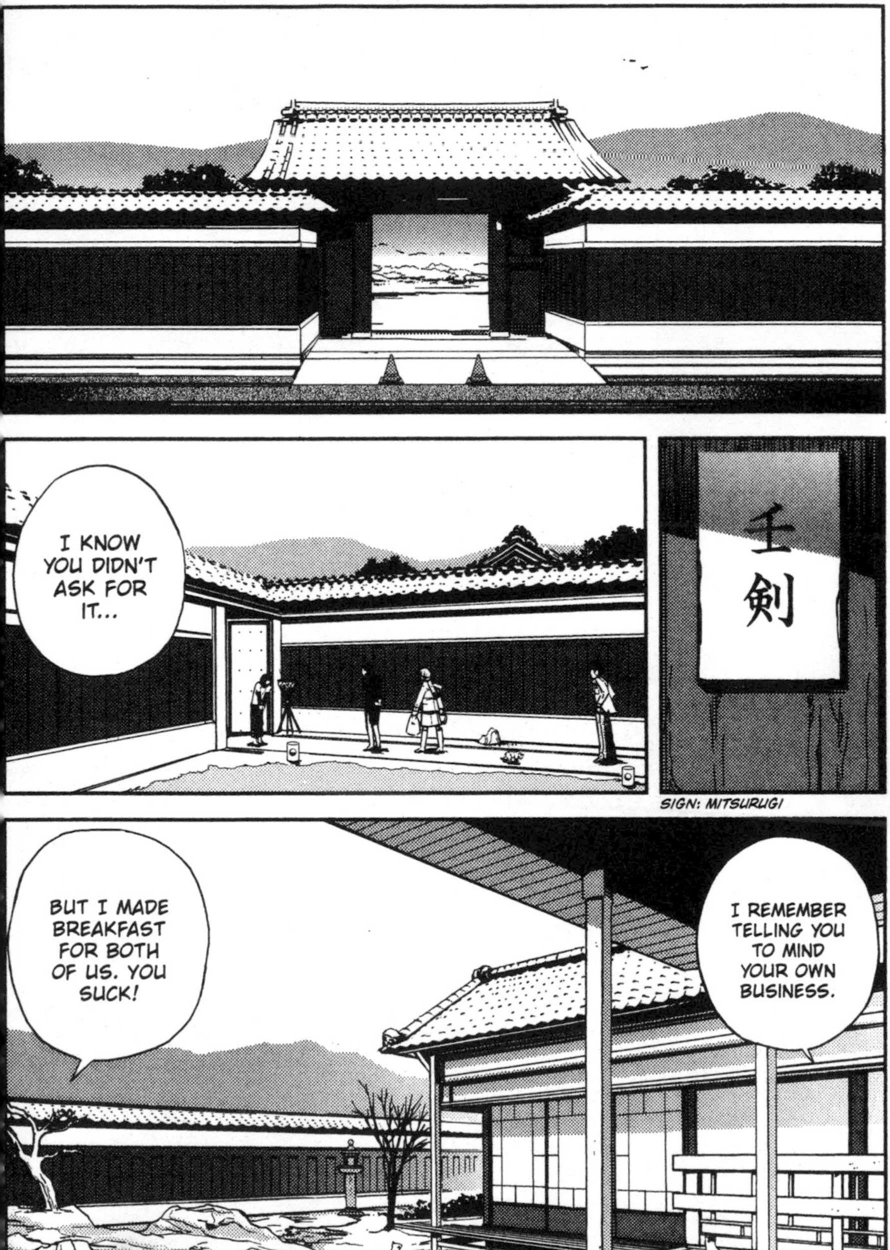
壬剣
SIGN: MITSURUGI
I KNOW YOU DIDN'T ASK FOR IT...
I REMEMBER TELLING YOU TO MIND YOUR OWN BUSINESS.
BUT I MADE BREAKFAST FOR BOTH OF US. YOU SUCK!

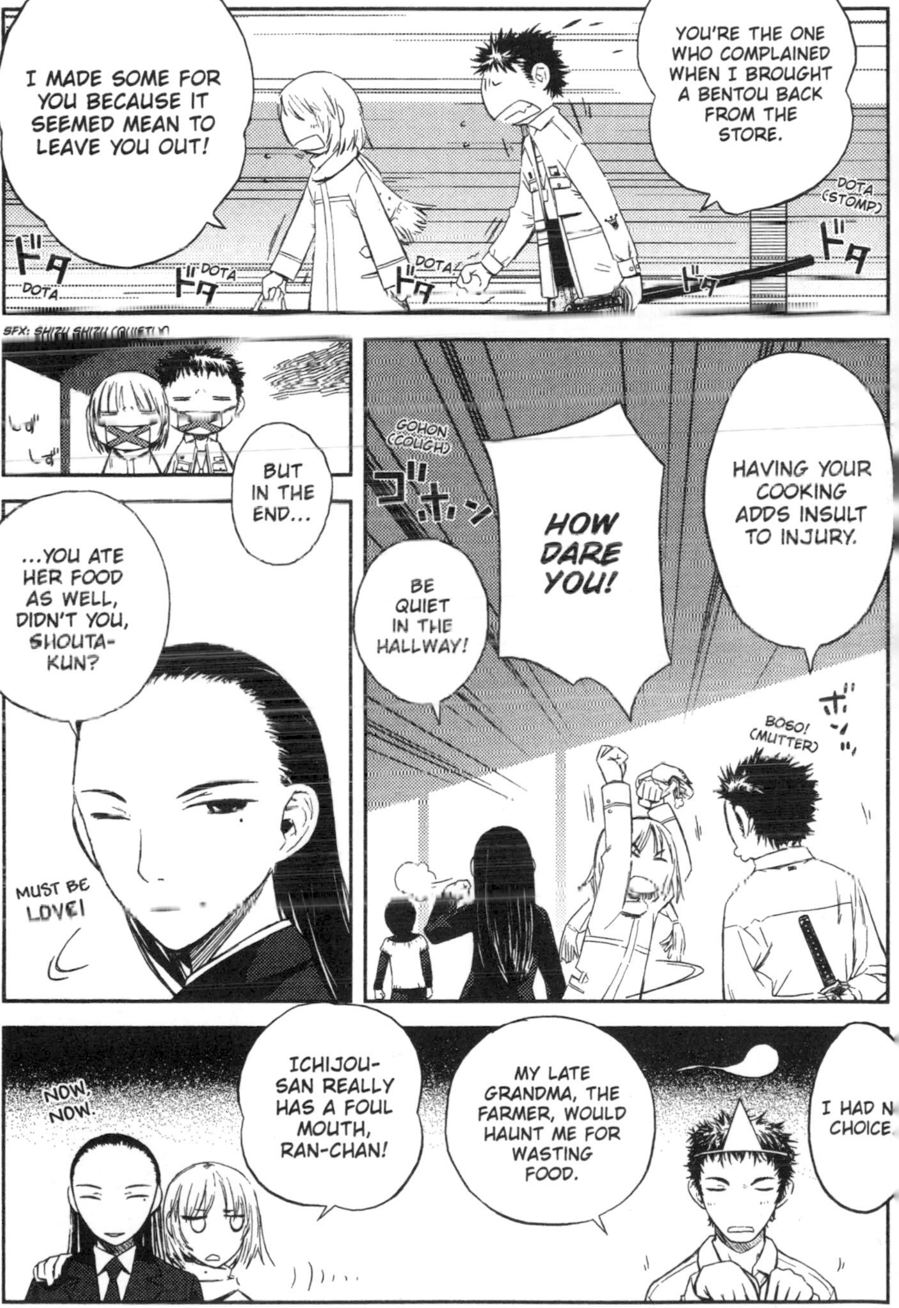
YOU'RE THE ONE WHO COMPLAINED WHEN I BROUGHT A BENTOU BACK FROM THE STORE.
DOTA (STOMP)
I MADE SOME FOR YOU BECAUSE IT SEEMED MEAN TO LEAVE YOU OUT!
DOTA
DOTA
DOTA
SFX: SHIZU SHIZU (QUIETLY)
HAVING YOUR COOKING ADDS INSULT TO INJURY.
HOW DARE YOU!
GOHON (COUGH)
BE QUIET IN THE HALLWAY!
BOSO! (MUTTER)
BUT IN THE END...
...YOU ATE HER FOOD AS WELL, DIDN'T YOU, SHOUTA-KUN?
MUST BE LOVE!
I HAD N CHOICE.
MY LATE GRANDMA, THE FARMER, WOULD HAUNT ME FOR WASTING FOOD.
ICHIJOU-SAN REALLY HAS A FOUL MOUTH, RAN-CHAN!
NOW, NOW.

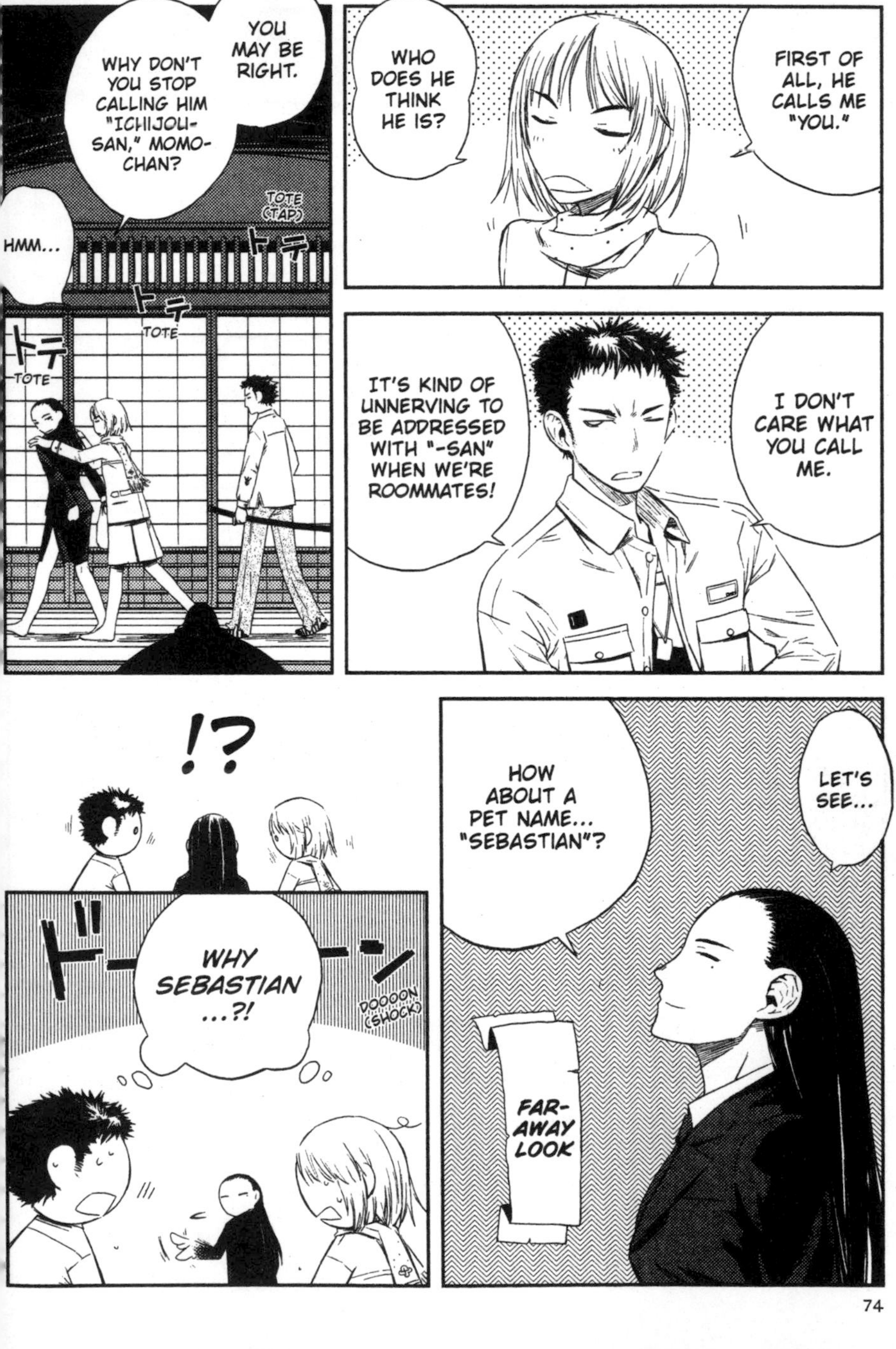
FIRST OF ALL, HE CALLS ME "YOU."
WHO DOES HE THINK HE IS?
I DON'T CARE WHAT YOU CALL ME.
IT'S KIND OF UNNERVING TO BE ADDRESSED WITH "-SAN" WHEN WE'RE ROOMMATES!
YOU MAY BE RIGHT.
WHY DON'T YOU STOP CALLING HIM "ICHIJOU-SAN," MOMO-CHAN?
TOTE (TAP)
HMM...
TOTE
TOTE
LET'S SEE...
HOW ABOUT A PET NAME... "SEBASTIAN"?
FAR-AWAY LOOK
!?
WHY SEBASTIAN ...?!
DOOOON (SHOCK)

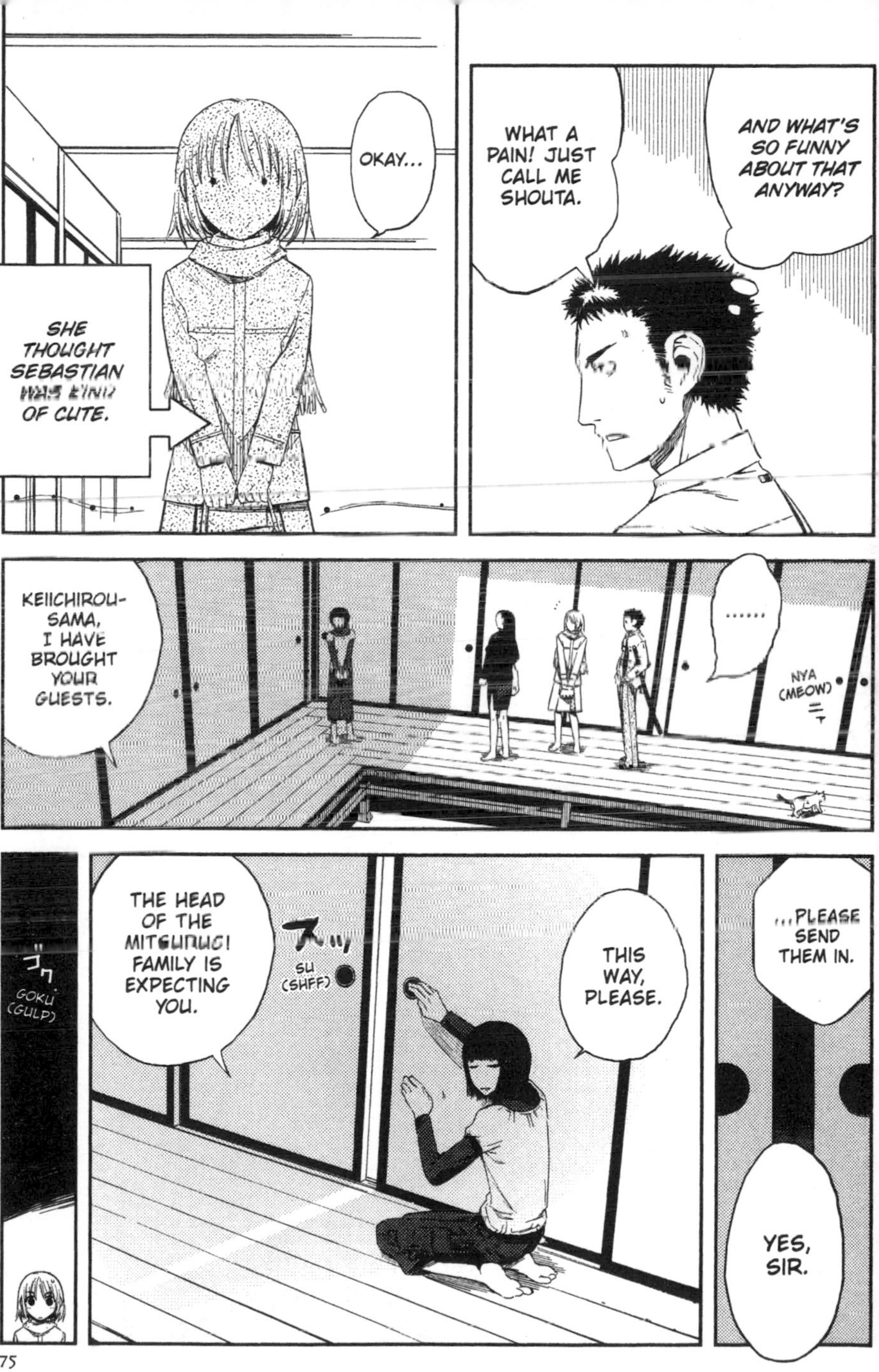
WHAT A PAIN! JUST CALL ME SHOUTA.
AND WHAT'S SO FUNNY ABOUT THAT ANYWAY?
OKAY...
SHE THOUGHT SEBASTIAN WAS KIND OF CUTE.
......
NYA (MEOW)
KEIICHIROU-SAMA, I HAVE BROUGHT YOUR GUESTS.
...PLEASE SEND THEM IN.
YES, SIR.
THIS WAY, PLEASE.
SU (SHFF)
THE HEAD OF THE MITSURUGI FAMILY IS EXPECTING YOU.
GOKU (GULP)

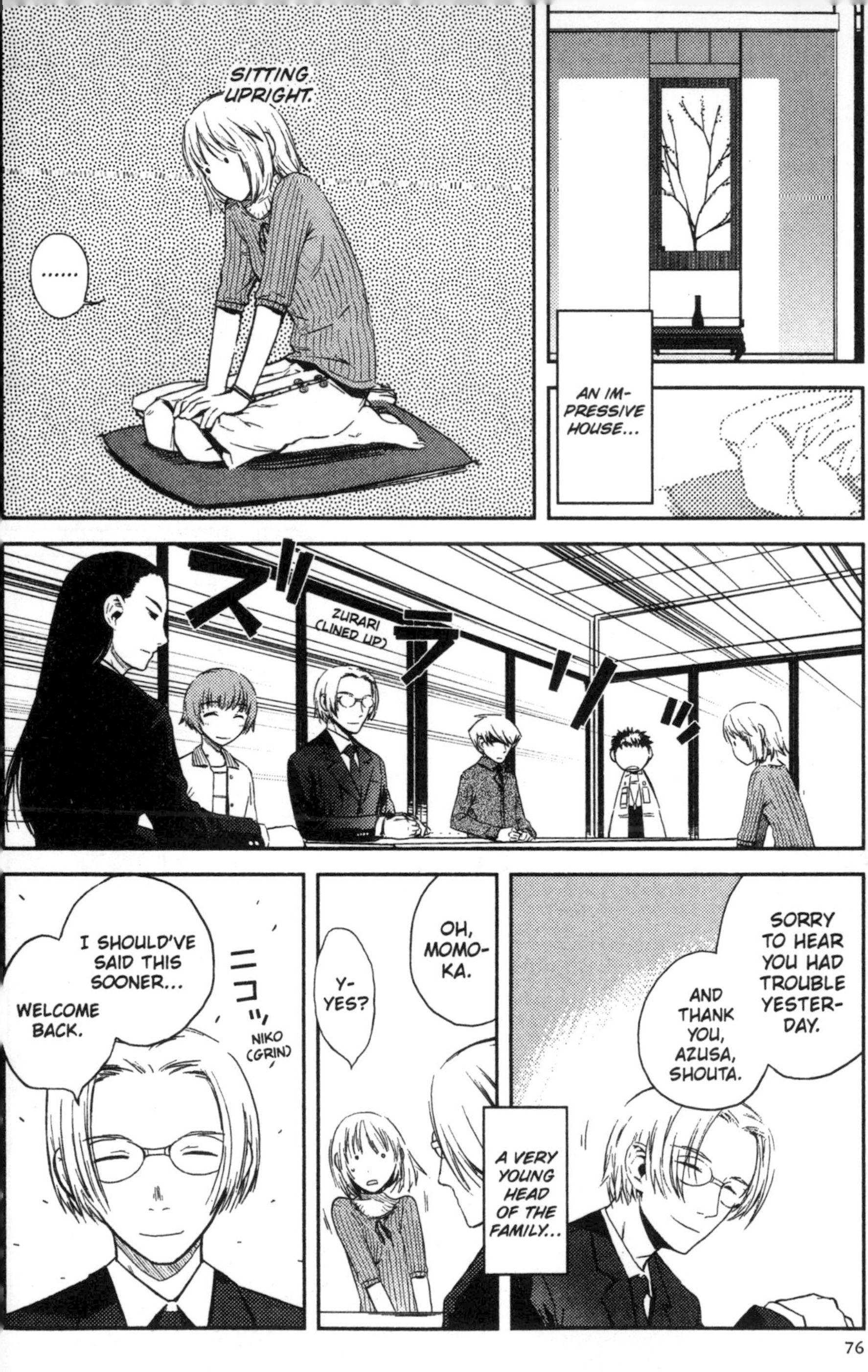
AN IM-PRESSIVE HOUSE...
SITTING UPRIGHT.
......
ZURARI (LINED UP)
SORRY TO HEAR YOU HAD TROUBLE YESTER-DAY.
AND THANK YOU, AZUSA, SHOUTA.
A VERY YOUNG HEAD OF THE FAMILY...
OH, MOMO-KA.
Y-YES?
I SHOULD'VE SAID THIS SOONER...
WELCOME BACK.
NIKO (GRIN)

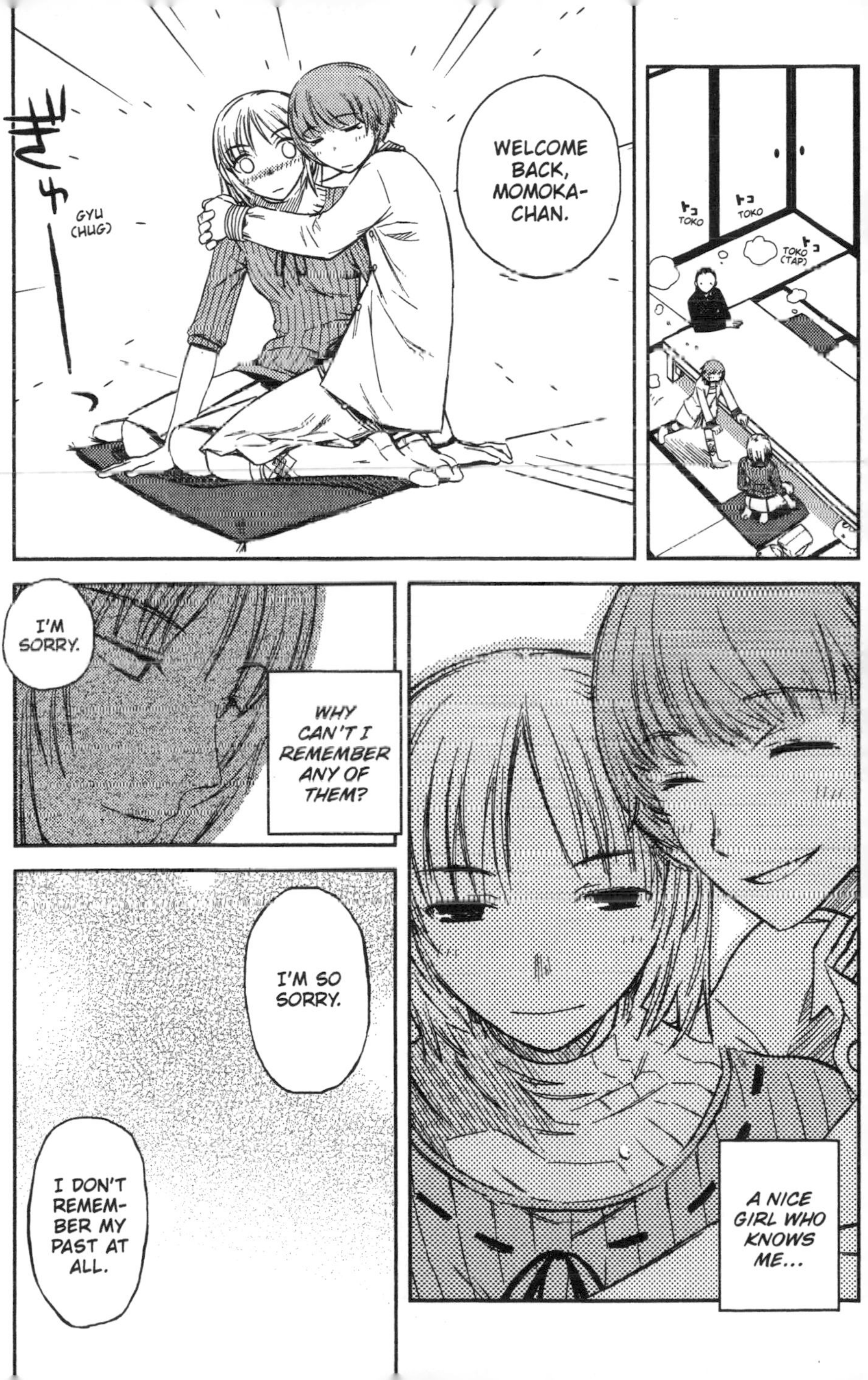
トコ
TOKO
トコ
TOKO
トコ
TOKO (TAP)
WELCOME BACK, MOMOKA-CHAN.
GYU (HUG)
A NICE GIRL WHO KNOWS ME...
I'M SORRY.
WHY CAN'T I REMEMBER ANY OF THEM?
I'M SO SORRY.
I DON'T REMEM-BER MY PAST AT ALL.

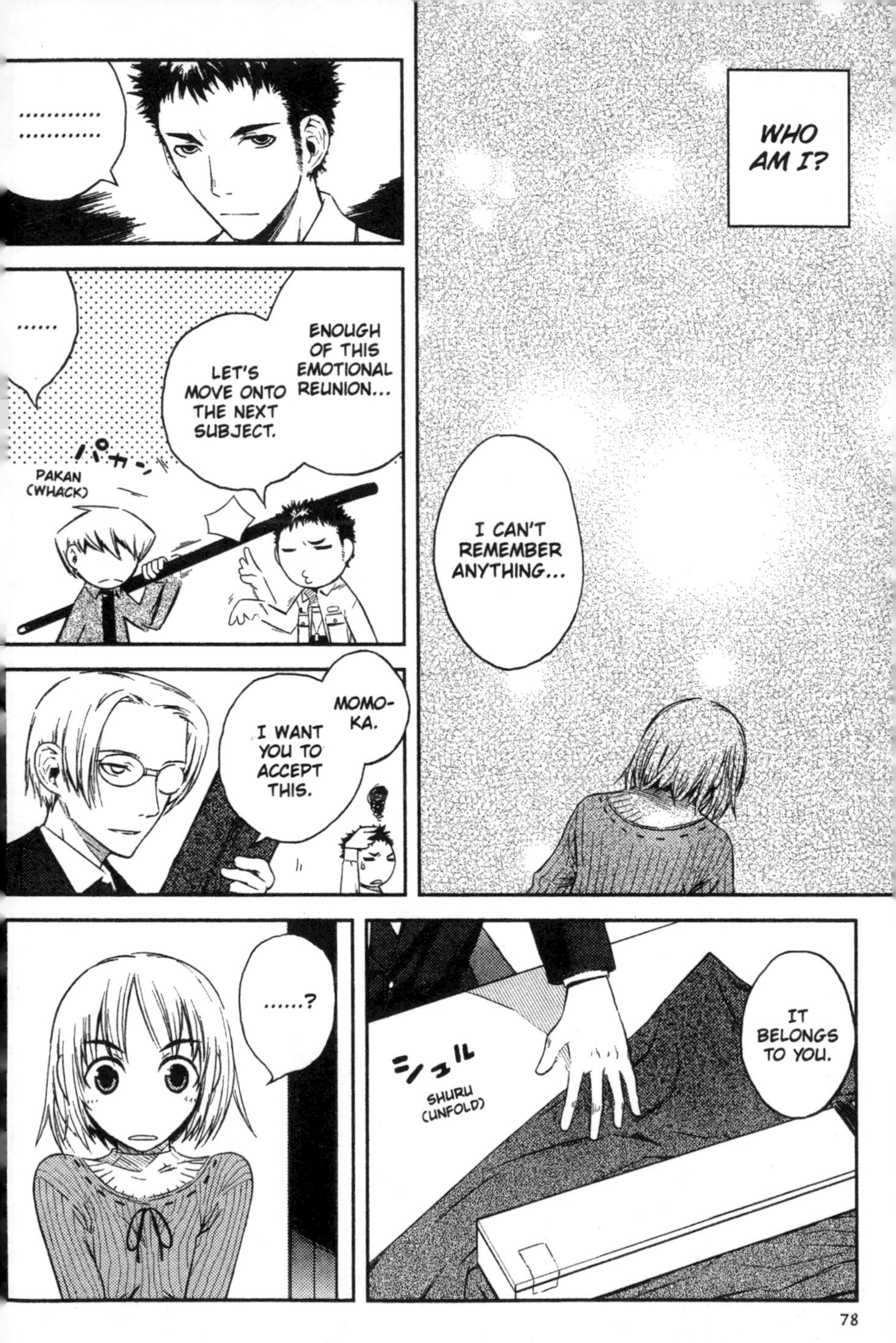
WHO AM I?
I CAN'T REMEMBER ANYTHING...
....
ENOUGH OF THIS EMOTIONAL REUNION... LET'S MOVE ONTO THE NEXT SUBJECT.
......
パカーン
PAKAN (WHACK)
MOMOKA. I WANT YOU TO ACCEPT THIS.
IT BELONGS TO YOU.
シュル
SHURU (UNFOLD)
......?

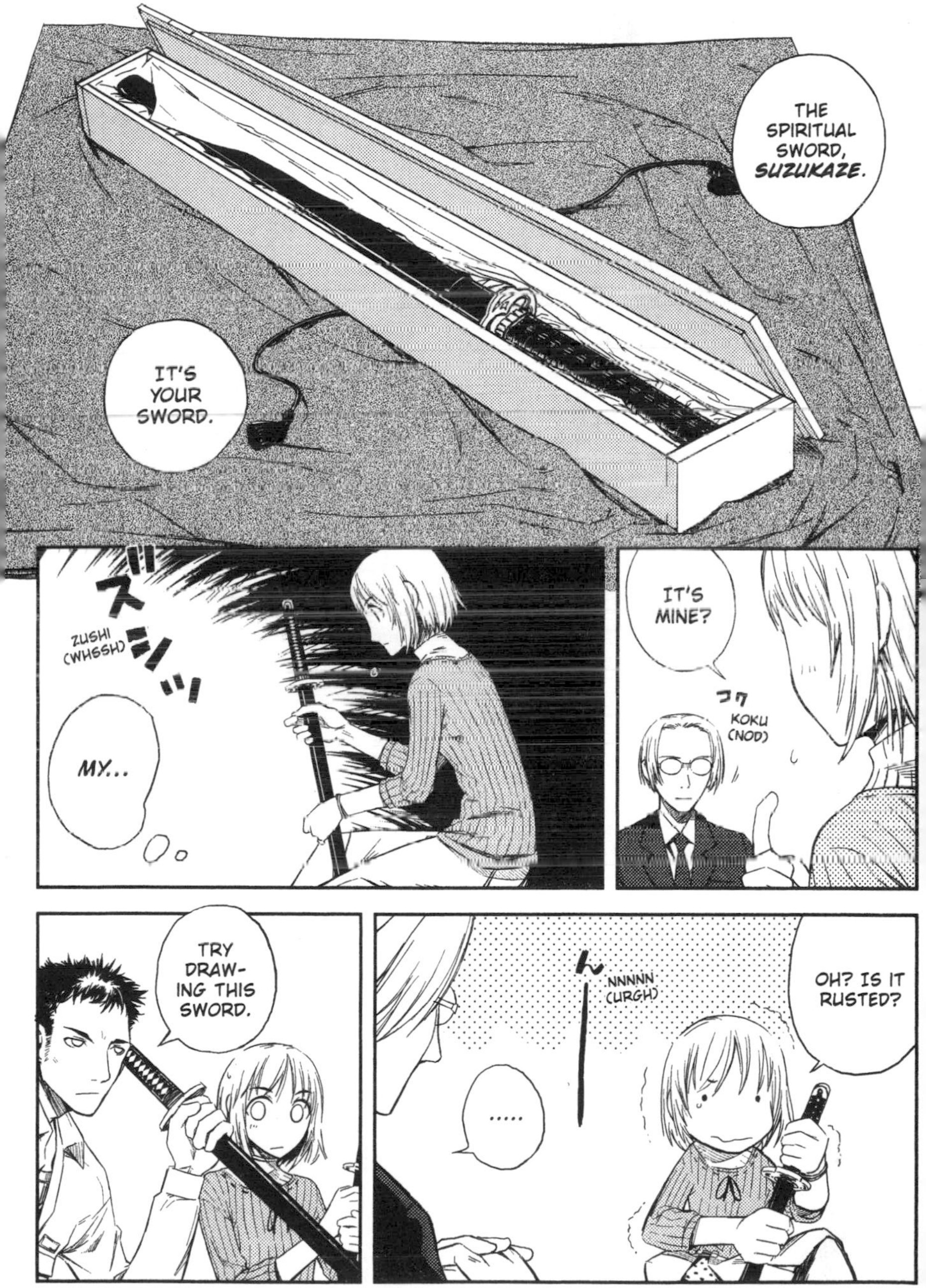
THE SPIRITUAL SWORD, SUZUKAZE.
IT'S YOUR SWORD.
IT'S MINE?
コク
KOKU (NOD)
ズシッ
ZUSHI (WHSSH)
MY...
OH? IS IT RUSTED?
ん
NNNNN (URGH)
.....
TRY DRAWING THIS SWORD.

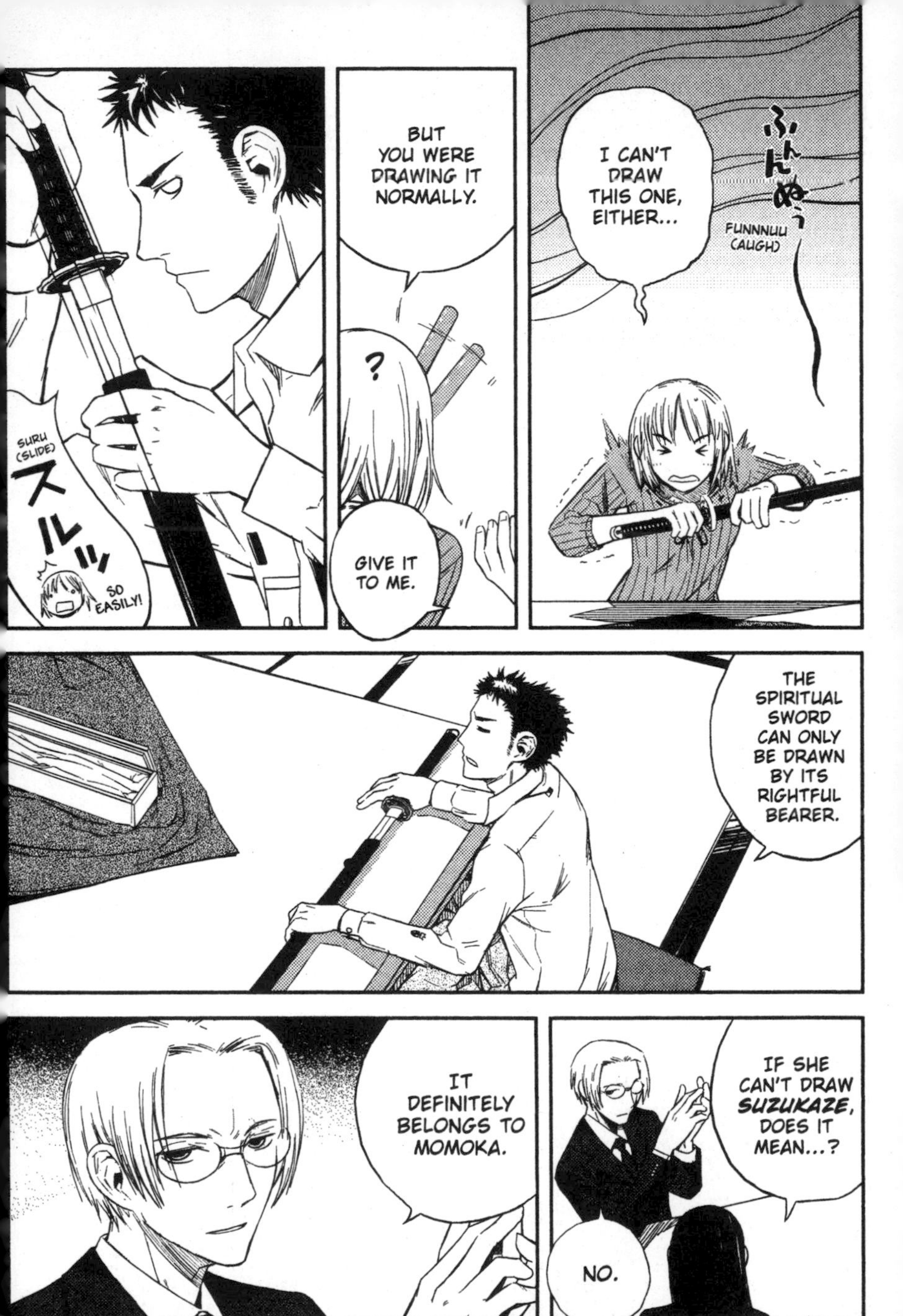
ふんぬぅ
FUNNNUU (AUGH)
I CAN'T DRAW THIS ONE, EITHER...
BUT YOU WERE DRAWING IT NORMALLY.
?
GIVE IT TO ME.
SURU (SLIDE)
スルッ
SO EASILY!
THE SPIRITUAL SWORD CAN ONLY BE DRAWN BY ITS RIGHTFUL BEARER.
IF SHE CAN'T DRAW *SUZUKAZE*, DOES IT MEAN...?
NO.
IT DEFINITELY BELONGS TO MOMOKA.

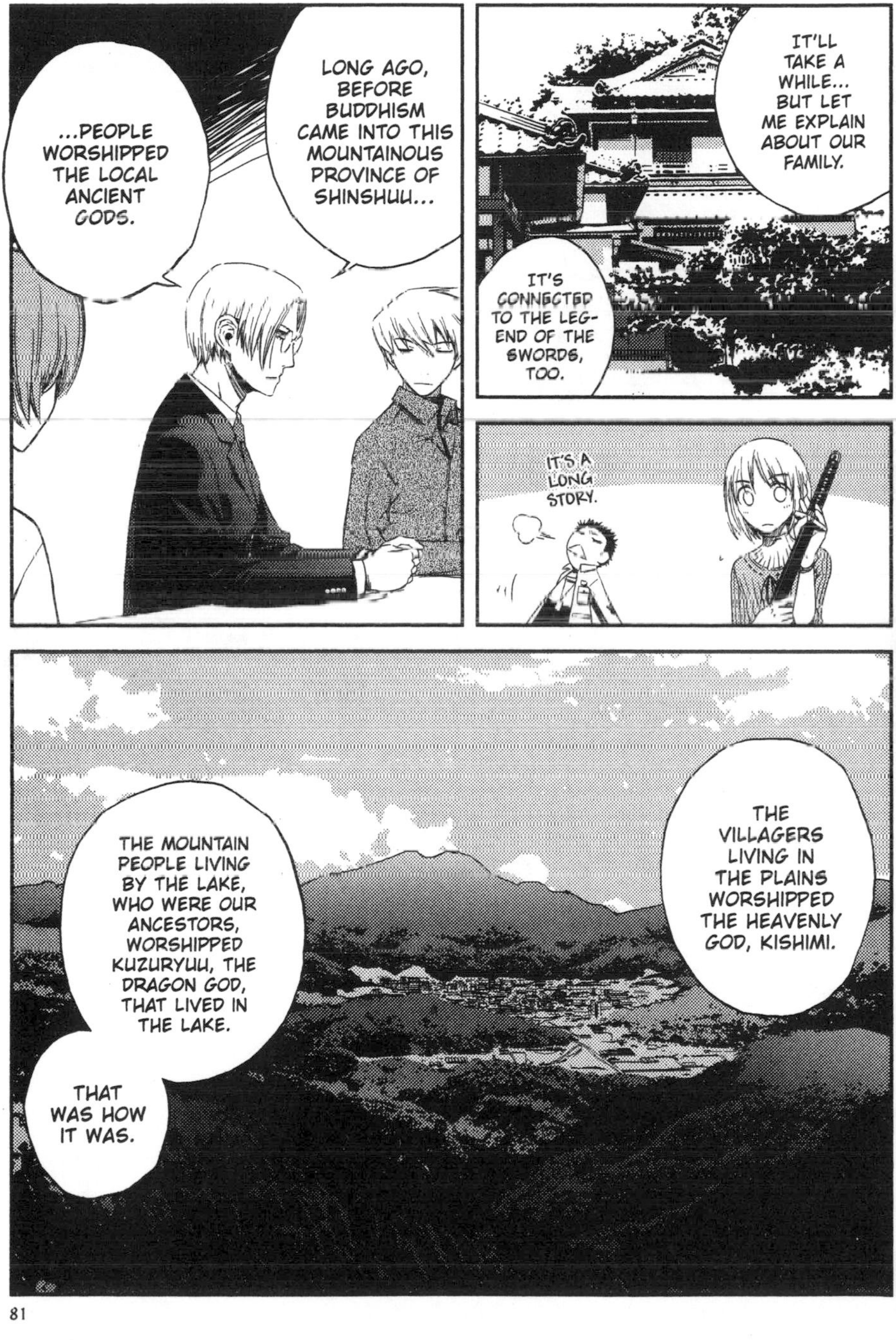
IT'LL TAKE A WHILE... BUT LET ME EXPLAIN ABOUT OUR FAMILY.
IT'S CONNECTED TO THE LEG-END OF THE SWORDS, TOO.
IT'S A LONG STORY.
LONG AGO, BEFORE BUDDHISM CAME INTO THIS MOUNTAINOUS PROVINCE OF SHINSHUU...
...PEOPLE WORSHIPPED THE LOCAL ANCIENT GODS.
THE VILLAGERS LIVING IN THE PLAINS WORSHIPPED THE HEAVENLY GOD, KISHIMI.
THE MOUNTAIN PEOPLE LIVING BY THE LAKE, WHO WERE OUR ANCESTORS, WORSHIPPED KUZURYUU, THE DRAGON GOD, THAT LIVED IN THE LAKE.
THAT WAS HOW IT WAS.

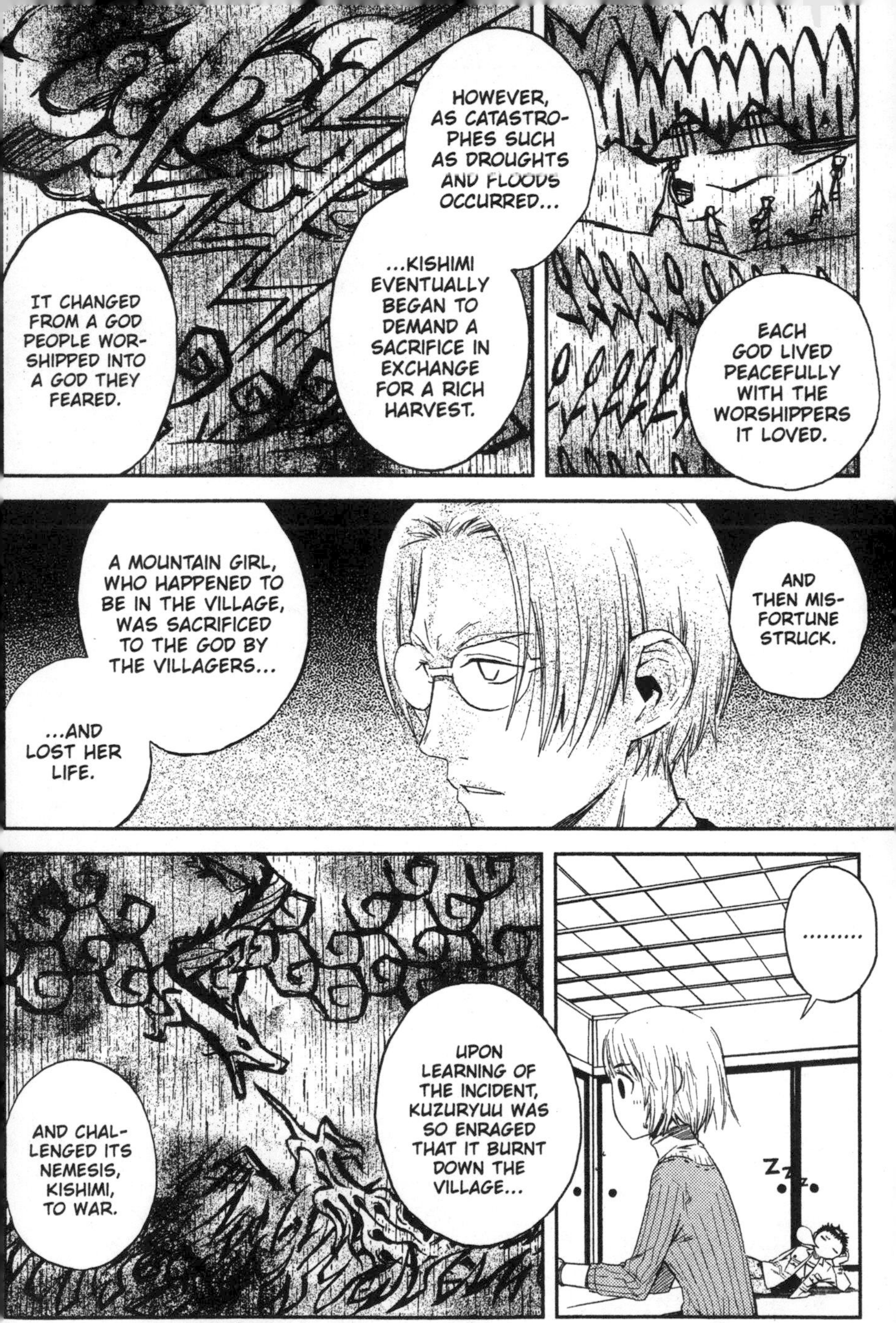
EACH GOD LIVED PEACEFULLY WITH THE WORSHIPPERS IT LOVED.
HOWEVER, AS CATASTRO-PHES SUCH AS DROUGHTS AND FLOODS OCCURRED...
...KISHIMI EVENTUALLY BEGAN TO DEMAND A SACRIFICE IN EXCHANGE FOR A RICH HARVEST.
IT CHANGED FROM A GOD PEOPLE WOR-SHIPPED INTO A GOD THEY FEARED.
AND THEN MIS-FORTUNE STRUCK.
A MOUNTAIN GIRL, WHO HAPPENED TO BE IN THE VILLAGE, WAS SACRIFICED TO THE GOD BY THE VILLAGERS...
...AND LOST HER LIFE.
....
Zzz
UPON LEARNING OF THE INCIDENT, KUZURYUU WAS SO ENRAGED THAT IT BURNT DOWN THE VILLAGE...
AND CHAL-LENGED ITS NEMESIS, KISHIMI, TO WAR.

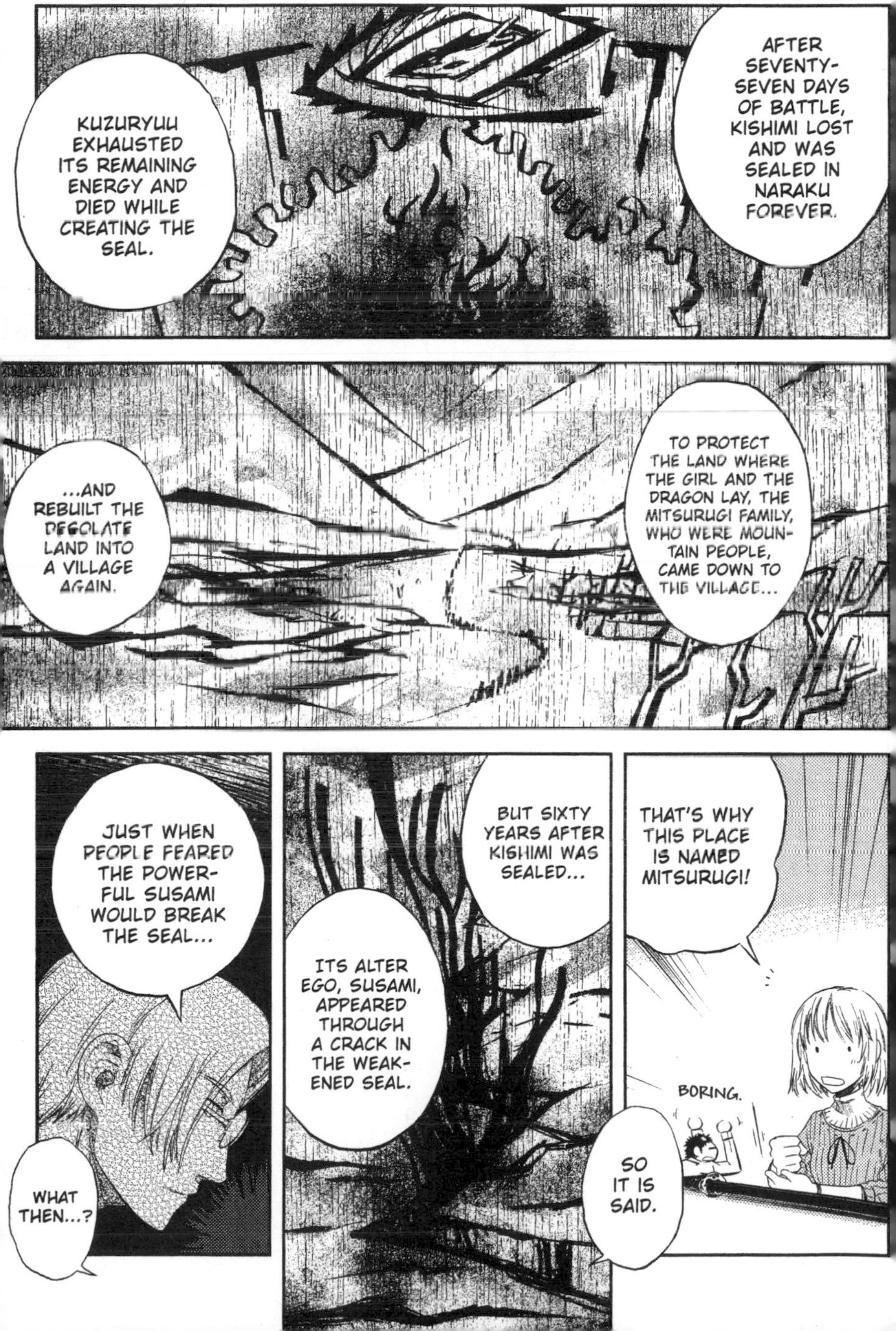
AFTER SEVENTY-SEVEN DAYS OF BATTLE, KISHIMI LOST AND WAS SEALED IN NARAKU FOREVER.
KUZURYUU EXHAUSTED ITS REMAINING ENERGY AND DIED WHILE CREATING THE SEAL.
TO PROTECT THE LAND WHERE THE GIRL AND THE DRAGON LAY, THE MITSURUGI FAMILY, WHO WERE MOUNTAIN PEOPLE, CAME DOWN TO THE VILLAGE...
...AND REBUILT THE DESOLATE LAND INTO A VILLAGE AGAIN.
THAT'S WHY THIS PLACE IS NAMED MITSURUGI!
BORING.
SO IT IS SAID.
BUT SIXTY YEARS AFTER KISHIMI WAS SEALED...
ITS ALTER EGO, SUSAMI, APPEARED THROUGH A CRACK IN THE WEAKENED SEAL.
JUST WHEN PEOPLE FEARED THE POWERFUL SUSAMI WOULD BREAK THE SEAL...
WHAT THEN...?

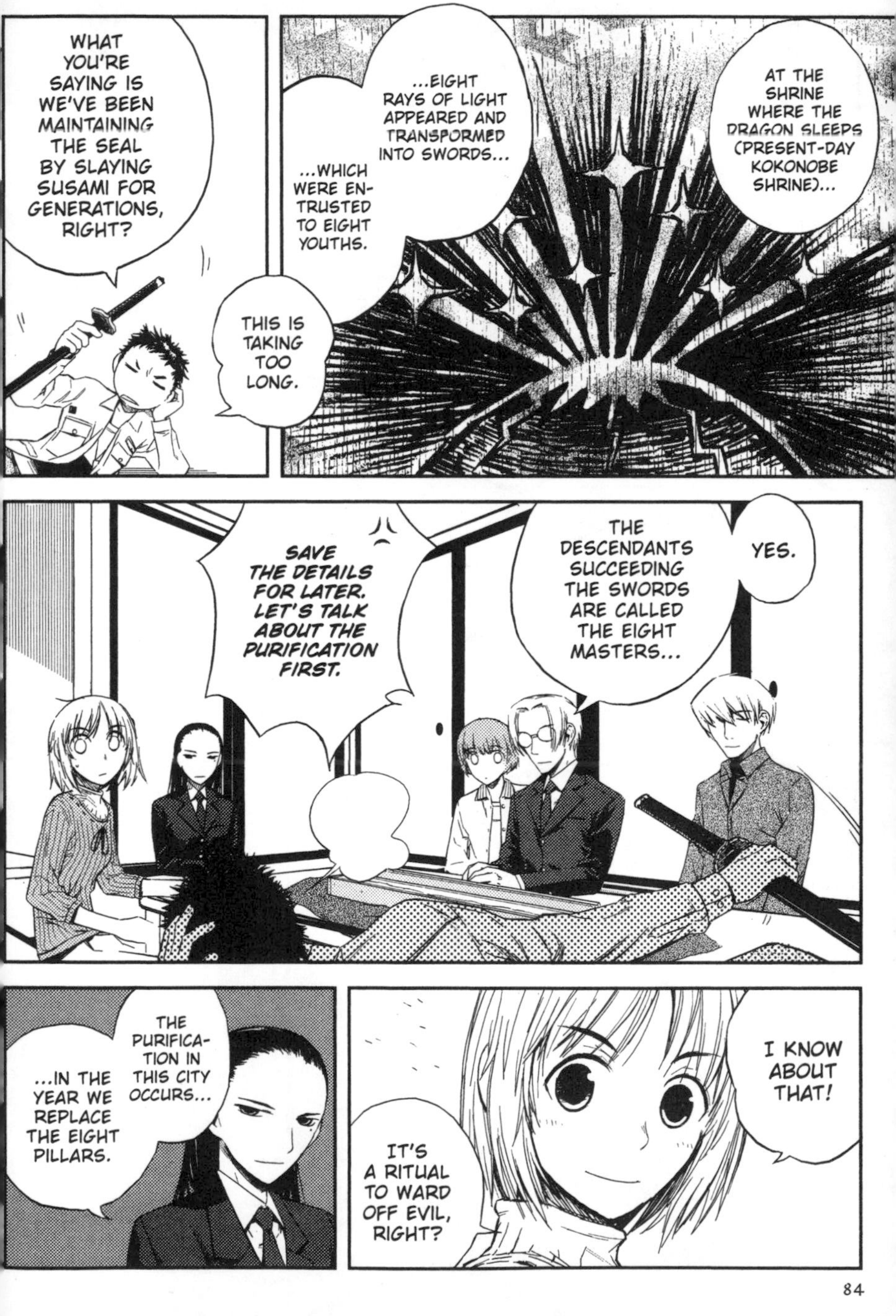
AT THE SHRINE WHERE THE DRAGON SLEEPS (PRESENT-DAY KOKONOBE SHRINE)...
...EIGHT RAYS OF LIGHT APPEARED AND TRANSPORMED INTO SWORDS...
...WHICH WERE EN-TRUSTED TO EIGHT YOUTHS.
WHAT YOU'RE SAYING IS WE'VE BEEN MAINTAINING THE SEAL BY SLAYING SUSAMI FOR GENERATIONS, RIGHT?
THIS IS TAKING TOO LONG.
YES.
THE DESCENDANTS SUCCEEDING THE SWORDS ARE CALLED THE EIGHT MASTERS...
SAVE THE DETAILS FOR LATER. LET'S TALK ABOUT THE PURIFICATION FIRST.
I KNOW ABOUT THAT!
IT'S A RITUAL TO WARD OFF EVIL, RIGHT?
THE PURIFICA-TION IN THIS CITY OCCURS...
...IN THE YEAR WE REPLACE THE EIGHT PILLARS.

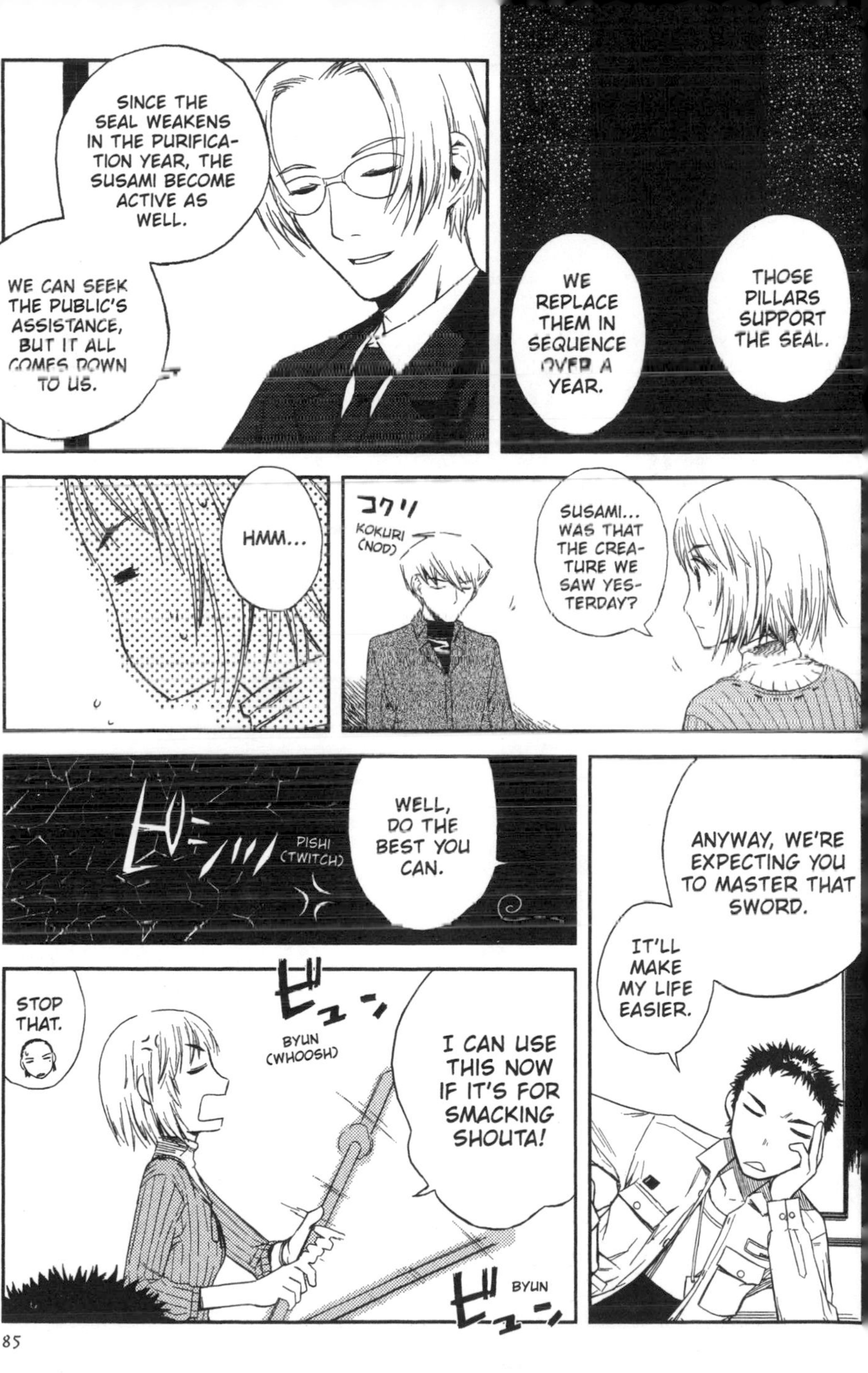
THOSE PILLARS SUPPORT THE SEAL.
WE REPLACE THEM IN SEQUENCE OVER A YEAR.
SINCE THE SEAL WEAKENS IN THE PURIFICATION YEAR, THE SUSAMI BECOME ACTIVE AS WELL.
WE CAN SEEK THE PUBLIC'S ASSISTANCE, BUT IT ALL COMES DOWN TO US.
SUSAMI... WAS THAT THE CREATURE WE SAW YESTERDAY?
コクリ
KOKURI (NOD)
HMM...
ANYWAY, WE'RE EXPECTING YOU TO MASTER THAT SWORD.
IT'LL MAKE MY LIFE EASIER.
WELL, DO THE BEST YOU CAN.
PISHI (TWITCH)
I CAN USE THIS NOW IF IT'S FOR SMACKING SHOUTA!
BYUN (WHOOSH)
BYUN
STOP THAT.

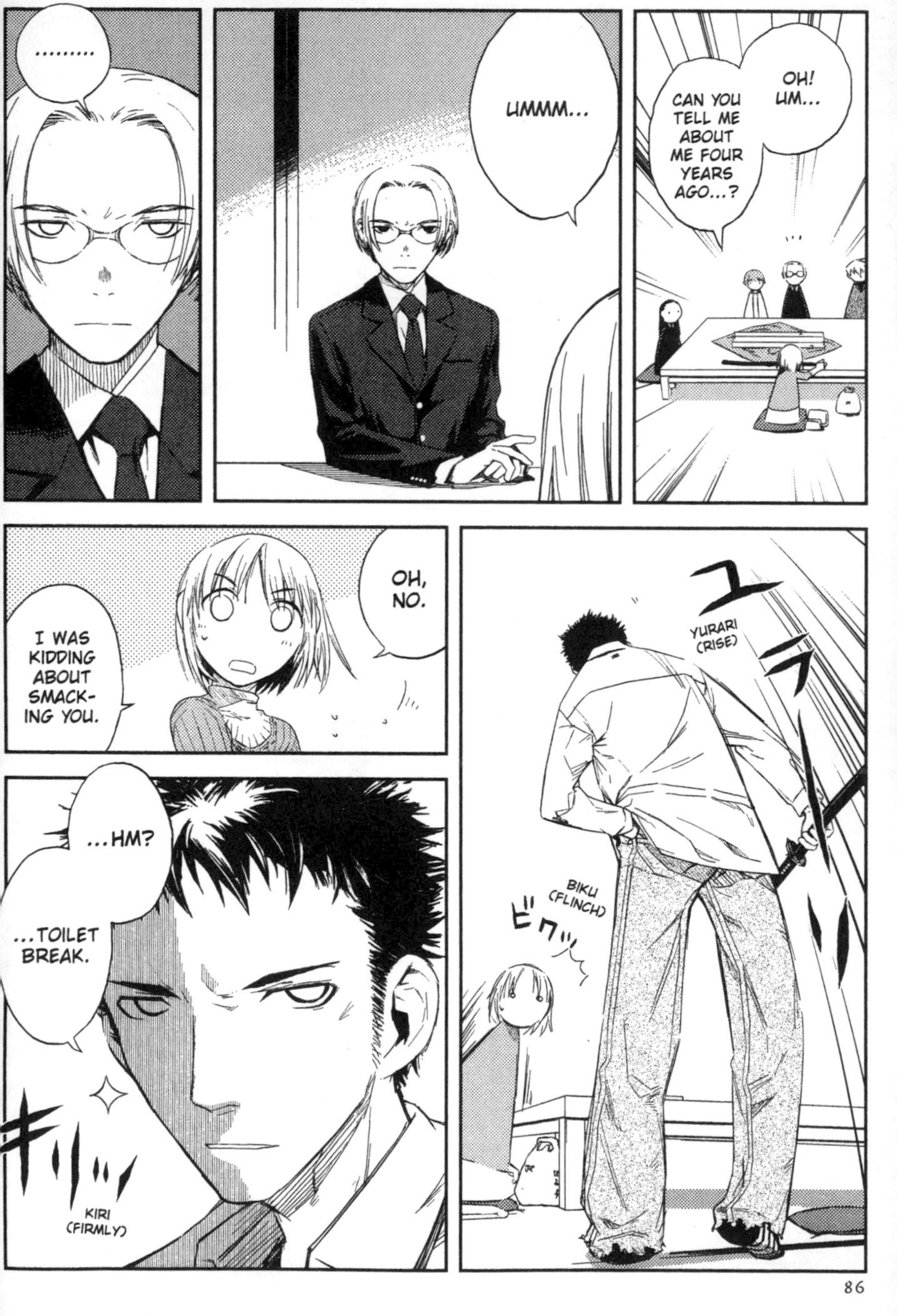
OH! UM...
CAN YOU TELL ME ABOUT ME FOUR YEARS AGO...?
...
UMMM...
....
YURARI (RISE)
BIKU (FLINCH)
OH, NO.
I WAS KIDDING ABOUT SMACKING YOU.
...HM?
...TOILET BREAK.
KIRI (FIRMLY)

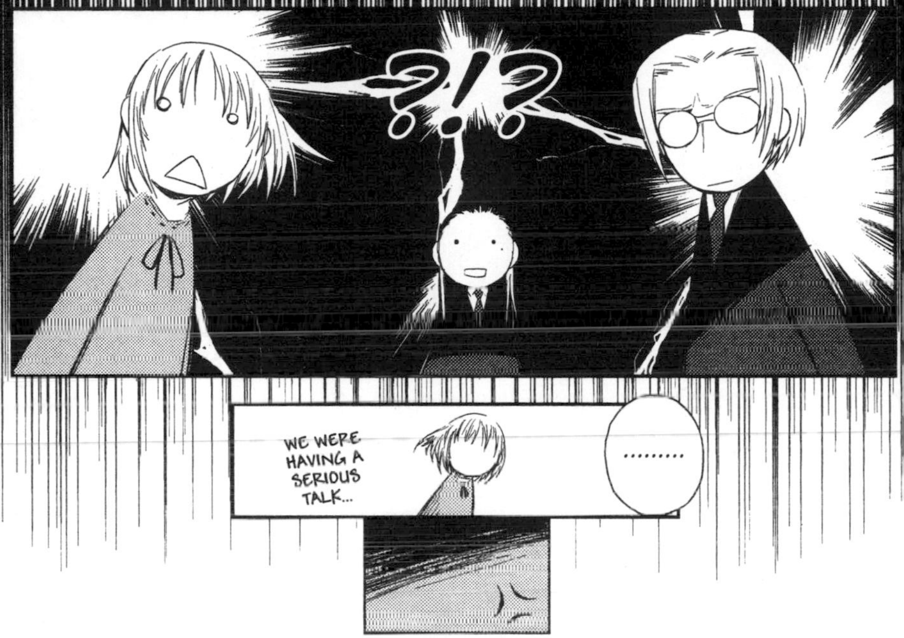
?!?
....
WE WERE HAVING A SERIOUS TALK...

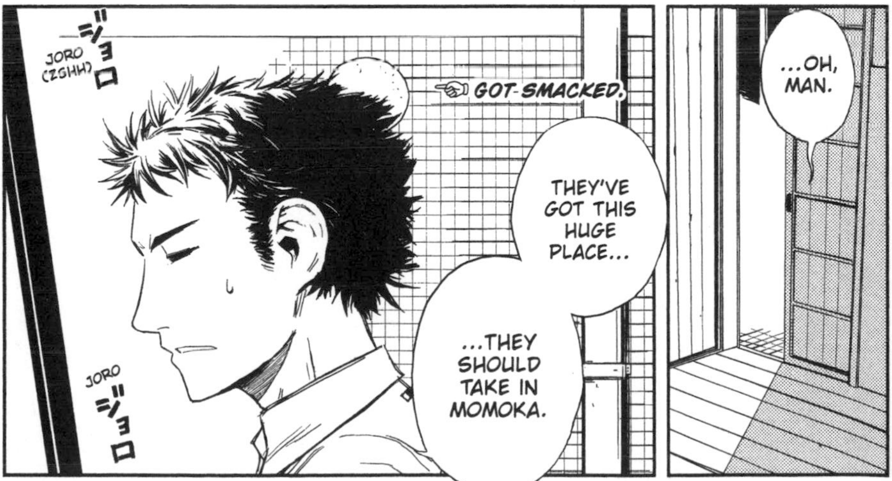
...OH, MAN.
GOT-SMACKED.
JORO (ZGHH) ジョロ
THEY'VE GOT THIS HUGE PLACE...
...THEY SHOULD TAKE IN MOMOKA.
JORO ジョロ

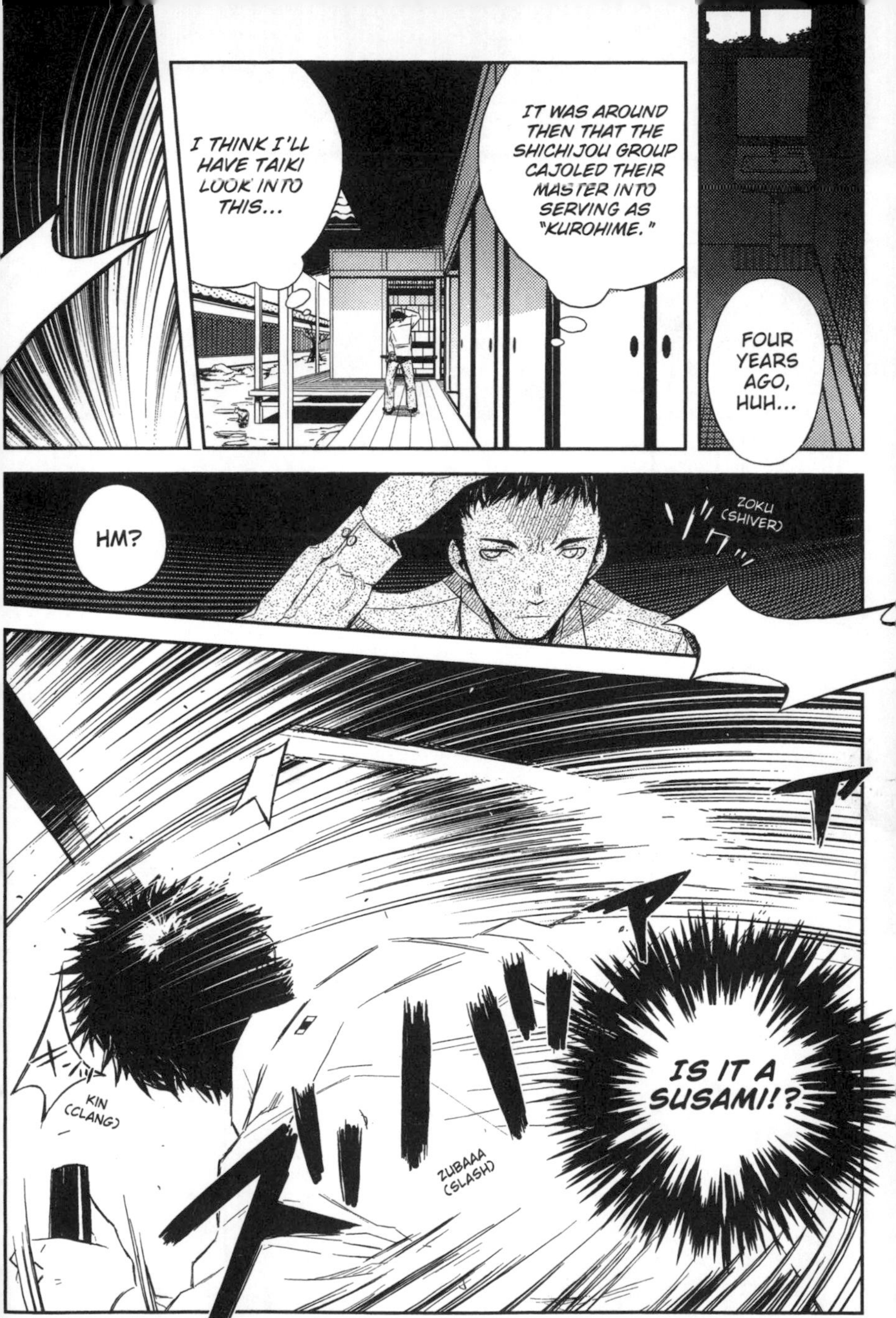
FOUR YEARS AGO, HUH...
IT WAS AROUND THEN THAT THE SHICHIJOU GROUP CAJOLED THEIR MASTER INTO SERVING AS "KUROHIME."
I THINK I'LL HAVE TAIKI LOOK INTO THIS...
ZOKU (SHIVER)
HM?
IS IT A SUSAMI!?
ZUBAAA (SLASH)
KIN (CLANG)

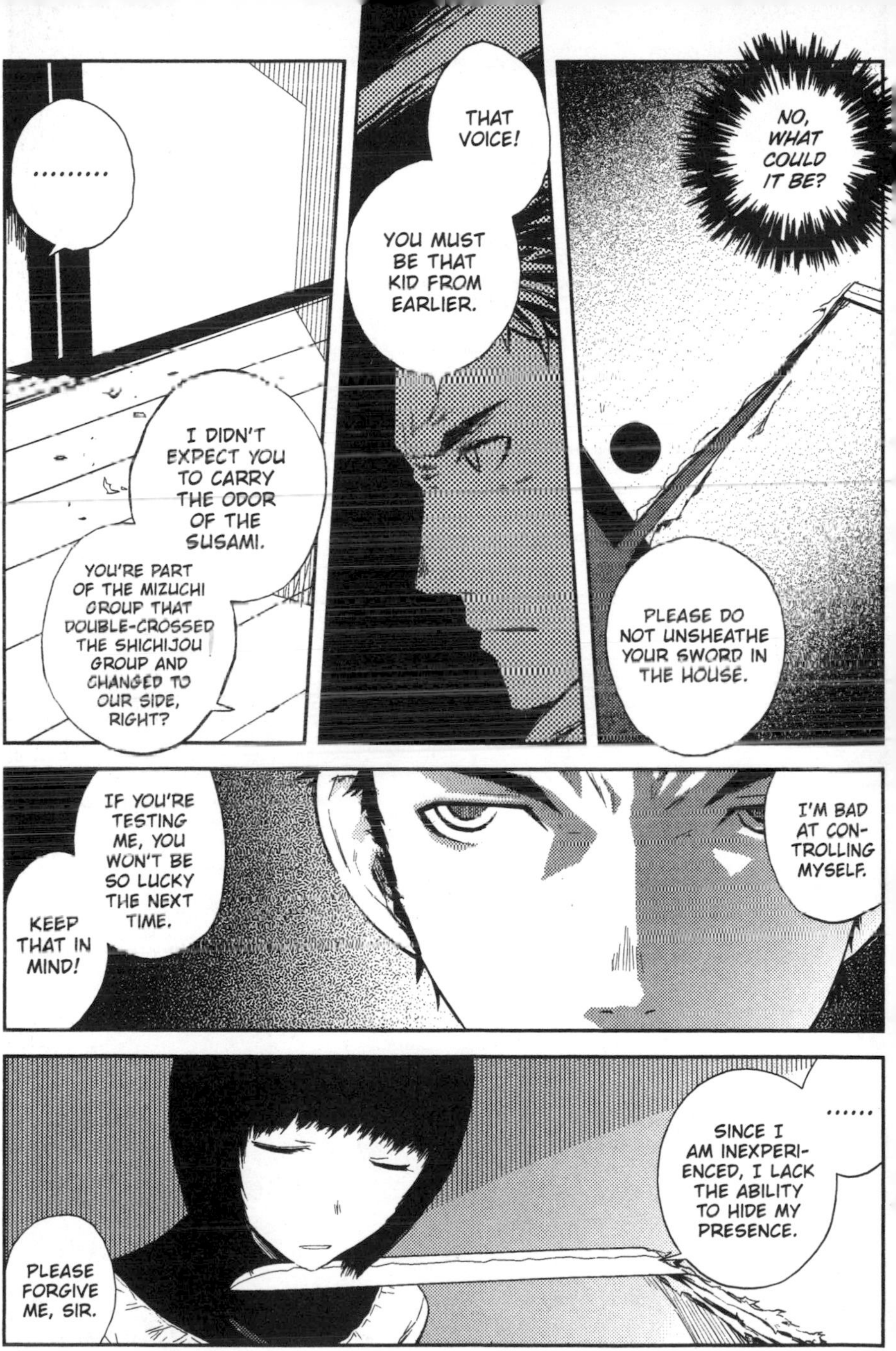
NO, WHAT COULD IT BE?
PLEASE DO NOT UNSHEATHE YOUR SWORD IN THE HOUSE.
THAT VOICE!
YOU MUST BE THAT KID FROM EARLIER.
....
I DIDN'T EXPECT YOU TO CARRY THE ODOR OF THE SUSAMI.
YOU'RE PART OF THE MIZUCHI GROUP THAT DOUBLE-CROSSED THE SHICHIJOU GROUP AND CHANGED TO OUR SIDE, RIGHT?
I'M BAD AT CON-TROLLING MYSELF.
IF YOU'RE TESTING ME, YOU WON'T BE SO LUCKY THE NEXT TIME.
KEEP THAT IN MIND!
......
SINCE I AM INEXPERI-ENCED, I LACK THE ABILITY TO HIDE MY PRESENCE.
PLEASE FORGIVE ME, SIR.

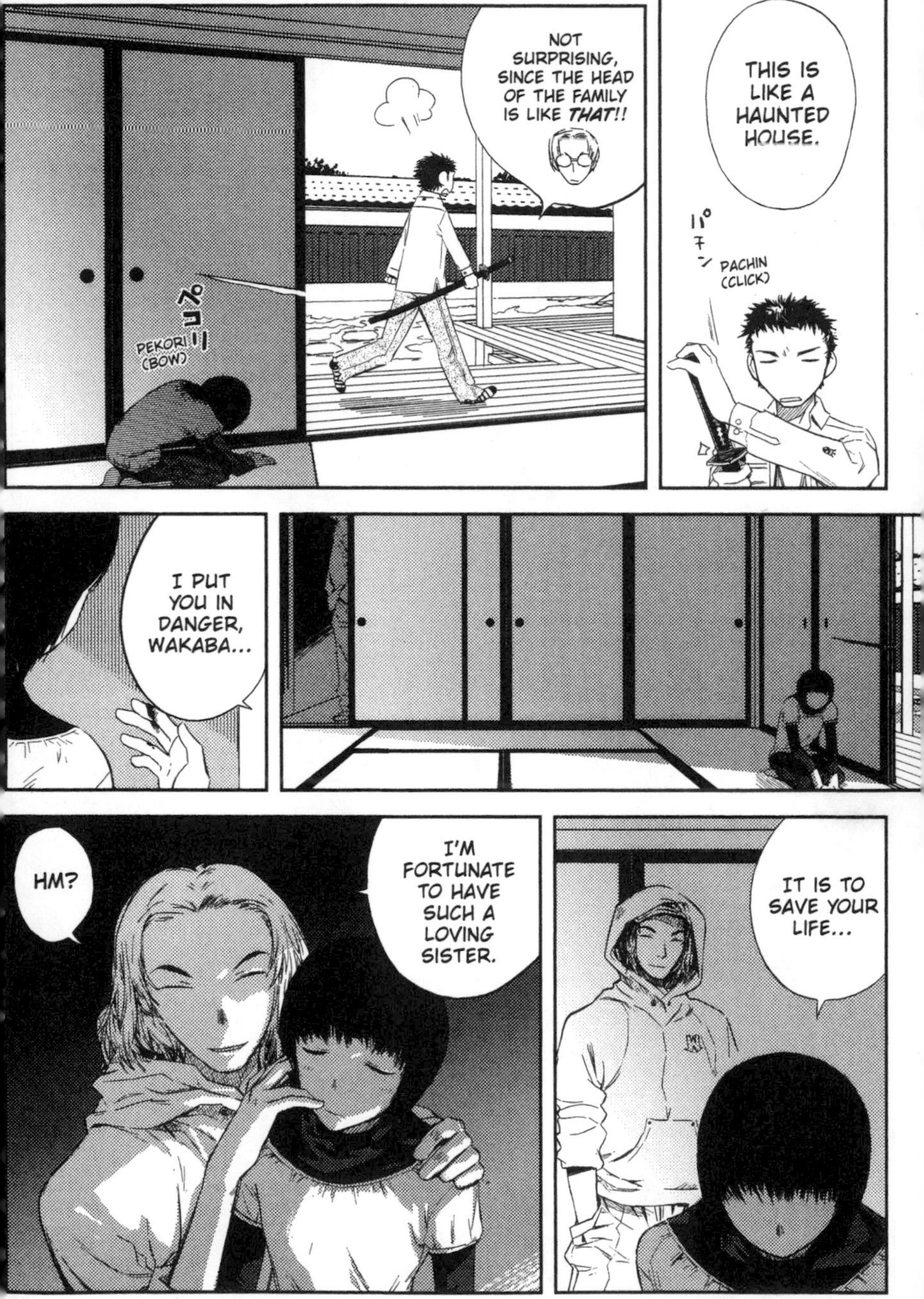
THIS IS LIKE A HAUNTED HOUSE.
パチン
PACHIN (CLICK)
NOT SURPRISING, SINCE THE HEAD OF THE FAMILY IS LIKE *THAT*!!
ペコリ
PEKORI (BOW)
I PUT YOU IN DANGER, WAKABA...
IT IS TO SAVE YOUR LIFE...
I'M FORTUNATE TO HAVE SUCH A LOVING SISTER.
HM?

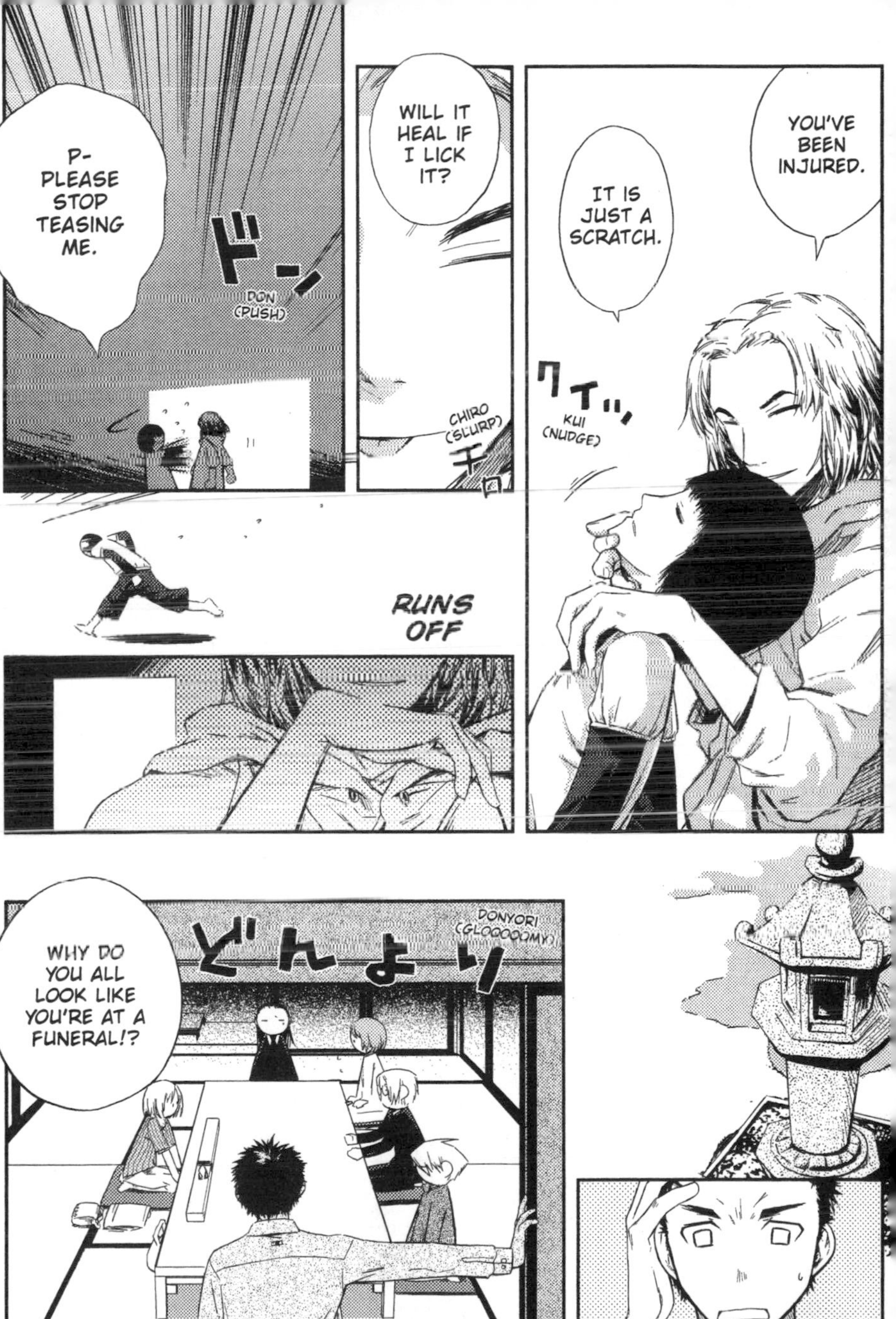
YOU'VE BEEN INJURED.
IT IS JUST A SCRATCH.
KUI (NUDGE)
WILL IT HEAL IF I LICK IT?
CHIRO (SLURP)
P- PLEASE STOP TEASING ME.
DON (PUSH)
RUNS OFF
DONYORI (GLOOOOOMY)
WHY DO YOU ALL LOOK LIKE YOU'RE AT A FUNERAL!?

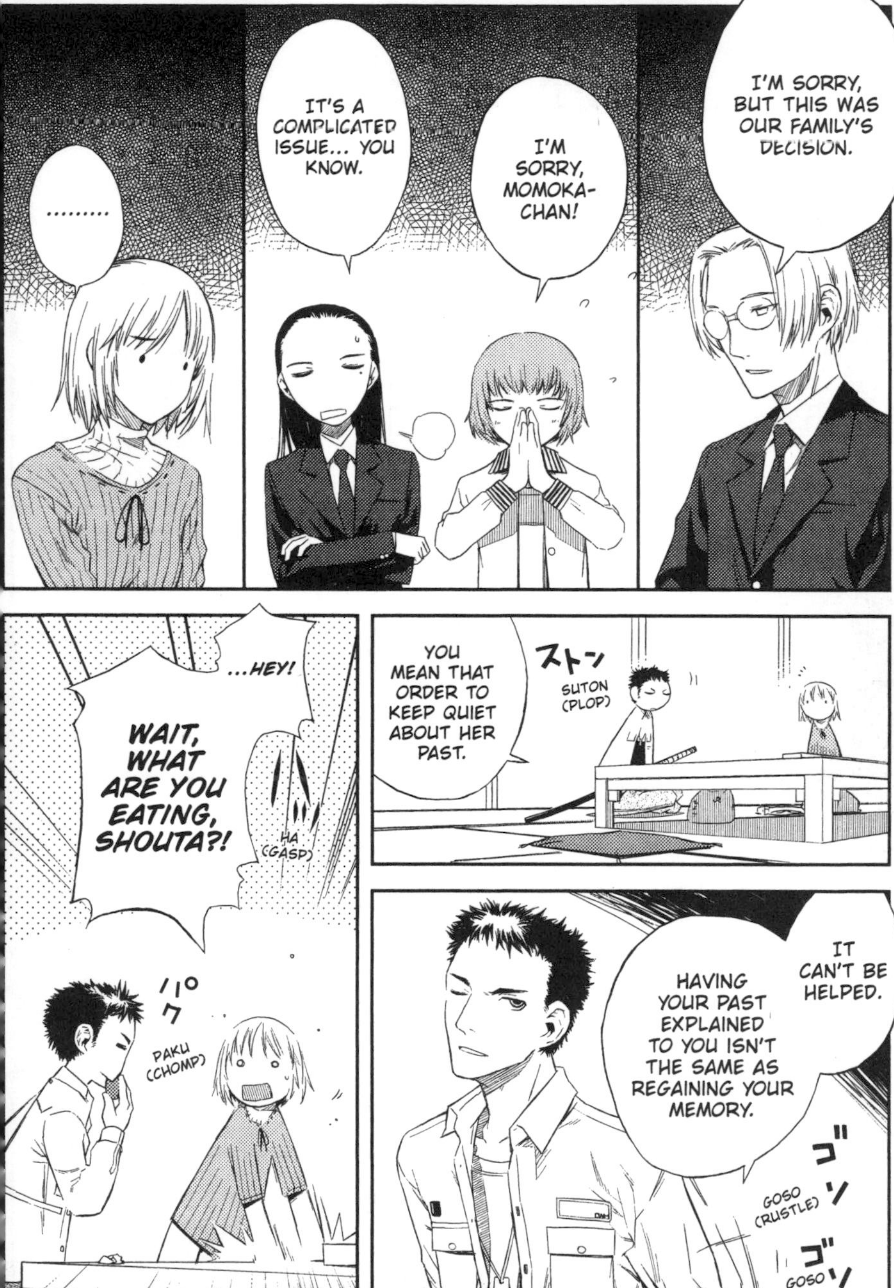
I'M SORRY, BUT THIS WAS OUR FAMILY'S DECISION.
I'M SORRY, MOMOKA-CHAN!
IT'S A COMPLICATED ISSUE... YOU KNOW.
....
ストン
SUTON (PLOP)
YOU MEAN THAT ORDER TO KEEP QUIET ABOUT HER PAST.
IT CAN'T BE HELPED.
HAVING YOUR PAST EXPLAINED TO YOU ISN'T THE SAME AS REGAINING YOUR MEMORY.
ゴソ
GOSO (RUSTLE)
ゴソ
GOSO
...HEY!
WAIT, WHAT ARE YOU EATING, SHOUTA?!
HA (GASP)
パク
PAKU (CHOMP)

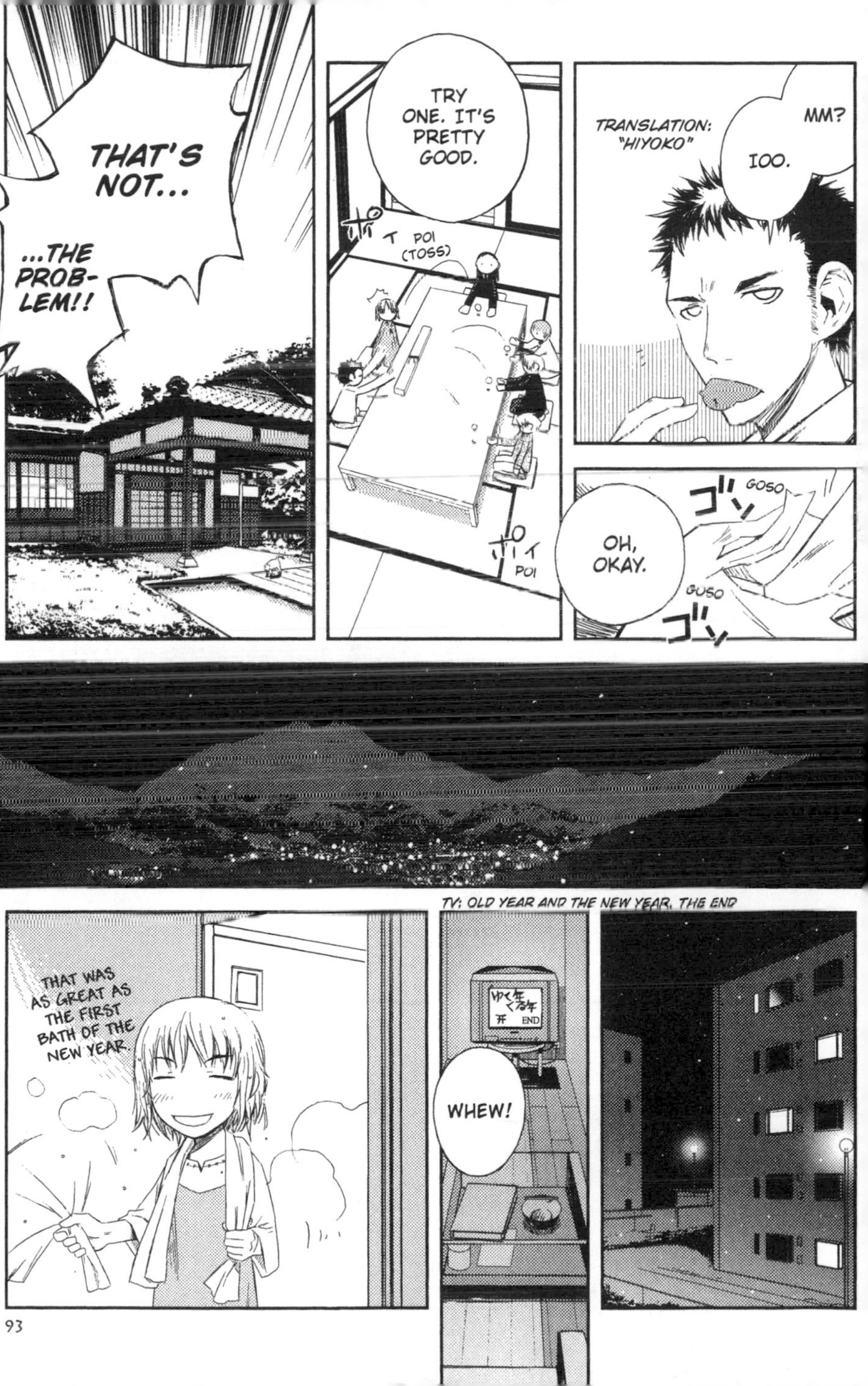
MM?
IOO.
TRANSLATION: "HIYOKO"
OH, OKAY.
GOSO
GOSO
TRY ONE. IT'S PRETTY GOOD.
POI (TOSS)
POI
THAT'S NOT...
...THE PROB-LEM!!
TV: OLD YEAR AND THE NEW YEAR, THE END
END
WHEW!
THAT WAS AS GREAT AS THE FIRST BATH OF THE NEW YEAR.

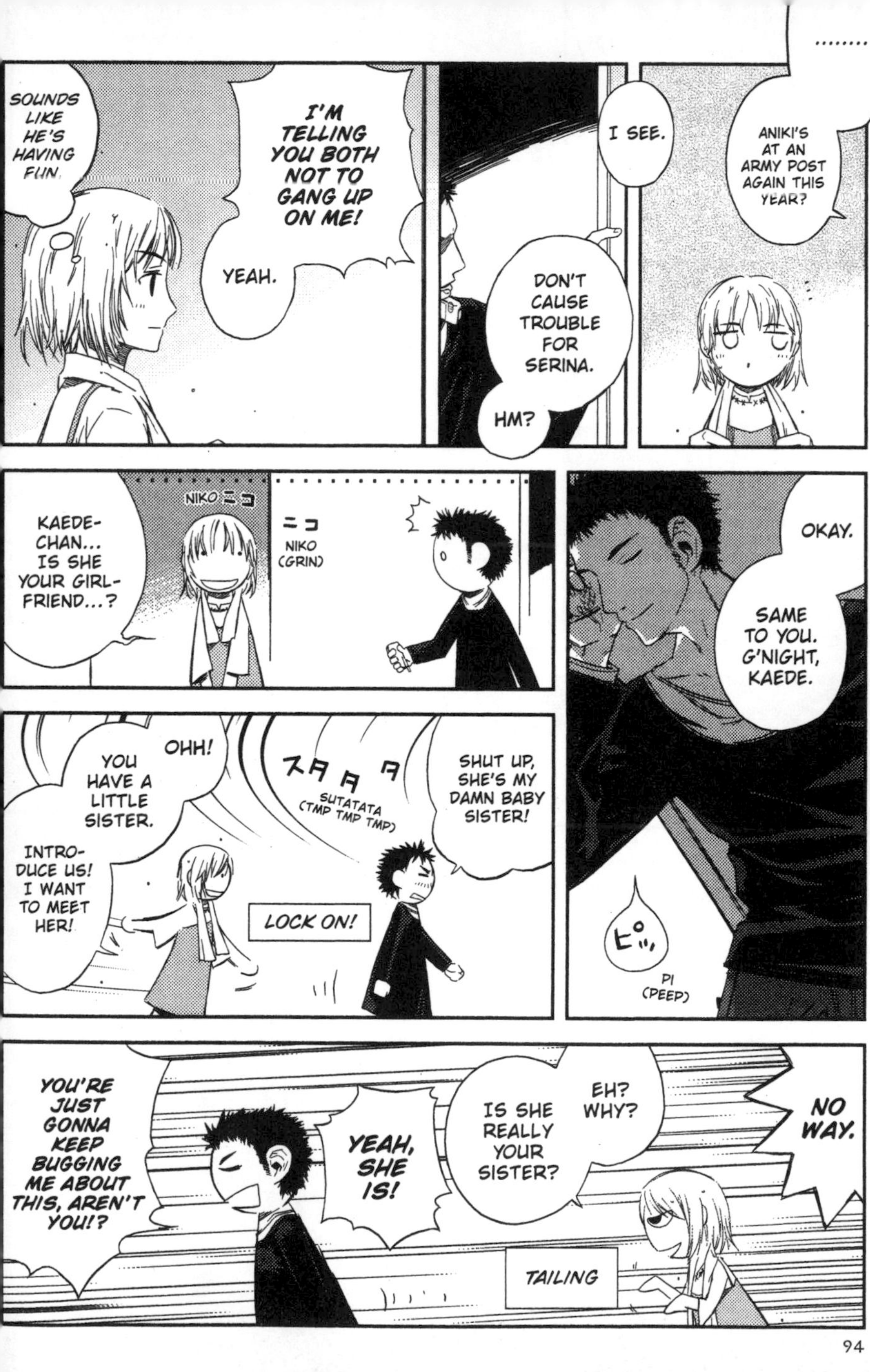
....
ANIKI'S AT AN ARMY POST AGAIN THIS YEAR?
I SEE.
DON'T CAUSE TROUBLE FOR SERINA.
HM?
I'M TELLING YOU BOTH NOT TO GANG UP ON ME!
YEAH.
SOUNDS LIKE HE'S HAVING FUN.
OKAY.
SAME TO YOU. G'NIGHT, KAEDE.
ピッ
PI (PEEP)
ニコ
NIKO (GRIN)
NIKO ニコ
KAEDE-CHAN... IS SHE YOUR GIRL-FRIEND...?
SHUT UP, SHE'S MY DAMN BABY SISTER!
スタタタ
SUTATATA (TMP TMP TMP)
OHH!
YOU HAVE A LITTLE SISTER.
LOCK ON!
INTRO-DUCE US! I WANT TO MEET HER!
NO WAY.
EH? WHY?
IS SHE REALLY YOUR SISTER?
YEAH, SHE IS!
TAILING
YOU'RE JUST GONNA KEEP BUGGING ME ABOUT THIS, AREN'T YOU!?

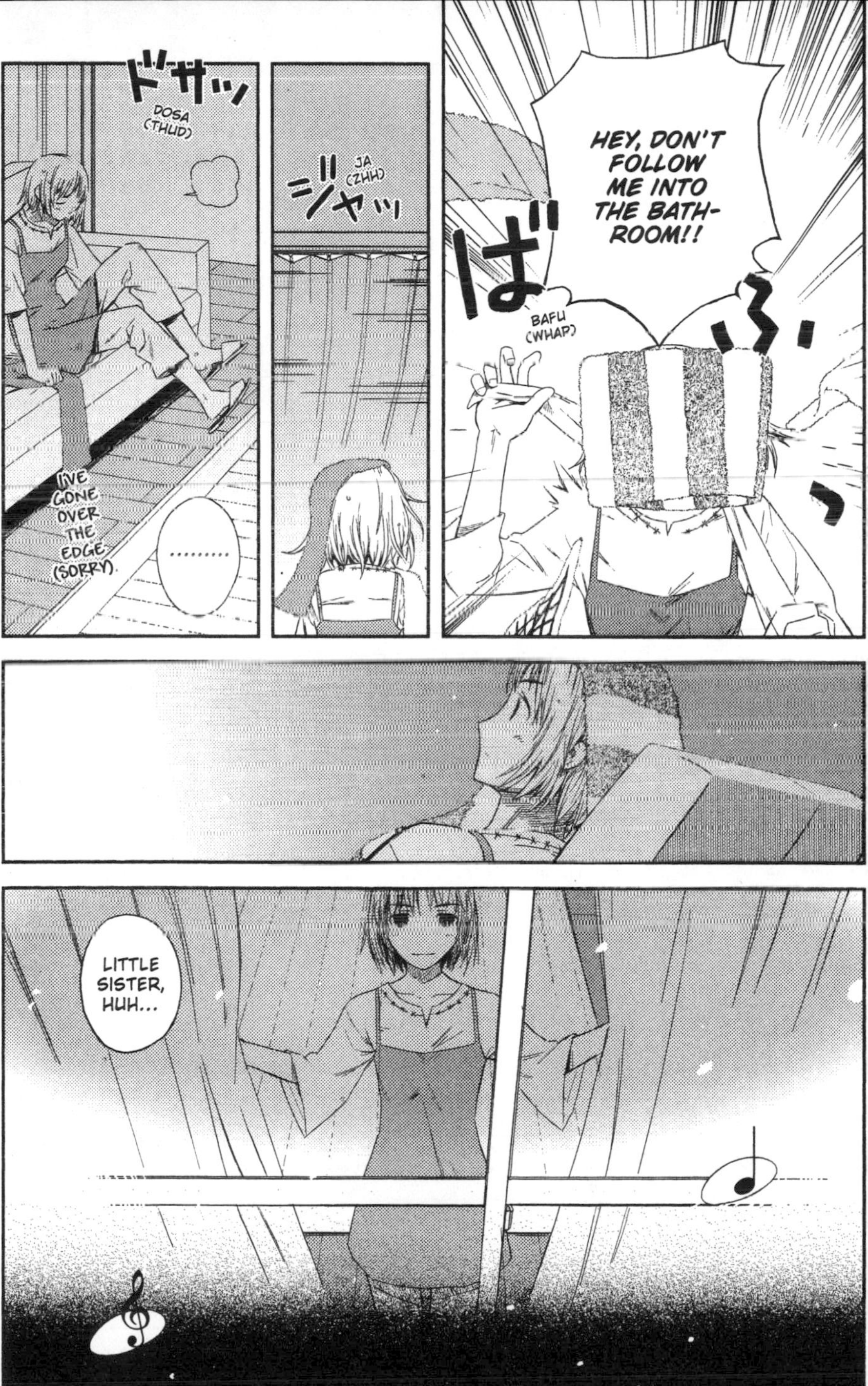
HEY, DON'T FOLLOW ME INTO THE BATH-ROOM!!
ばふ
BAFU (WHAP)
ジャッ
JA (ZHH)
ドサッ
DOSA (THUD)
....
I'VE GONE OVER THE EDGE (SORRY)
LITTLE SISTER, HUH...

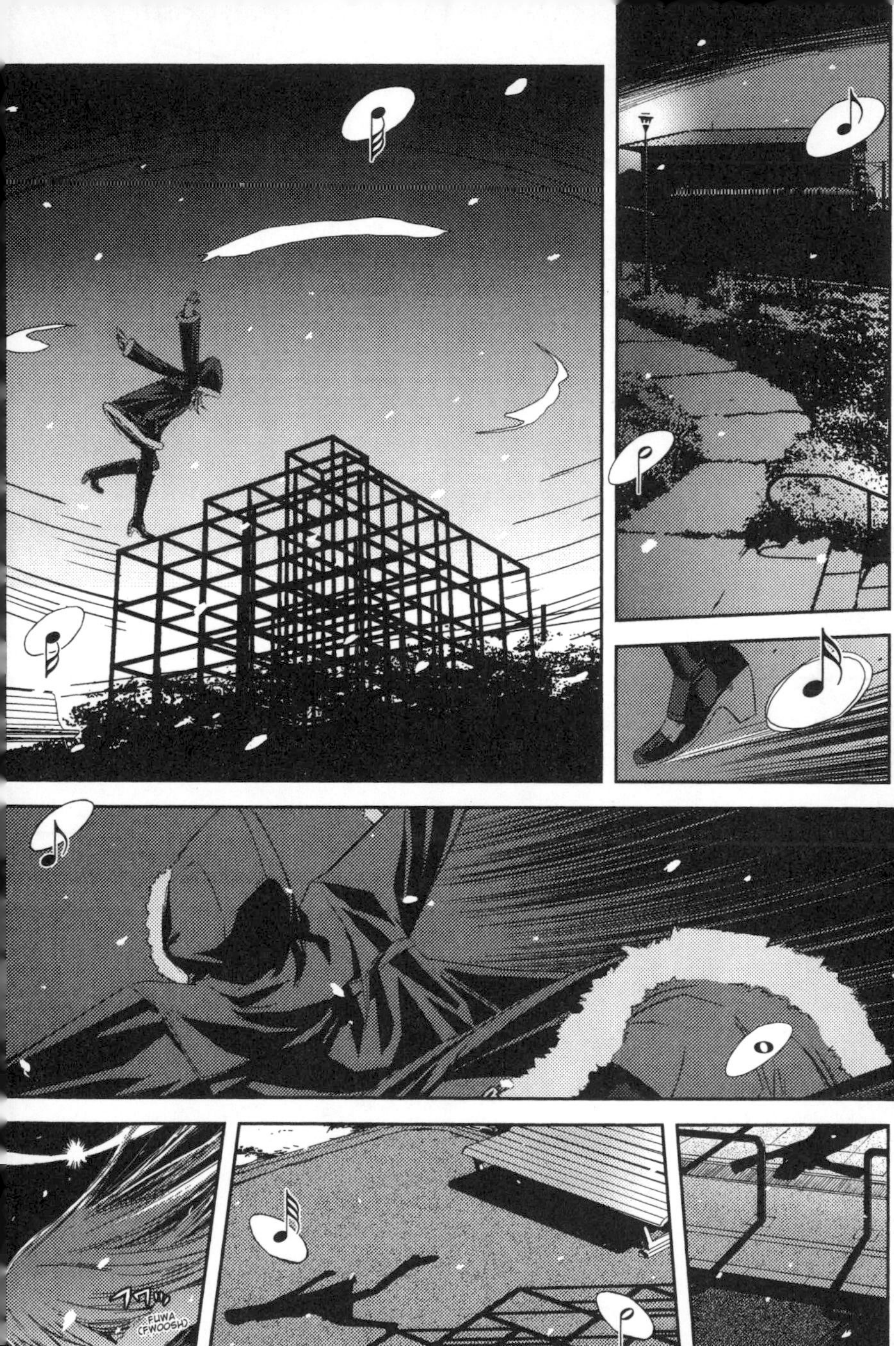
FUWA
(FWOOSH)

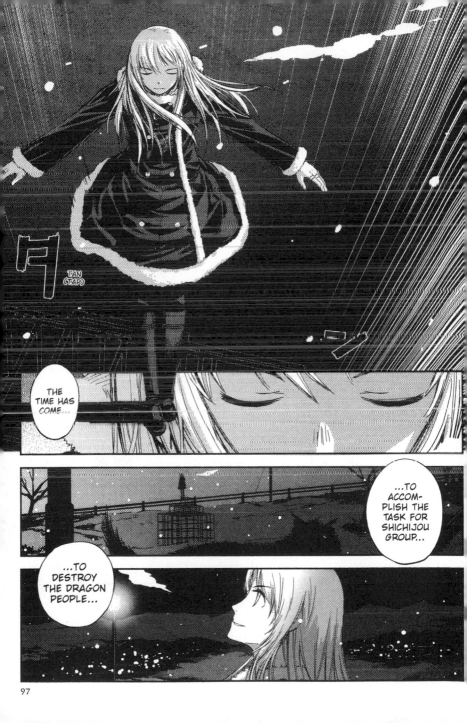

TAN
(TAP)

THE
TIME HAS
COME...

...TO
ACCOM-
PLISH THE
TASK FOR
SHICHIJOU
GROUP...

...TO
DESTROY
THE DRAGON
PEOPLE...

SEBASTIAN...

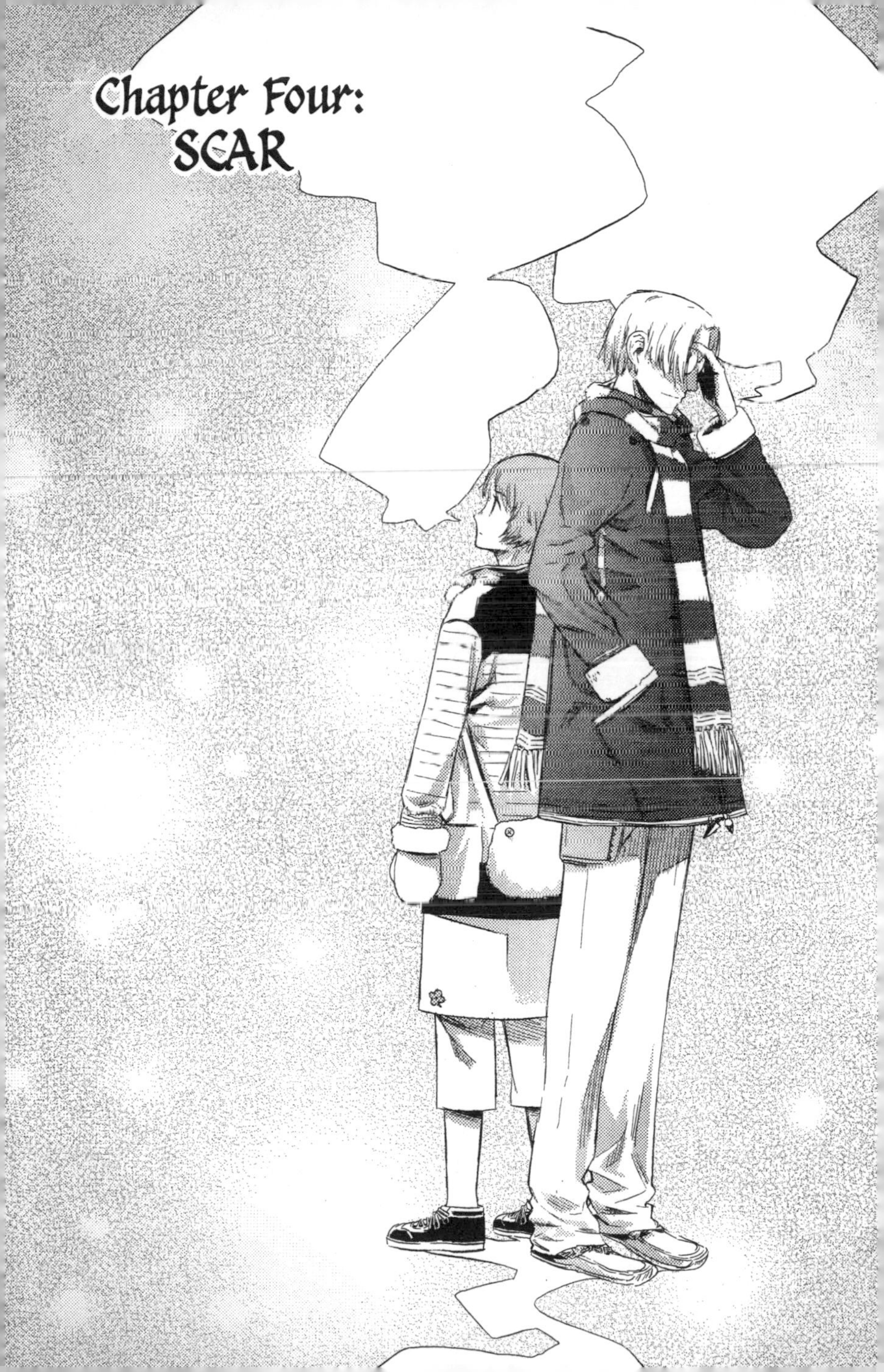
Chapter Four:
SCAR

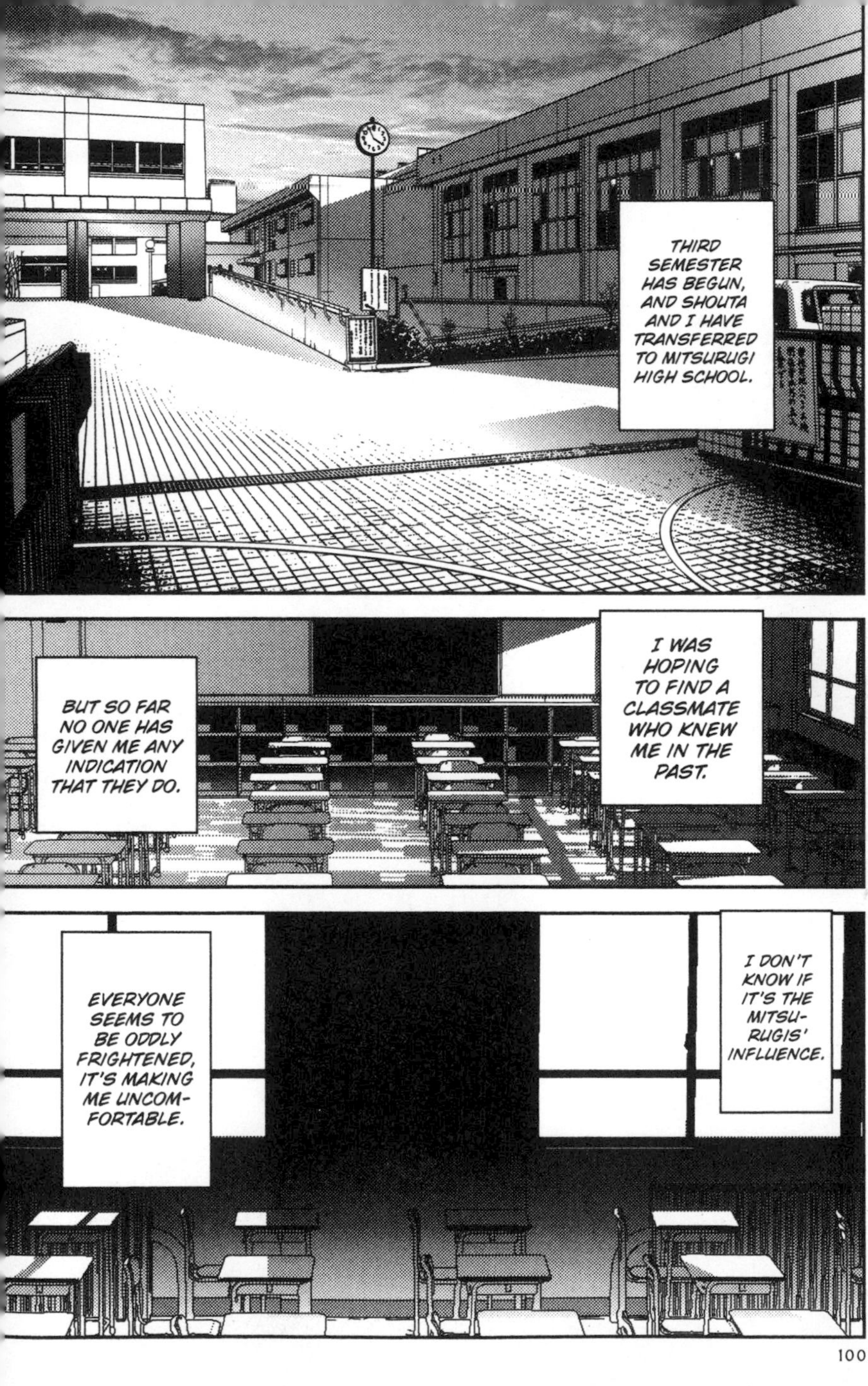
THIRD SEMESTER HAS BEGUN, AND SHOUTA AND I HAVE TRANSFERRED TO MITSURUGI HIGH SCHOOL.
I WAS HOPING TO FIND A CLASSMATE WHO KNEW ME IN THE PAST.
BUT SO FAR NO ONE HAS GIVEN ME ANY INDICATION THAT THEY DO.
I DON'T KNOW IF IT'S THE MITSU-RUGIS' INFLUENCE.
EVERYONE SEEMS TO BE ODDLY FRIGHTENED, IT'S MAKING ME UNCOM-FORTABLE.

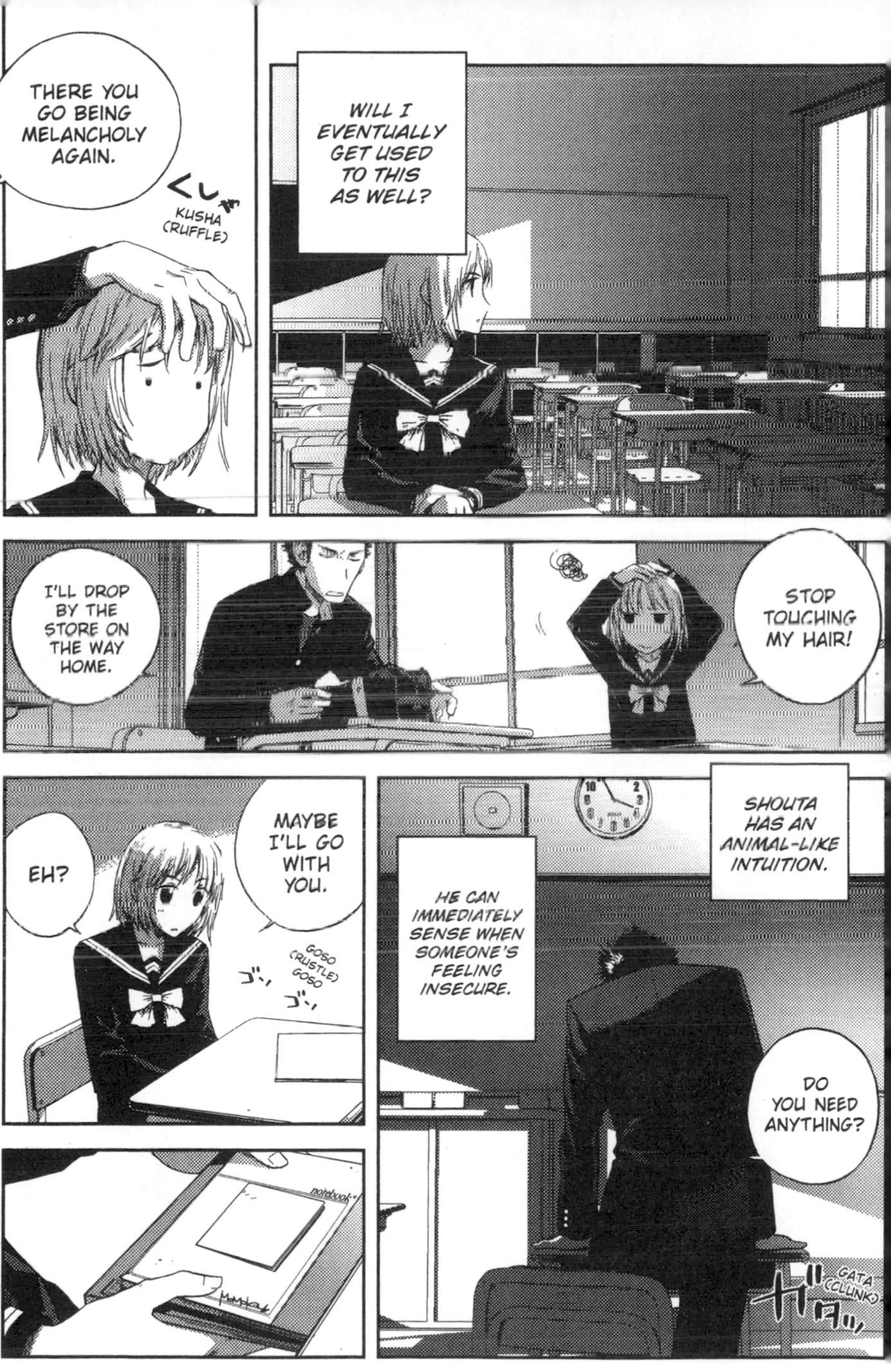
WILL I EVENTUALLY GET USED TO THIS AS WELL?
THERE YOU GO BEING MELANCHOLY AGAIN.
くしゃ
KUSHA (RUFFLE)
STOP TOUCHING MY HAIR!
I'LL DROP BY THE STORE ON THE WAY HOME.
SHOUTA HAS AN ANIMAL-LIKE INTUITION.
HE CAN IMMEDIATELY SENSE WHEN SOMEONE'S FEELING INSECURE.
DO YOU NEED ANYTHING?
ガタッ
GATA (CLUNK)
MAYBE I'LL GO WITH YOU.
EH?
ゴソ ゴソ
GOSO (RUSTLE) GOSO

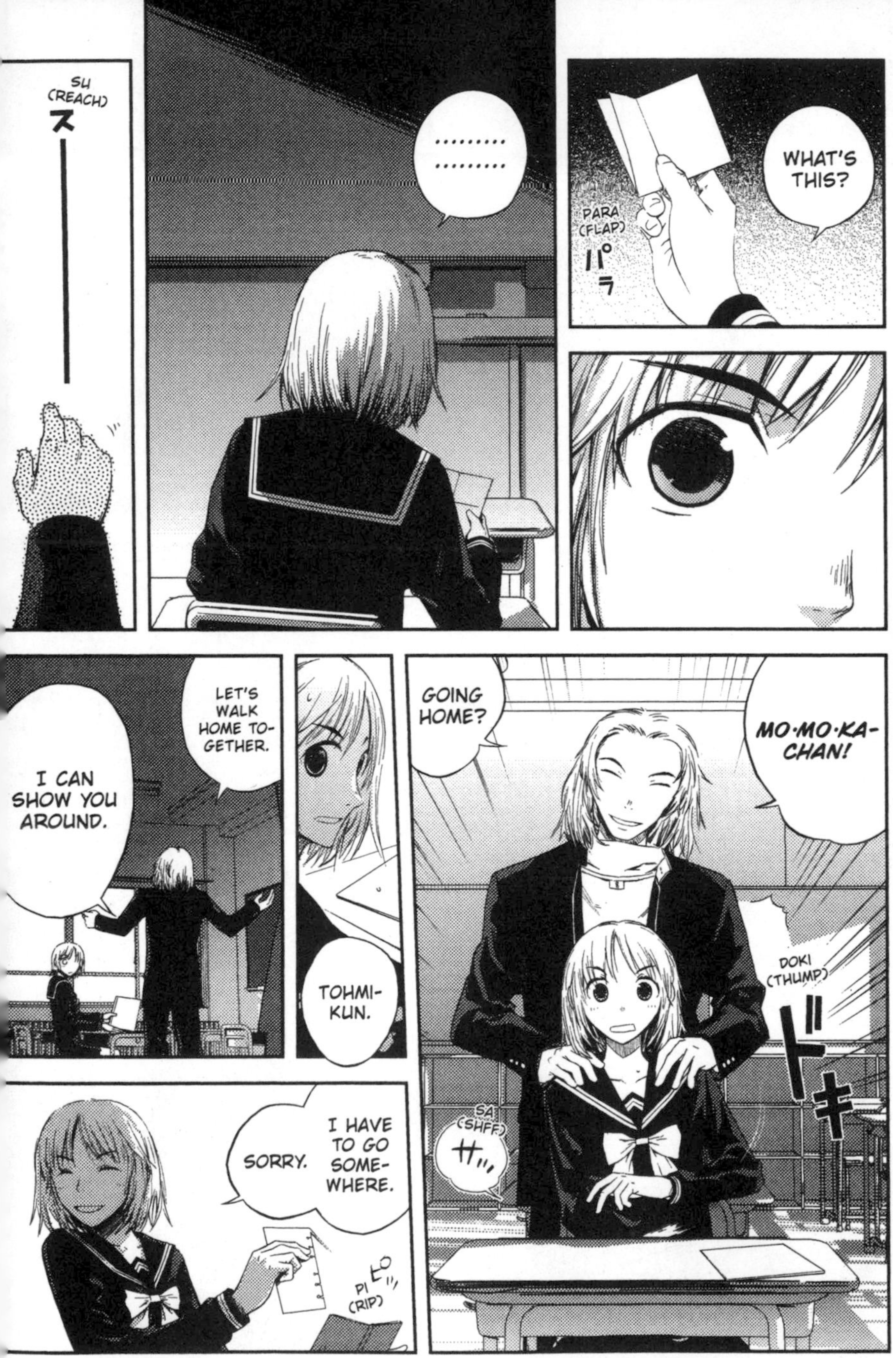
WHAT'S THIS?
PARA (FLAP)
パラ
....
....
SU (REACH)
ス—
MO·MO·KA-CHAN!
GOING HOME?
DOKI (THUMP)
ドキ
SA (SHFF)
サッ
TOHMI-KUN.
LET'S WALK HOME TO-GETHER.
I CAN SHOW YOU AROUND.
SORRY. I HAVE TO GO SOME-WHERE.
PI (RIP)
ピッ

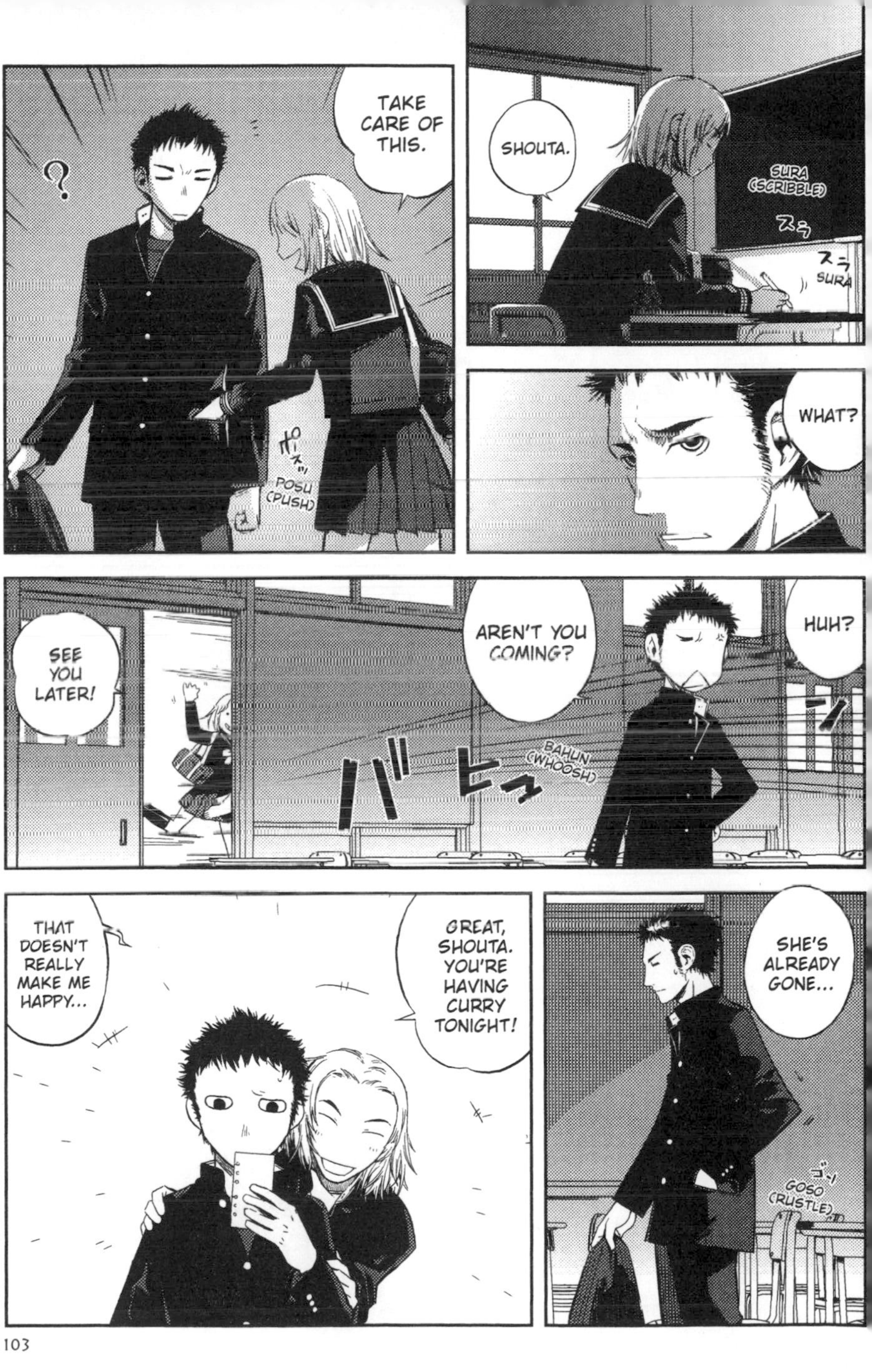
SHOUTA.
SURA (SCRIBBLE)
SURA
WHAT?
TAKE CARE OF THIS.
?
POSU (PUSH)
HUH?
AREN'T YOU COMING?
BAHUN (WHOOSH)
SEE YOU LATER!
SHE'S ALREADY GONE...
GOSO (RUSTLE)
GREAT, SHOUTA. YOU'RE HAVING CURRY TONIGHT!
THAT DOESN'T REALLY MAKE ME HAPPY...

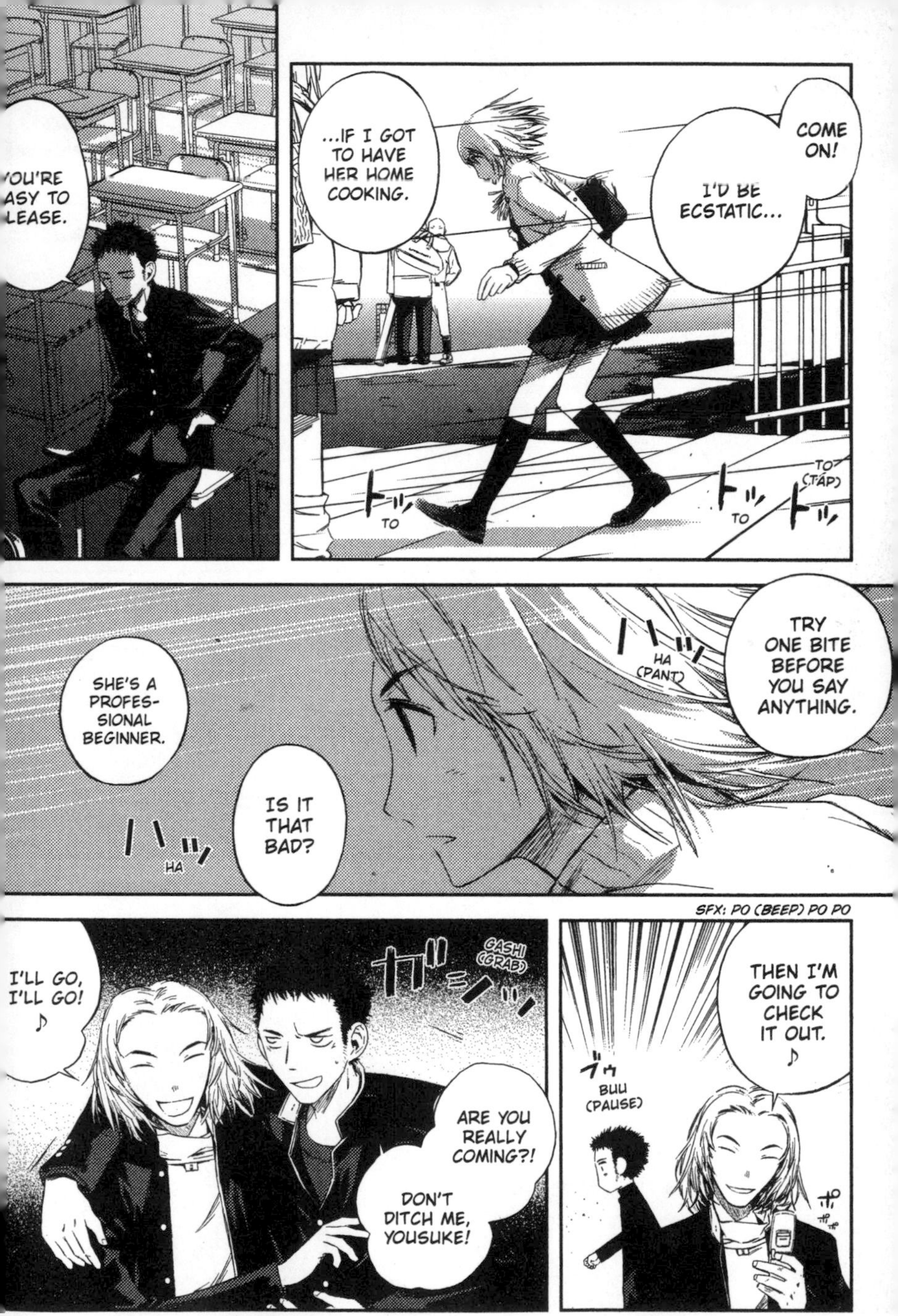
COME ON!
I'D BE ECSTATIC...
...IF I GOT TO HAVE HER HOME COOKING.
TO (TAP)
TO
TO
OU'RE ASY TO LEASE.
TRY ONE BITE BEFORE YOU SAY ANYTHING.
HA (PANT)
SHE'S A PROFES-SIONAL BEGINNER.
IS IT THAT BAD?
HA
SFX: PO (BEEP) PO PO
THEN I'M GOING TO CHECK IT OUT. ♪
BUU (PAUSE)
GASHI (GRAB)
I'LL GO, I'LL GO! ♪
ARE YOU REALLY COMING?!
DON'T DITCH ME, YOUSUKE!

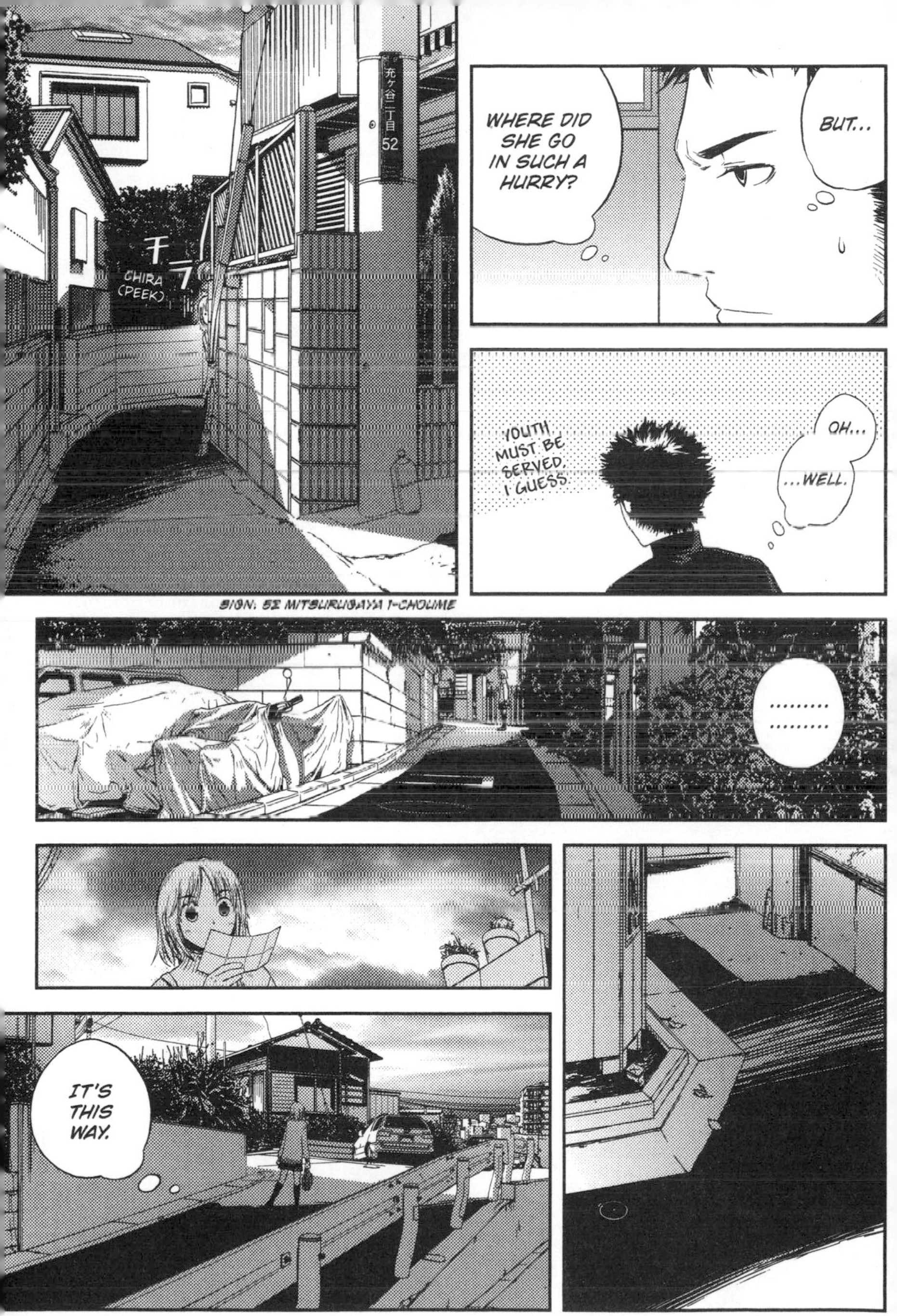
BUT...
WHERE DID SHE GO IN SUCH A HURRY?
OH...
...WELL.
YOUTH MUST BE SERVED, I GUESS.
チラ
CHIRA (PEEK)
SIGN: 52 MITSURUGAYA 1-CHOUME
....
....
IT'S THIS WAY.

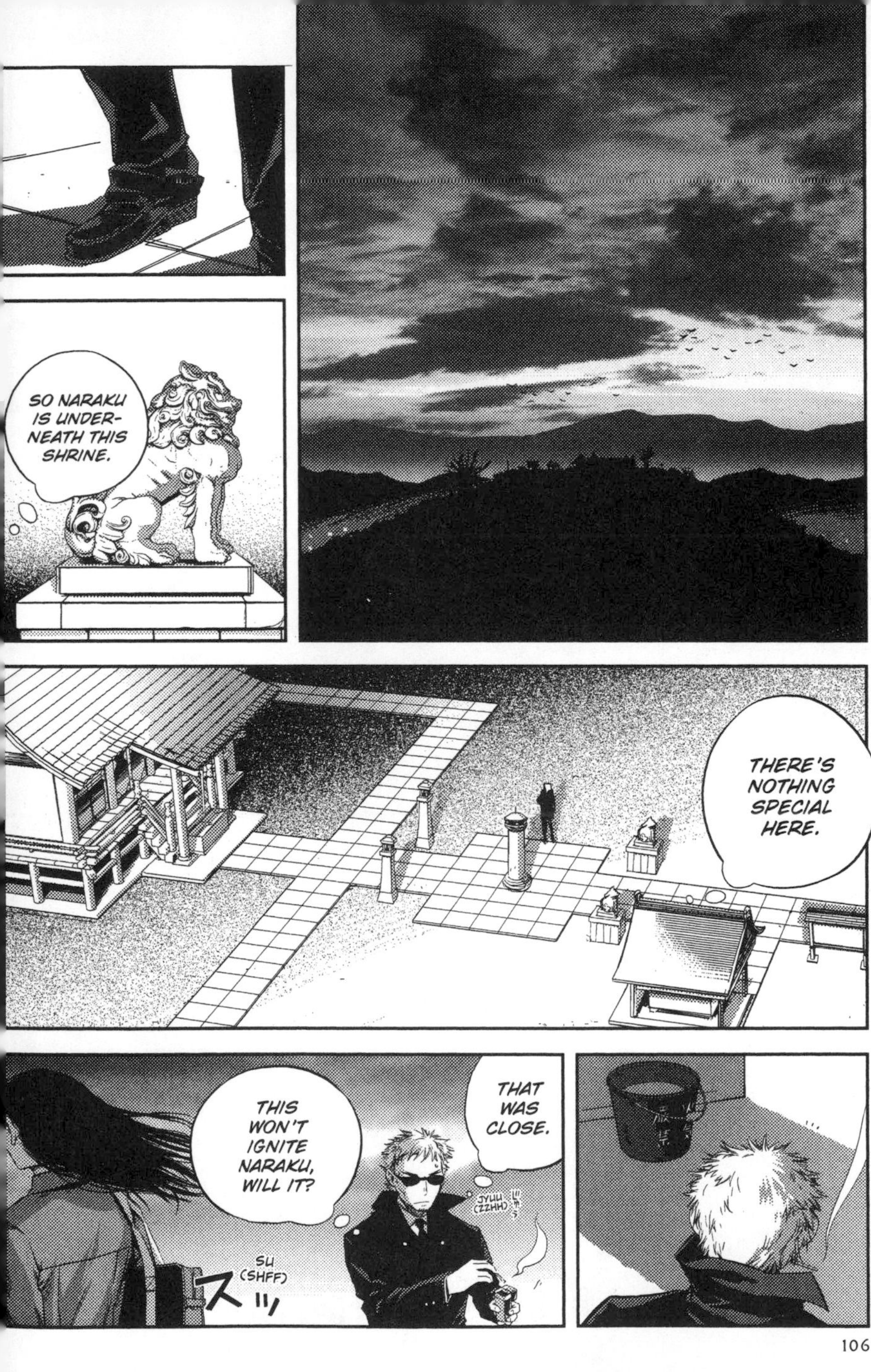
SO NARAKU IS UNDERNEATH THIS SHRINE.
THERE'S NOTHING SPECIAL HERE.
...
THAT WAS CLOSE.
THIS WON'T IGNITE NARAKU, WILL IT?
JYUU (ZZHH)
SU (SHFF)

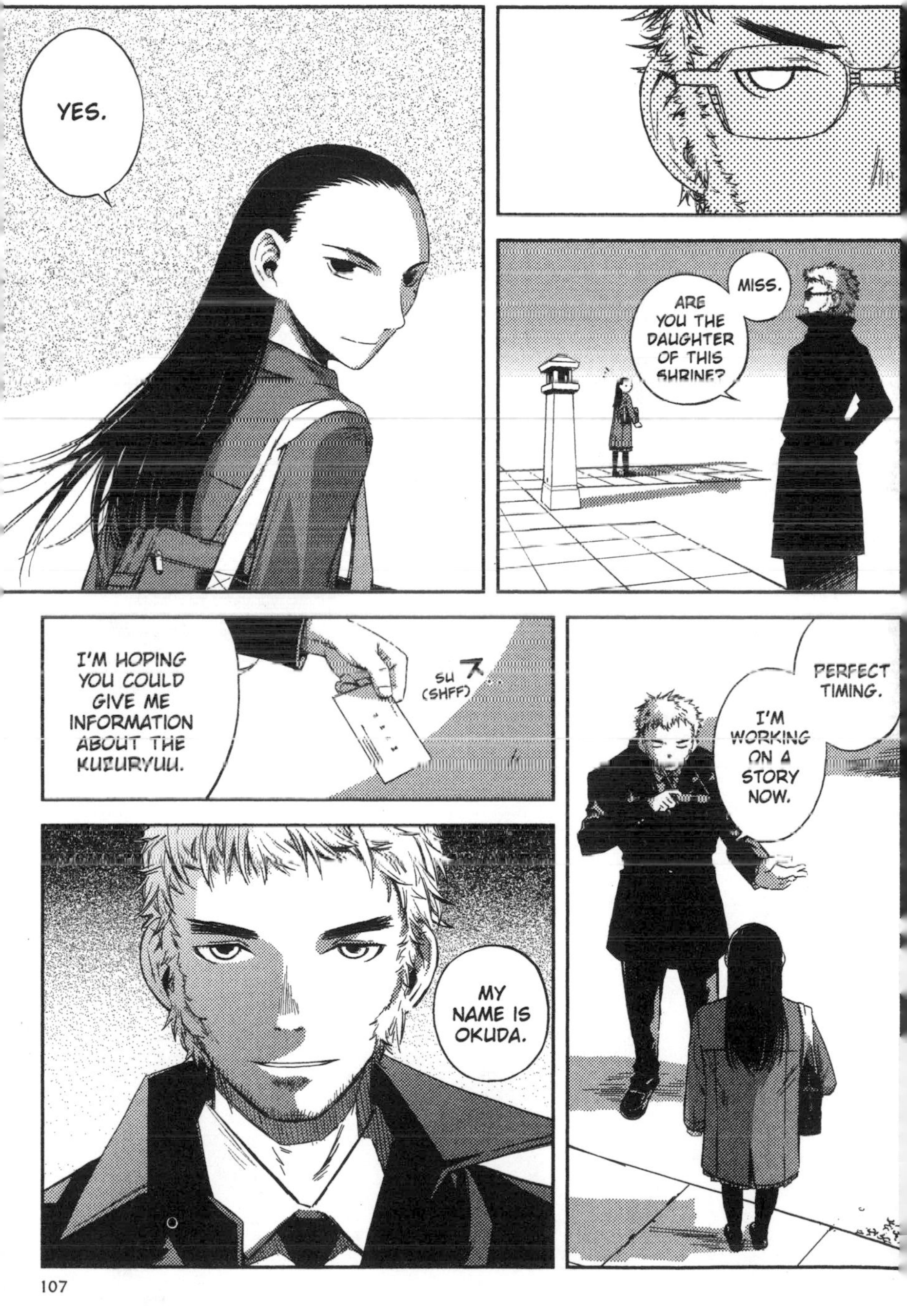
MISS.
ARE YOU THE DAUGHTER OF THIS SHRINE?
YES.
PERFECT TIMING.
I'M WORKING ON A STORY NOW.
I'M HOPING YOU COULD GIVE ME INFORMATION ABOUT THE KUZURYUU.
SU ス (SHFF)
MY NAME IS OKUDA.

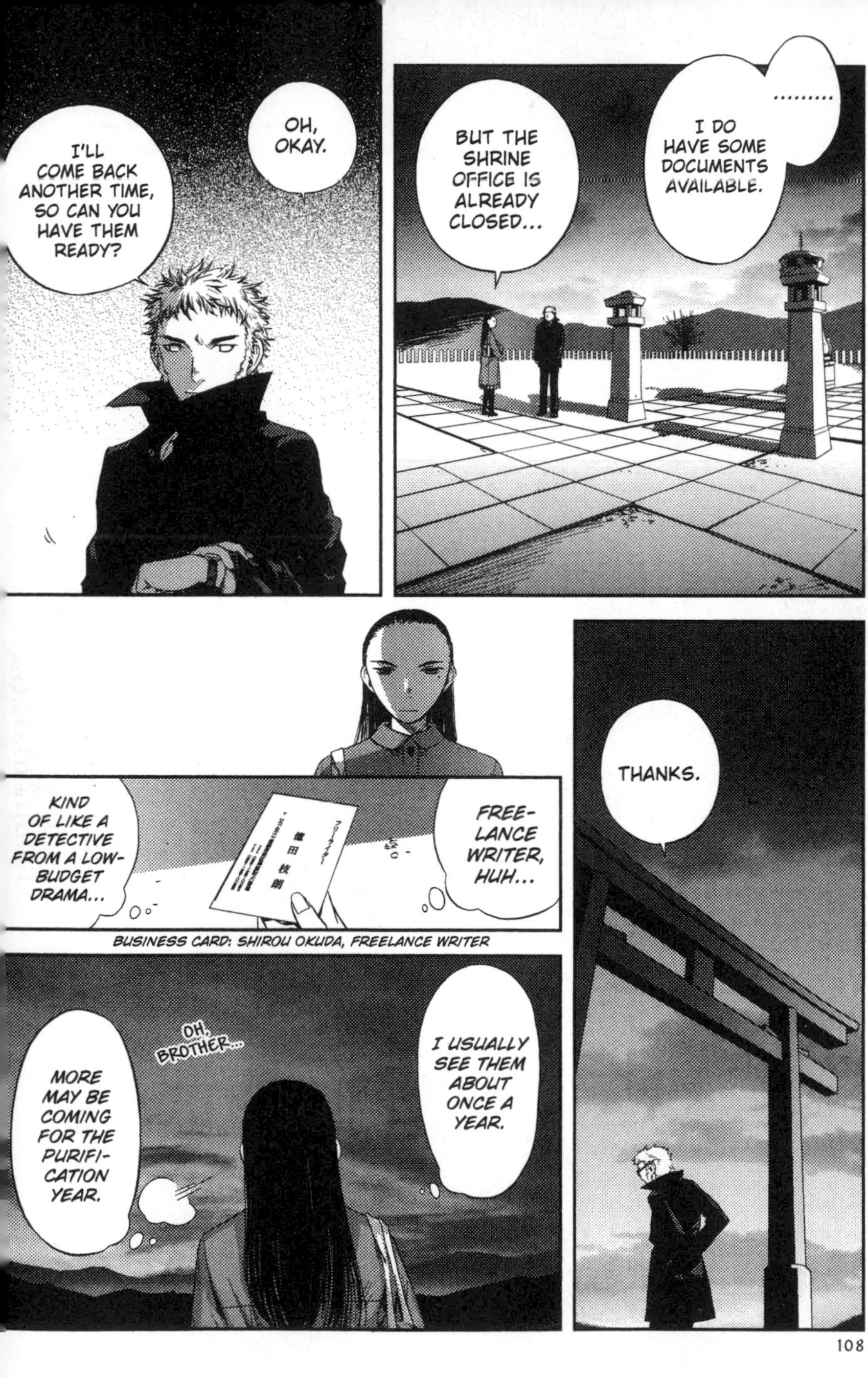
....
I DO HAVE SOME DOCUMENTS AVAILABLE.
BUT THE SHRINE OFFICE IS ALREADY CLOSED...
OH, OKAY.
I'LL COME BACK ANOTHER TIME, SO CAN YOU HAVE THEM READY?
THANKS.
FREE-LANCE WRITER, HUH...
KIND OF LIKE A DETECTIVE FROM A LOW-BUDGET DRAMA...
BUSINESS CARD: SHIROU OKUDA, FREELANCE WRITER
I USUALLY SEE THEM ABOUT ONCE A YEAR.
OH, BROTHER...
MORE MAY BE COMING FOR THE PURIFI-CATION YEAR.

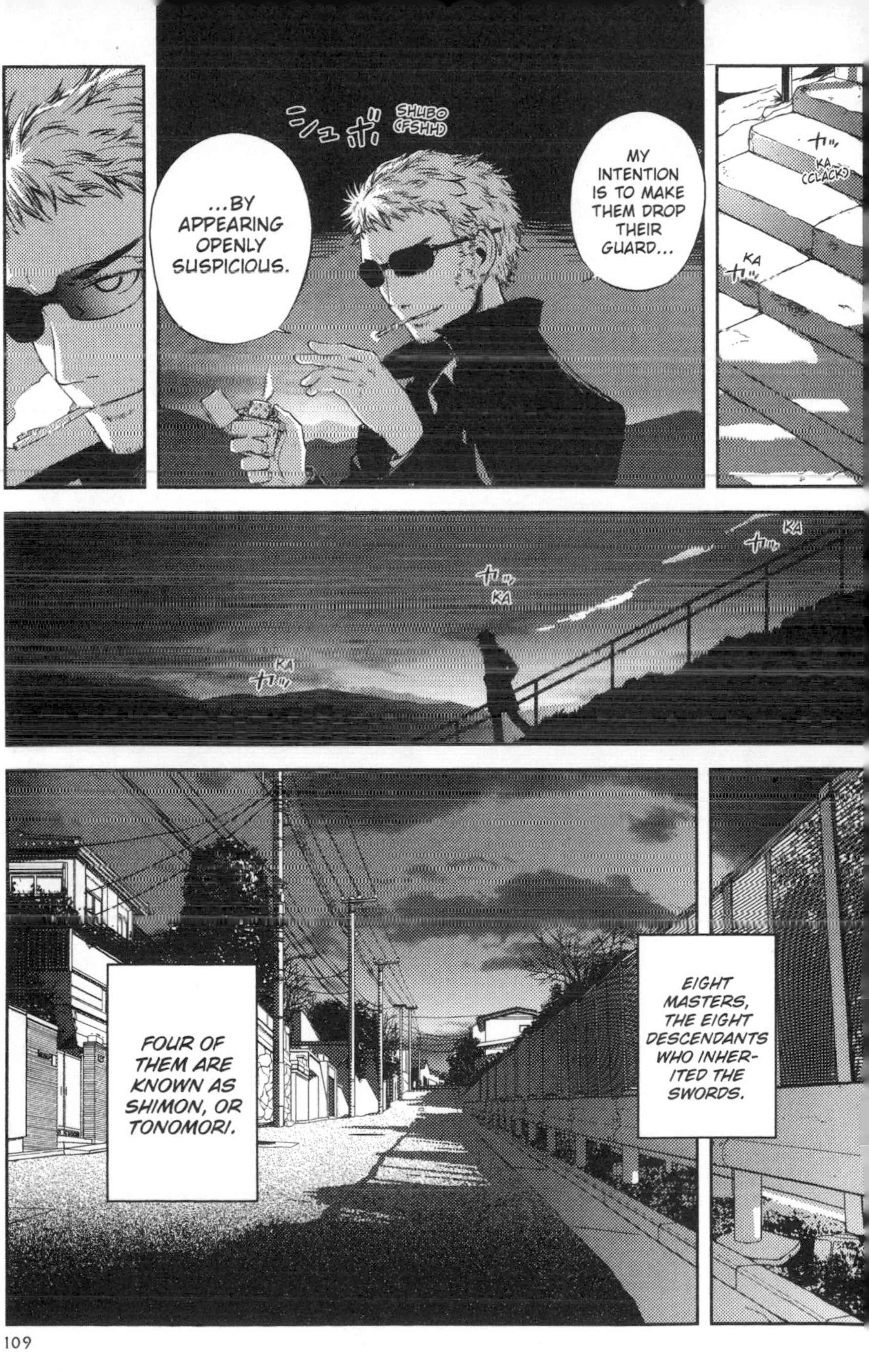
KA (CLACK)
KA
MY INTENTION IS TO MAKE THEM DROP THEIR GUARD...
SHUBO (FSHHD)
...BY APPEARING OPENLY SUSPICIOUS.
KA
KA
KA
EIGHT MASTERS, THE EIGHT DESCENDANTS WHO INHERITED THE SWORDS.
FOUR OF THEM ARE KNOWN AS SHIMON, OR TONOMORI.

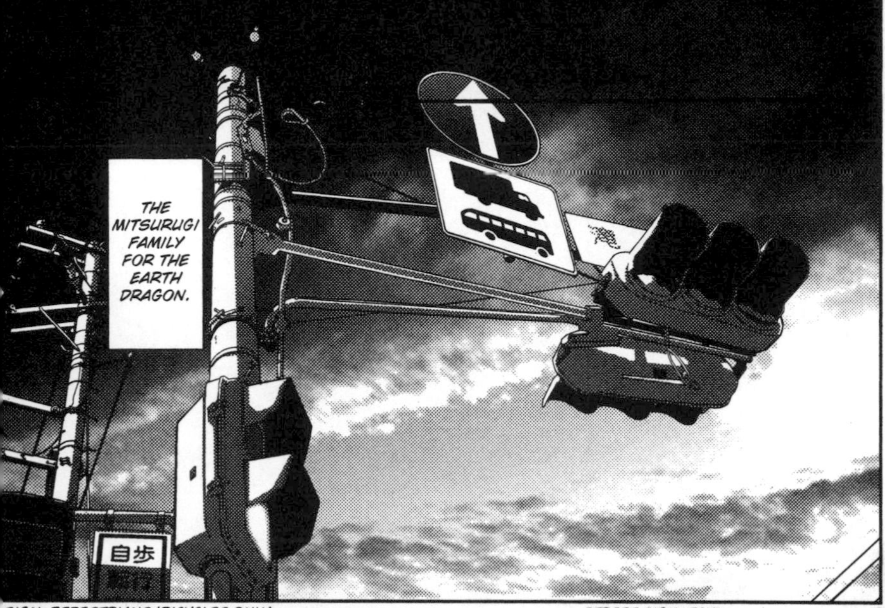
THE MITSURUGI FAMILY FOR THE EARTH DRAGON.
自歩

SIGN: PEDESTRIANS/BICYCLES ONLY

STREET SIGN: TAKI

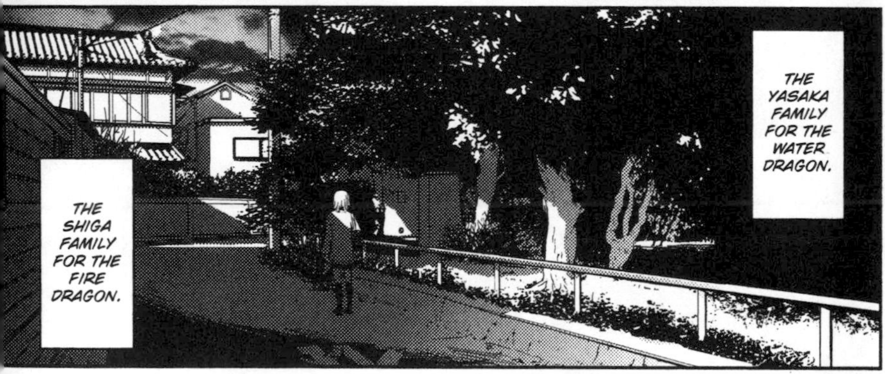
THE YASAKA FAMILY FOR THE WATER DRAGON.
THE SHIGA FAMILY FOR THE FIRE DRAGON.

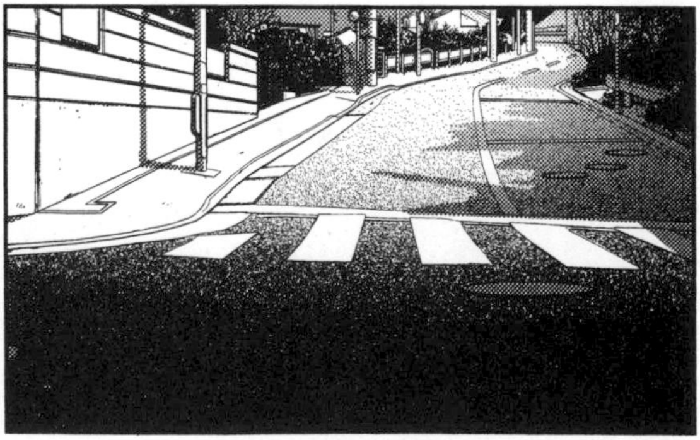

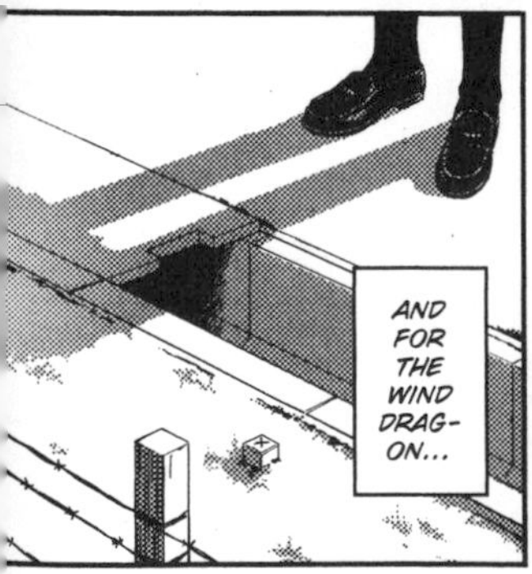
AND FOR THE WIND DRAG-ON...

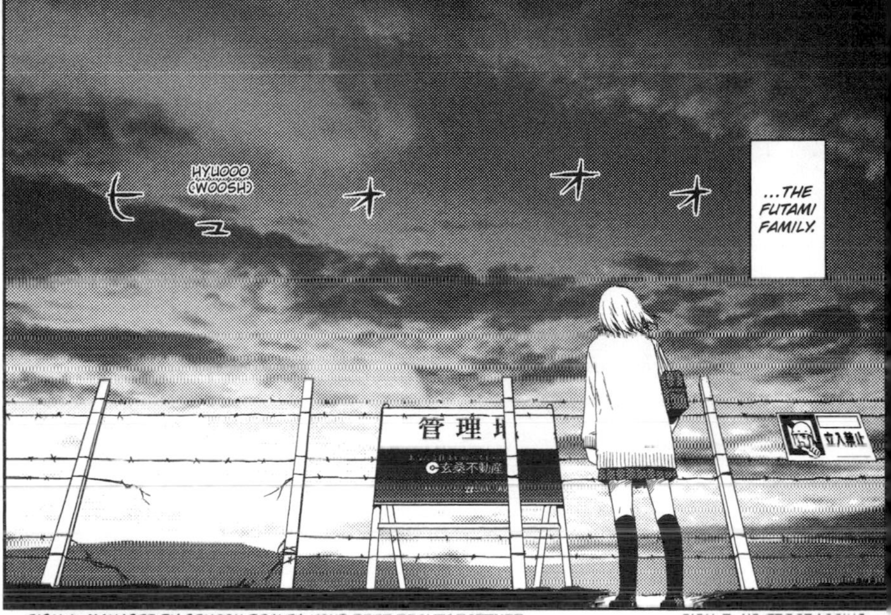
...THE FUTAMI FAMILY.
管理地
玄桑不動産
立入禁止
HYUOOO (WOOSH)

SIGN-L: MANAGED BY GENSOU REALTY, YOUR BEST REALTY PARTNER; SIGN-R: NO TRESPASSING

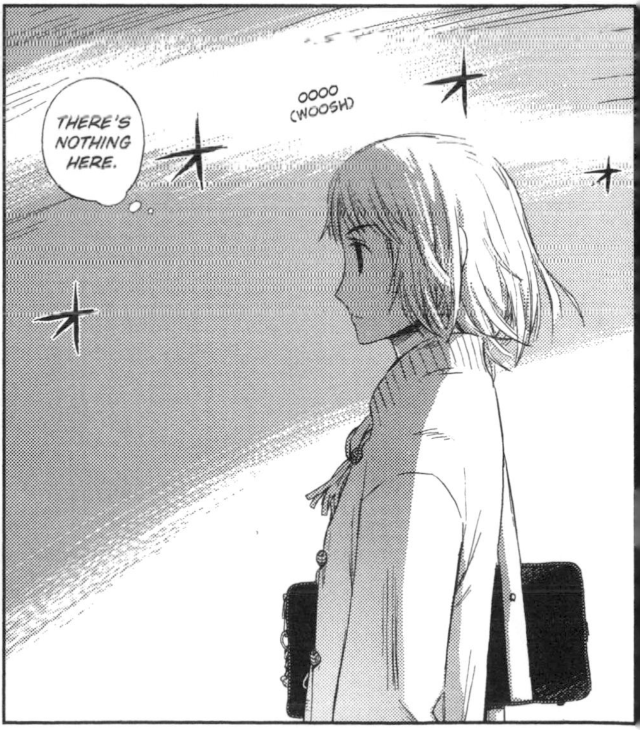
OOOO (WOOSH)
THERE'S NOTHING HERE.

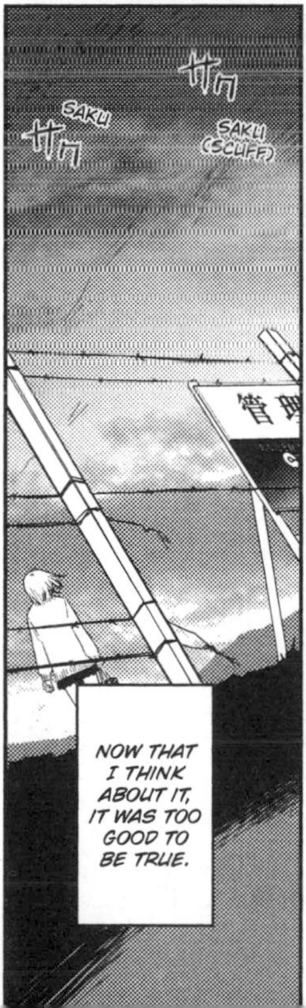
SAKU
SAKU (SCUFF)
NOW THAT I THINK ABOUT IT, IT WAS TOO GOOD TO BE TRUE.

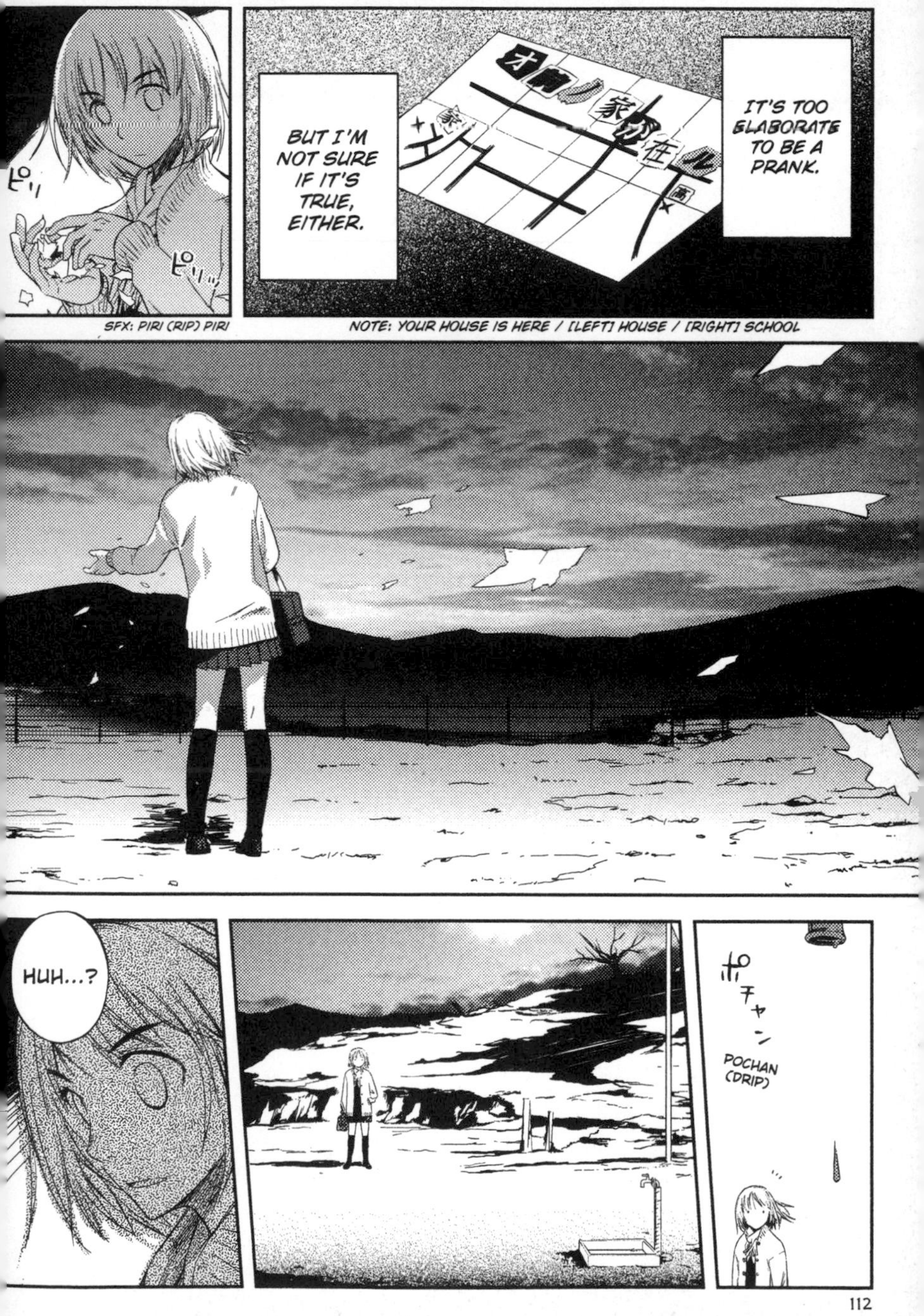
IT'S TOO ELABORATE TO BE A PRANK.
BUT I'M NOT SURE IF IT'S TRUE, EITHER.
ピリッ
ピリッ
NOTE: YOUR HOUSE IS HERE / [LEFT] HOUSE / [RIGHT] SCHOOL
SFX: PIRI (RIP) PIRI
ポチャン
POCHAN (DRIP)
HUH...?

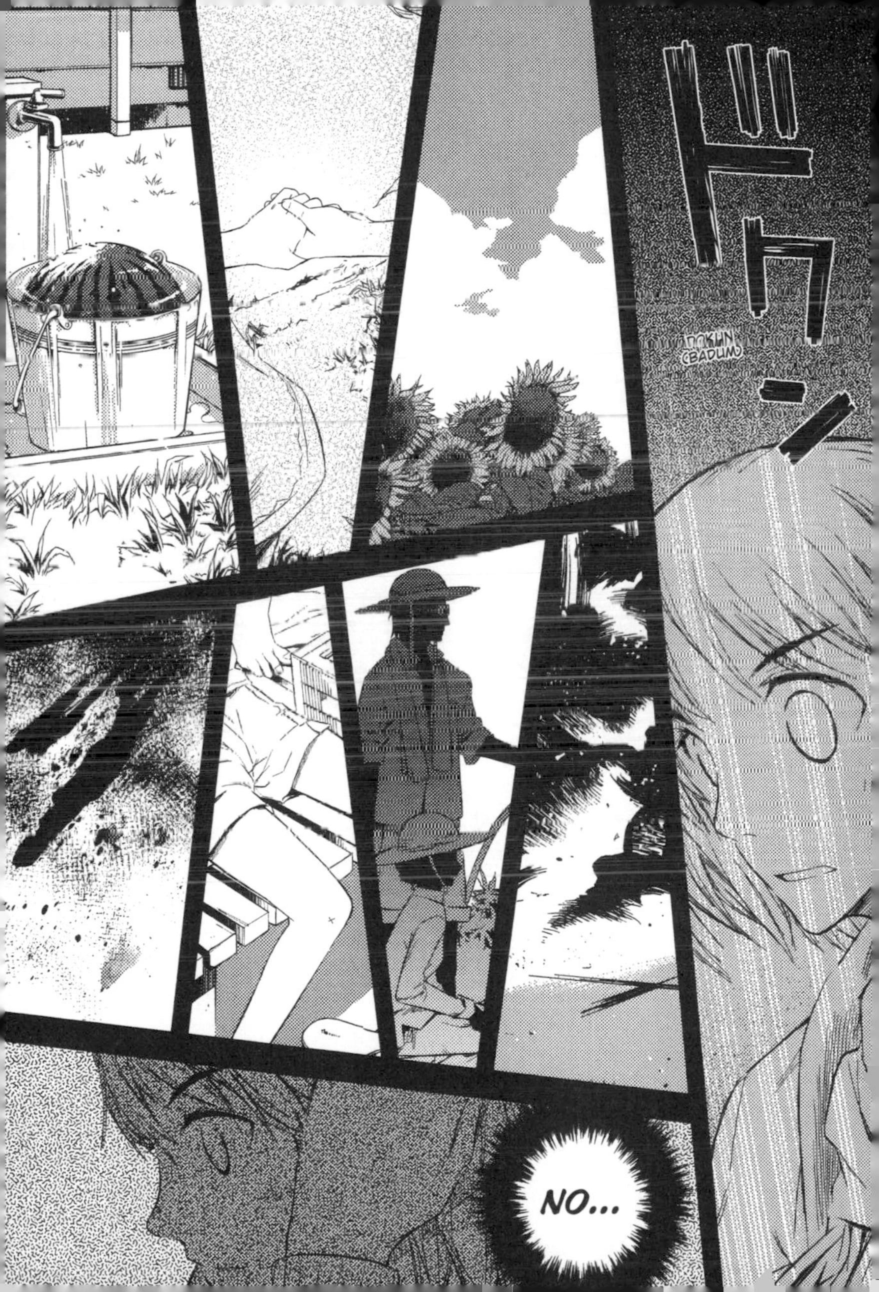
ドクン
DOKUN
(BADUM)
NO...

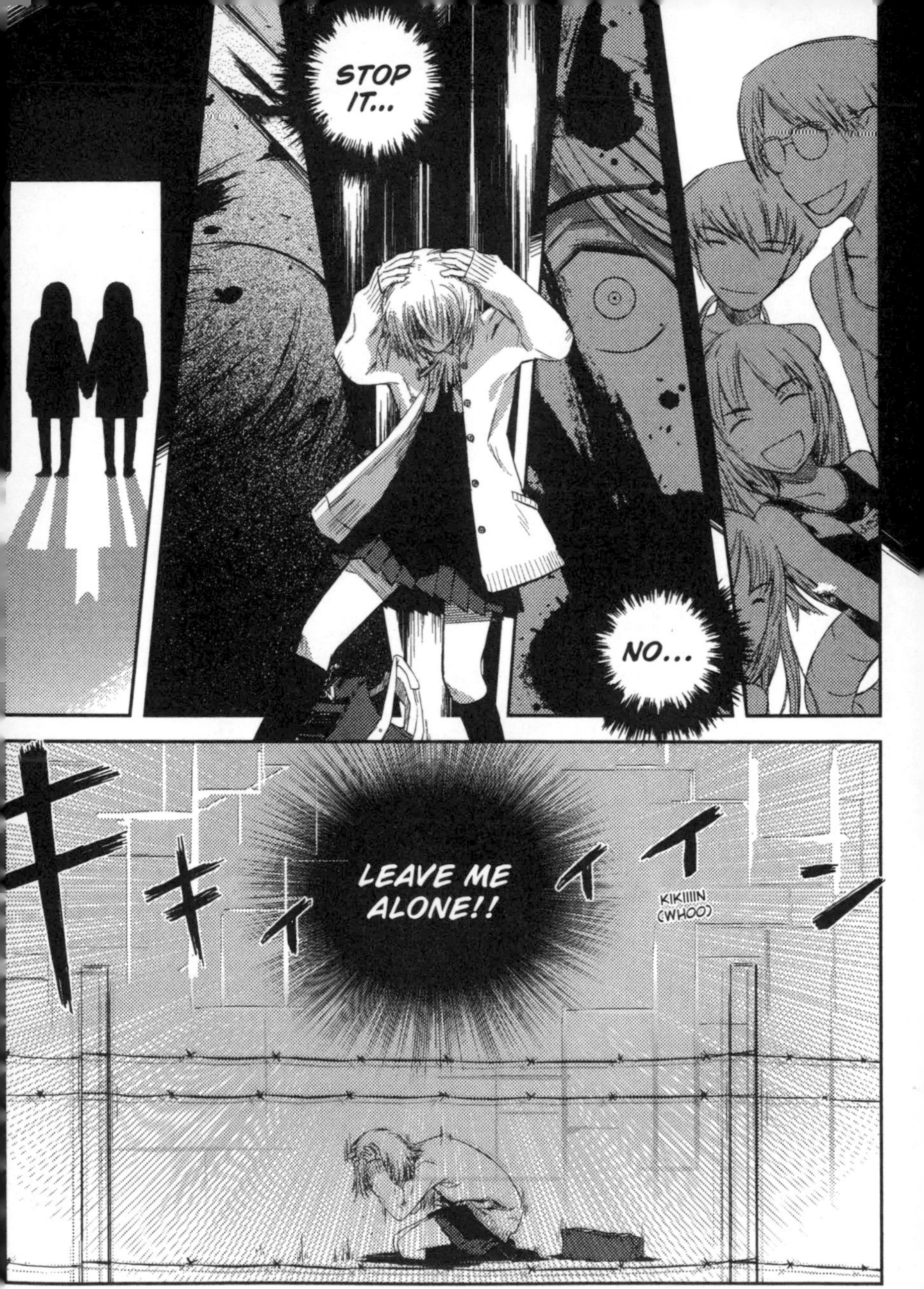
STOP IT...
NO...
LEAVE ME ALONE!!
KIKIIIIN (WHOO)

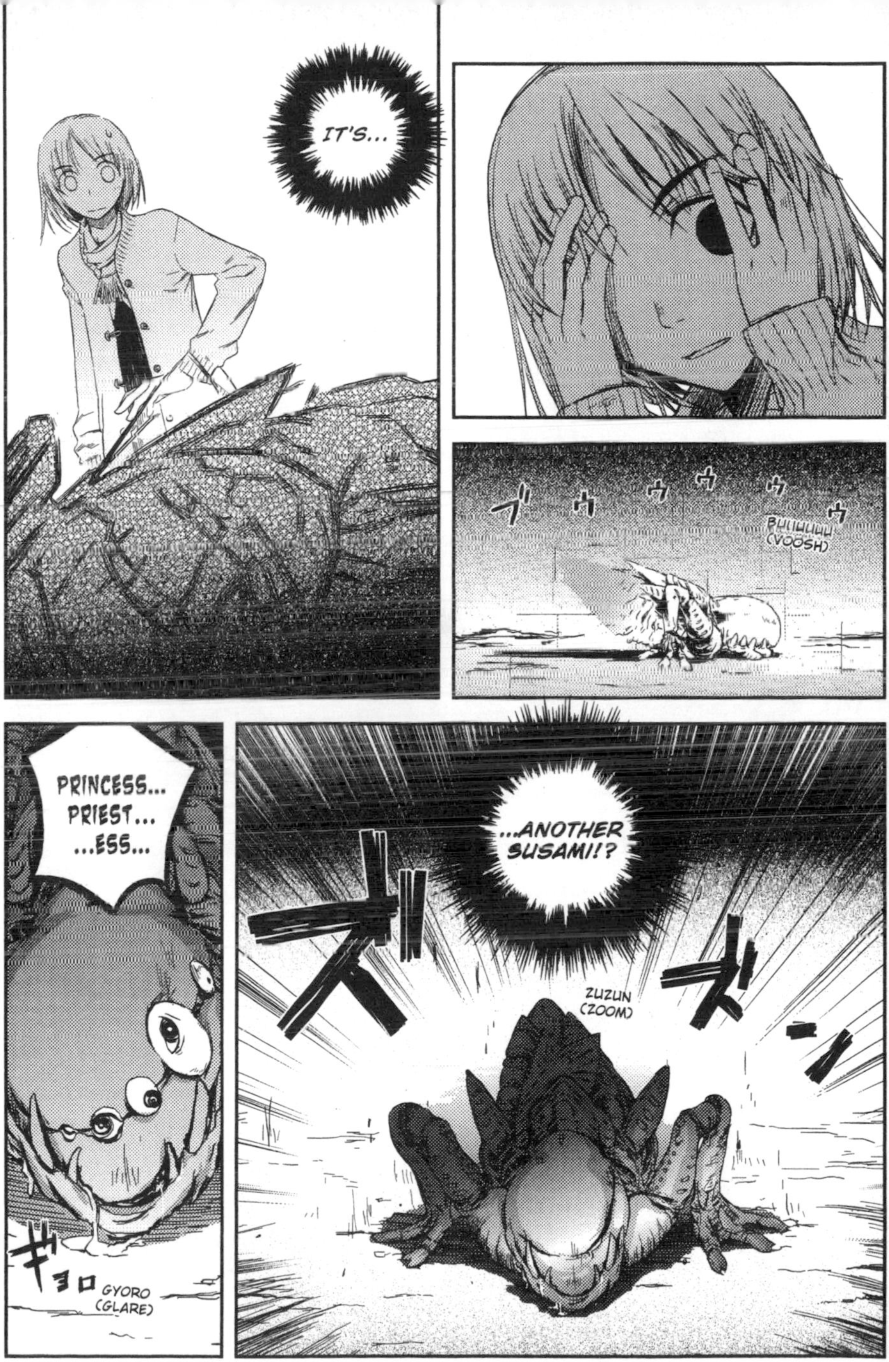
ブゥゥゥゥゥ
BUUUUUU (VOOSH)
IT'S...
...ANOTHER SUSAMI!?
ズズン
ZUZUN (ZOOM)
PRINCESS... PRIEST... ...ESS...
ギョロ
GYORO (GLARE)

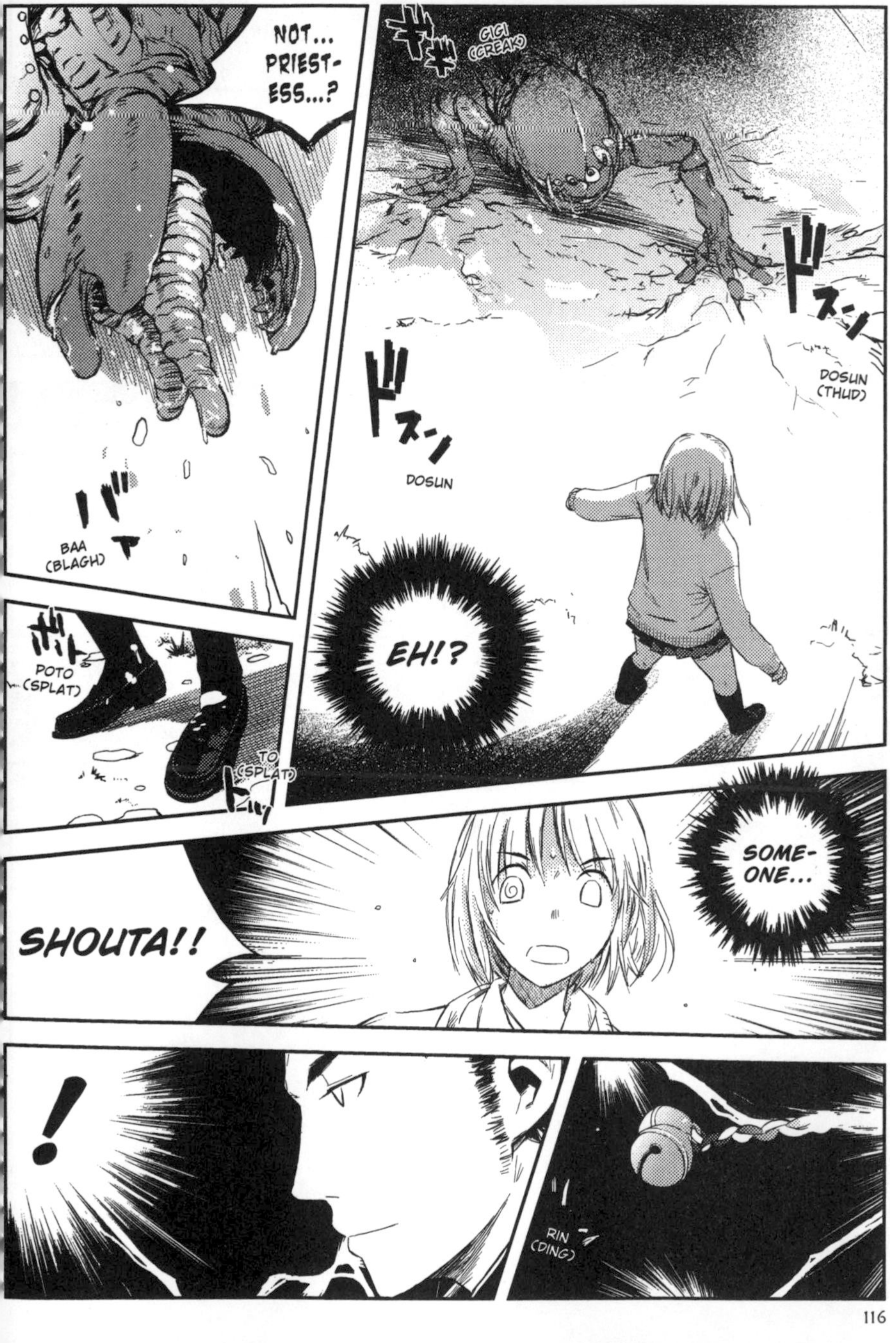
GIGI (CREAK)
DOSUN (THUD)
DOSUN
EH!?
NOT... PRIEST-ESS...?
BAA (BLAGH)
POTO (SPLAT)
TO (SPLAT)
SOME-ONE...
SHOUTA!!
RIN (DING)
!

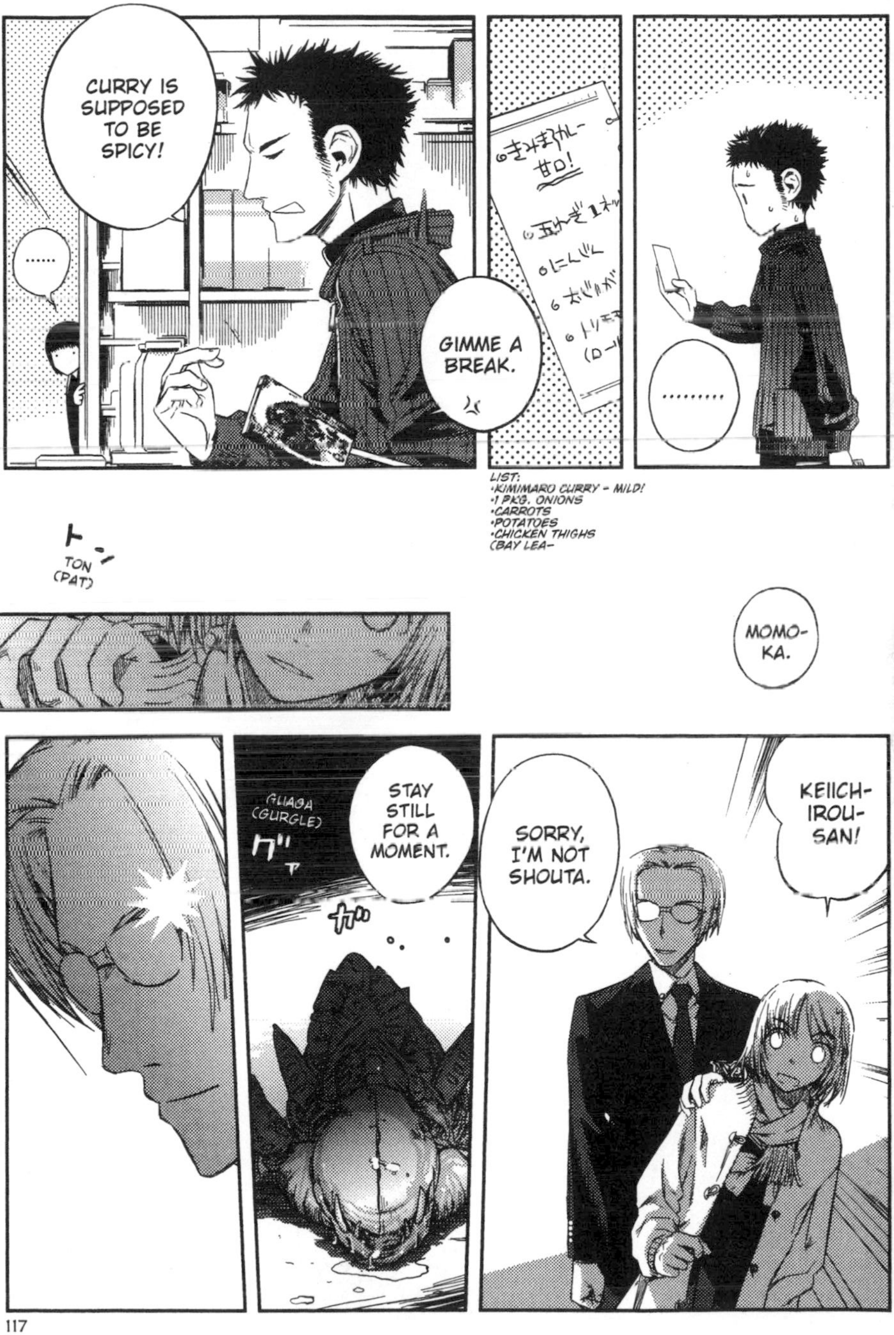
....
LIST:
·KIMIMARO CURRY - MILD!
·1 PKG. ONIONS
·CARROTS
·POTATOES
·CHICKEN THIGHS
(BAY LEA-
GIMME A BREAK.
CURRY IS SUPPOSED TO BE SPICY!
......
MOMO-KA.
TON (PAT)
KEIICH-IROU-SAN!
SORRY, I'M NOT SHOUTA.
STAY STILL FOR A MOMENT.
GUAGA (GURGLE)

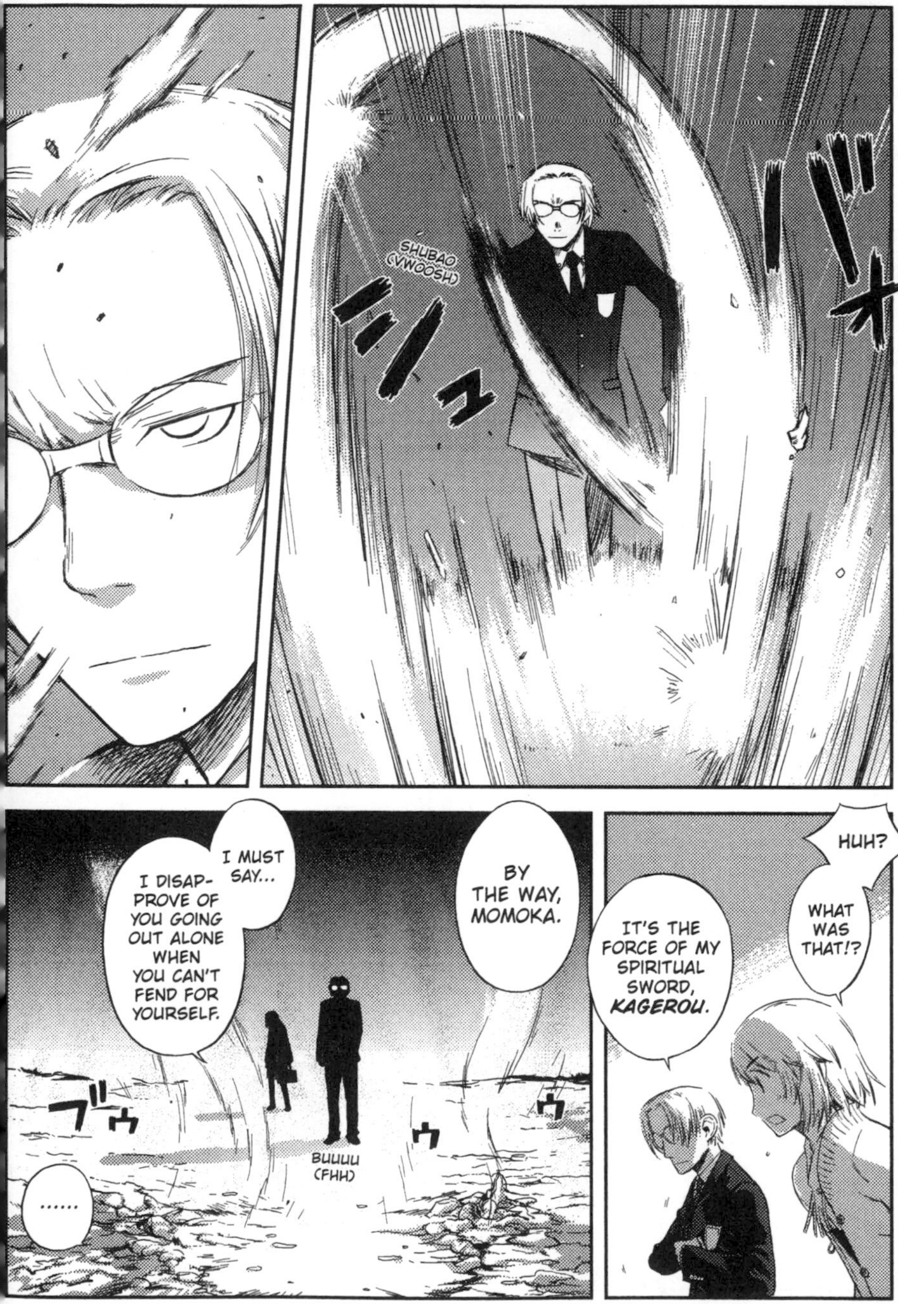
SHUBAO (VWOOSH)
HUH?
WHAT WAS THAT!?
IT'S THE FORCE OF MY SPIRITUAL SWORD, *KAGEROU*.
BY THE WAY, MOMOKA.
I MUST SAY...
I DISAPPROVE OF YOU GOING OUT ALONE WHEN YOU CAN'T FEND FOR YOURSELF.
BUUUU (FHH)
......

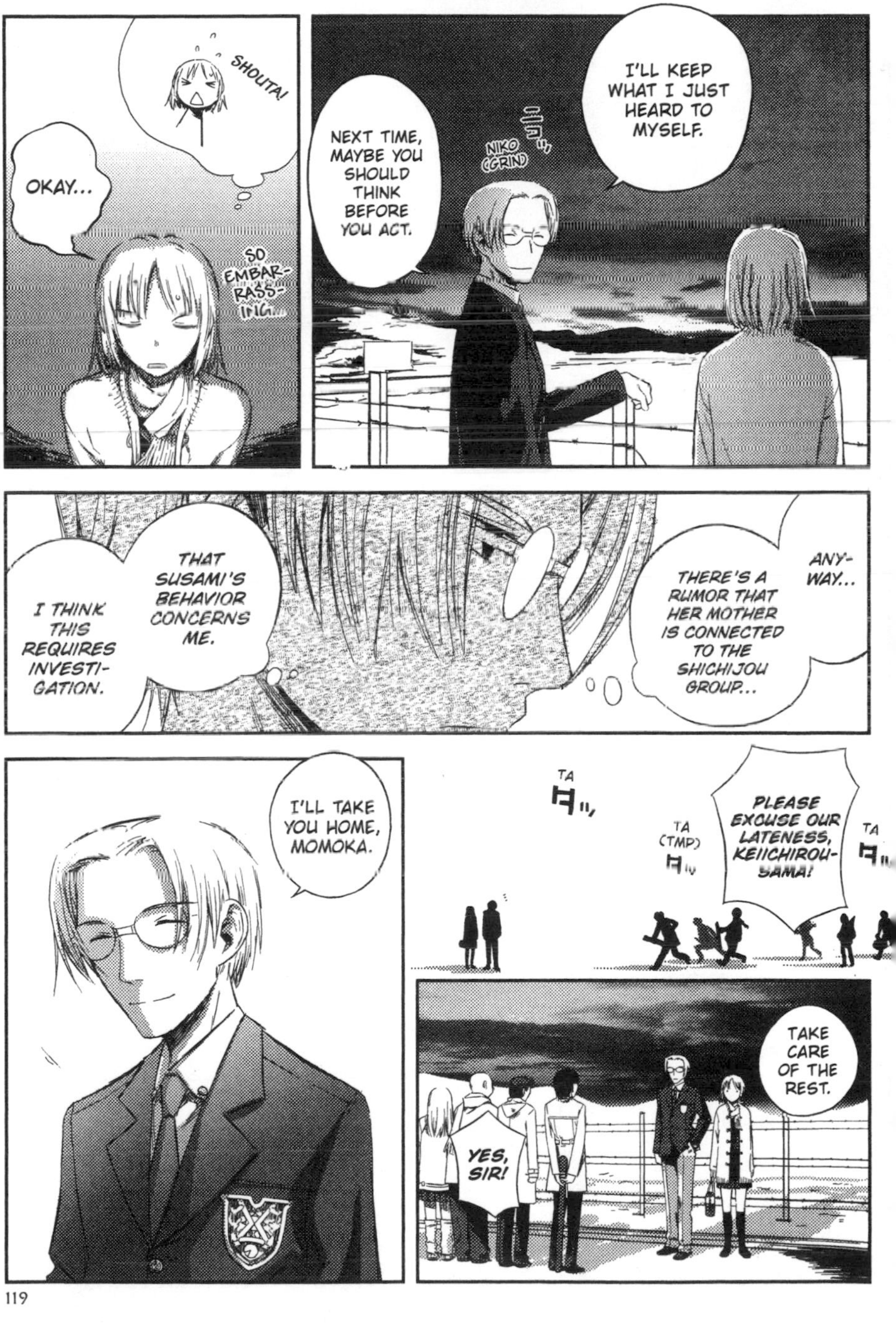
I'LL KEEP WHAT I JUST HEARD TO MYSELF.
NIKO (GRIN)
NEXT TIME, MAYBE YOU SHOULD THINK BEFORE YOU ACT.
SHOUTA!
OKAY...
SO EMBARRASSING...
ANYWAY...
THERE'S A RUMOR THAT HER MOTHER IS CONNECTED TO THE SHICHIJOU GROUP...
THAT SUSAMI'S BEHAVIOR CONCERNS ME.
I THINK THIS REQUIRES INVESTIGATION.
TA
TA
PLEASE EXCUSE OUR LATENESS, KEIICHIROU-SAMA!
TA (TMP)
TAKE CARE OF THE REST.
YES, SIR!
I'LL TAKE YOU HOME, MOMOKA.

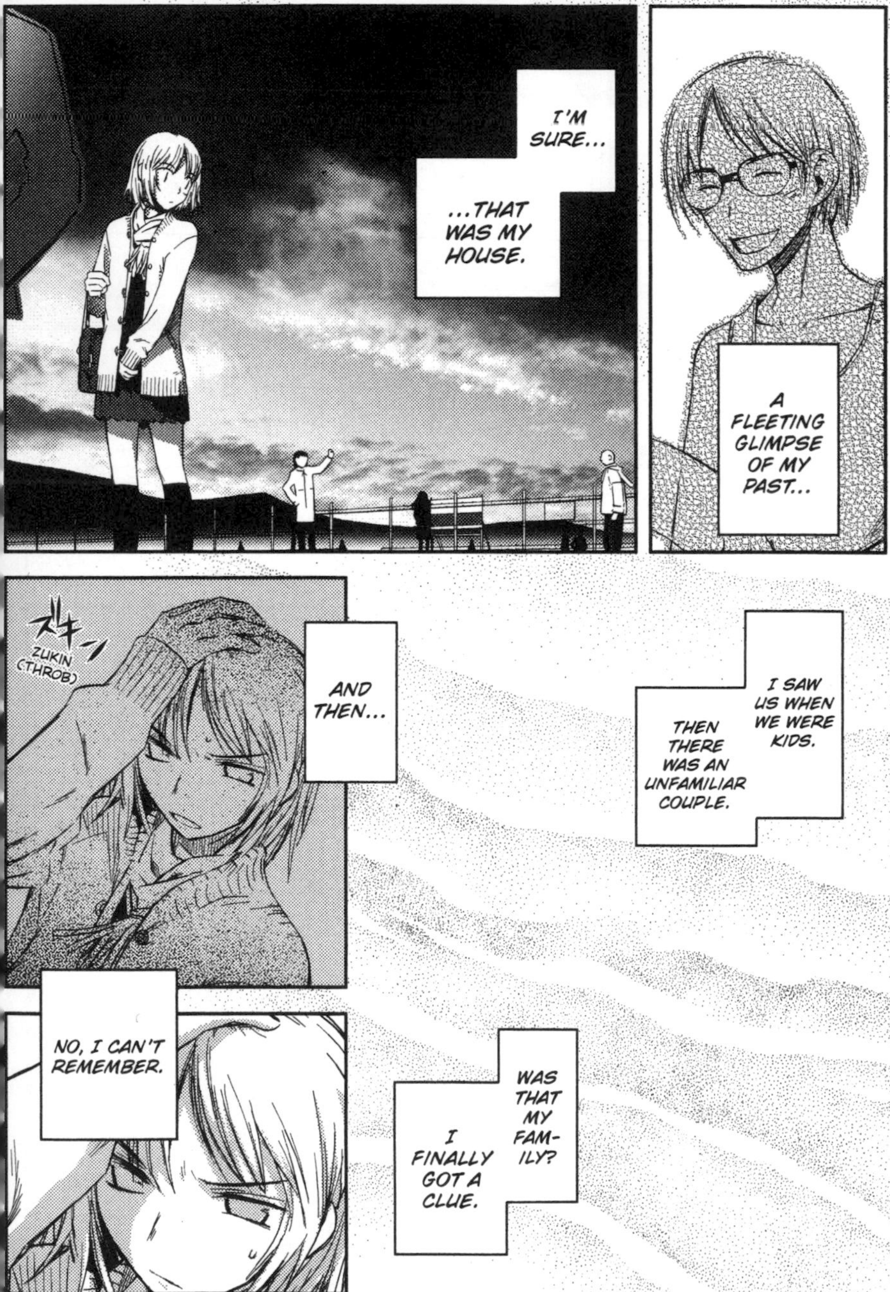
A FLEETING GLIMPSE OF MY PAST...
I'M SURE...
...THAT WAS MY HOUSE.
I SAW US WHEN WE WERE KIDS.
THEN THERE WAS AN UNFAMILIAR COUPLE.
AND THEN...
ZUKIN (THROB)
WAS THAT MY FAM-ILY?
I FINALLY GOT A CLUE.
NO, I CAN'T REMEMBER.

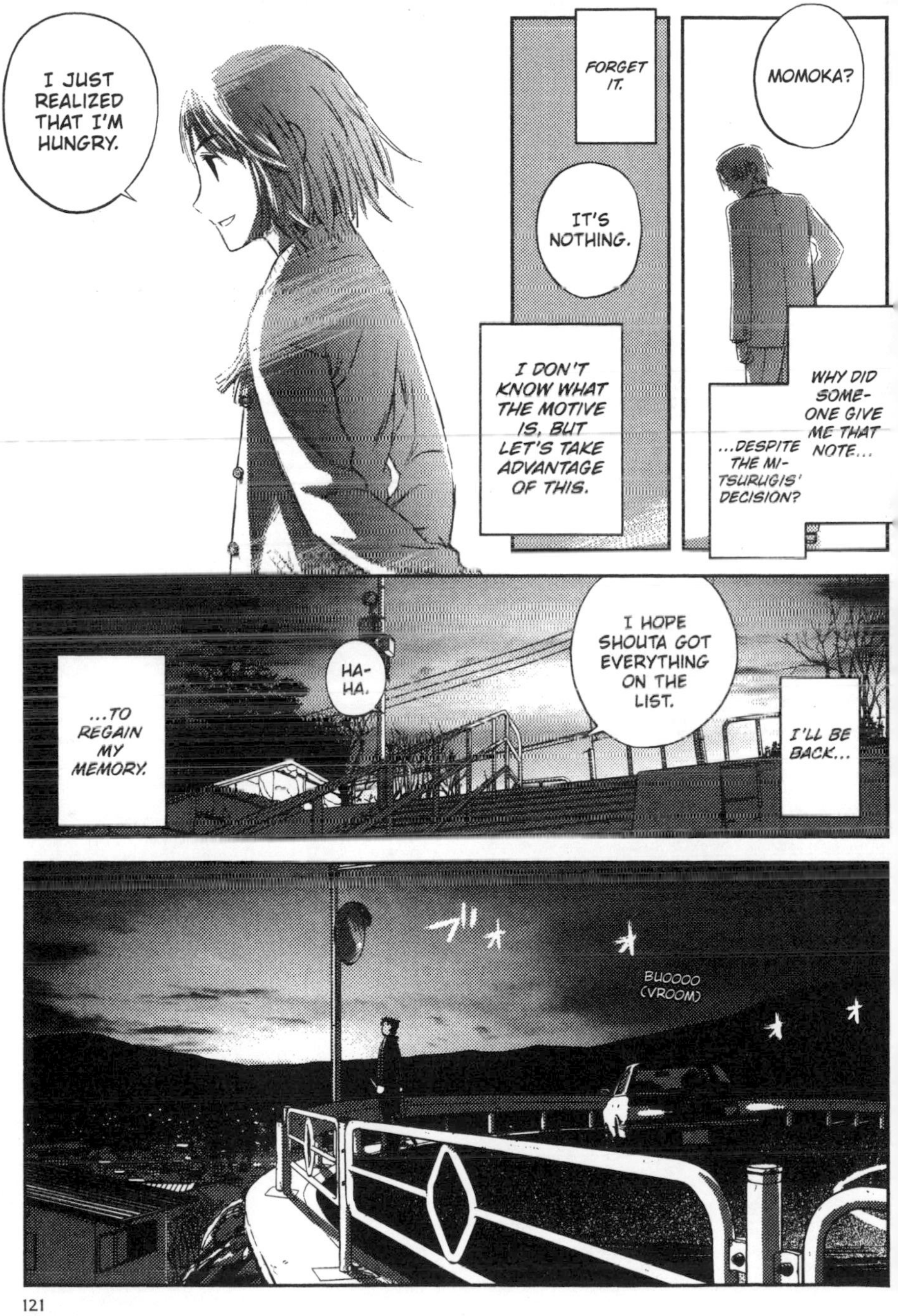
MOMOKA?
WHY DID SOME-ONE GIVE ME THAT NOTE...
...DESPITE THE MI-TSURUGIS' DECISION?
FORGET IT.
IT'S NOTHING.
I DON'T KNOW WHAT THE MOTIVE IS, BUT LET'S TAKE ADVANTAGE OF THIS.
I JUST REALIZED THAT I'M HUNGRY.
I'LL BE BACK...
I HOPE SHOUTA GOT EVERYTHING ON THE LIST.
HA-HA.
...TO REGAIN MY MEMORY.
BUOOOO (VROOM)

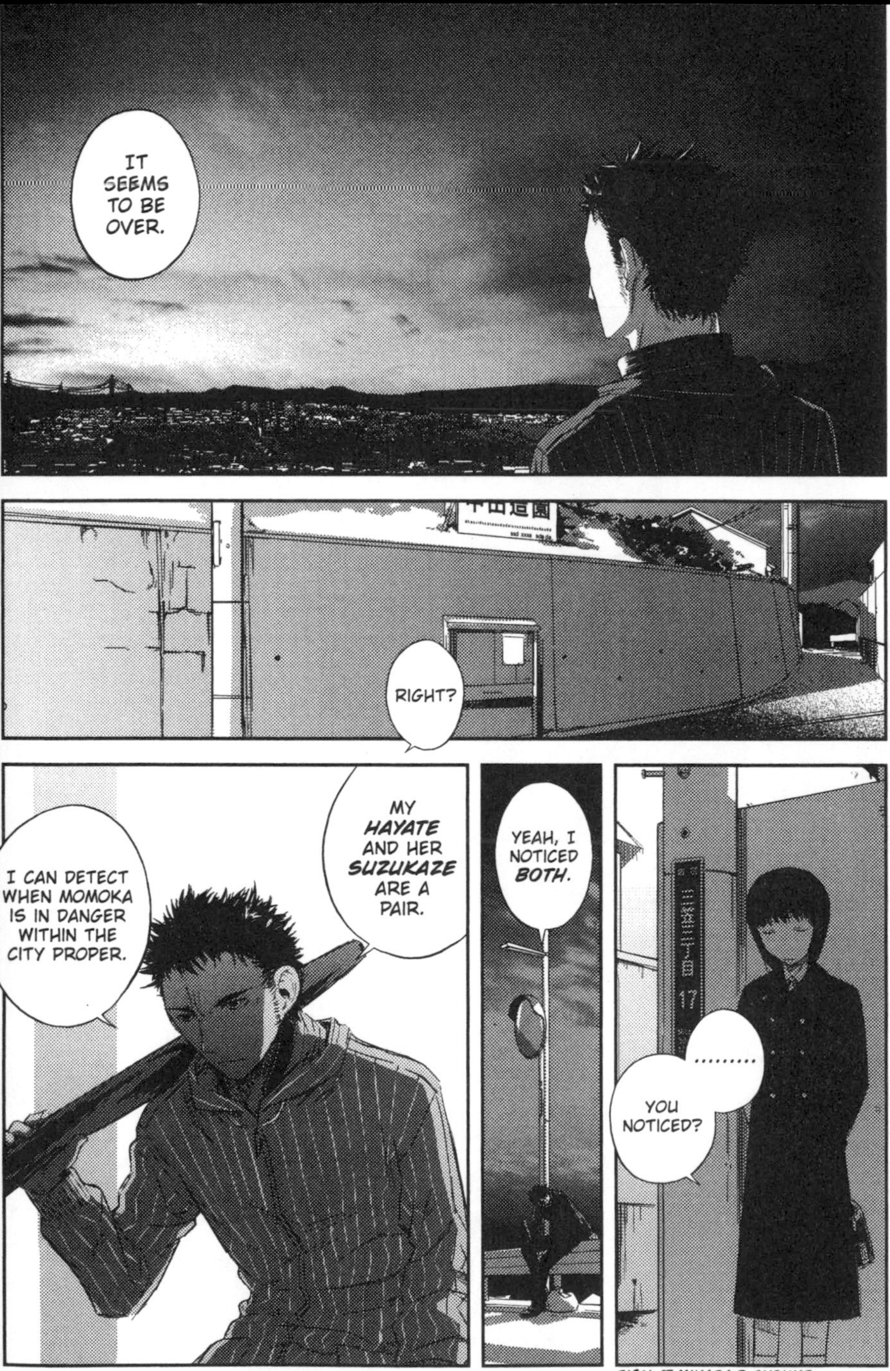
IT SEEMS TO BE OVER.
RIGHT?
....
YOU NOTICED?
YEAH, I NOTICED *BOTH*.
MY *HAYATE* AND HER *SUZUKAZE* ARE A PAIR.
I CAN DETECT WHEN MOMOKA IS IN DANGER WITHIN THE CITY PROPER.

SIGN: 17 MIKASA 3-CHOUME

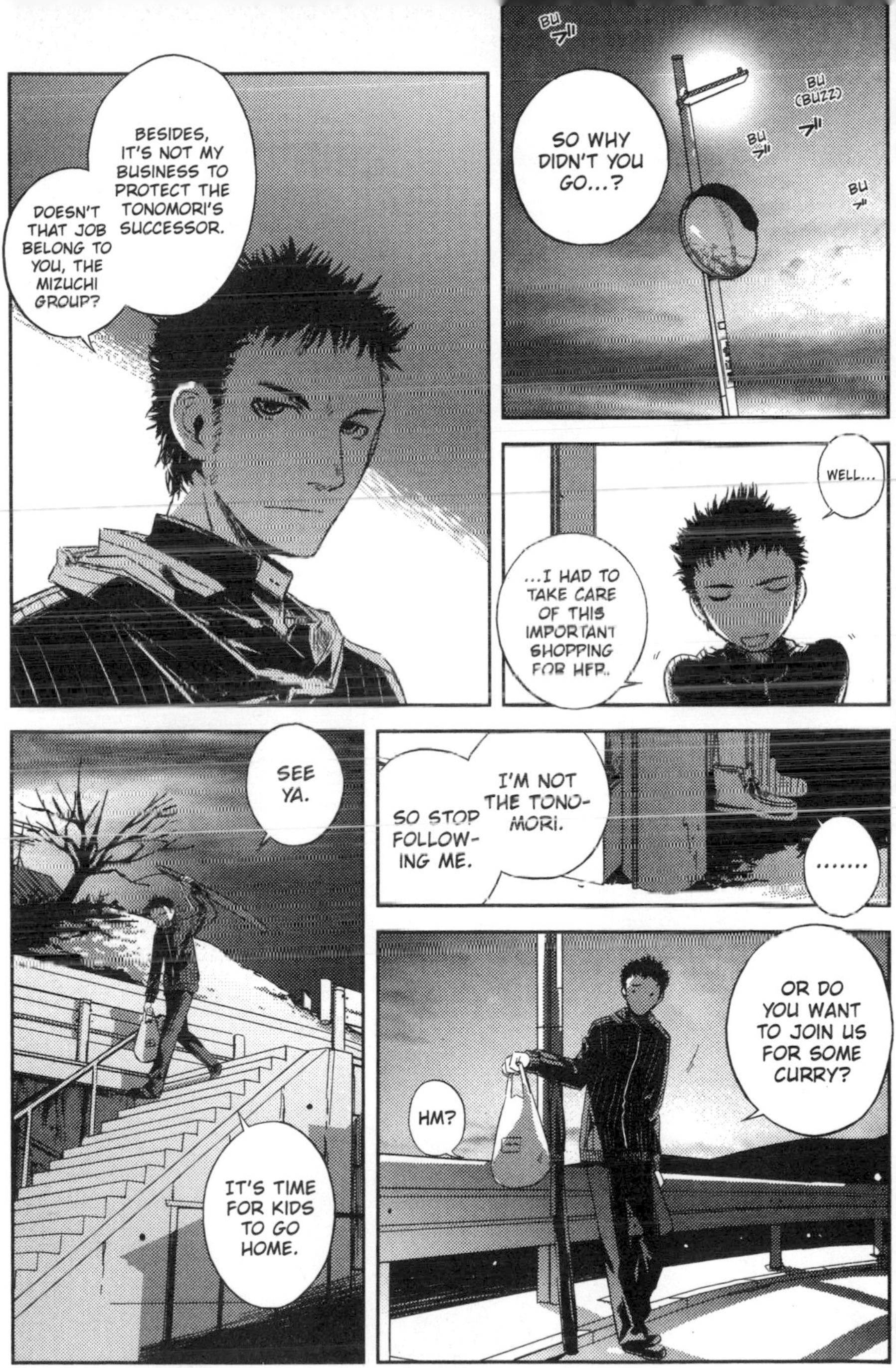
BU (BUZZ) ヅ
BU ヅ
BU ヅ
BU ヅ
SO WHY DIDN'T YOU GO...?
WELL...
...I HAD TO TAKE CARE OF THIS IMPORTANT SHOPPING FOR HER.
BESIDES, IT'S NOT MY BUSINESS TO PROTECT THE TONOMORI'S SUCCESSOR.
DOESN'T THAT JOB BELONG TO YOU, THE MIZUCHI GROUP?
....
I'M NOT THE TONO-MORI.
SO STOP FOLLOW-ING ME.
OR DO YOU WANT TO JOIN US FOR SOME CURRY?
HM?
SEE YA.
IT'S TIME FOR KIDS TO GO HOME.

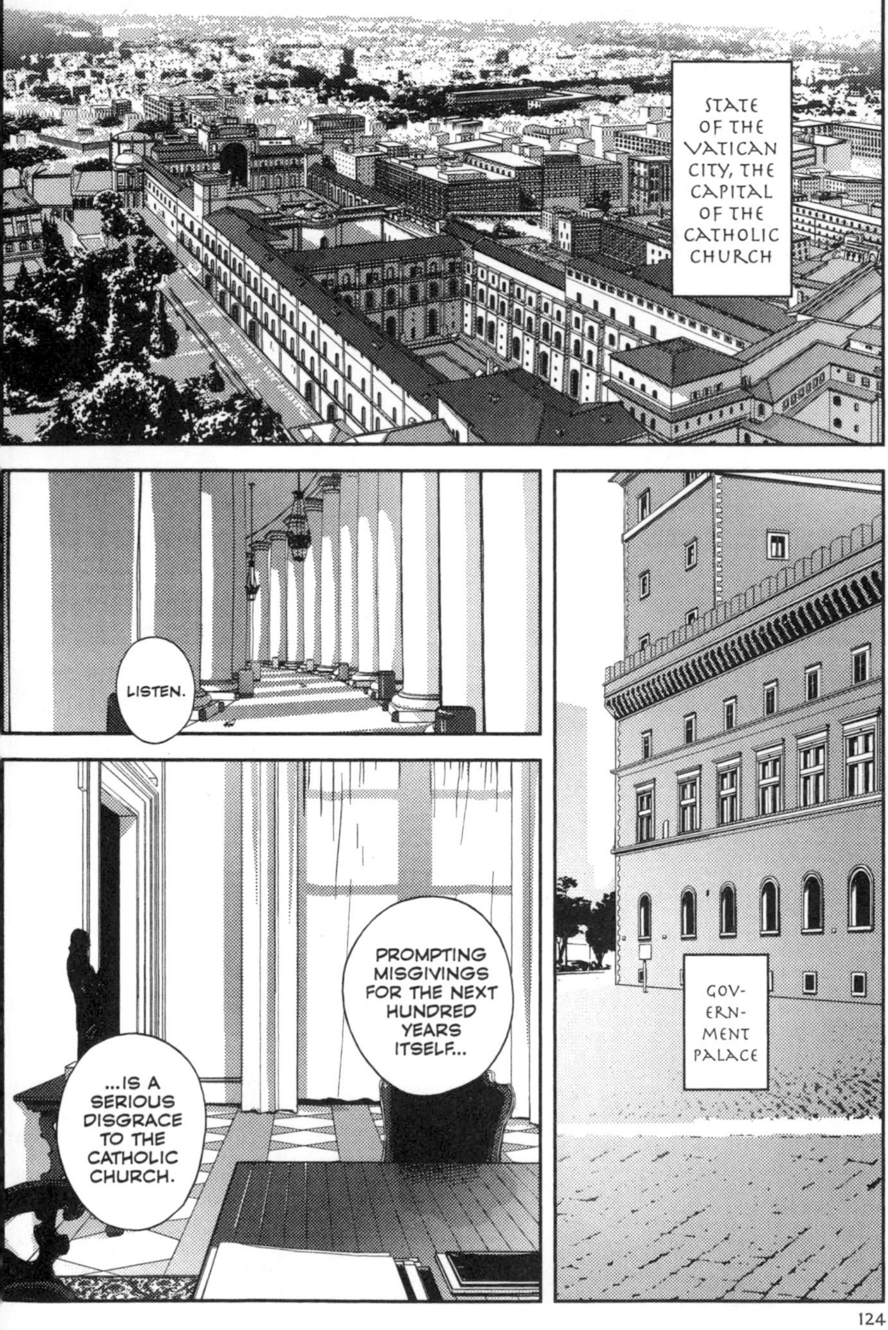
STATE OF THE VATICAN CITY, THE CAPITAL OF THE CATHOLIC CHURCH
GOV-ERN-MENT PALACE
LISTEN.
PROMPTING MISGIVINGS FOR THE NEXT HUNDRED YEARS ITSELF...
...IS A SERIOUS DISGRACE TO THE CATHOLIC CHURCH.

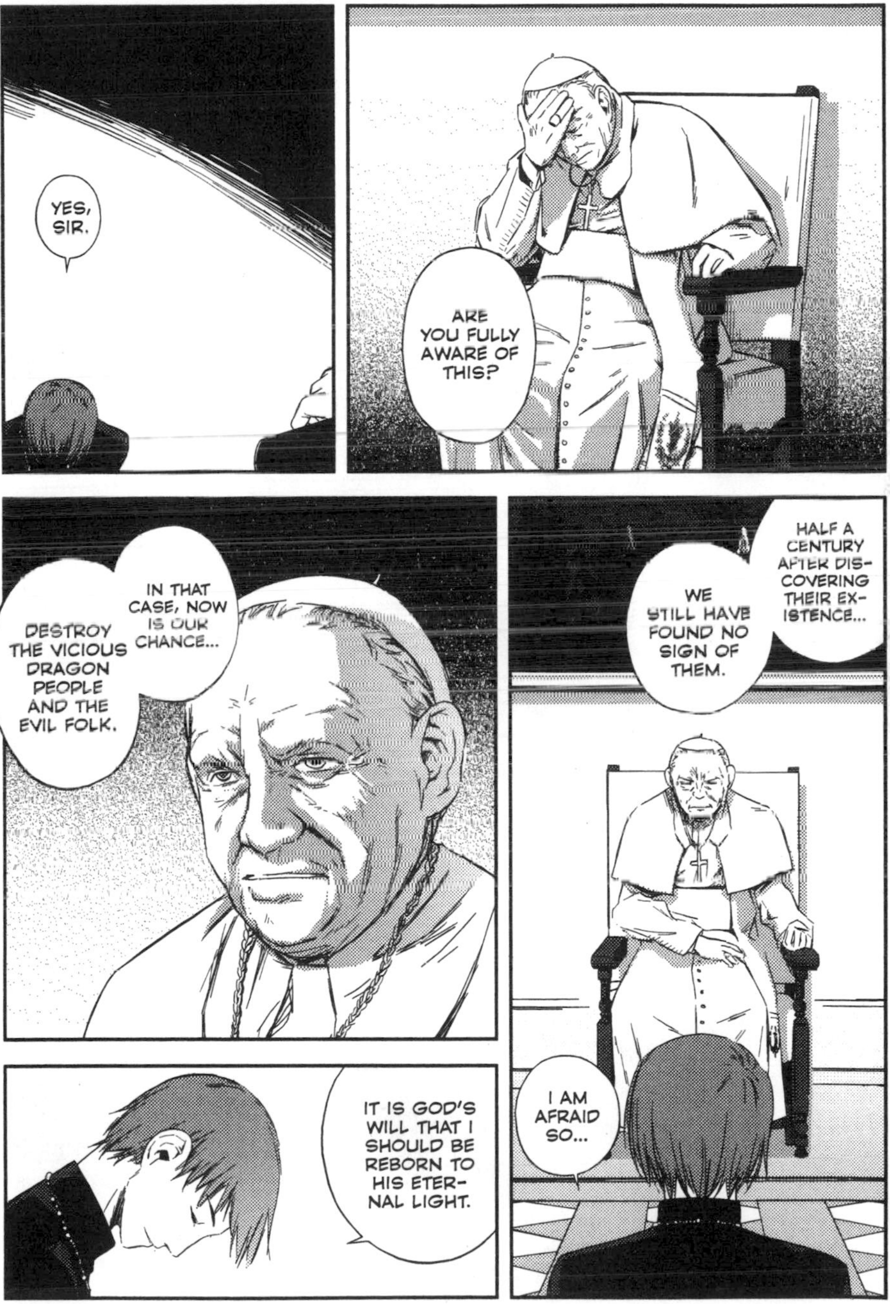

ARE YOU FULLY AWARE OF THIS?
YES, SIR.
HALF A CENTURY AFTER DIS-COVERING THEIR EX-ISTENCE...
WE STILL HAVE FOUND NO SIGN OF THEM.
I AM AFRAID SO...
IN THAT CASE, NOW IS OUR CHANCE...
DESTROY THE VICIOUS DRAGON PEOPLE AND THE EVIL FOLK.
IT IS GOD'S WILL THAT I SHOULD BE REBORN TO HIS ETER-NAL LIGHT.

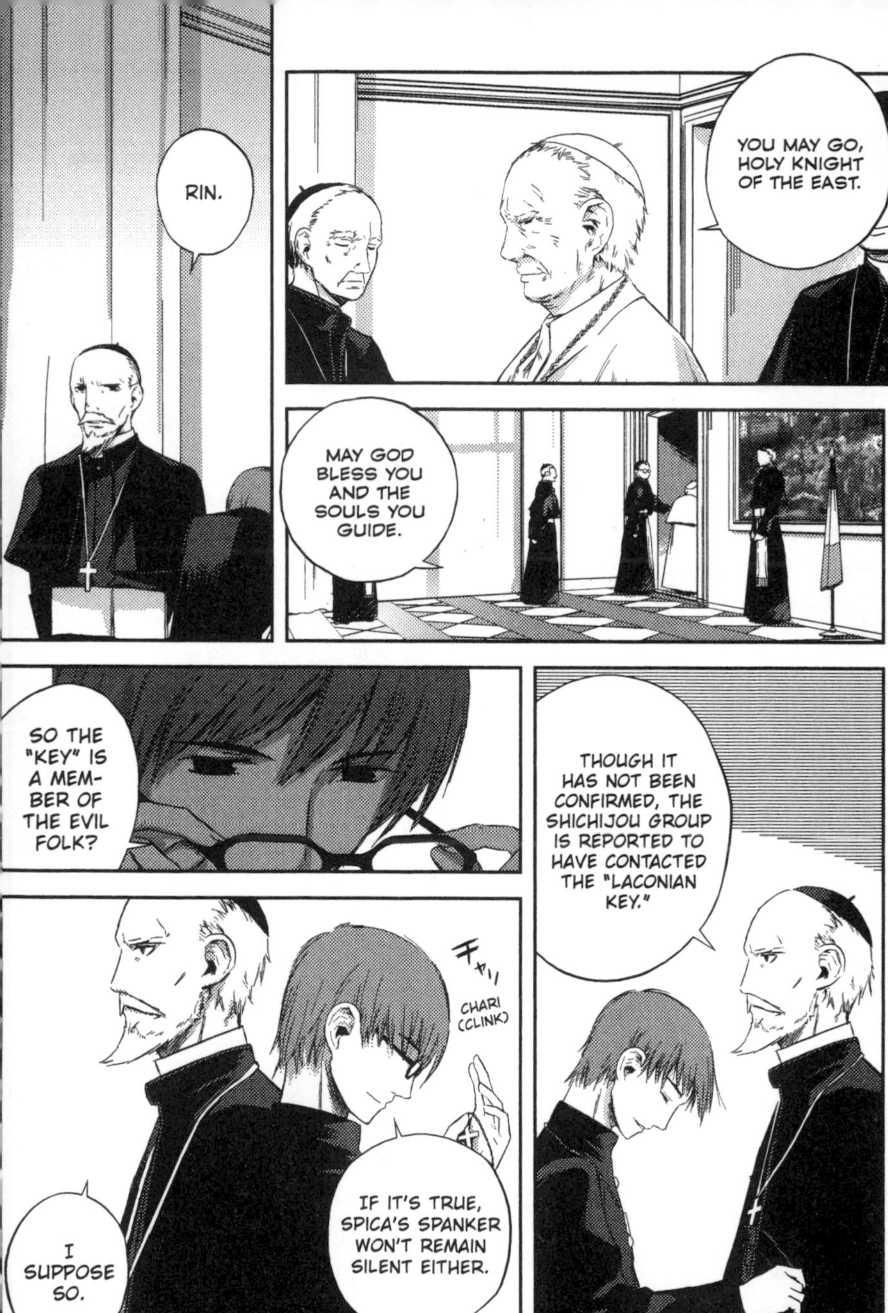
YOU MAY GO, HOLY KNIGHT OF THE EAST.
MAY GOD BLESS YOU AND THE SOULS YOU GUIDE.
RIN.
THOUGH IT HAS NOT BEEN CONFIRMED, THE SHICHIJOU GROUP IS REPORTED TO HAVE CONTACTED THE "LACONIAN KEY."
SO THE "KEY" IS A MEMBER OF THE EVIL FOLK?
チャリ
CHARI (CLINK)
IF IT'S TRUE, SPICA'S SPANKER WON'T REMAIN SILENT EITHER.
I SUPPOSE SO.

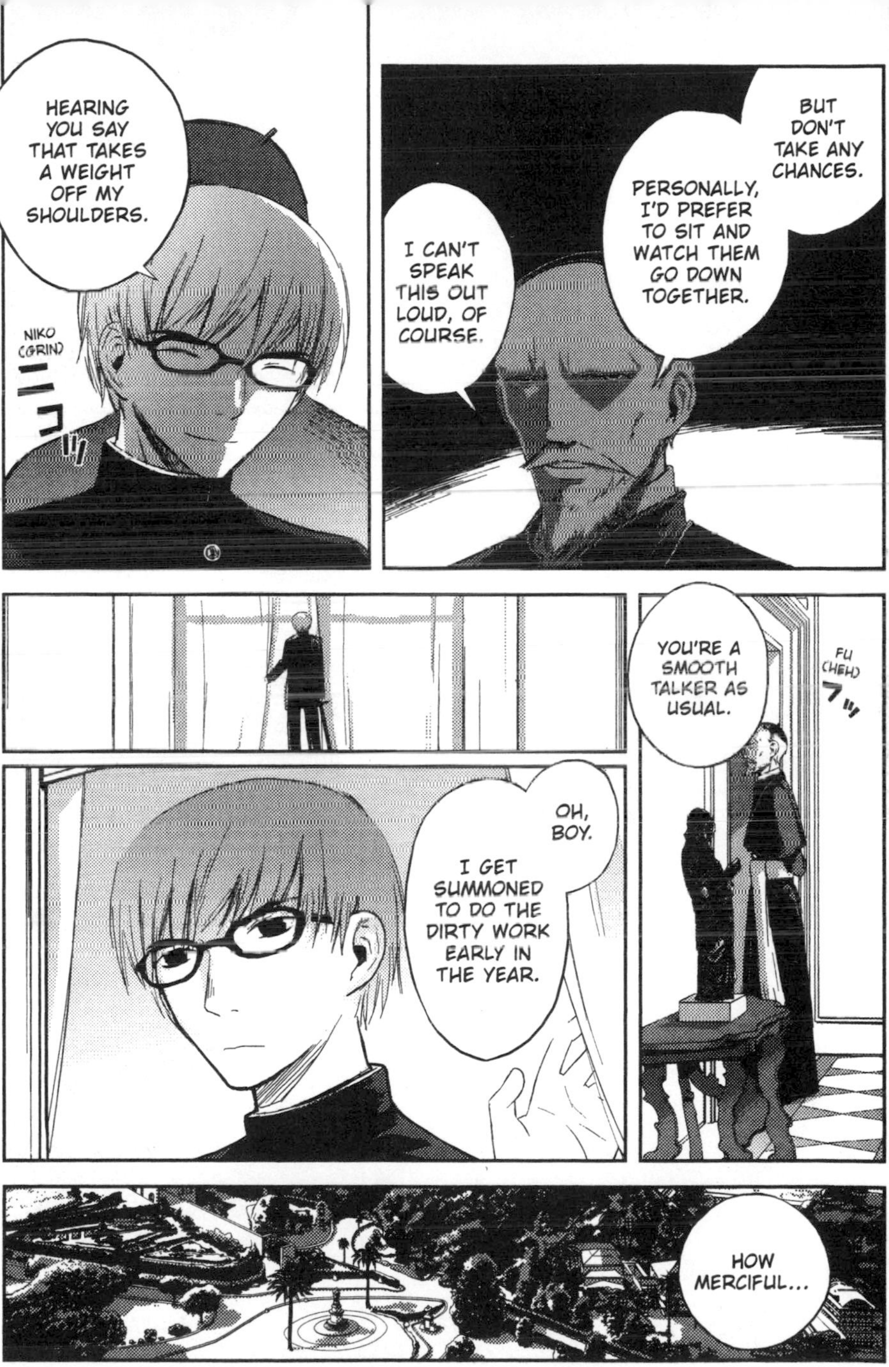
BUT DON'T TAKE ANY CHANCES.
PERSONALLY, I'D PREFER TO SIT AND WATCH THEM GO DOWN TOGETHER.
I CAN'T SPEAK THIS OUT LOUD, OF COURSE.
HEARING YOU SAY THAT TAKES A WEIGHT OFF MY SHOULDERS.
NIKO (GRIN)
FU (HEH)
YOU'RE A SMOOTH TALKER AS USUAL.
OH, BOY.
I GET SUMMONED TO DO THE DIRTY WORK EARLY IN THE YEAR.
HOW MERCIFUL...

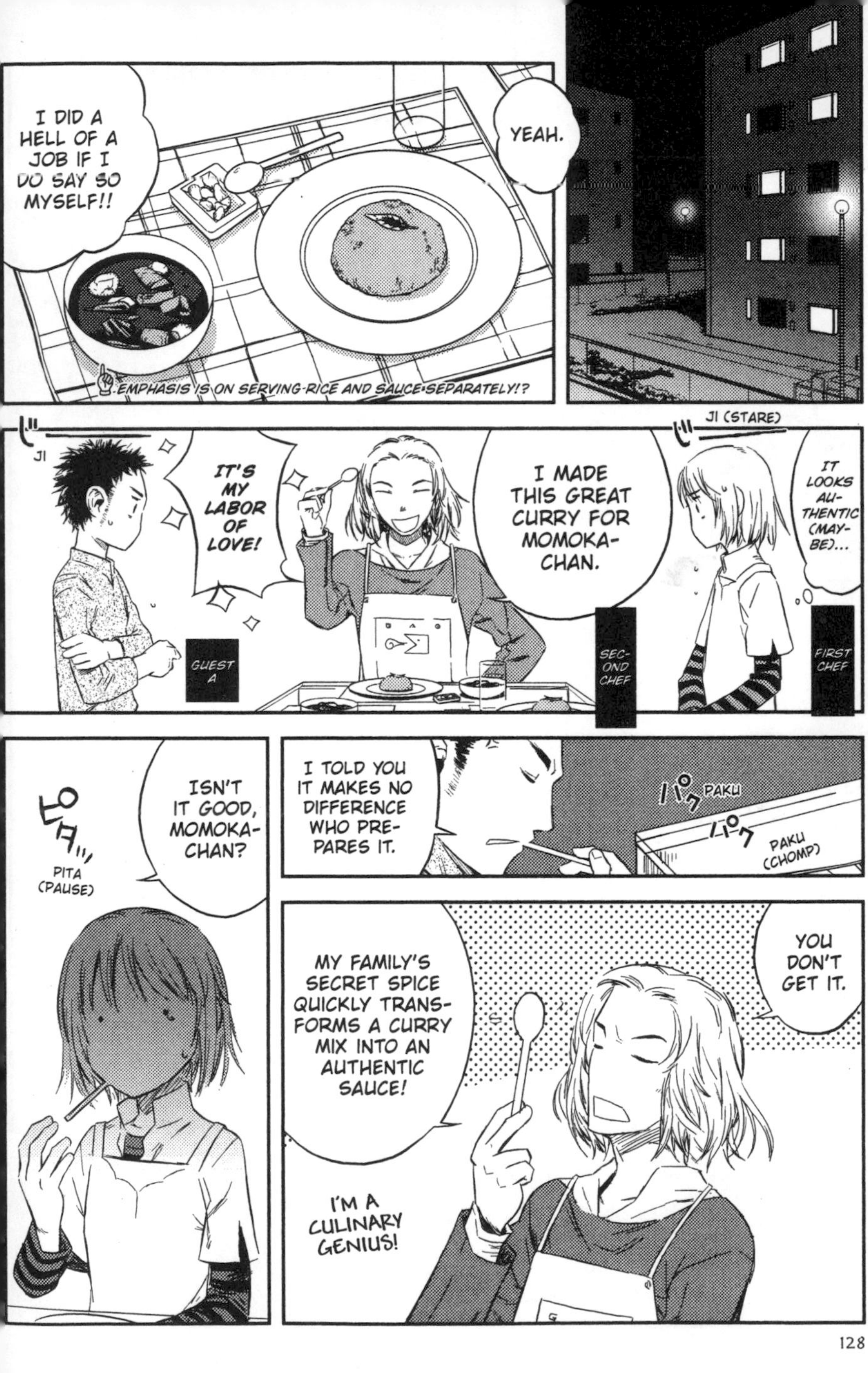
YEAH.
I DID A HELL OF A JOB IF I DO SAY SO MYSELF!!
EMPHASIS IS ON SERVING RICE AND SAUCE SEPARATELY!?
JI (STARE)
IT LOOKS AUTHENTIC (MAYBE)...
FIRST CHEF
I MADE THIS GREAT CURRY FOR MOMOKA-CHAN.
SECOND CHEF
IT'S MY LABOR OF LOVE!
GUEST A
JI
I TOLD YOU IT MAKES NO DIFFERENCE WHO PREPARES IT.
PAKU
PAKU (CHOMP)
YOU DON'T GET IT.
MY FAMILY'S SECRET SPICE QUICKLY TRANSFORMS A CURRY MIX INTO AN AUTHENTIC SAUCE!
I'M A CULINARY GENIUS!
ISN'T IT GOOD, MOMOKA-CHAN?
PITA (PAUSE)

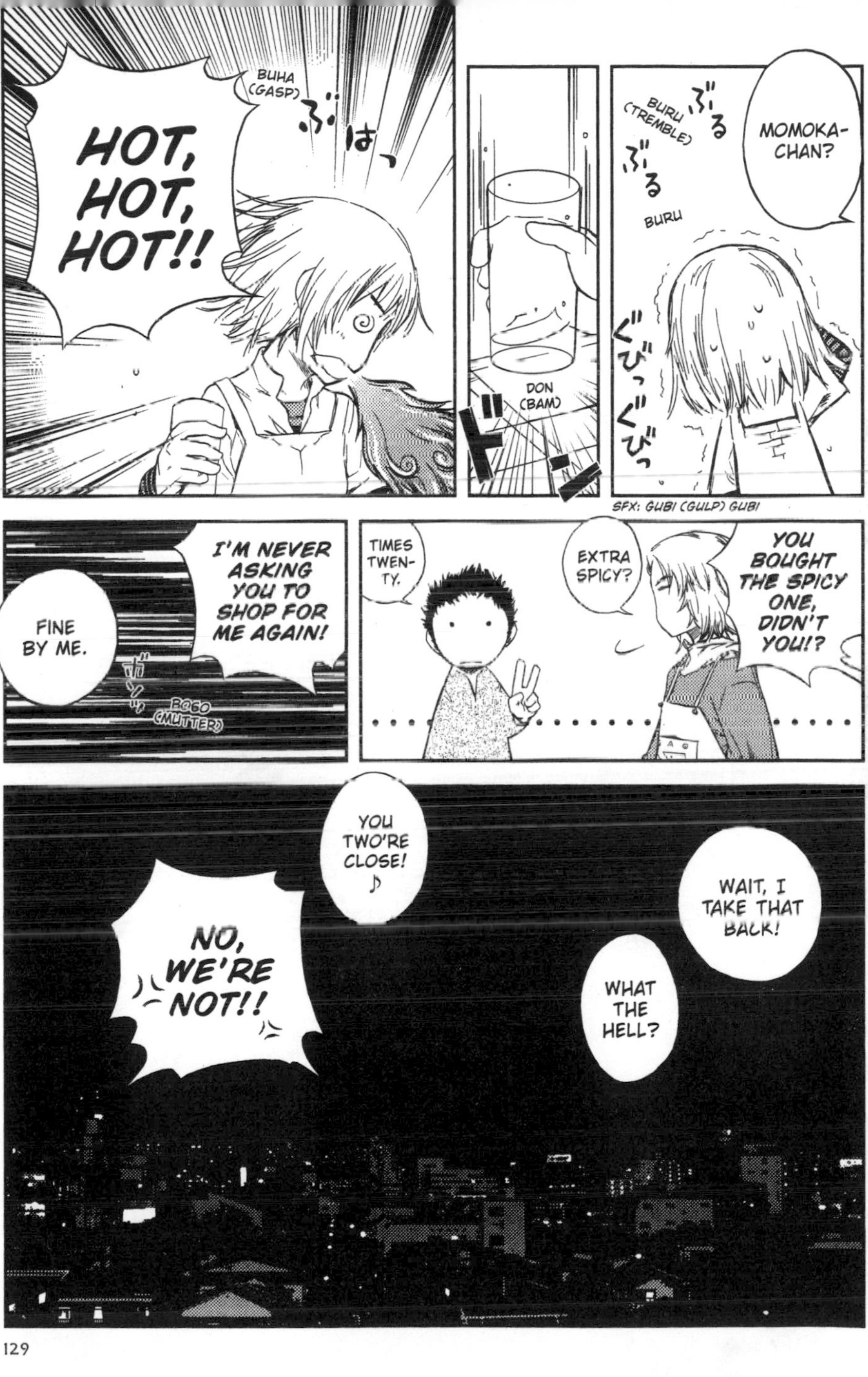
MOMOKA-CHAN?
BURU (TREMBLE)
ぶる
ぶる
BURU
ぐびっ
ぐびっ
DON (BAM)
BUHA (GASP)
ぶはっ
HOT, HOT, HOT!!
SFX: GUBI (GULP) GUBI
YOU BOUGHT THE SPICY ONE, DIDN'T YOU!?
EXTRA SPICY?
TIMES TWENTY.
I'M NEVER ASKING YOU TO SHOP FOR ME AGAIN!
FINE BY ME.
BOSO (MUTTER)
WAIT, I TAKE THAT BACK!
WHAT THE HELL?
YOU TWO'RE CLOSE! ♪
NO, WE'RE NOT!!

BY MOMOKA, THE FIRST CHEF
SAMPLE MEAL BY THE PROFESSIONAL BEGINNER: HAMBURGER
OVERCOOKED MISO SOUP
RICE BURNT IN AN EARTHENWARE POT
UNDERCOOKED CARROTS AND POTATOES
SUPPOSED TO BE JAPANESE PICKLES
BROKEN EGG YOLK
THE HAMBURGER IS TOO RARE, OF COURSE.

Chapter Five: OMEN

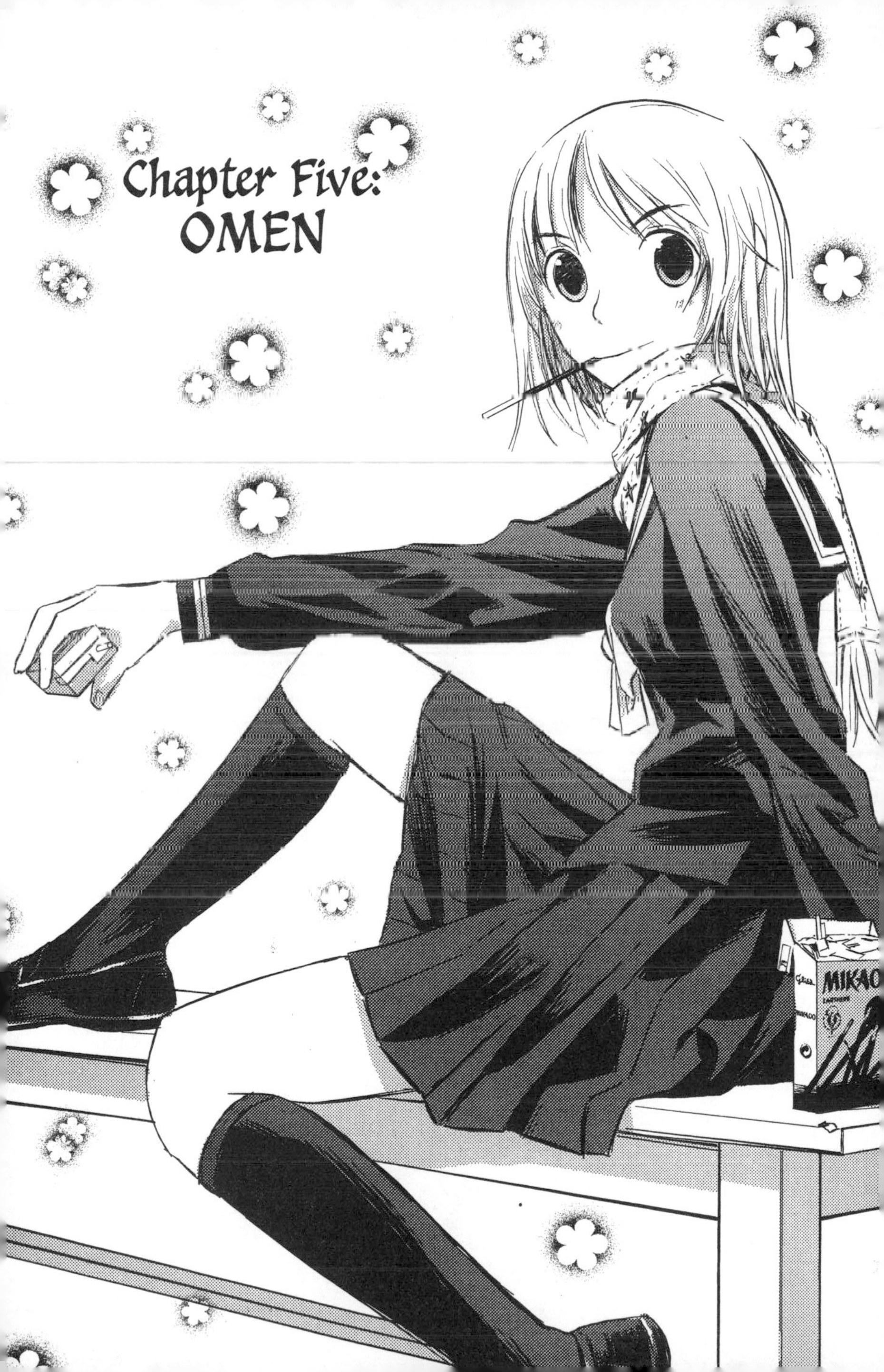
MIKAO

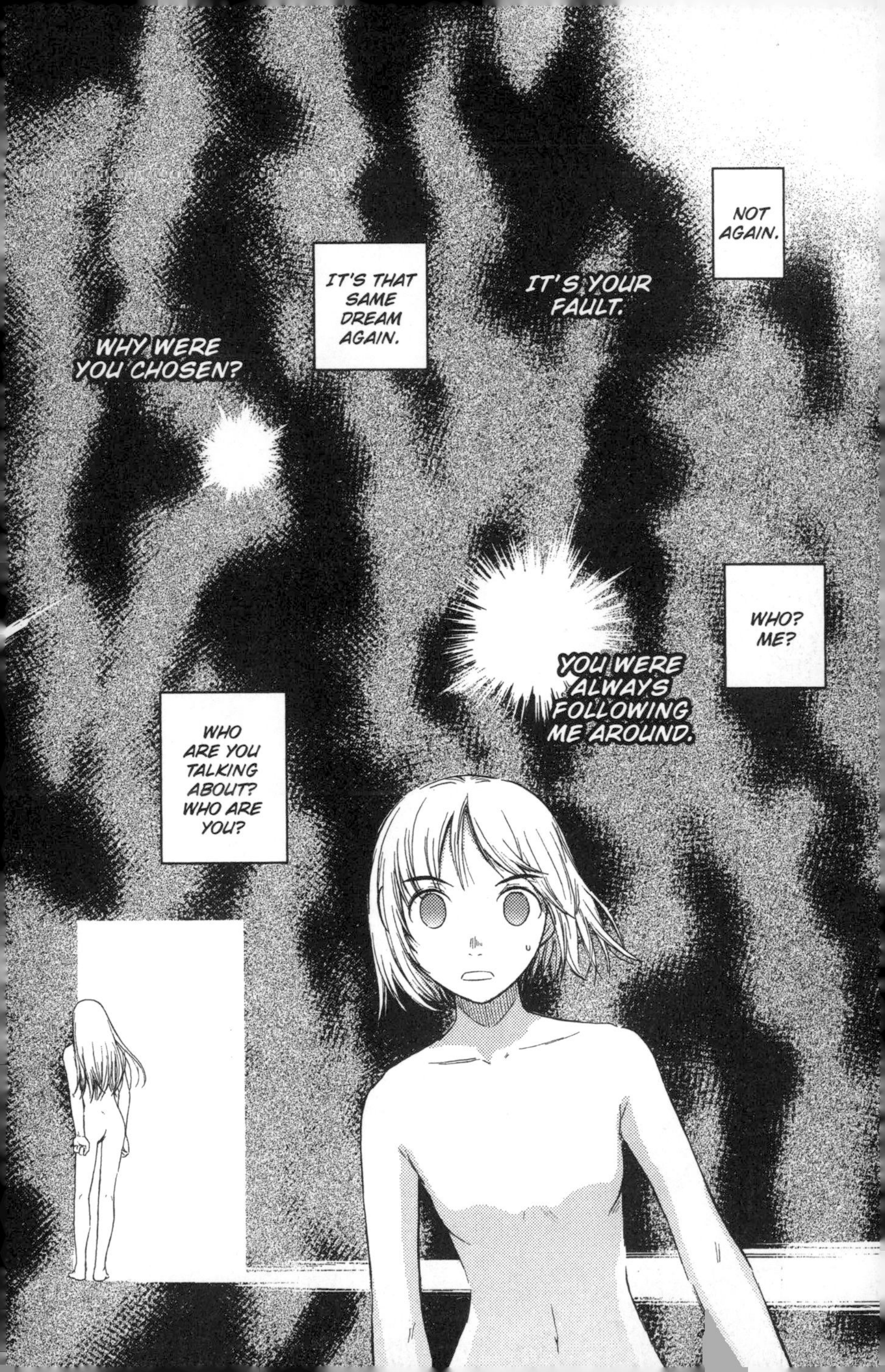
NOT AGAIN.
IT'S YOUR FAULT.
IT'S THAT SAME DREAM AGAIN.
WHY WERE YOU CHOSEN?
WHO? ME?
YOU WERE ALWAYS FOLLOWING ME AROUND.
WHO ARE YOU TALKING ABOUT? WHO ARE YOU?

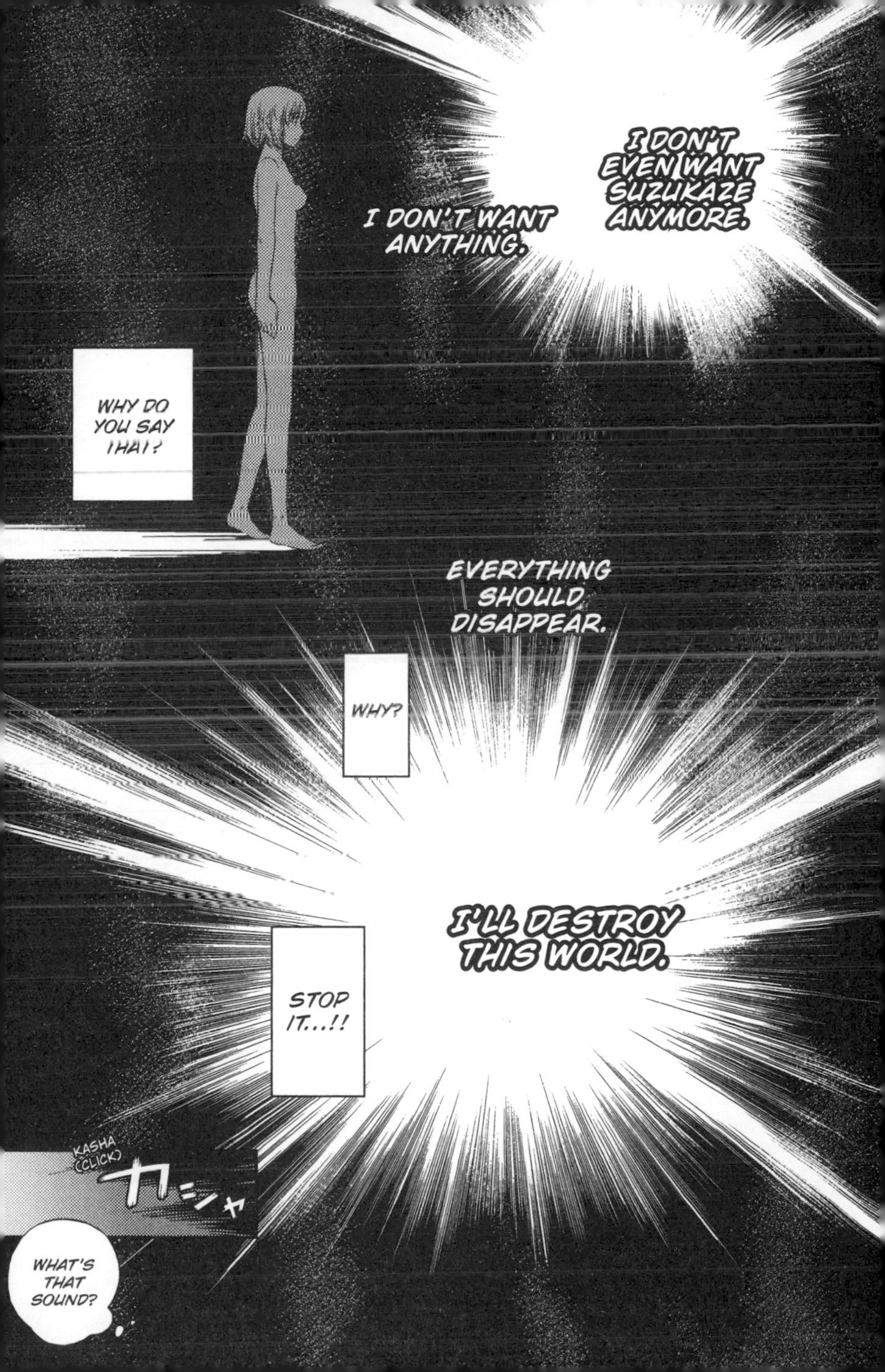
I DON'T EVEN WANT SUZUKAZE ANYMORE.
I DON'T WANT ANYTHING.
WHY DO YOU SAY THAT?
EVERYTHING SHOULD DISAPPEAR.
WHY?
I'LL DESTROY THIS WORLD.
STOP IT...!!
KASHA (CLICK)
カシャ
WHAT'S THAT SOUND?

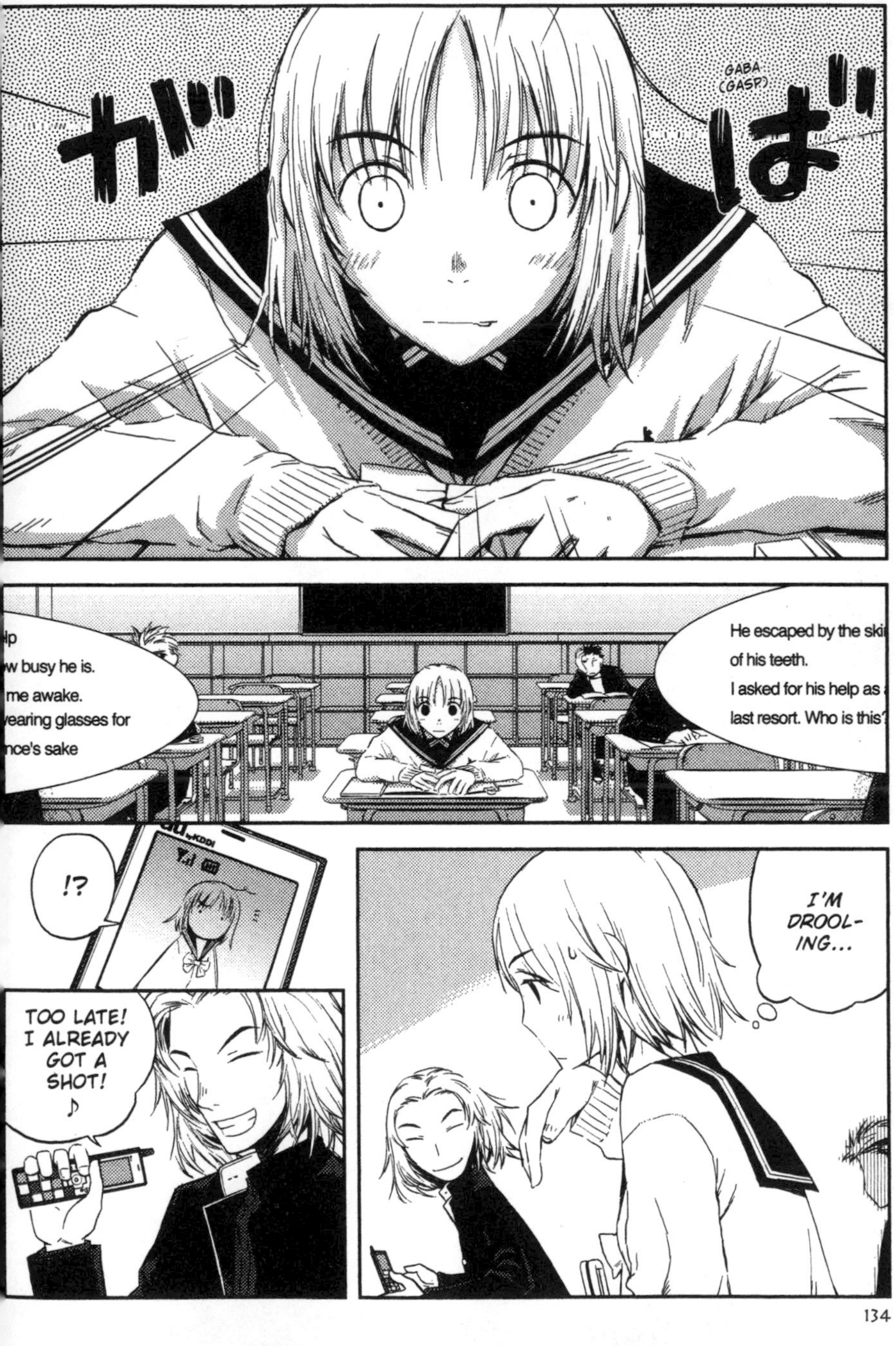

GABA (GASP)
He escaped by the ski of his teeth. I asked for his help as last resort. Who is this?
lp w busy he is. me awake. vearing glasses for nce's sake
I'M DROOLING...
!?
TOO LATE! I ALREADY GOT A SHOT! ♪

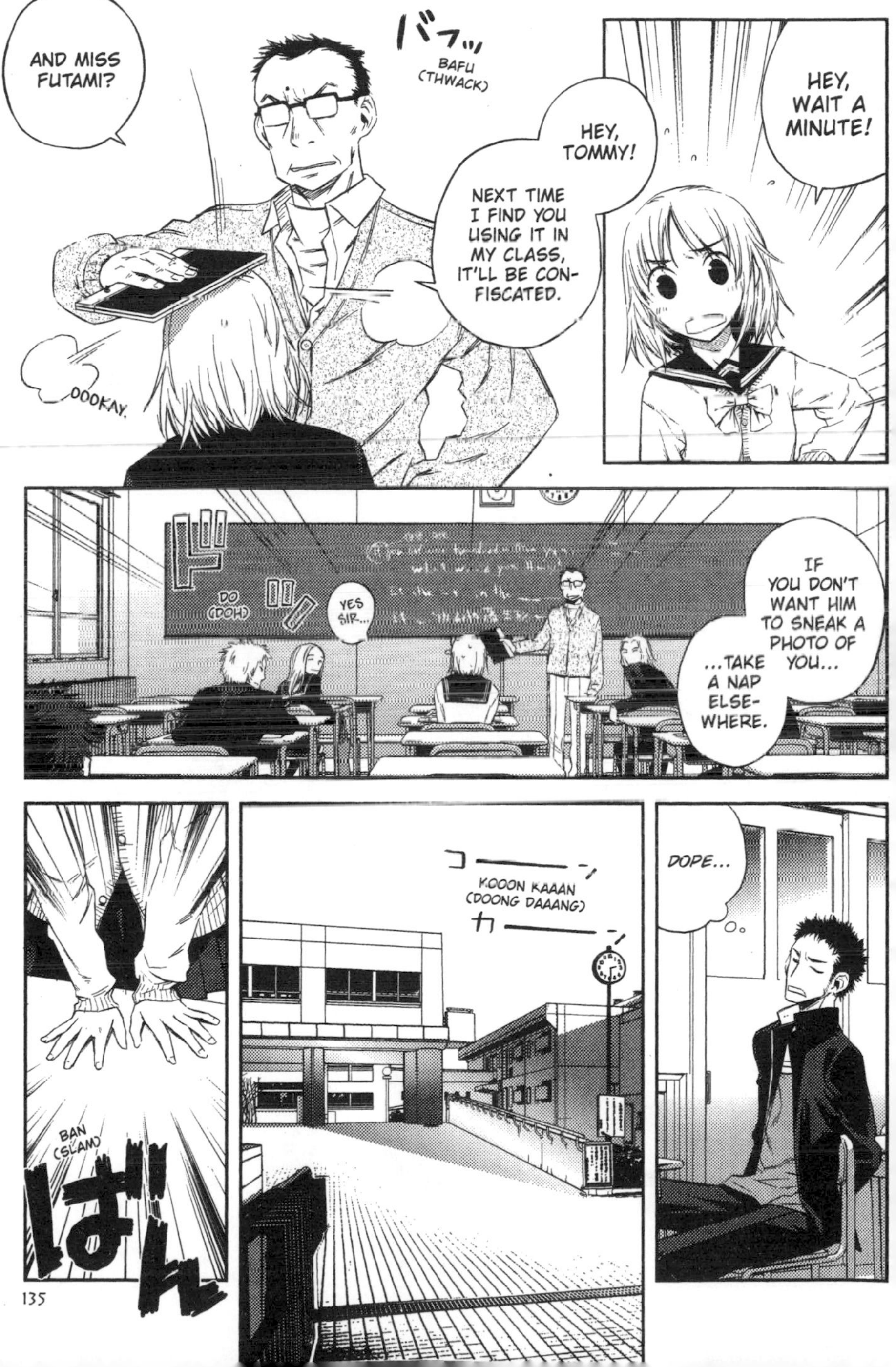
HEY, WAIT A MINUTE!
HEY, TOMMY!
NEXT TIME I FIND YOU USING IT IN MY CLASS, IT'LL BE CON-FISCATED.
バフッ
BAFU (THWACK)
AND MISS FUTAMI?
OOOKAY.
IF YOU DON'T WANT HIM TO SNEAK A PHOTO OF YOU...
...TAKE A NAP ELSE-WHERE.
YES SIR...
DO (DOH)
DOPE...
KOOON KAAAN (DOONG DAAANG)
BAN (SLAM)
ばん

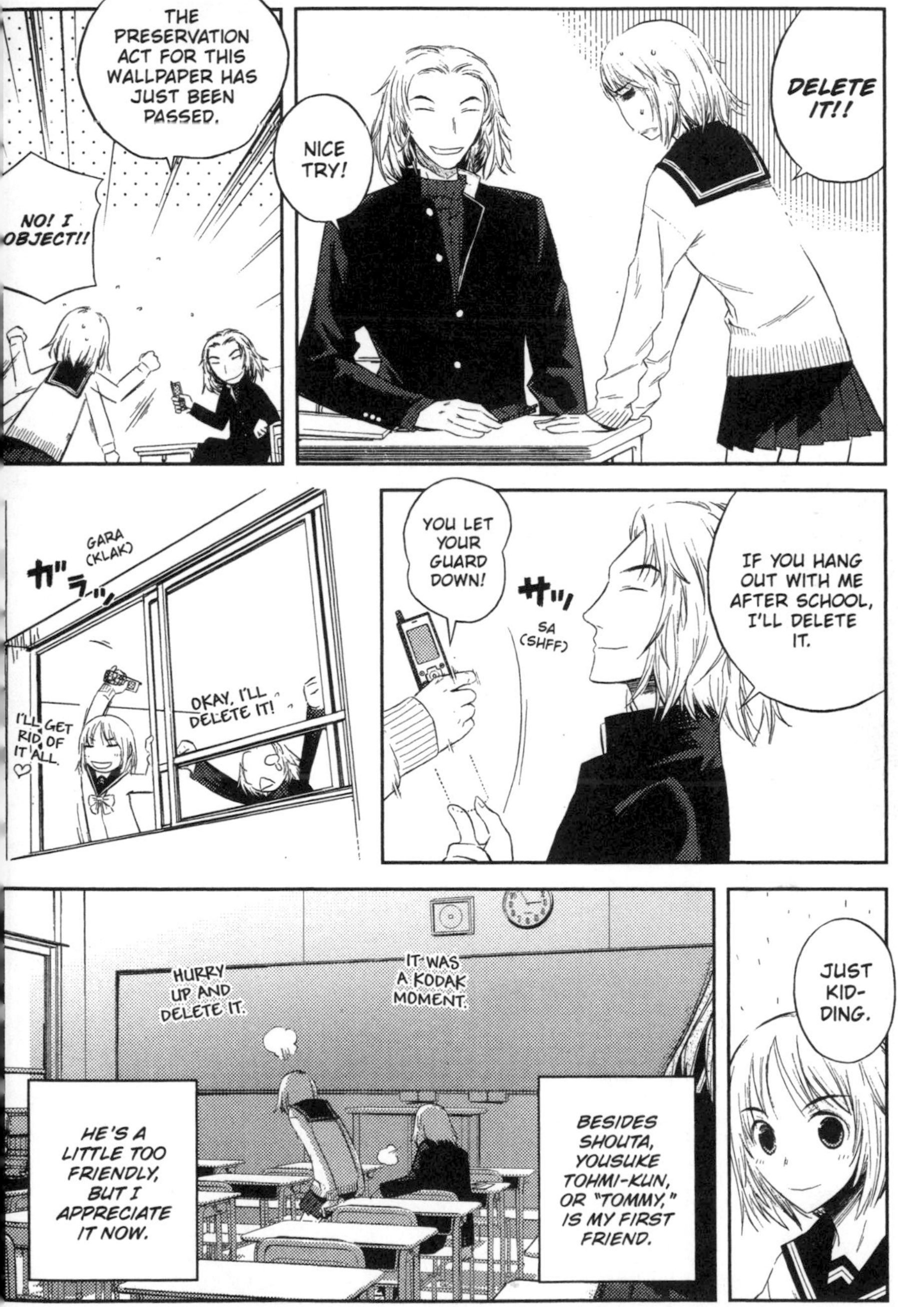
DELETE IT!!
NICE TRY!
THE PRESERVATION ACT FOR THIS WALLPAPER HAS JUST BEEN PASSED.
NO! I OBJECT!!
IF YOU HANG OUT WITH ME AFTER SCHOOL, I'LL DELETE IT.
サッ
SA (SHFF)
YOU LET YOUR GUARD DOWN!
ガラッ
GARA (KLAK)
OKAY, I'LL DELETE IT!
I'LL GET RID OF IT ALL. ♡
JUST KID-DING.
BESIDES SHOUTA, YOUSUKE TOHMI-KUN, OR "TOMMY," IS MY FIRST FRIEND.
IT WAS A KODAK MOMENT.
HURRY UP AND DELETE IT.
HE'S A LITTLE TOO FRIENDLY, BUT I APPRECIATE IT NOW.

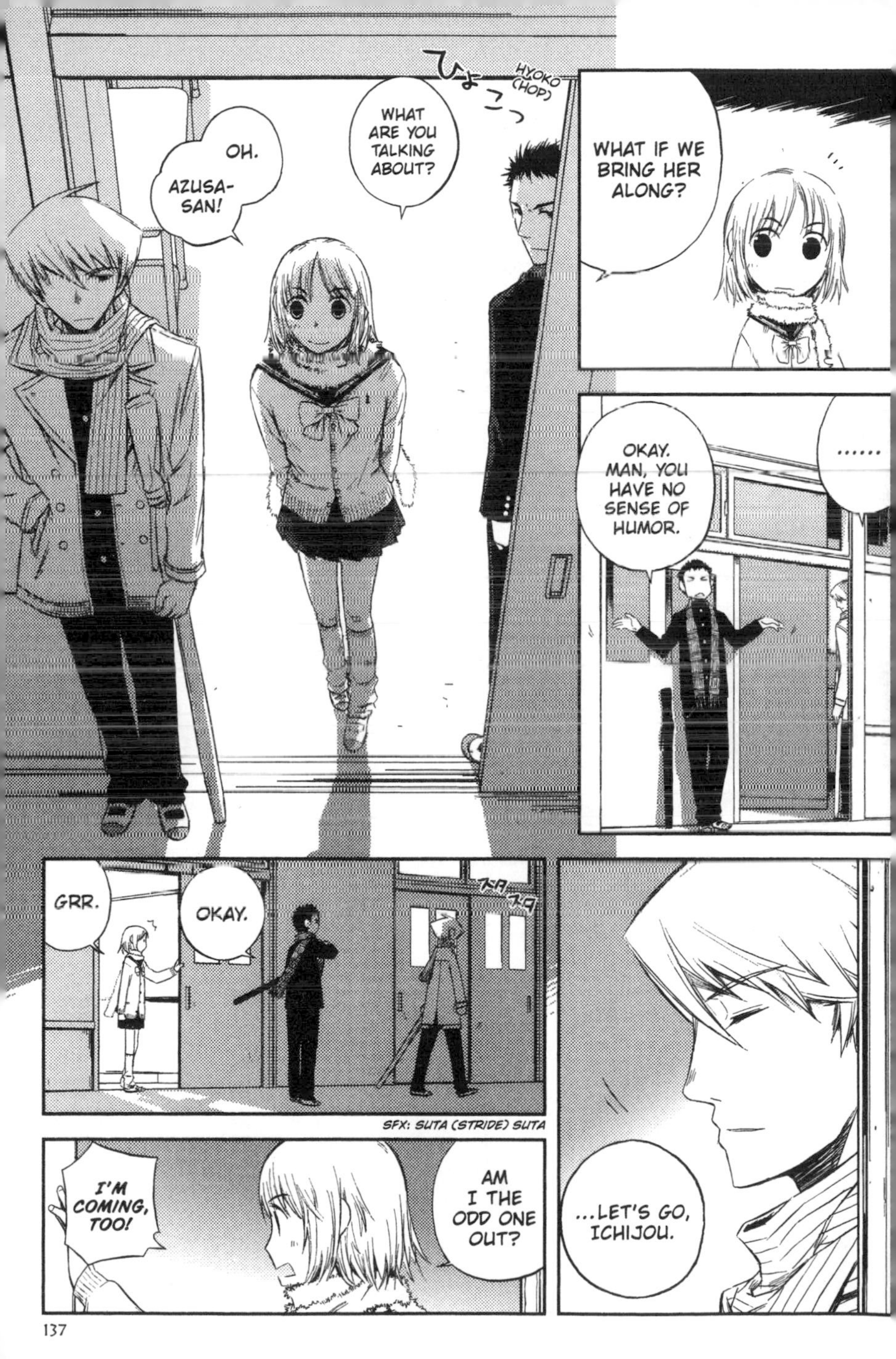
WHAT IF WE BRING HER ALONG?
......
OKAY. MAN, YOU HAVE NO SENSE OF HUMOR.
ひょこっ
HYOKO (HOP)
WHAT ARE YOU TALKING ABOUT?
OH. AZUSA-SAN!
...LET'S GO, ICHIJOU.
スタ スタ
OKAY.
GRR.
SFX: SUTA (STRIDE) SUTA
AM I THE ODD ONE OUT?
I'M COMING, TOO!

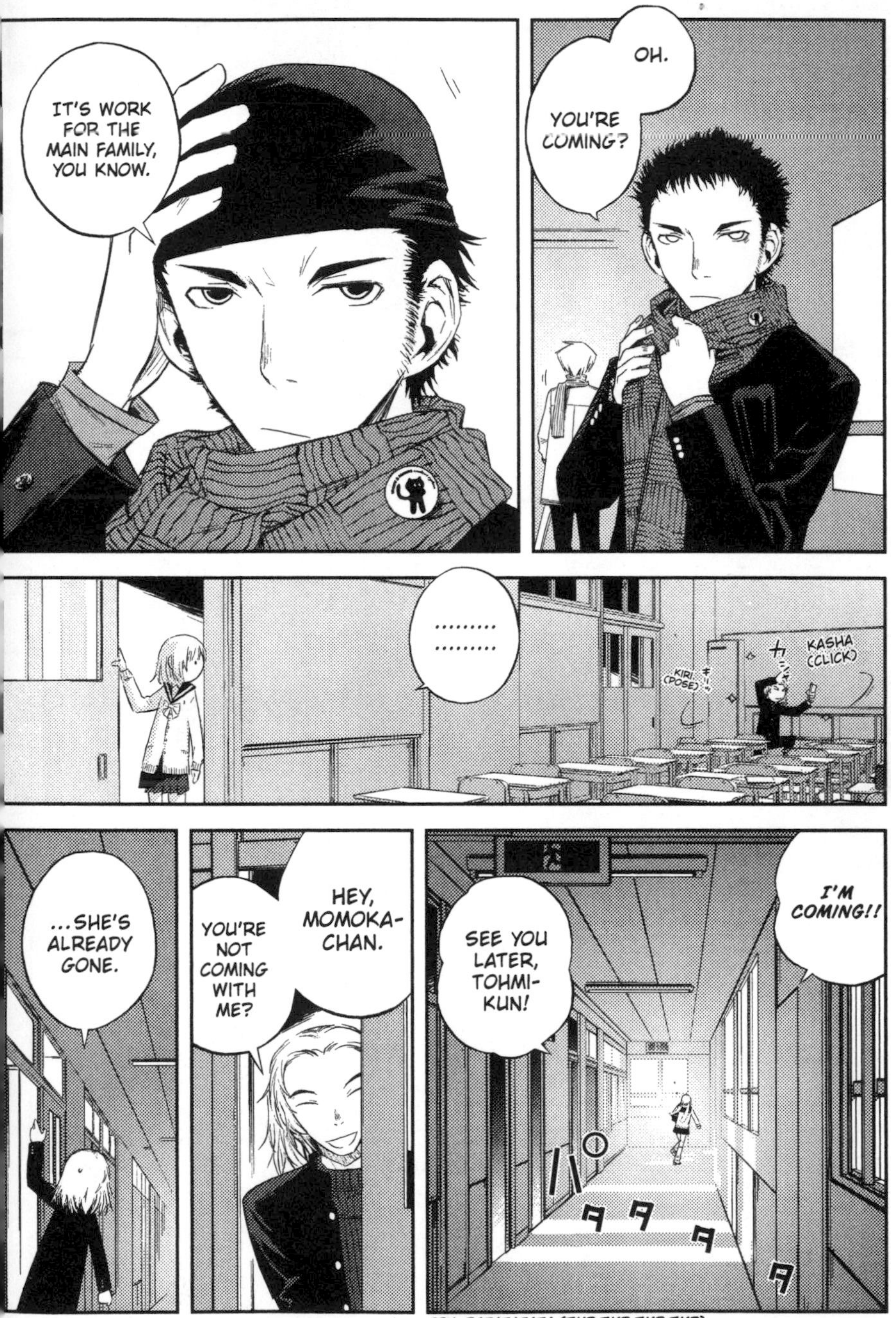
OH.
YOU'RE COMING?
IT'S WORK FOR THE MAIN FAMILY, YOU KNOW.
KASHA (CLICK)
KIRI (POSE)
....
....
I'M COMING!!
SEE YOU LATER, TOHMI-KUN!
HEY, MOMOKA-CHAN.
YOU'RE NOT COMING WITH ME?
...SHE'S ALREADY GONE.

SFX: PATATATATA (TMP TMP TMP TMP)

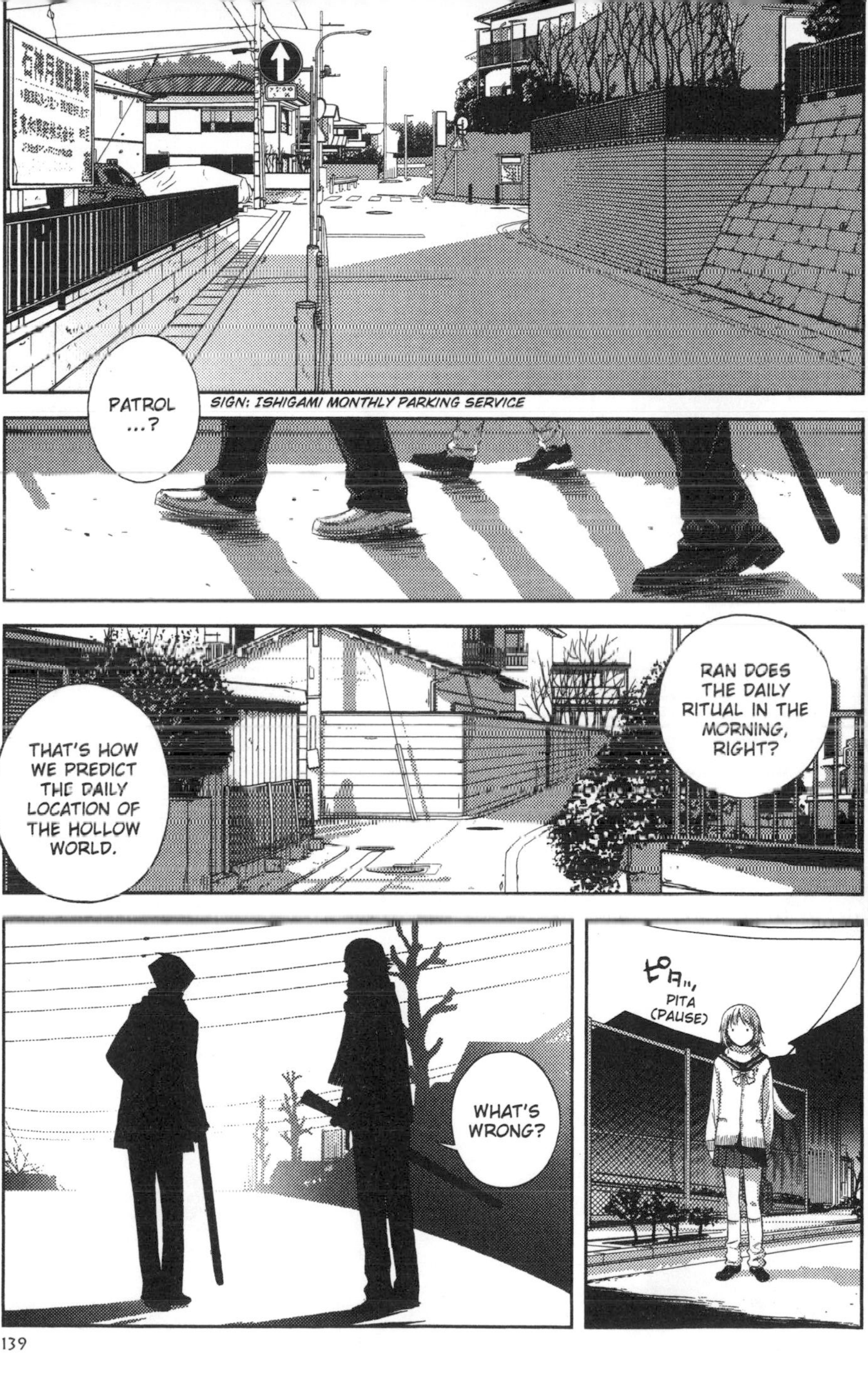
PATROL ...?
SIGN: ISHIGAMI MONTHLY PARKING SERVICE
RAN DOES THE DAILY RITUAL IN THE MORNING, RIGHT?
THAT'S HOW WE PREDICT THE DAILY LOCATION OF THE HOLLOW WORLD.
ピタッ
PITA (PAUSE)
WHAT'S WRONG?

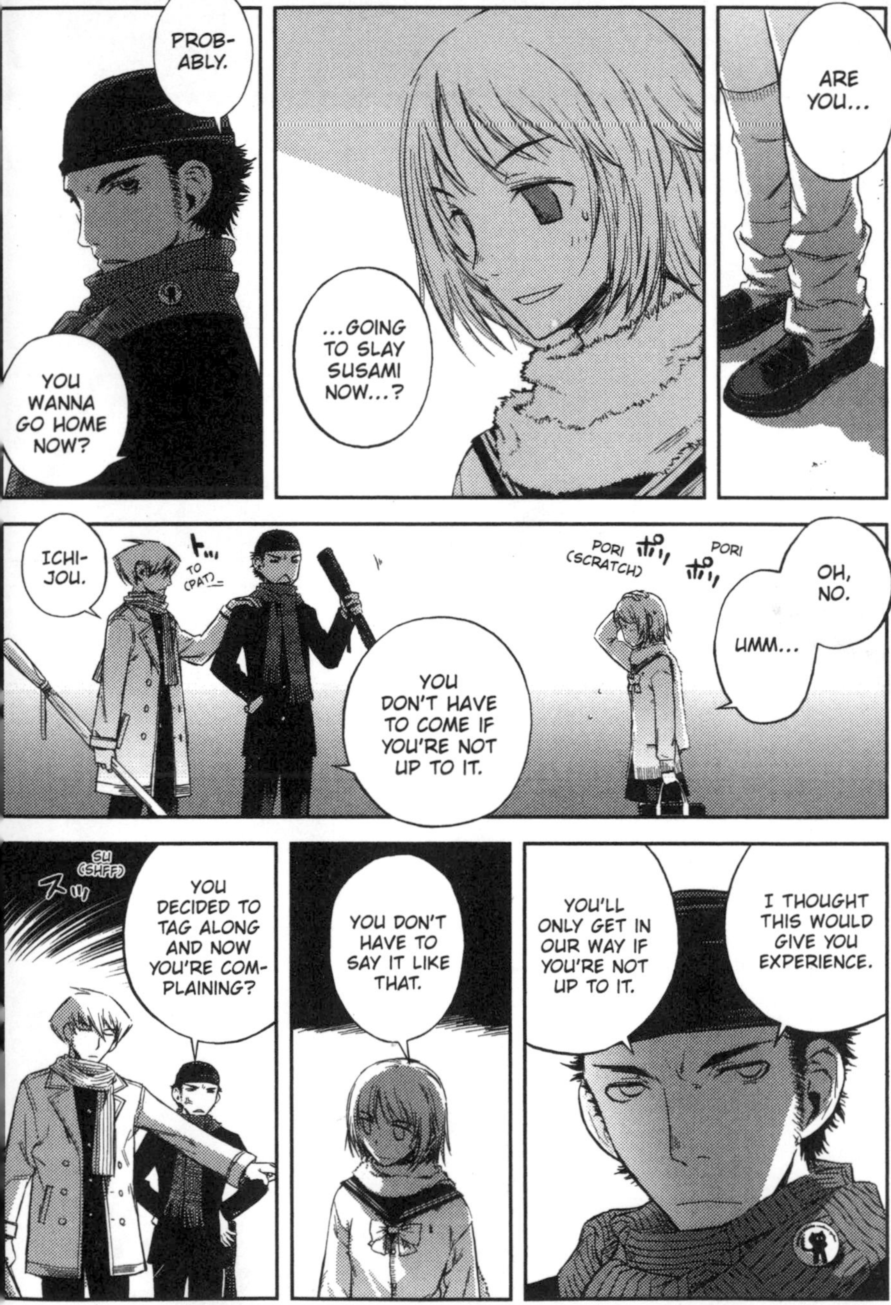
ARE YOU...
...GOING TO SLAY SUSAMI NOW...?
PROB-ABLY.
YOU WANNA GO HOME NOW?
PORI
OH, NO.
UMM...
PORI (SCRATCH)
YOU DON'T HAVE TO COME IF YOU'RE NOT UP TO IT.
TO (PAT)
ICHI-JOU.
I THOUGHT THIS WOULD GIVE YOU EXPERIENCE.
YOU'LL ONLY GET IN OUR WAY IF YOU'RE NOT UP TO IT.
YOU DON'T HAVE TO SAY IT LIKE THAT.
YOU DECIDED TO TAG ALONG AND NOW YOU'RE COM-PLAINING?
SU (SHFF)

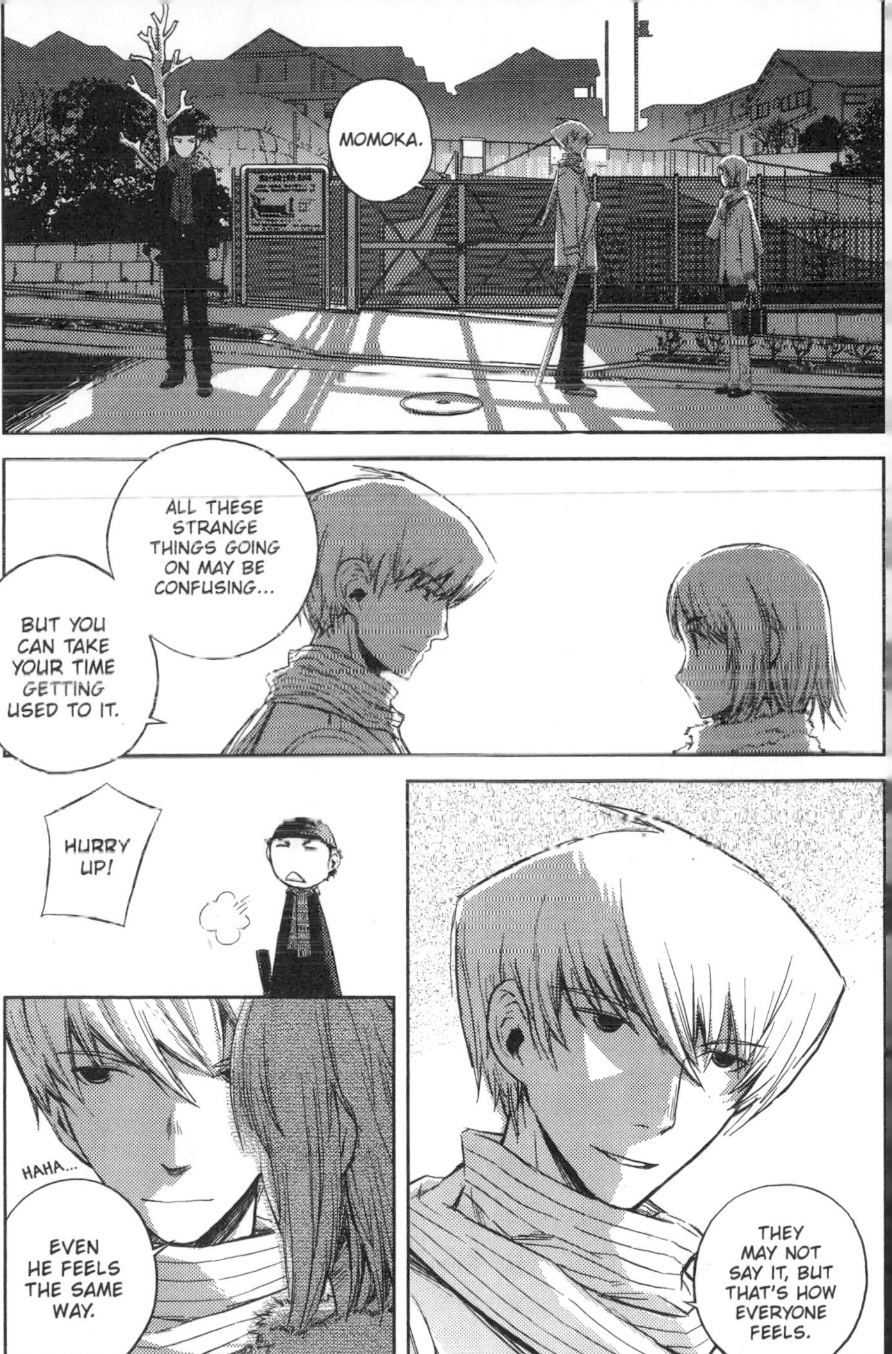
MOMOKA.
ALL THESE STRANGE THINGS GOING ON MAY BE CONFUSING...
BUT YOU CAN TAKE YOUR TIME GETTING USED TO IT.
THEY MAY NOT SAY IT, BUT THAT'S HOW EVERYONE FEELS.
HURRY UP!
HAHA...
EVEN HE FEELS THE SAME WAY.

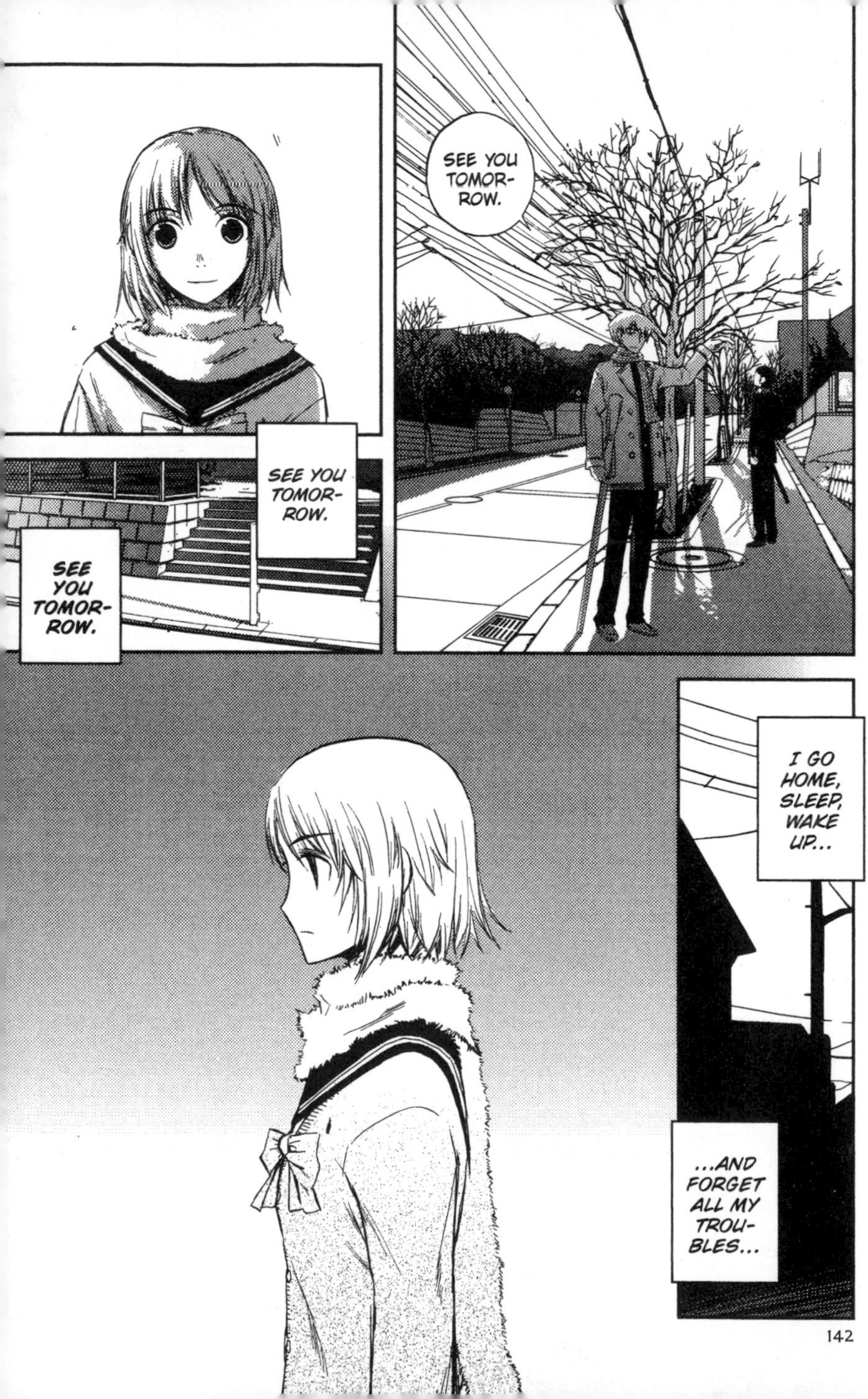
SEE YOU TOMOR-ROW.
SEE YOU TOMOR-ROW.
SEE YOU TOMOR-ROW.
I GO HOME, SLEEP, WAKE UP...
...AND FORGET ALL MY TROU-BLES...

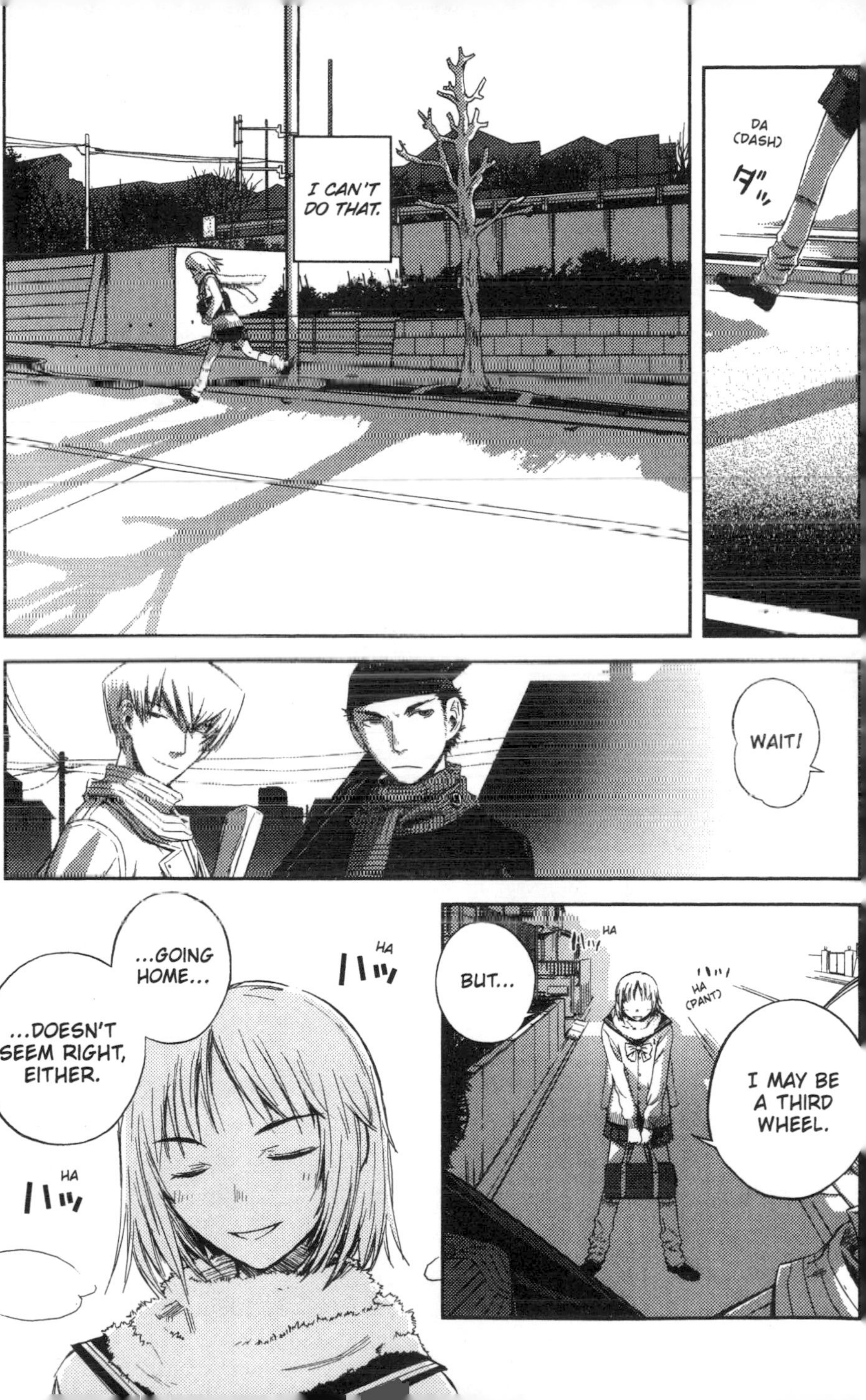

DA (DASH)
ダッ
I CAN'T DO THAT.
WAIT!
HA (PANT)
ハッ
I MAY BE A THIRD WHEEL.
HA
ハッ
BUT...
HA
ハッ
...GOING HOME...
...DOESN'T SEEM RIGHT, EITHER.
HA
ハッ

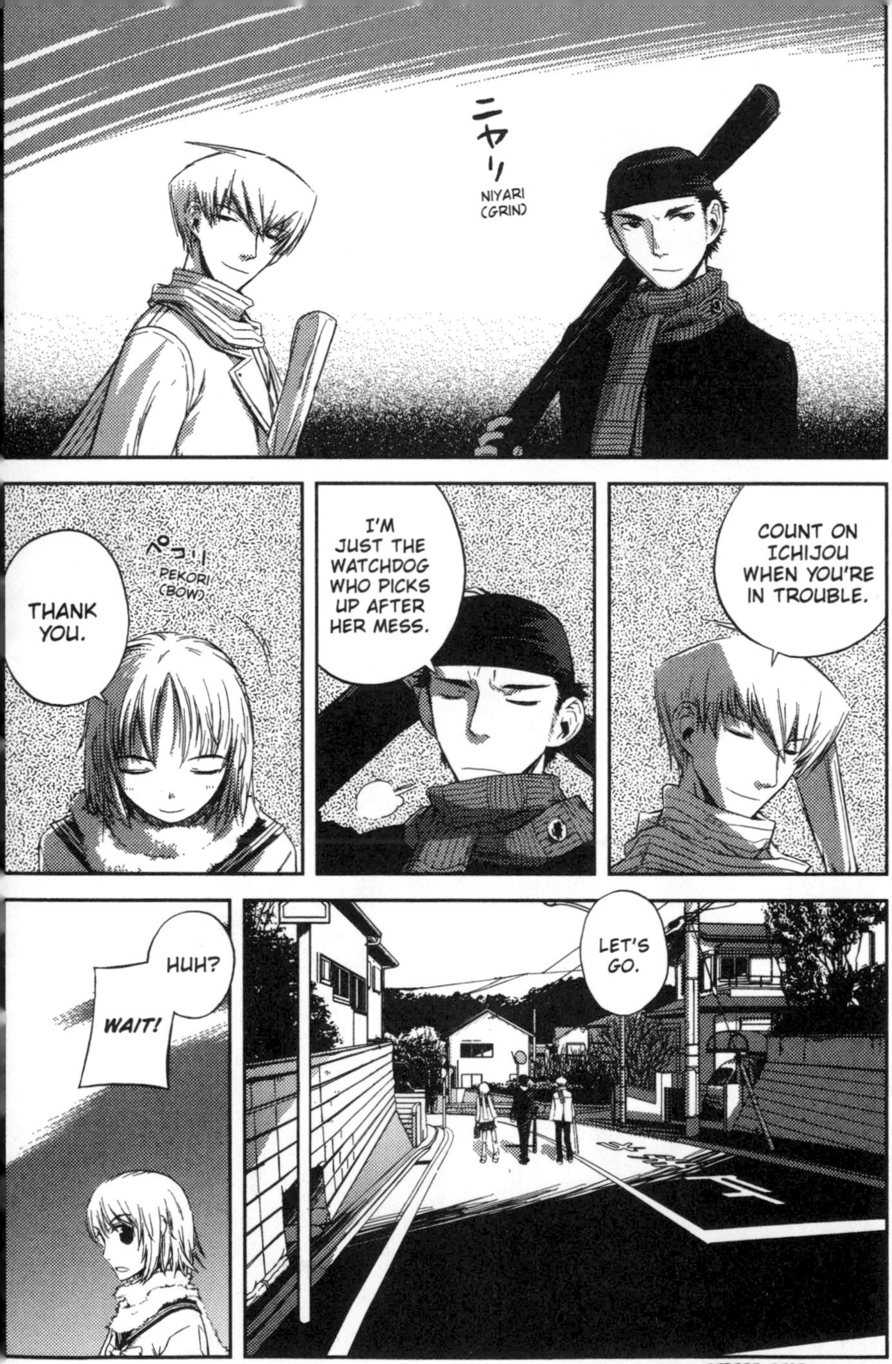
ニヤリ
NIYARI (GRIN)
COUNT ON ICHIJOU WHEN YOU'RE IN TROUBLE.
I'M JUST THE WATCHDOG WHO PICKS UP AFTER HER MESS.
ペコリ
PEKORI (BOW)
THANK YOU.
LET'S GO.
HUH?
WAIT!

STREET: STOP

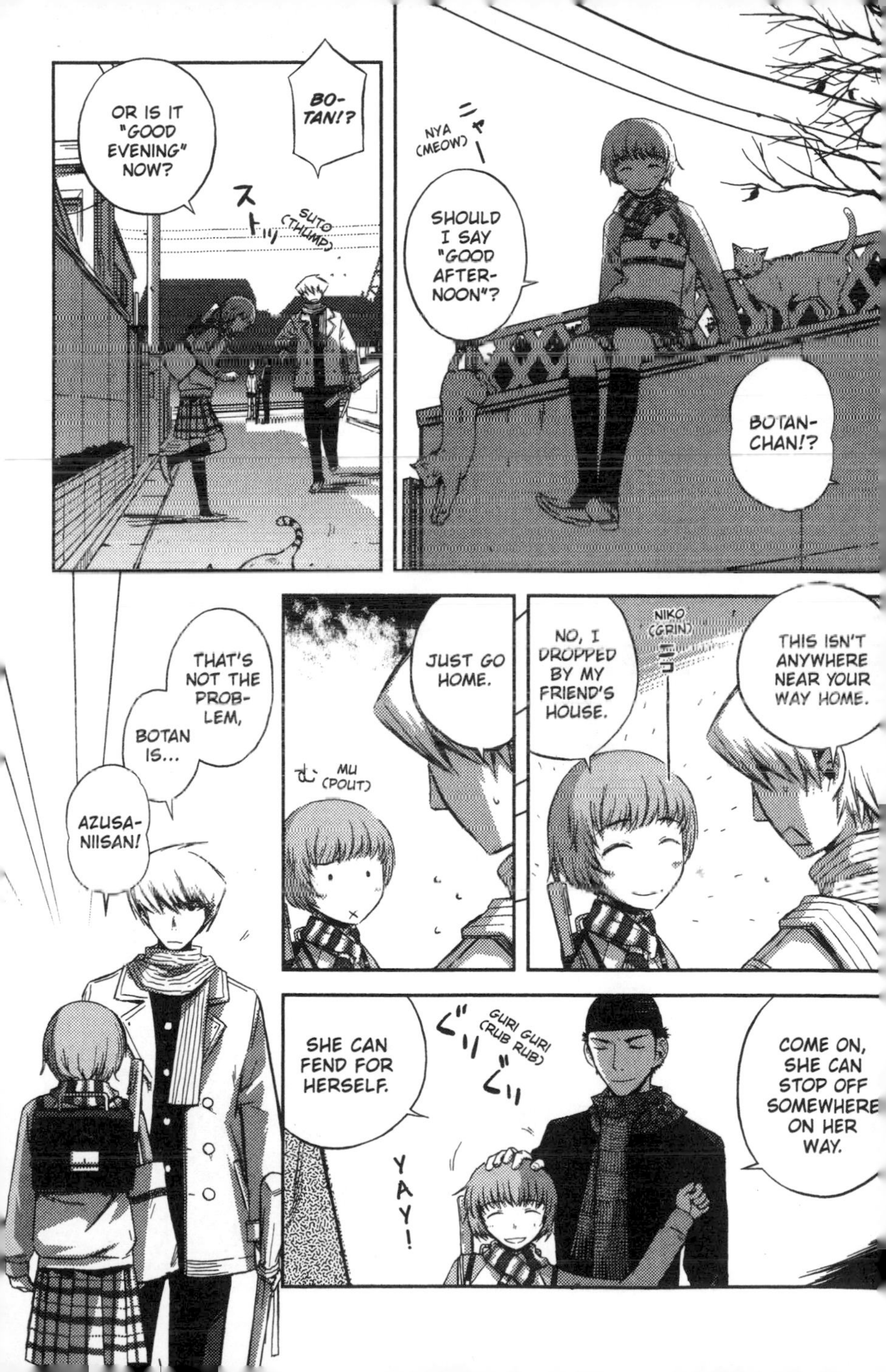

ニャー
NYA (MEOW)
SHOULD I SAY "GOOD AFTER-NOON"?
BOTAN-CHAN!?
BO-TAN!?
OR IS IT "GOOD EVENING" NOW?
ストッ
SUTO (THUMP)
THIS ISN'T ANYWHERE NEAR YOUR WAY HOME.
NIKO (GRIN)
ニコ
NO, I DROPPED BY MY FRIEND'S HOUSE.
JUST GO HOME.
む
MU (POUT)
COME ON, SHE CAN STOP OFF SOMEWHERE ON HER WAY.
ぐりぐり
GURI GURI (RUB RUB)
SHE CAN FEND FOR HERSELF.
YAY!
THAT'S NOT THE PROB-LEM,
BOTAN IS...
AZUSA-NIISAN!

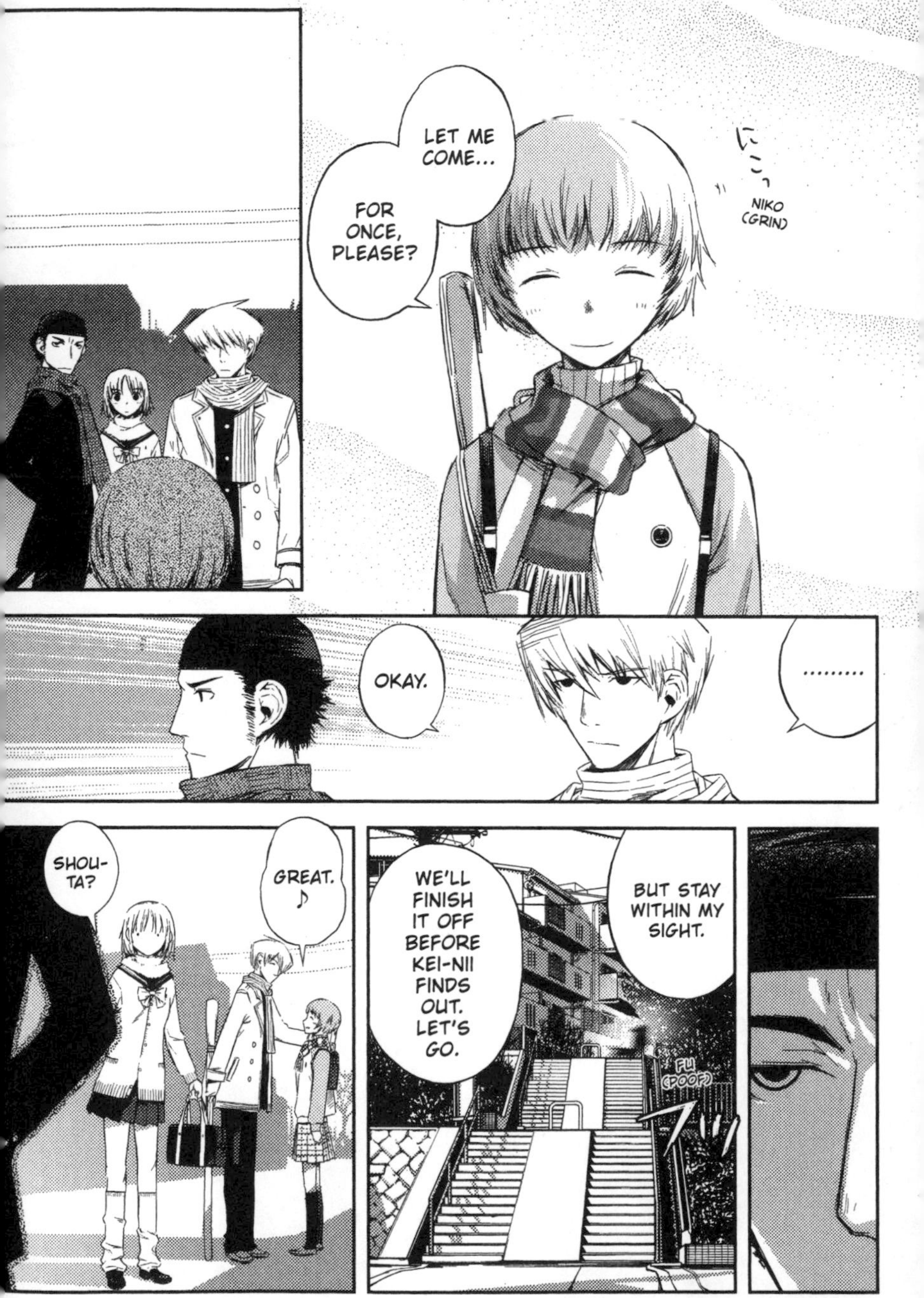
にこっ
NIKO (GRIN)
LET ME COME...
FOR ONCE, PLEASE?
....
OKAY.
BUT STAY WITHIN MY SIGHT.
FU (POOF)
WE'LL FINISH IT OFF BEFORE KEI-NII FINDS OUT. LET'S GO.
GREAT. ♪
SHOU-TA?

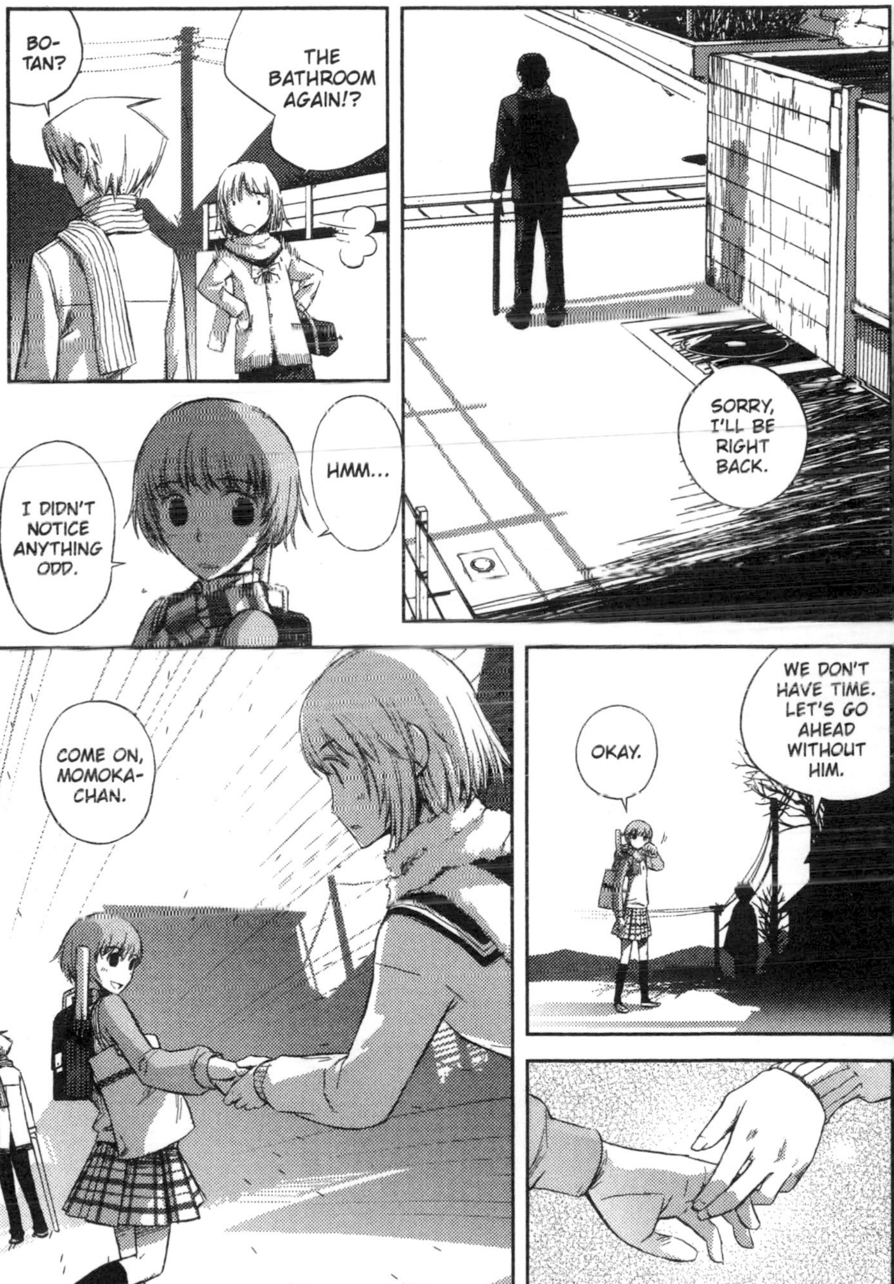
SORRY, I'LL BE RIGHT BACK.
THE BATHROOM AGAIN!?
BO-TAN?
HMM...
I DIDN'T NOTICE ANYTHING ODD.
WE DON'T HAVE TIME. LET'S GO AHEAD WITHOUT HIM.
OKAY.
COME ON, MOMOKA-CHAN.

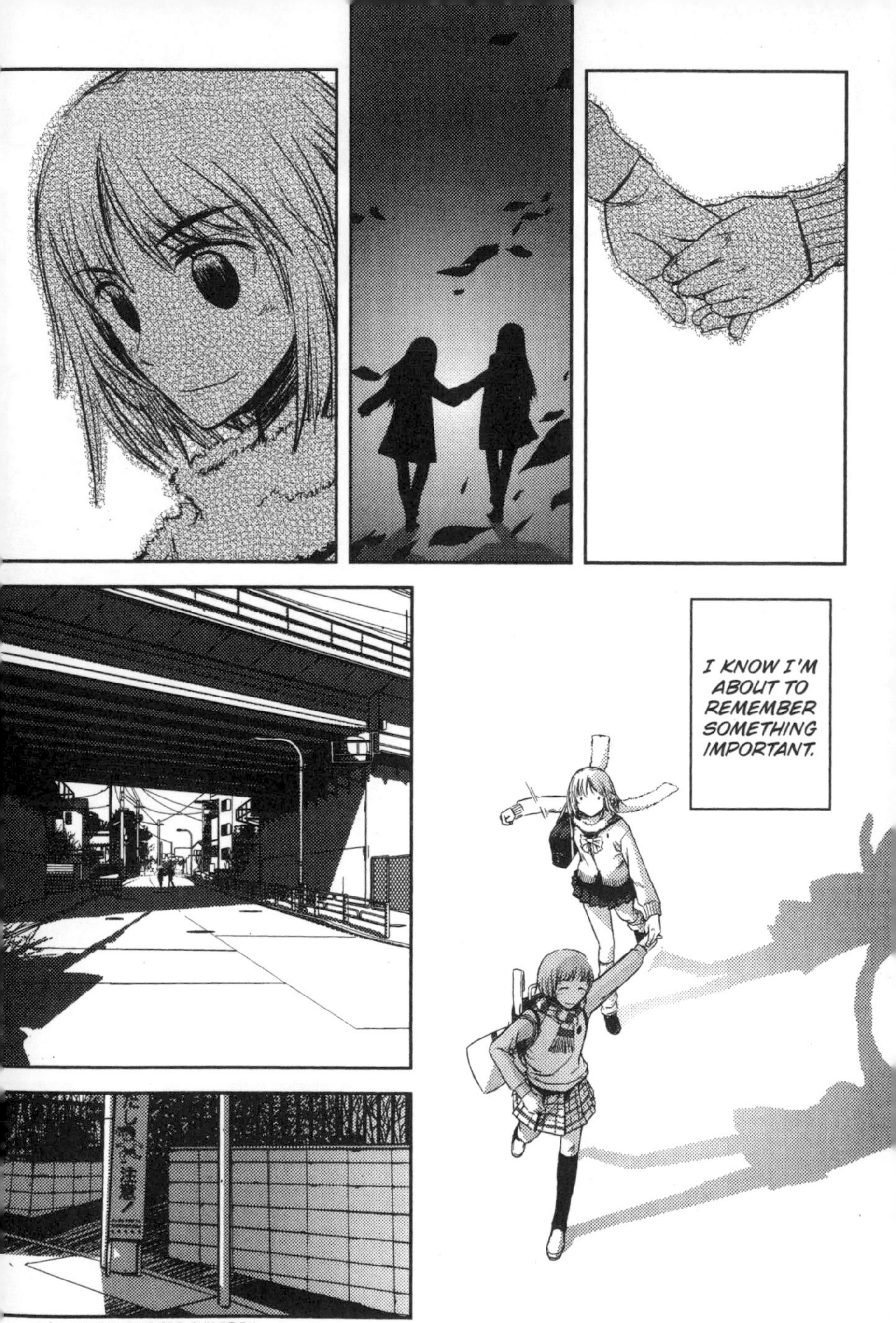
I KNOW I'M ABOUT TO REMEMBER SOMETHING IMPORTANT.

SIGN: WATCH OUT FOR CHILDREN

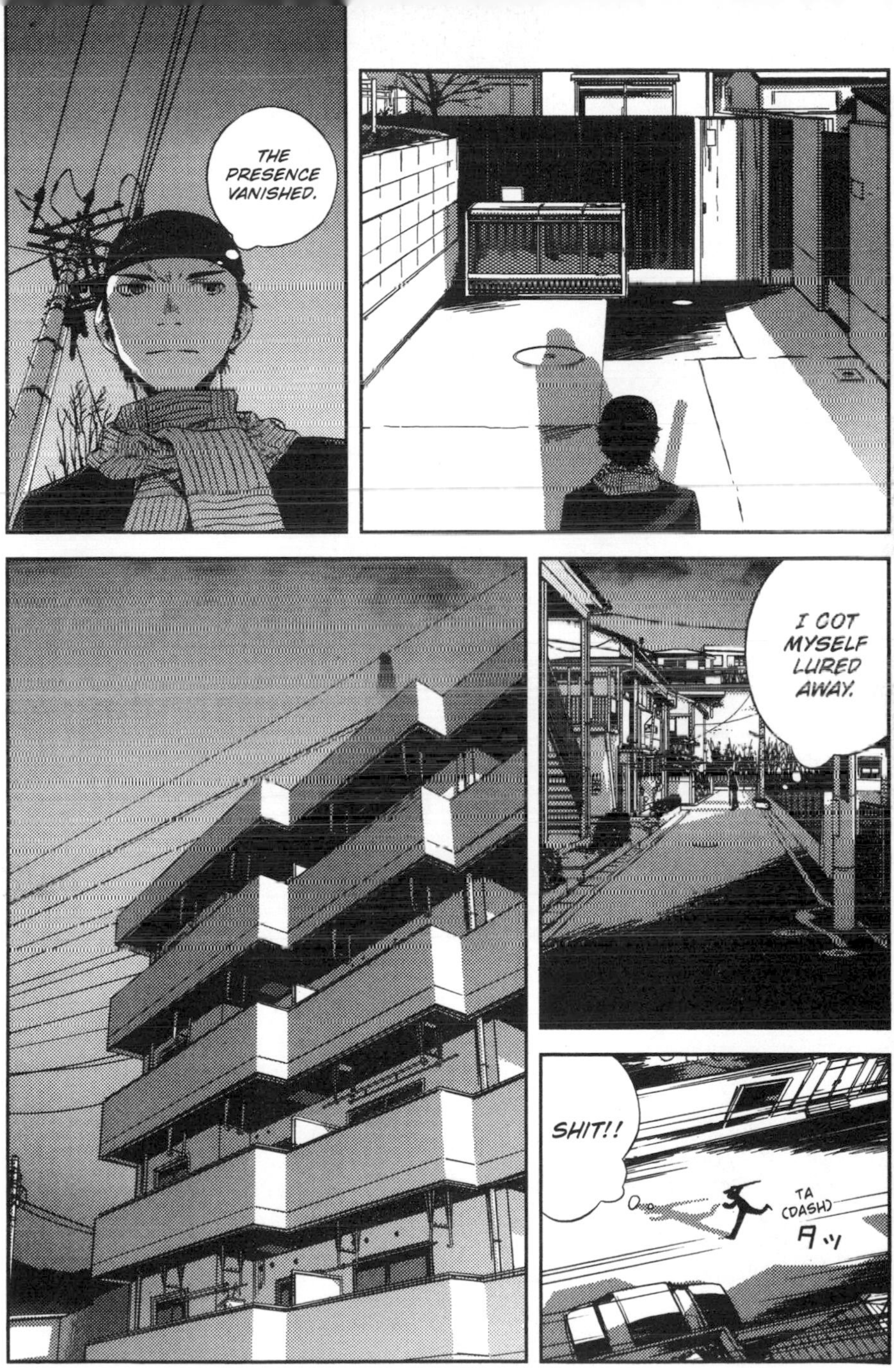
THE PRESENCE VANISHED.
I GOT MYSELF LURED AWAY.
SHIT!!
TA (DASH)
タッ

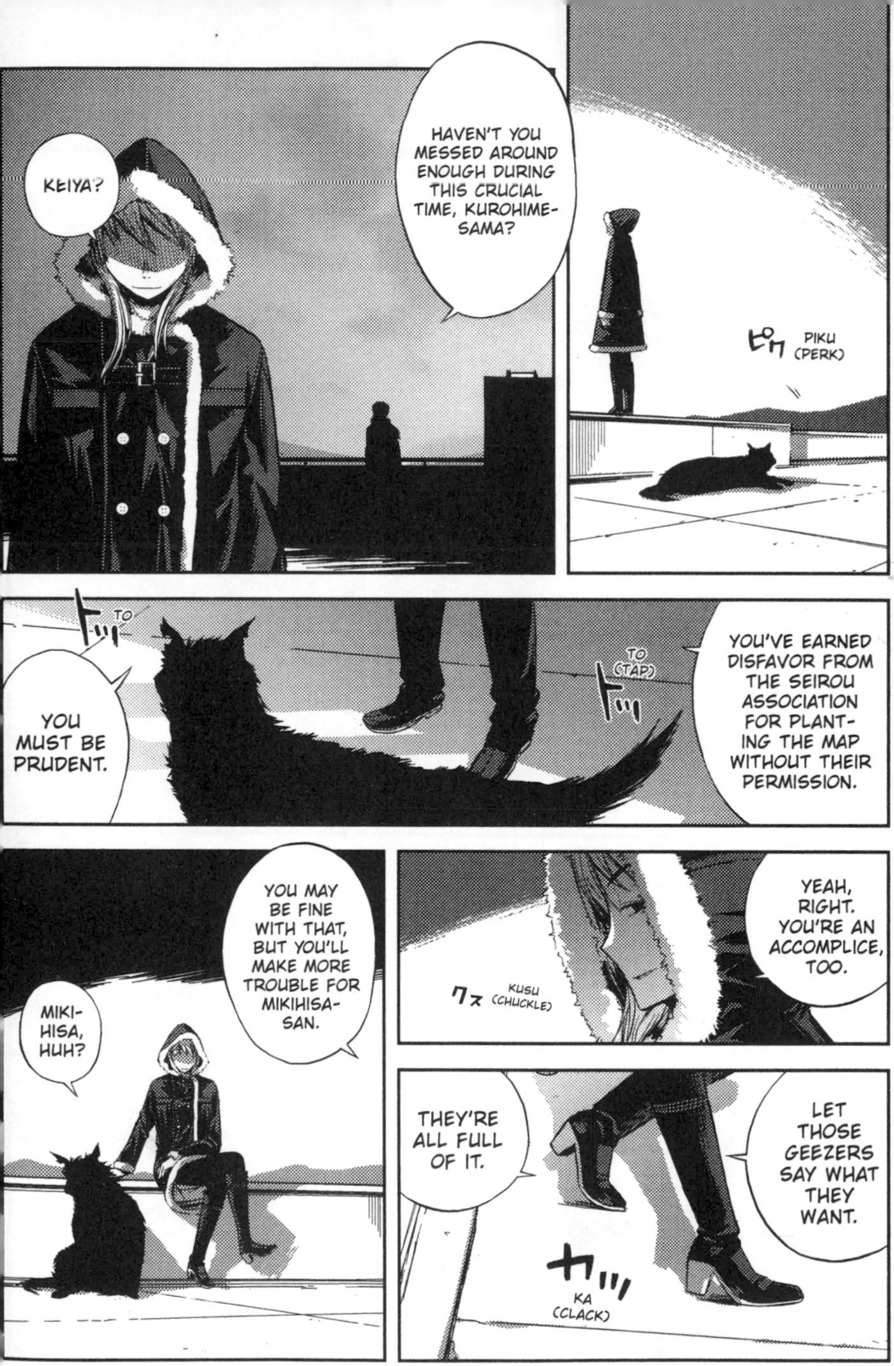
ピク PIKU (PERK)
HAVEN'T YOU MESSED AROUND ENOUGH DURING THIS CRUCIAL TIME, KUROHIME-SAMA?
KEIYA?
YOU'VE EARNED DISFAVOR FROM THE SEIROU ASSOCIATION FOR PLANTING THE MAP WITHOUT THEIR PERMISSION.
トッ TO (TAP)
トッ TO
YOU MUST BE PRUDENT.
YEAH, RIGHT. YOU'RE AN ACCOMPLICE, TOO.
クス KUSU (CHUCKLE)
LET THOSE GEEZERS SAY WHAT THEY WANT.
THEY'RE ALL FULL OF IT.
カッ KA (CLACK)
YOU MAY BE FINE WITH THAT, BUT YOU'LL MAKE MORE TROUBLE FOR MIKIHISA-SAN.
MIKI-HISA, HUH?

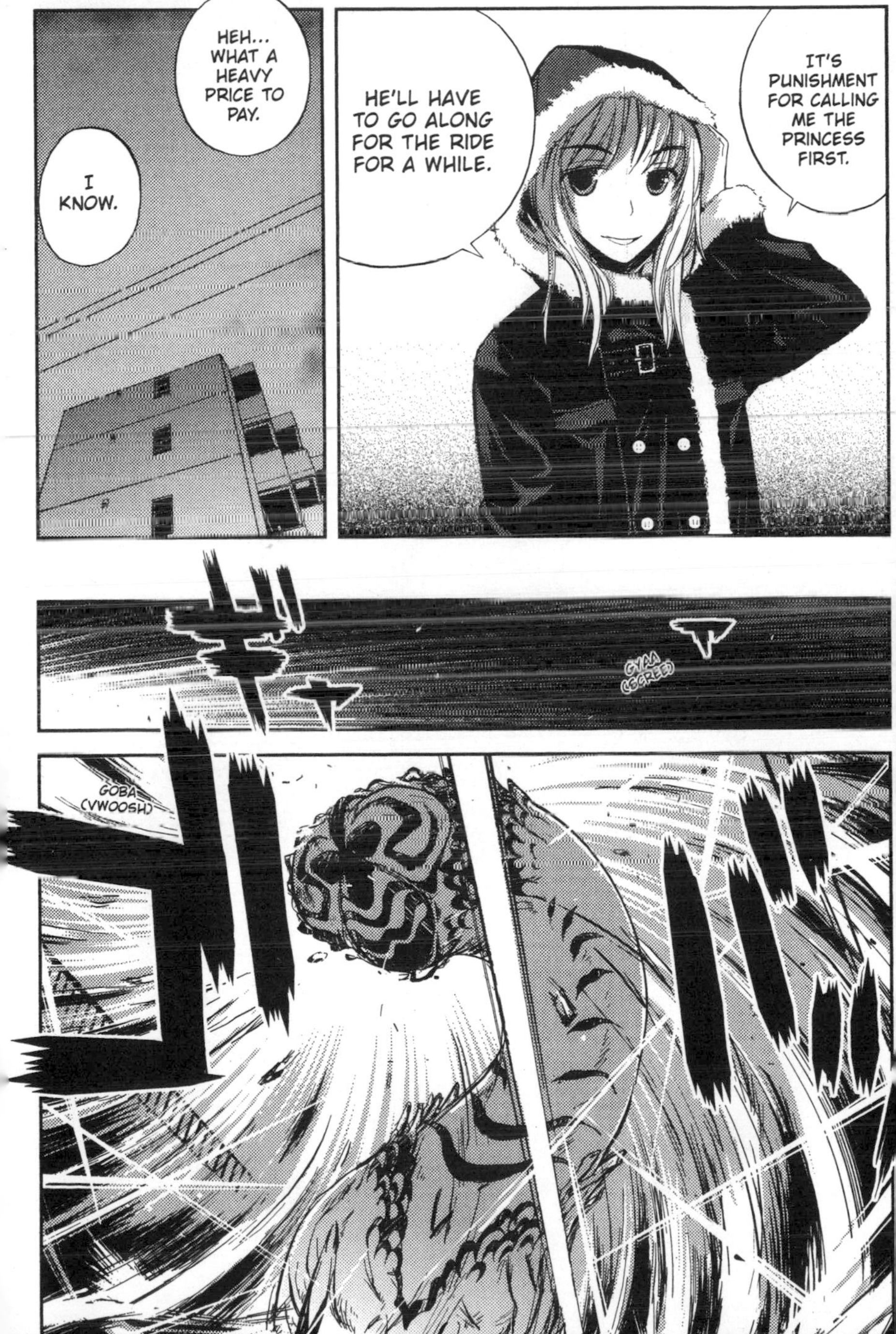
IT'S PUNISHMENT FOR CALLING ME THE PRINCESS FIRST.
HE'LL HAVE TO GO ALONG FOR THE RIDE FOR A WHILE.
HEH... WHAT A HEAVY PRICE TO PAY.
I KNOW.
GYAA (SCREE)
GOBA (VWOOSH)

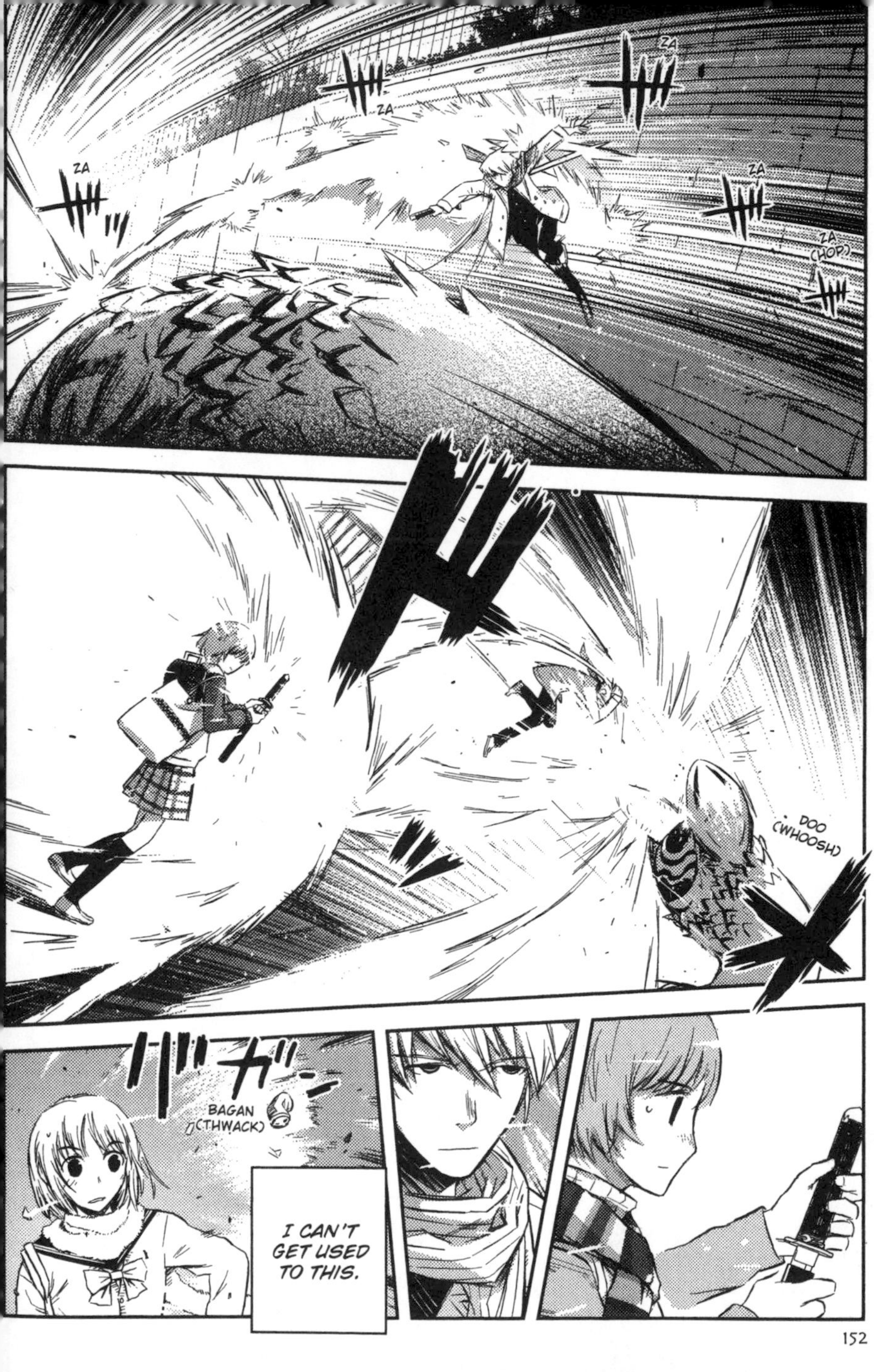
ZA
ZA
ZA (CHOP)
ZA
ZA
DOO (WHOOSH)
BAGAN (CTHWACK)
I CAN'T GET USED TO THIS.

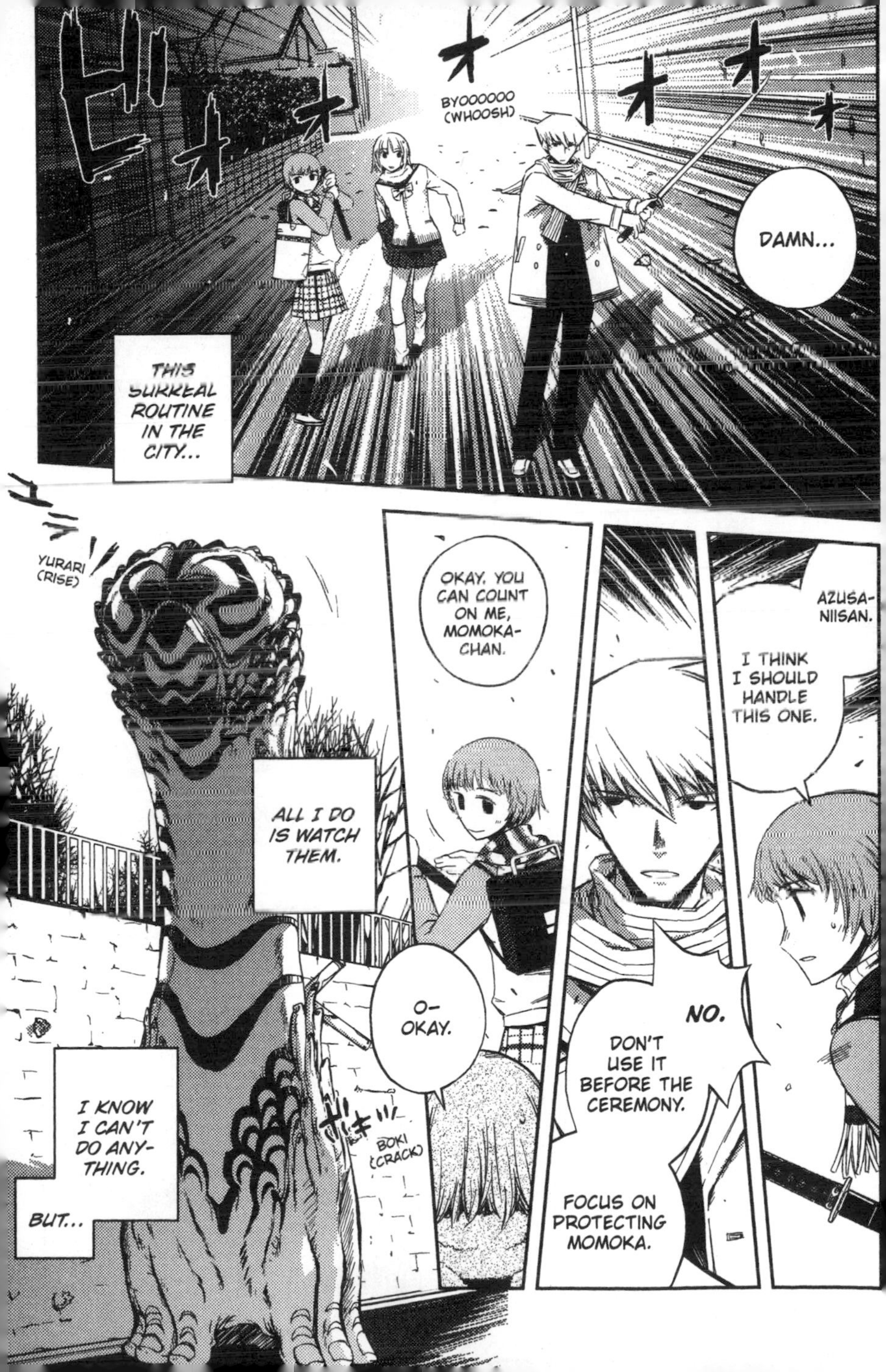
DAMN...
BYOOOOOO (WHOOSH)
THIS SURREAL ROUTINE IN THE CITY...
AZUSA-NIISAN.
I THINK I SHOULD HANDLE THIS ONE.
NO.
DON'T USE IT BEFORE THE CEREMONY.
FOCUS ON PROTECTING MOMOKA.
OKAY. YOU CAN COUNT ON ME, MOMOKA-CHAN.
O-OKAY.
YURARI (RISE)
ALL I DO IS WATCH THEM.
BOKI (CRACK)
I KNOW I CAN'T DO ANYTHING.
BUT...

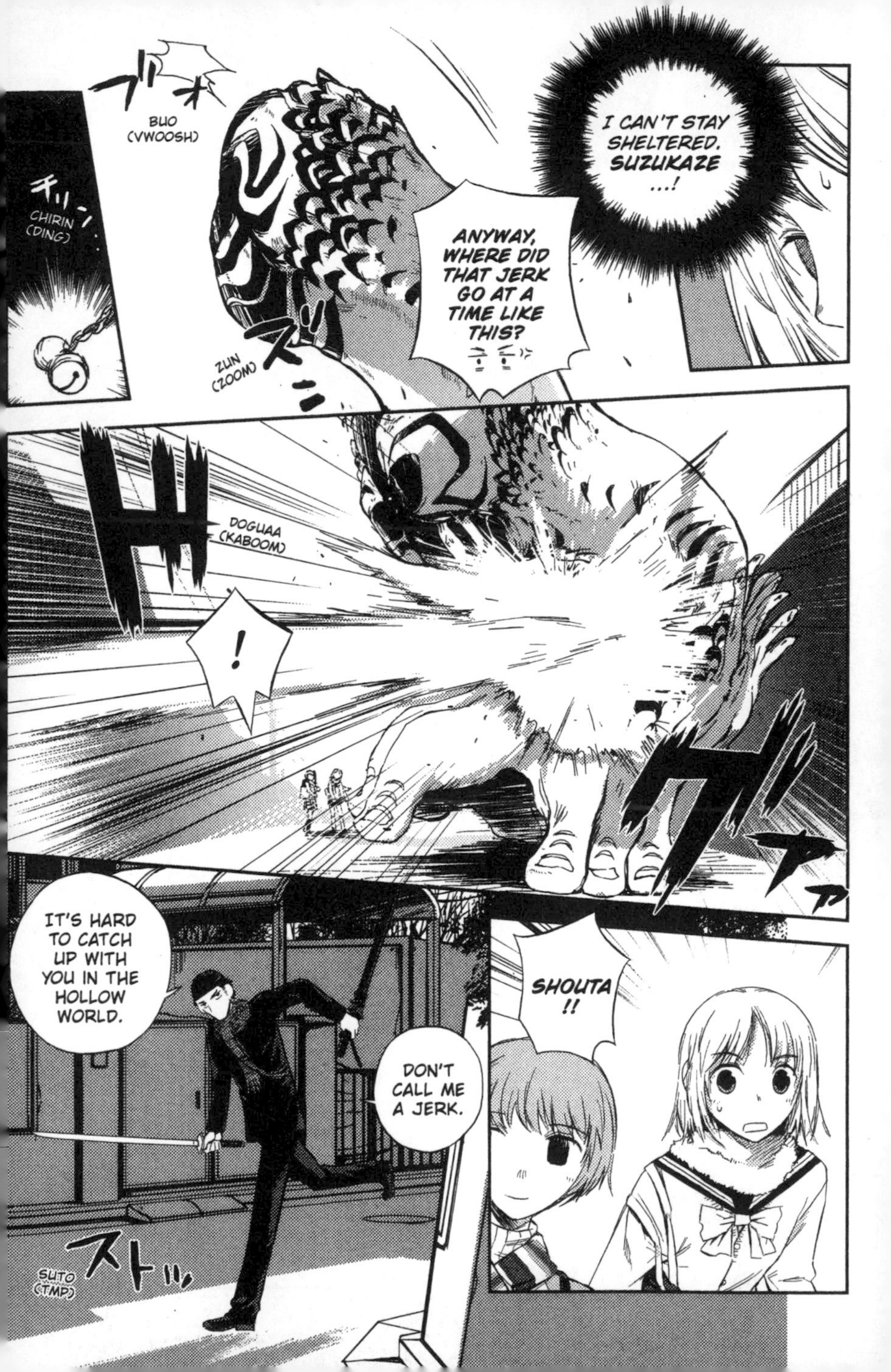

I CAN'T STAY SHELTERED. SUZUKAZE ...!
BUO (VWOOSH)
ANYWAY, WHERE DID THAT JERK GO AT A TIME LIKE THIS?
ZUN (ZOOM)
CHIRIN (DING)
DOGUAA (KABOOM)
!
SHOUTA !!
DON'T CALL ME A JERK.
IT'S HARD TO CATCH UP WITH YOU IN THE HOLLOW WORLD.
SUTO (TMP)

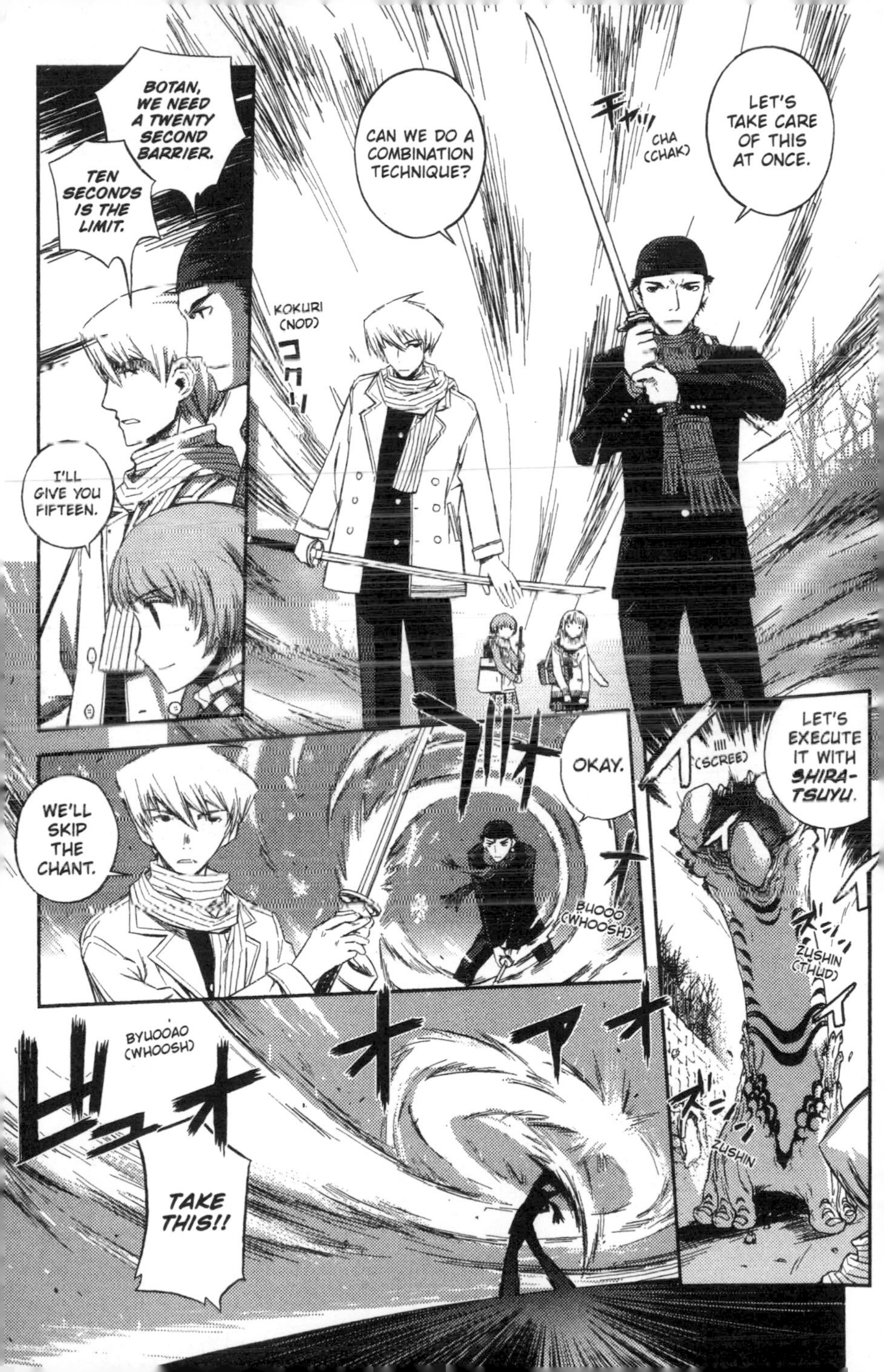
LET'S TAKE CARE OF THIS AT ONCE.
CHA (CHAK)
CAN WE DO A COMBINATION TECHNIQUE?
KOKURI (NOD)
BOTAN, WE NEED A TWENTY SECOND BARRIER.
TEN SECONDS IS THE LIMIT.
I'LL GIVE YOU FIFTEEN.
LET'S EXECUTE IT WITH SHIRA-TSUYU.
IIII (SCREE)
ZUSHIN (THUD)
ZUSHIN
OKAY.
BHOOO (WHOOSH)
WE'LL SKIP THE CHANT.
BYUOOAO (WHOOSH)
TAKE THIS!!

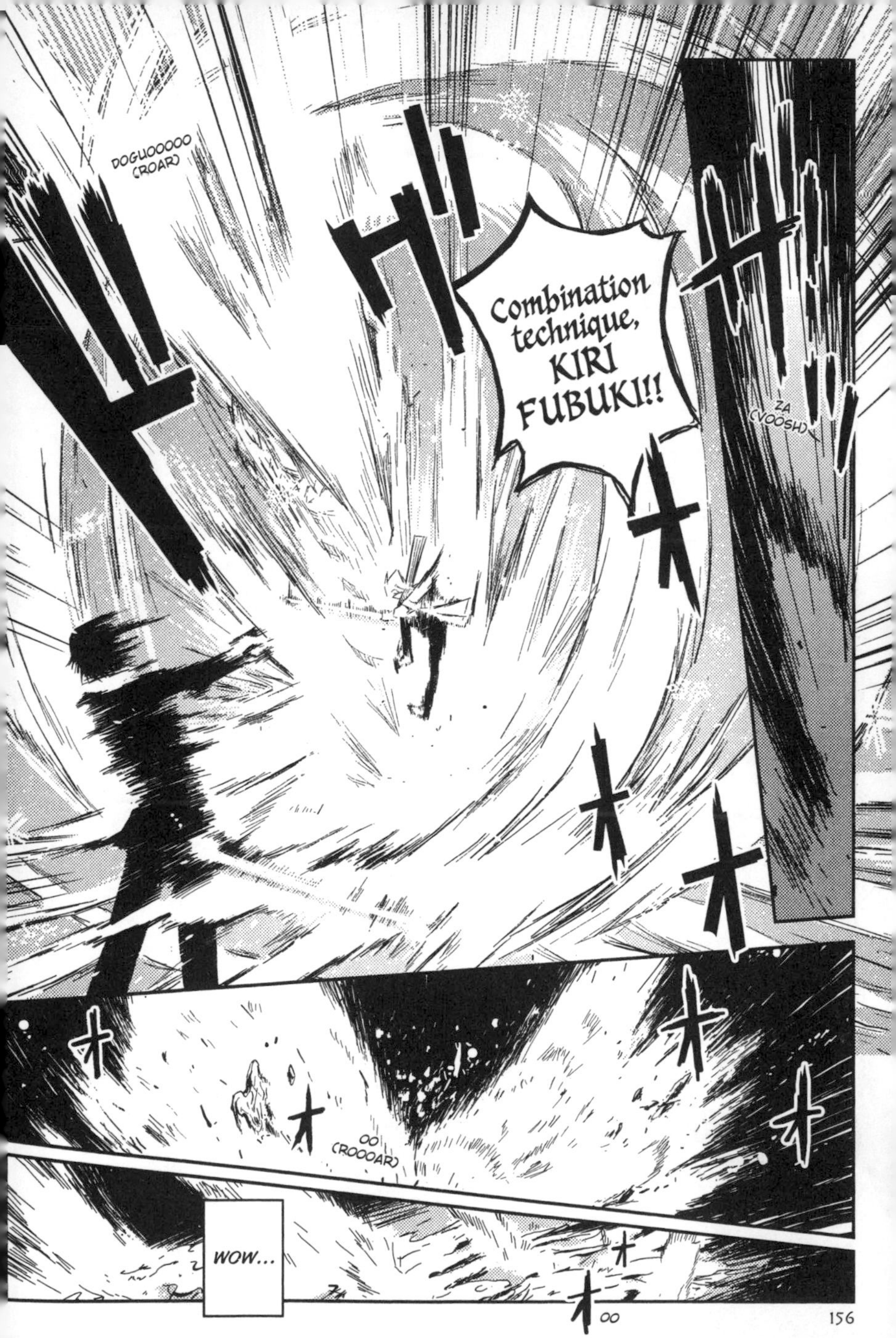
ZA (VOOSH)
Combination technique, KIRI FUBUKI!!
DOGUOOOOO (ROAR)
OO (ROOOAR)
WOW...
OO

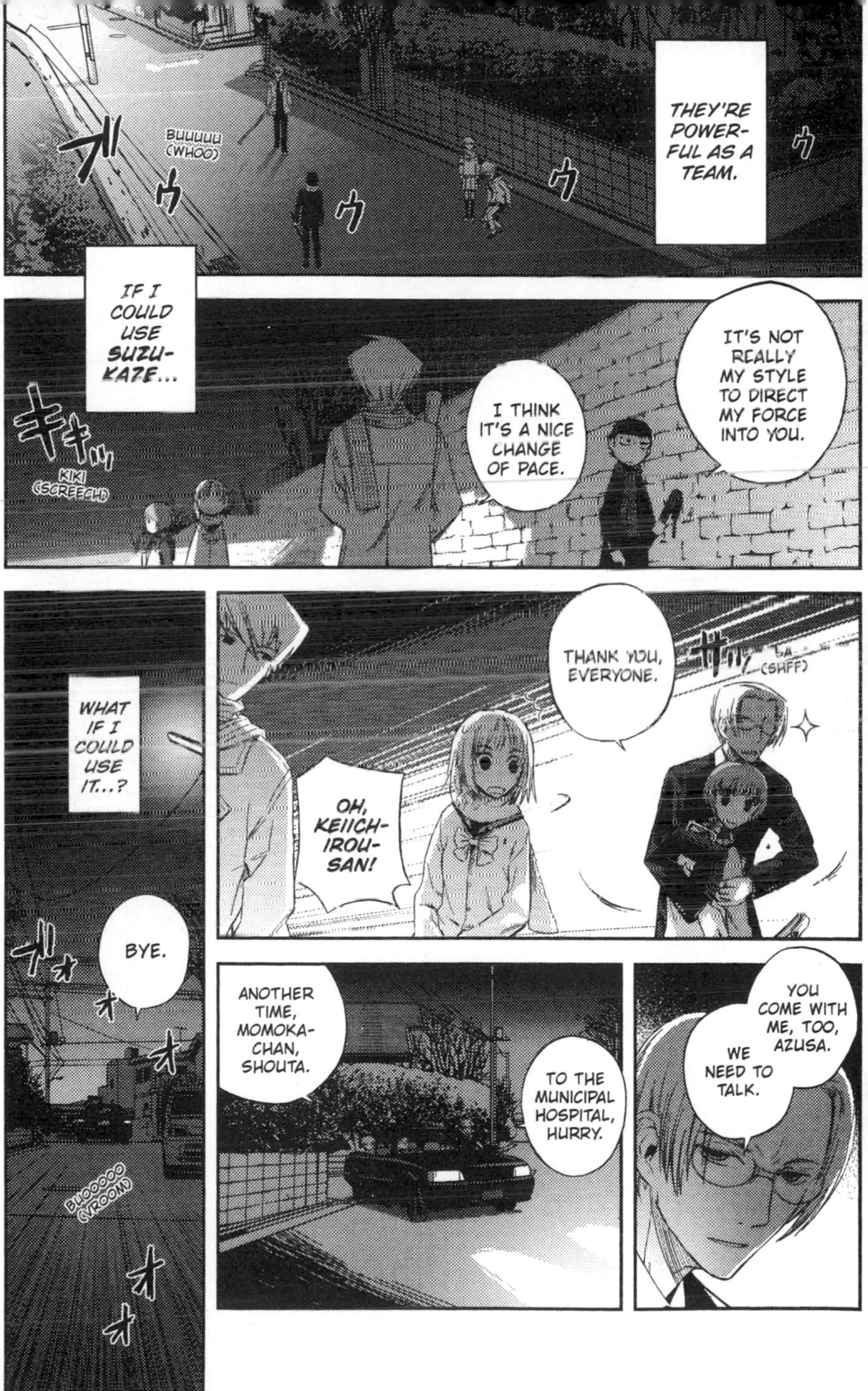
THEY'RE POWERFUL AS A TEAM.
BUUUUU (WHOO)
IT'S NOT REALLY MY STYLE TO DIRECT MY FORCE INTO YOU.
I THINK IT'S A NICE CHANGE OF PACE.
IF I COULD USE SUZUKAZE...
KIKI (SCREECH)
THANK YOU, EVERYONE.
SA (SHFF)
OH, KEIICHIROU-SAN!
YOU COME WITH ME, TOO, AZUSA.
WE NEED TO TALK.
TO THE MUNICIPAL HOSPITAL, HURRY.
ANOTHER TIME, MOMOKA-CHAN, SHOUTA.
WHAT IF I COULD USE IT...?
BYE.
BUOOOOO (VROOM)

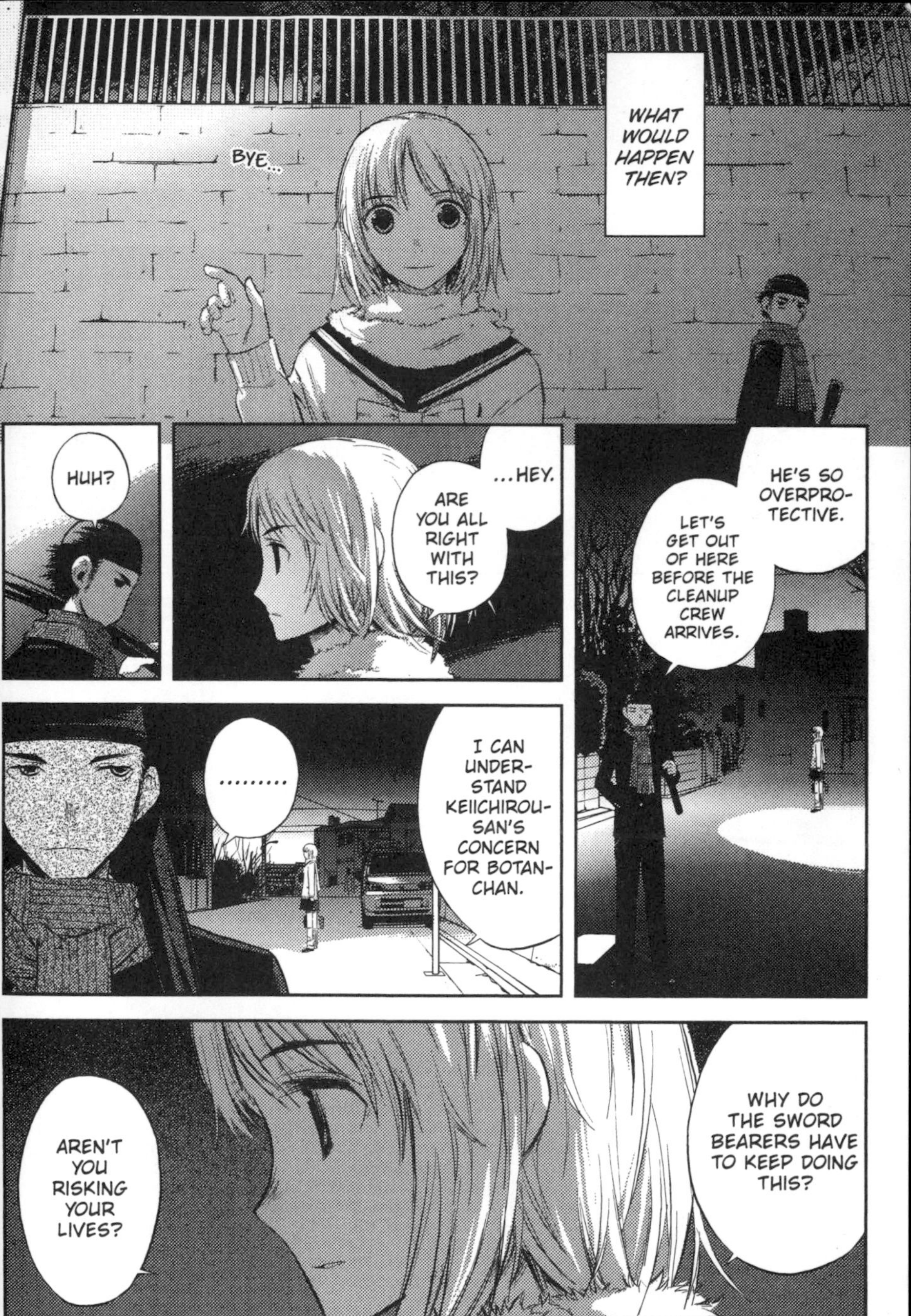
WHAT WOULD HAPPEN THEN?
BYE...
HE'S SO OVERPROTECTIVE.
LET'S GET OUT OF HERE BEFORE THE CLEANUP CREW ARRIVES.
...HEY.
ARE YOU ALL RIGHT WITH THIS?
HUH?
I CAN UNDERSTAND KEIICHIROU-SAN'S CONCERN FOR BOTAN-CHAN.
....
WHY DO THE SWORD BEARERS HAVE TO KEEP DOING THIS?
AREN'T YOU RISKING YOUR LIVES?

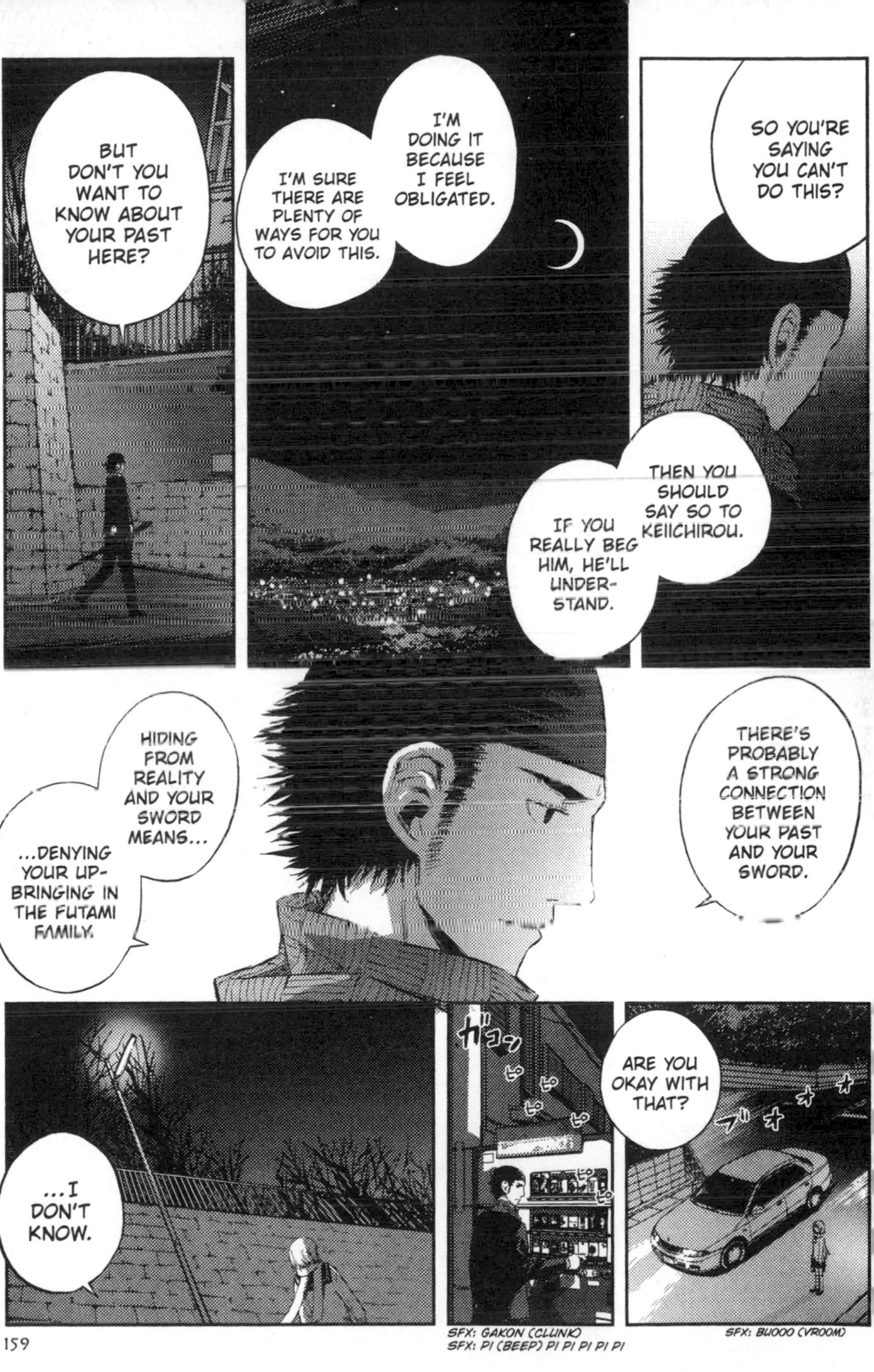
SO YOU'RE SAYING YOU CAN'T DO THIS?
THEN YOU SHOULD SAY SO TO KEIICHIROU.
IF YOU REALLY BEG HIM, HE'LL UNDER-STAND.
I'M DOING IT BECAUSE I FEEL OBLIGATED.
I'M SURE THERE ARE PLENTY OF WAYS FOR YOU TO AVOID THIS.
BUT DON'T YOU WANT TO KNOW ABOUT YOUR PAST HERE?
THERE'S PROBABLY A STRONG CONNECTION BETWEEN YOUR PAST AND YOUR SWORD.
HIDING FROM REALITY AND YOUR SWORD MEANS...
...DENYING YOUR UP-BRINGING IN THE FUTAMI FAMILY.
ARE YOU OKAY WITH THAT?
...I DON'T KNOW.

SFX: BUOOO (VROOM)

SFX: GAKON (CLUNK)
SFX: PI (BEEP) PI PI PI PI PI

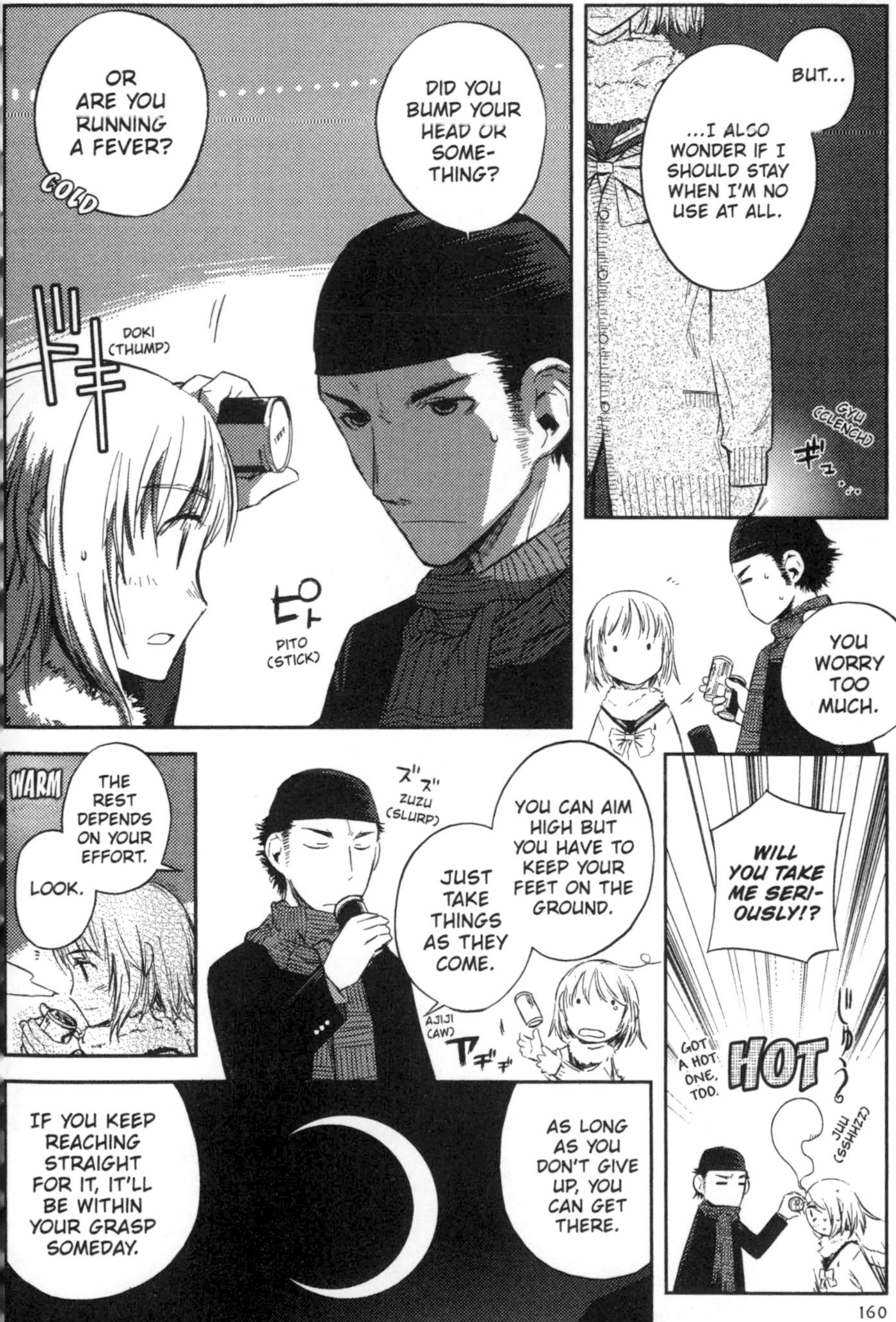
BUT...
...I ALSO WONDER IF I SHOULD STAY WHEN I'M NO USE AT ALL.
GYU (CLENCH)
DID YOU BUMP YOUR HEAD OR SOME-THING?
OR ARE YOU RUNNING A FEVER?
COLD
DOKI (THUMP)
PITO (STICK)
YOU WORRY TOO MUCH.
WILL YOU TAKE ME SERI-OUSLY!?
HOT
GOT A HOT ONE, TOO.
JUU (SSHHZZ)
ZUZU (SLURP)
YOU CAN AIM HIGH BUT YOU HAVE TO KEEP YOUR FEET ON THE GROUND.
JUST TAKE THINGS AS THEY COME.
AJIJI (AW)
WARM
THE REST DEPENDS ON YOUR EFFORT.
LOOK.
AS LONG AS YOU DON'T GIVE UP, YOU CAN GET THERE.
IF YOU KEEP REACHING STRAIGHT FOR IT, IT'LL BE WITHIN YOUR GRASP SOMEDAY.

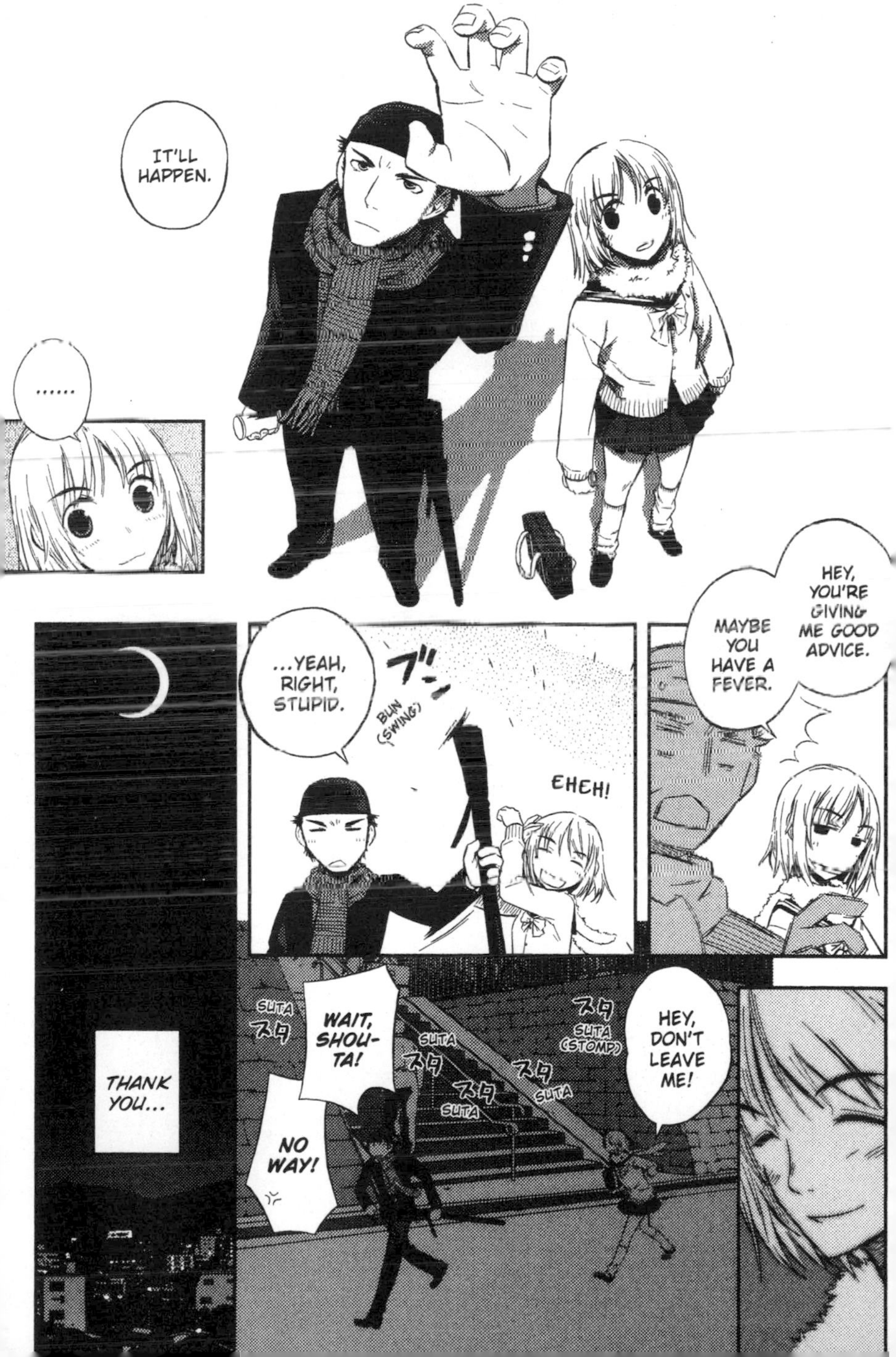
IT'LL HAPPEN.
......
HEY, YOU'RE GIVING ME GOOD ADVICE.
MAYBE YOU HAVE A FEVER.
...YEAH, RIGHT, STUPID.
ブン
BUN (SWING)
EHEH!
HEY, DON'T LEAVE ME!
スタ
SUTA (STOMP)
スタ
SUTA
スタ
SUTA
スタ
SUTA
WAIT, SHOU-TA!
スタ
SUTA
NO WAY!
THANK YOU...

THE KODAK MOMENT

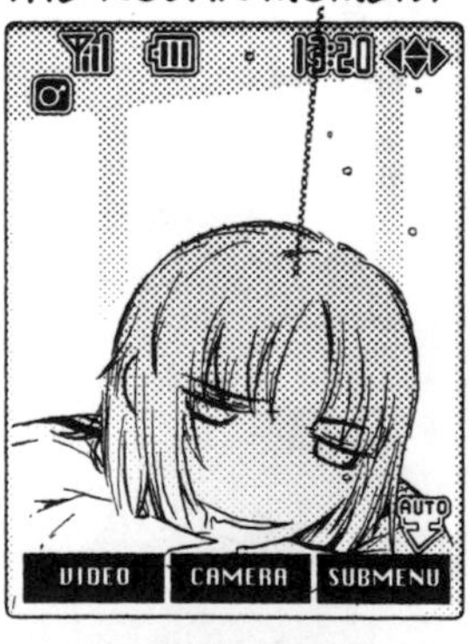
GU
(SNORE)
13:20
AUTO
VIDEO
CAMERA
SUBMENU

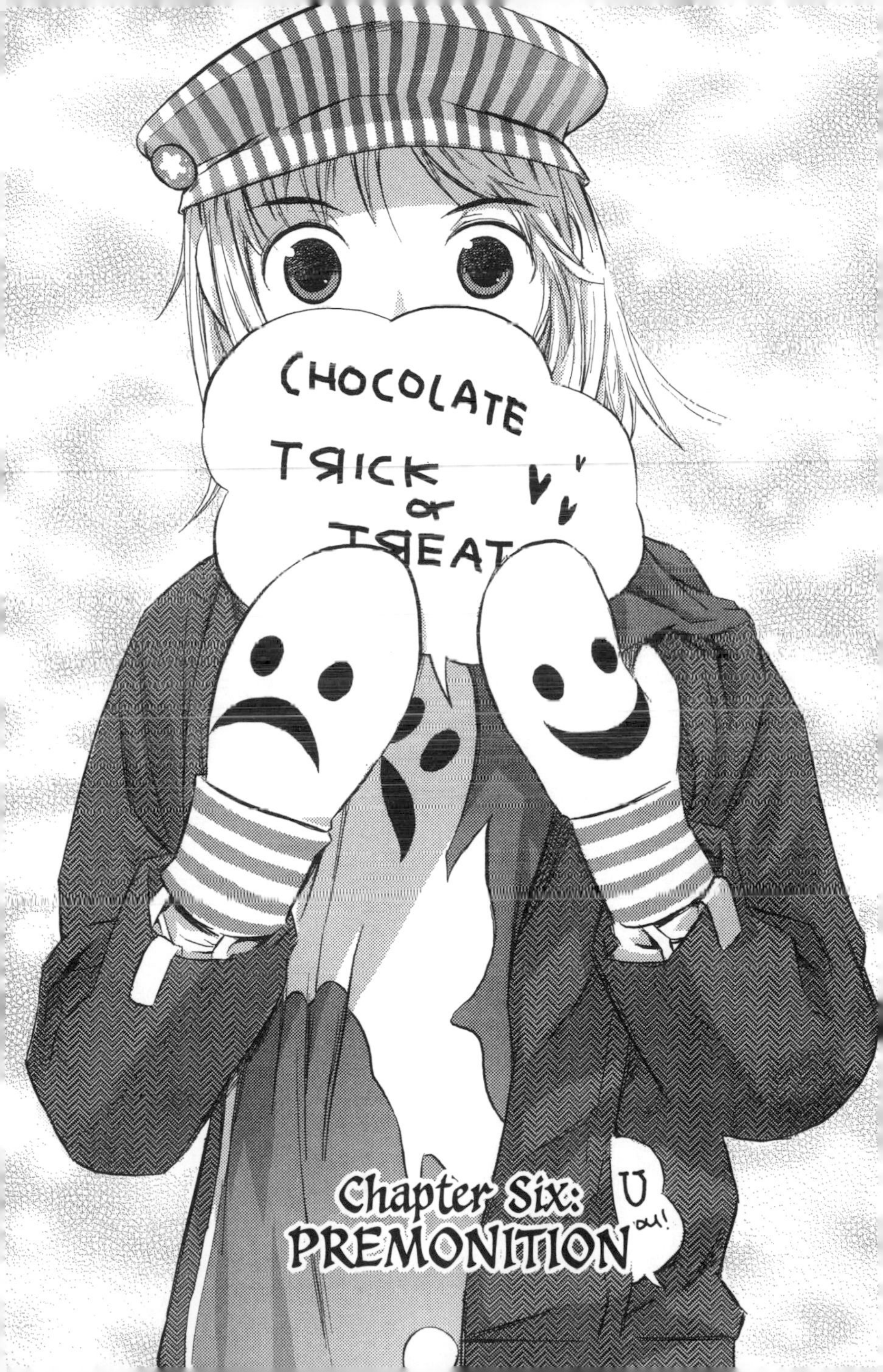
CHOCOLATE
TRICK
or
TREAT
Chapter Six:
PREMONITION

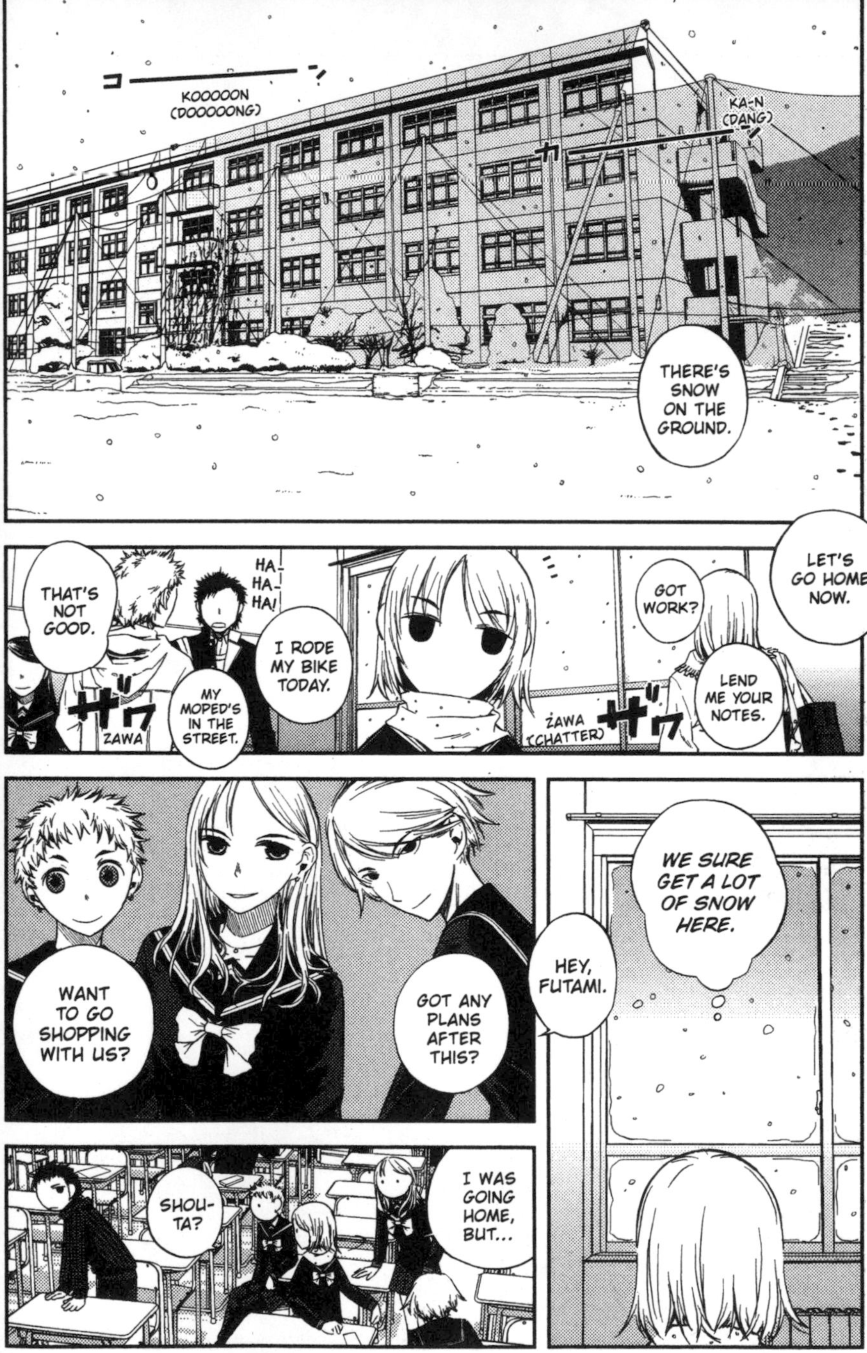
KA-N (DANG)
KOOOOON (DOOOOONG)
THERE'S SNOW ON THE GROUND.
LET'S GO HOME NOW.
GOT WORK?
LEND ME YOUR NOTES.
ZAWA (CHATTER)
HA-HA-HA!
I RODE MY BIKE TODAY.
MY MOPED'S IN THE STREET.
THAT'S NOT GOOD.
ZAWA
WE SURE GET A LOT OF SNOW HERE.
HEY, FUTAMI.
GOT ANY PLANS AFTER THIS?
WANT TO GO SHOPPING WITH US?
I WAS GOING HOME, BUT...
SHOU-TA?

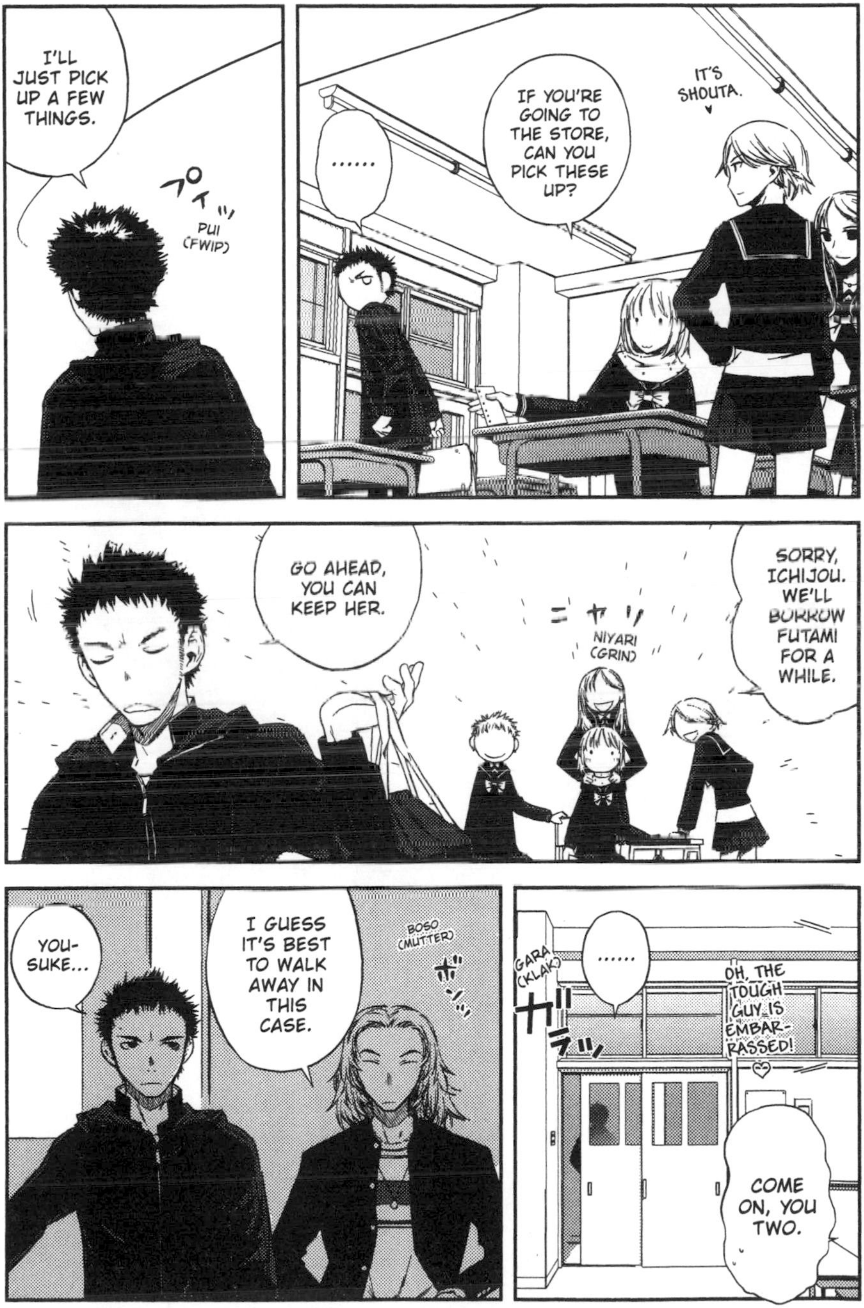
IT'S SHOUTA.
IF YOU'RE GOING TO THE STORE, CAN YOU PICK THESE UP?
......
I'LL JUST PICK UP A FEW THINGS.
PUI (FWIP)
SORRY, ICHIJOU. WE'LL BORROW FUTAMI FOR A WHILE.
NIYARI (GRIN)
GO AHEAD, YOU CAN KEEP HER.
OH, THE TOUGH GUY IS EMBARRASSED!
......
GARA (KLAK)
COME ON, YOU TWO.
BOSO (MUTTER)
I GUESS IT'S BEST TO WALK AWAY IN THIS CASE.
YOU-SUKE...

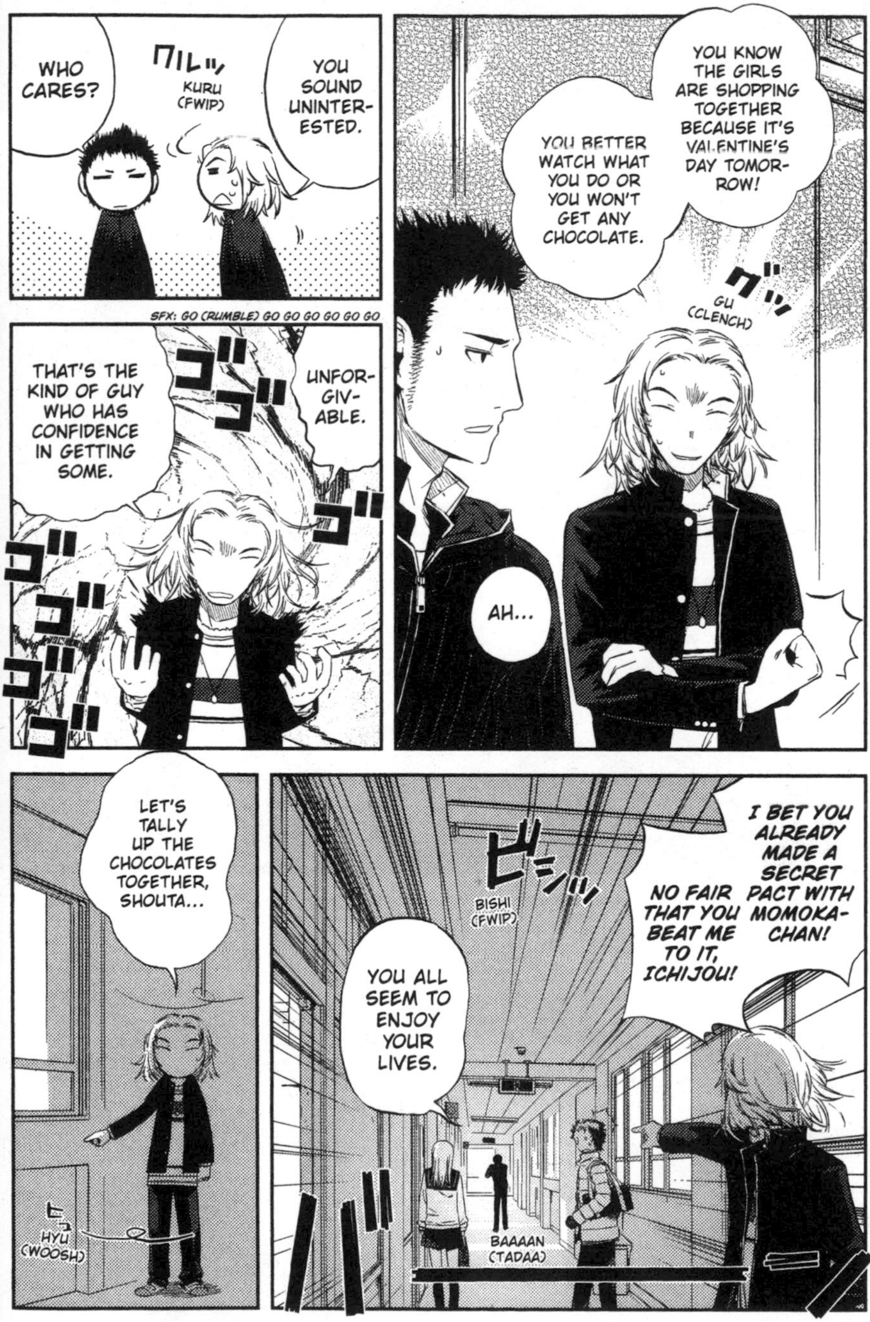
YOU KNOW THE GIRLS ARE SHOPPING TOGETHER BECAUSE IT'S VALENTINE'S DAY TOMOR-ROW!
YOU BETTER WATCH WHAT YOU DO OR YOU WON'T GET ANY CHOCOLATE.
GU (CLENCH)
AH...
YOU SOUND UNINTER-ESTED.
KURU (FWIP)
WHO CARES?
SFX: GO (RUMBLE) GO GO GO GO GO GO
UNFOR-GIV-ABLE.
THAT'S THE KIND OF GUY WHO HAS CONFIDENCE IN GETTING SOME.
I BET YOU ALREADY MADE A SECRET PACT WITH MOMOKA-CHAN!
NO FAIR THAT YOU BEAT ME TO IT, ICHIJOU!
BISHI (FWIP)
YOU ALL SEEM TO ENJOY YOUR LIVES.
BAAAAN (TADAA)
LET'S TALLY UP THE CHOCOLATES TOGETHER, SHOUTA...
HYU (WOOSH)

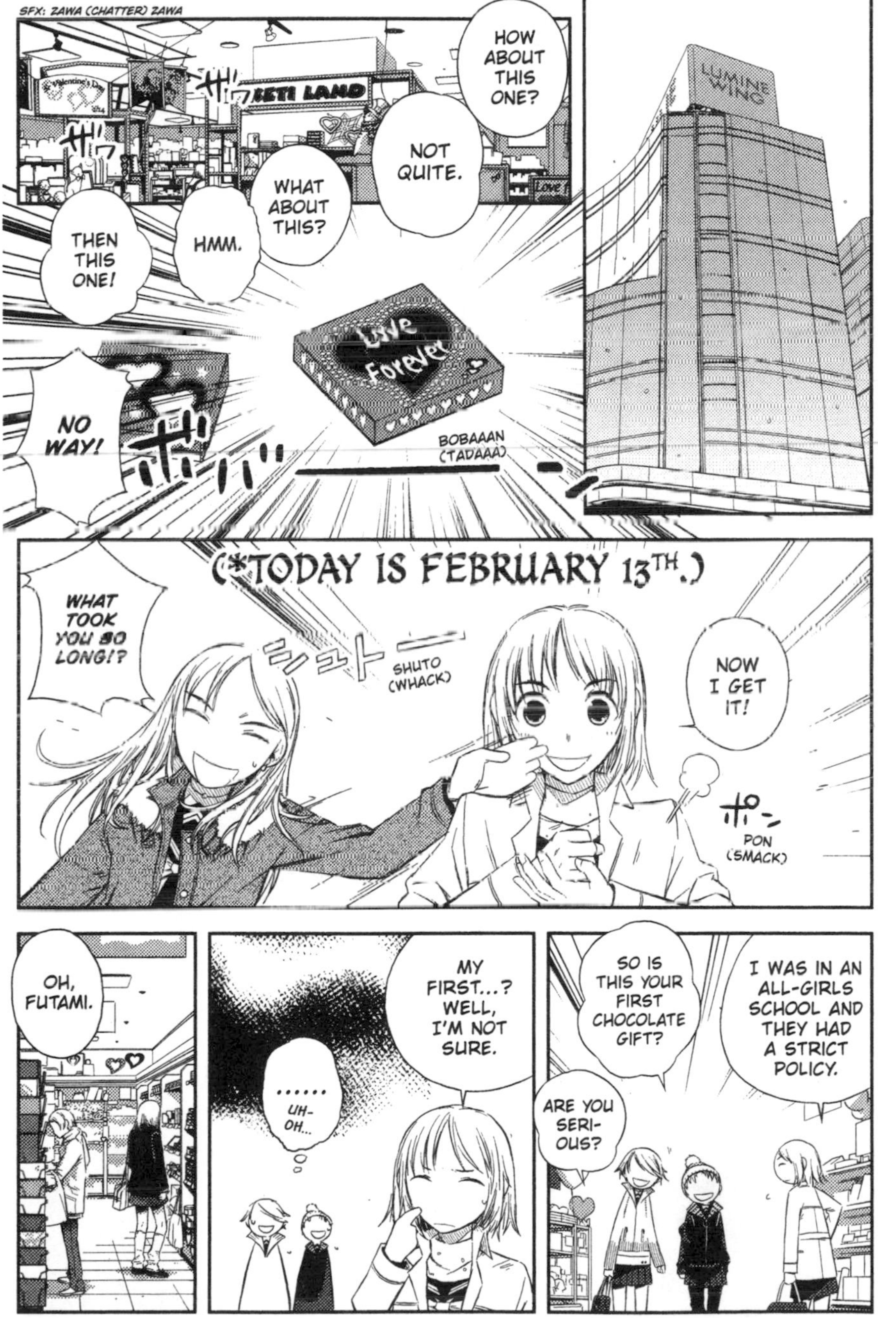
LUMINE WING
SFX: ZAWA (CHATTER) ZAWA
HOW ABOUT THIS ONE?
NOT QUITE.
WHAT ABOUT THIS?
HMM.
THEN THIS ONE!
Love Forever
BOBAAAN (TADAAA)
NO WAY!
(*TODAY IS FEBRUARY 13TH.)
NOW I GET IT!
PON (SMACK)
SHUTO (WHACK)
WHAT TOOK YOU SO LONG!?
I WAS IN AN ALL-GIRLS SCHOOL AND THEY HAD A STRICT POLICY.
SO IS THIS YOUR FIRST CHOCOLATE GIFT?
ARE YOU SERIOUS?
MY FIRST...? WELL, I'M NOT SURE.
.... UH-OH...
OH, FUTAMI.

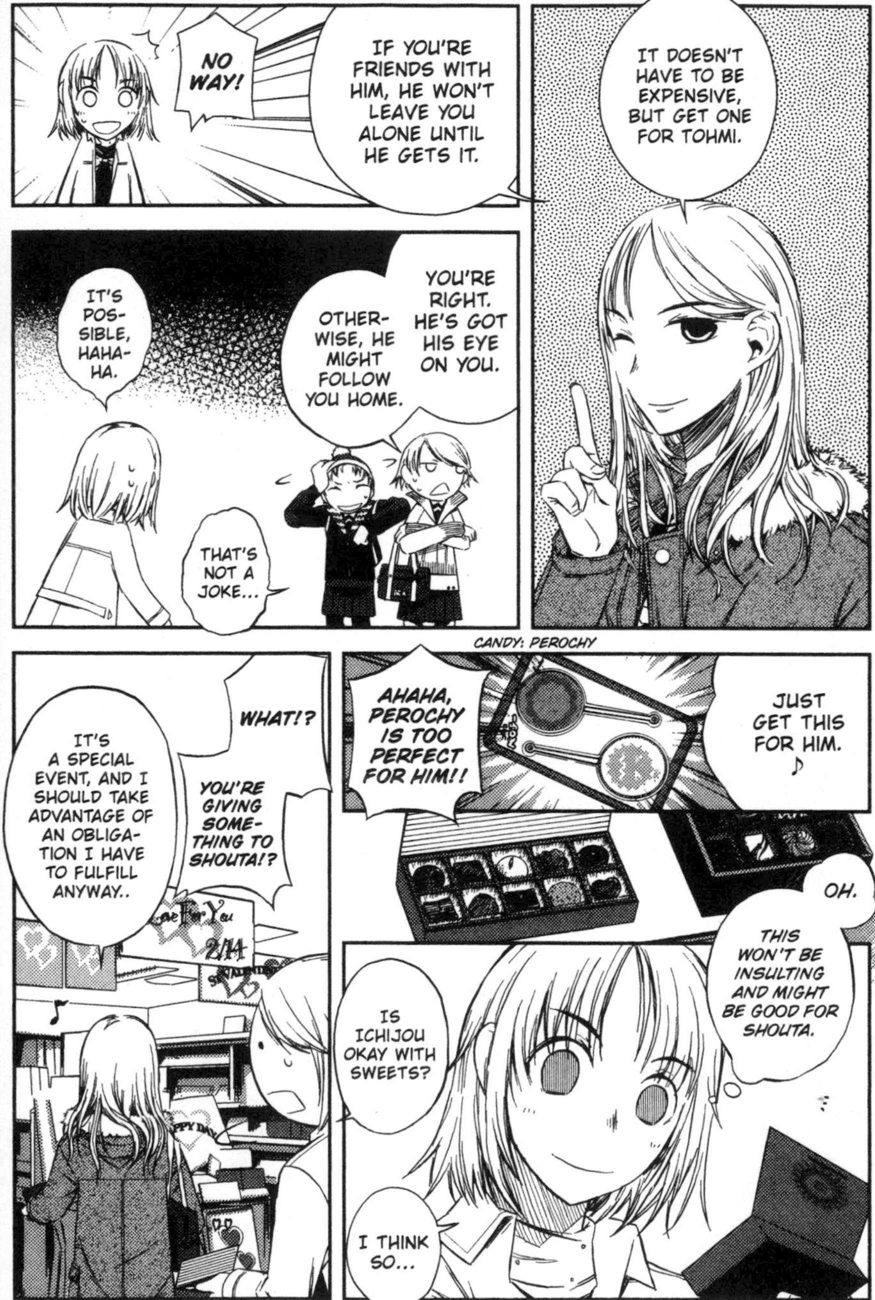
IT DOESN'T HAVE TO BE EXPENSIVE, BUT GET ONE FOR TOHMI.
IF YOU'RE FRIENDS WITH HIM, HE WON'T LEAVE YOU ALONE UNTIL HE GETS IT.
NO WAY!
YOU'RE RIGHT. HE'S GOT HIS EYE ON YOU.
OTHER-WISE, HE MIGHT FOLLOW YOU HOME.
IT'S POS-SIBLE, HAHA-HA.
THAT'S NOT A JOKE...
CANDY: PEROCHY
JUST GET THIS FOR HIM. ♪
AHAHA, PEROCHY IS TOO PERFECT FOR HIM!!
OH.
THIS WON'T BE INSULTING AND MIGHT BE GOOD FOR SHOUTA.
IS ICHIJOU OKAY WITH SWEETS?
I THINK SO...
WHAT!?
YOU'RE GIVING SOME-THING TO SHOUTA!?
IT'S A SPECIAL EVENT, AND I SHOULD TAKE ADVANTAGE OF AN OBLIGA-TION I HAVE TO FULFILL ANYWAY..
2/14

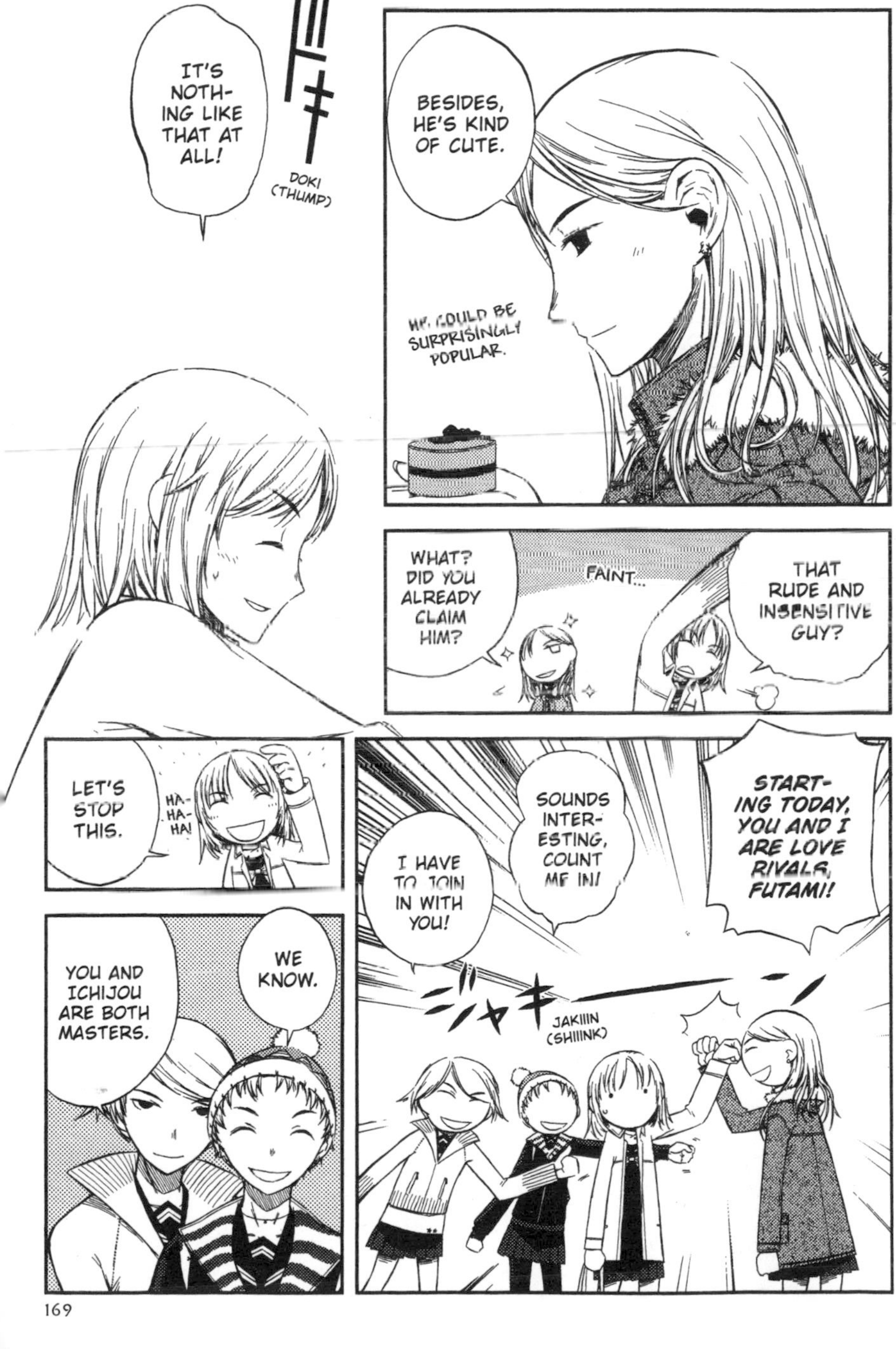
BESIDES, HE'S KIND OF CUTE.
HE COULD BE SURPRISINGLY POPULAR.
IT'S NOTHING LIKE THAT AT ALL!
DOKI (THUMP)
THAT RUDE AND INSENSITIVE GUY?
FAINT...
WHAT? DID YOU ALREADY CLAIM HIM?
STARTING TODAY, YOU AND I ARE LOVE RIVALS, FUTAMI!
SOUNDS INTERESTING, COUNT ME IN!
I HAVE TO JOIN IN WITH YOU!
JAKIIIN (SHIIINK)
LET'S STOP THIS.
HA-HA-HA!
WE KNOW.
YOU AND ICHIJOU ARE BOTH MASTERS.

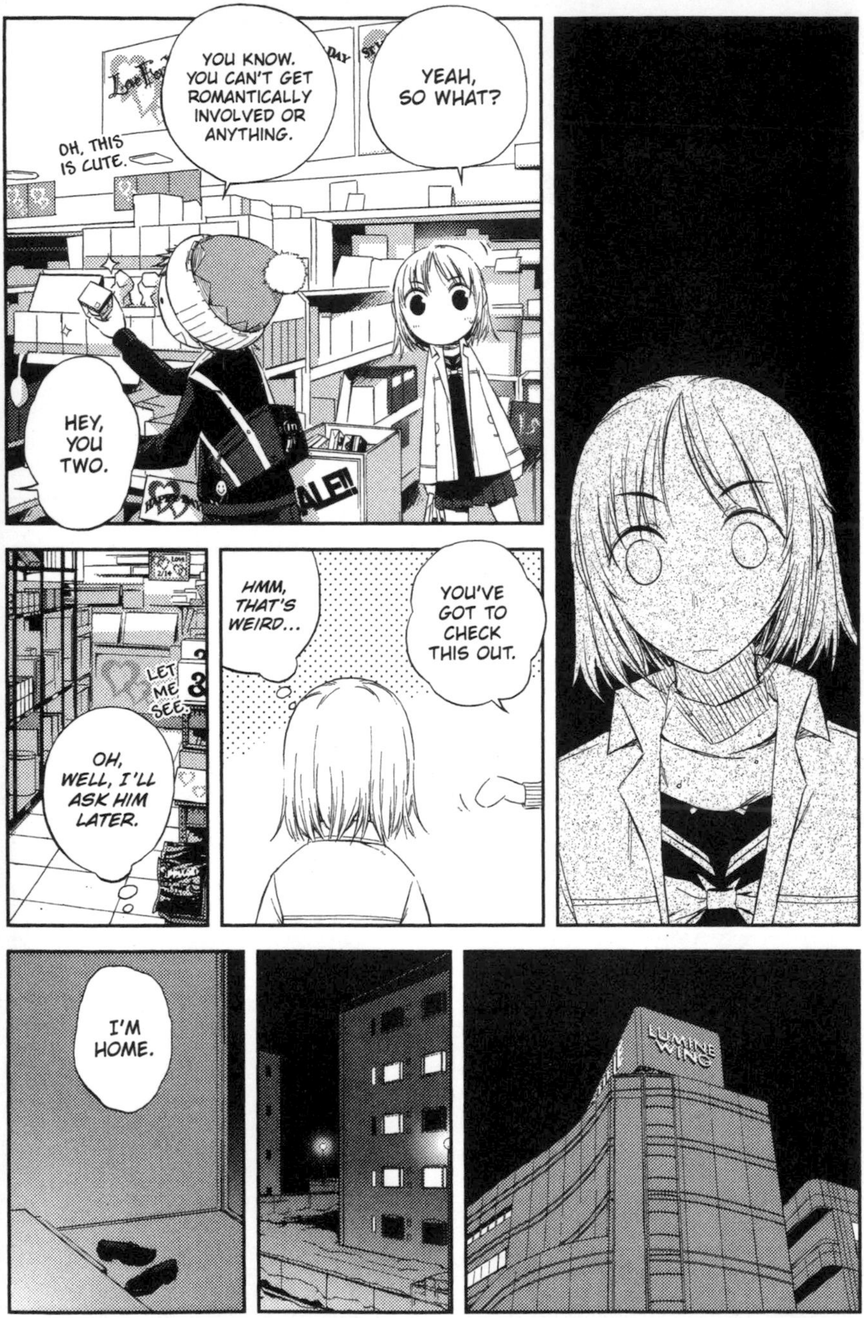
YEAH, SO WHAT?
YOU KNOW. YOU CAN'T GET ROMANTICALLY INVOLVED OR ANYTHING.
OH, THIS IS CUTE.
HEY, YOU TWO.
YOU'VE GOT TO CHECK THIS OUT.
HMM, THAT'S WEIRD...
LET ME SEE.
OH, WELL, I'LL ASK HIM LATER.
LUMINE WING
I'M HOME.

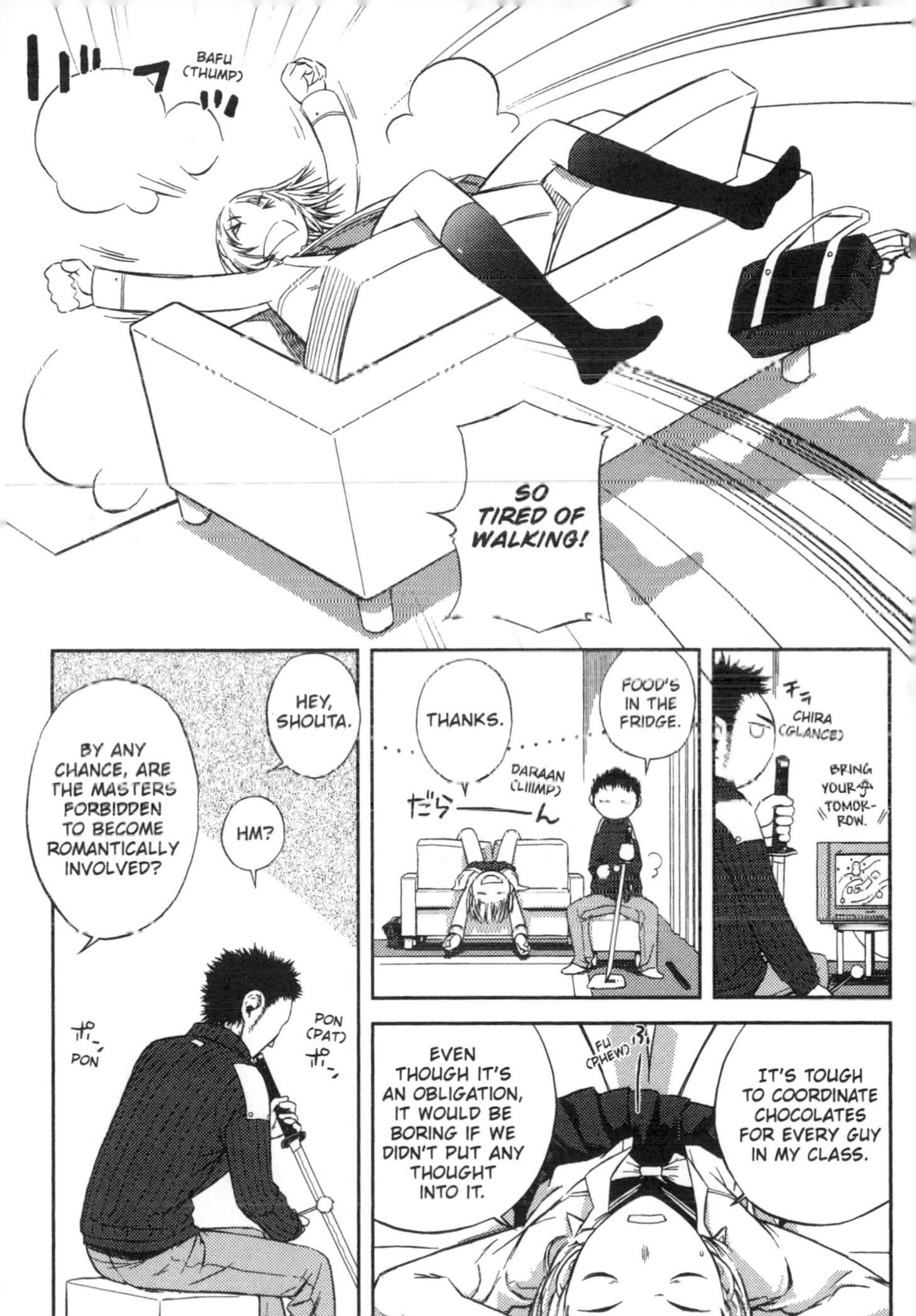
BAFU (THUMP)
SO TIRED OF WALKING!
CHIRA (GLANCE)
BRING YOUR TOMOR-ROW.
FOOD'S IN THE FRIDGE.
THANKS.
DARAAN (LIIIMP)
IT'S TOUGH TO COORDINATE CHOCOLATES FOR EVERY GUY IN MY CLASS.
FU (PHEW)
EVEN THOUGH IT'S AN OBLIGATION, IT WOULD BE BORING IF WE DIDN'T PUT ANY THOUGHT INTO IT.
HEY, SHOUTA.
HM?
BY ANY CHANCE, ARE THE MASTERS FORBIDDEN TO BECOME ROMANTICALLY INVOLVED?
PON (PAT)
PON

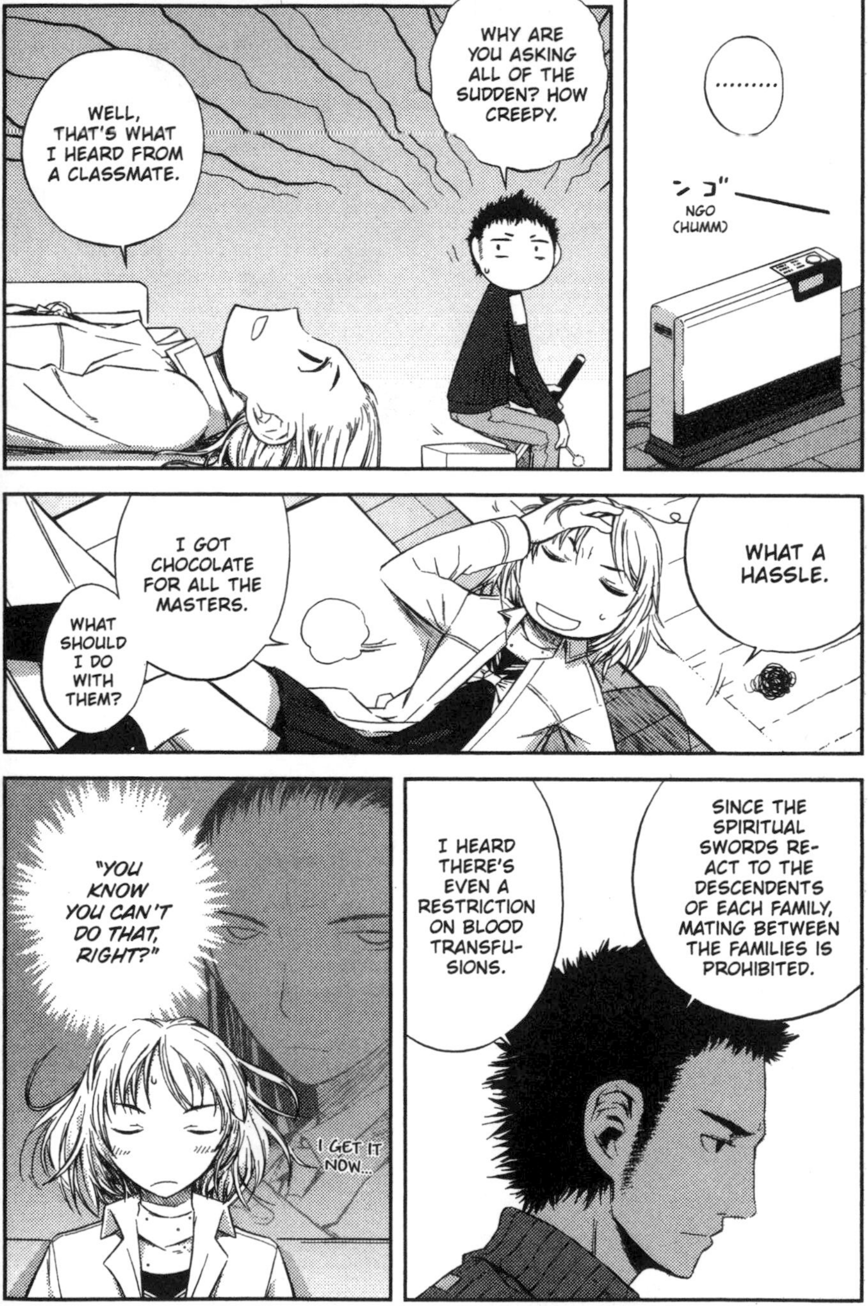

....
ンゴー
NGO (HUMM)
WHY ARE YOU ASKING ALL OF THE SUDDEN? HOW CREEPY.
WELL, THAT'S WHAT I HEARD FROM A CLASSMATE.
WHAT A HASSLE.
I GOT CHOCOLATE FOR ALL THE MASTERS.
WHAT SHOULD I DO WITH THEM?
SINCE THE SPIRITUAL SWORDS RE-ACT TO THE DESCENDENTS OF EACH FAMILY, MATING BETWEEN THE FAMILIES IS PROHIBITED.
I HEARD THERE'S EVEN A RESTRICTION ON BLOOD TRANSFU-SIONS.
"YOU KNOW YOU CAN'T DO THAT, RIGHT?"
I GET IT NOW...

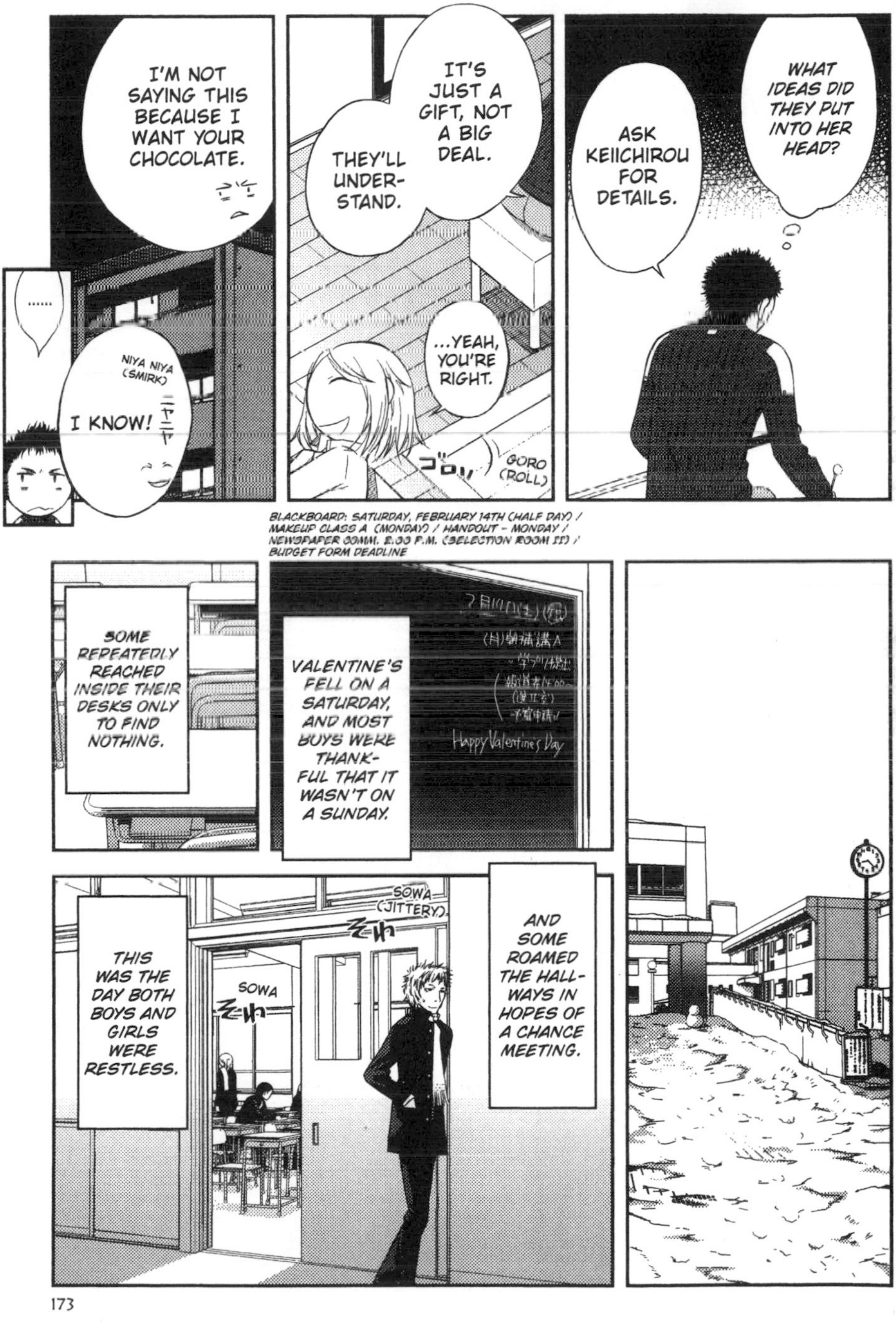
WHAT IDEAS DID THEY PUT INTO HER HEAD?
ASK KEIICHIROU FOR DETAILS.
IT'S JUST A GIFT, NOT A BIG DEAL.
THEY'LL UNDER-STAND.
...YEAH, YOU'RE RIGHT.
GORO (ROLL)
I'M NOT SAYING THIS BECAUSE I WANT YOUR CHOCOLATE.
......
NIYA NIYA (SMIRK)
I KNOW!
BLACKBOARD: SATURDAY, FEBRUARY 14TH (HALF DAY) / MAKEUP CLASS A (MONDAY) / HANDOUT - MONDAY / NEWSPAPER COMM. 2:00 P.M. (SELECTION ROOM II) / BUDGET FORM DEADLINE
Happy Valentine's Day
VALENTINE'S FELL ON A SATURDAY, AND MOST BOYS WERE THANK-FUL THAT IT WASN'T ON A SUNDAY.
SOME REPEATEDLY REACHED INSIDE THEIR DESKS ONLY TO FIND NOTHING.
AND SOME ROAMED THE HALL-WAYS IN HOPES OF A CHANCE MEETING.
SOWA (JITTERY)
THIS WAS THE DAY BOTH BOYS AND GIRLS WERE RESTLESS.
SOWA

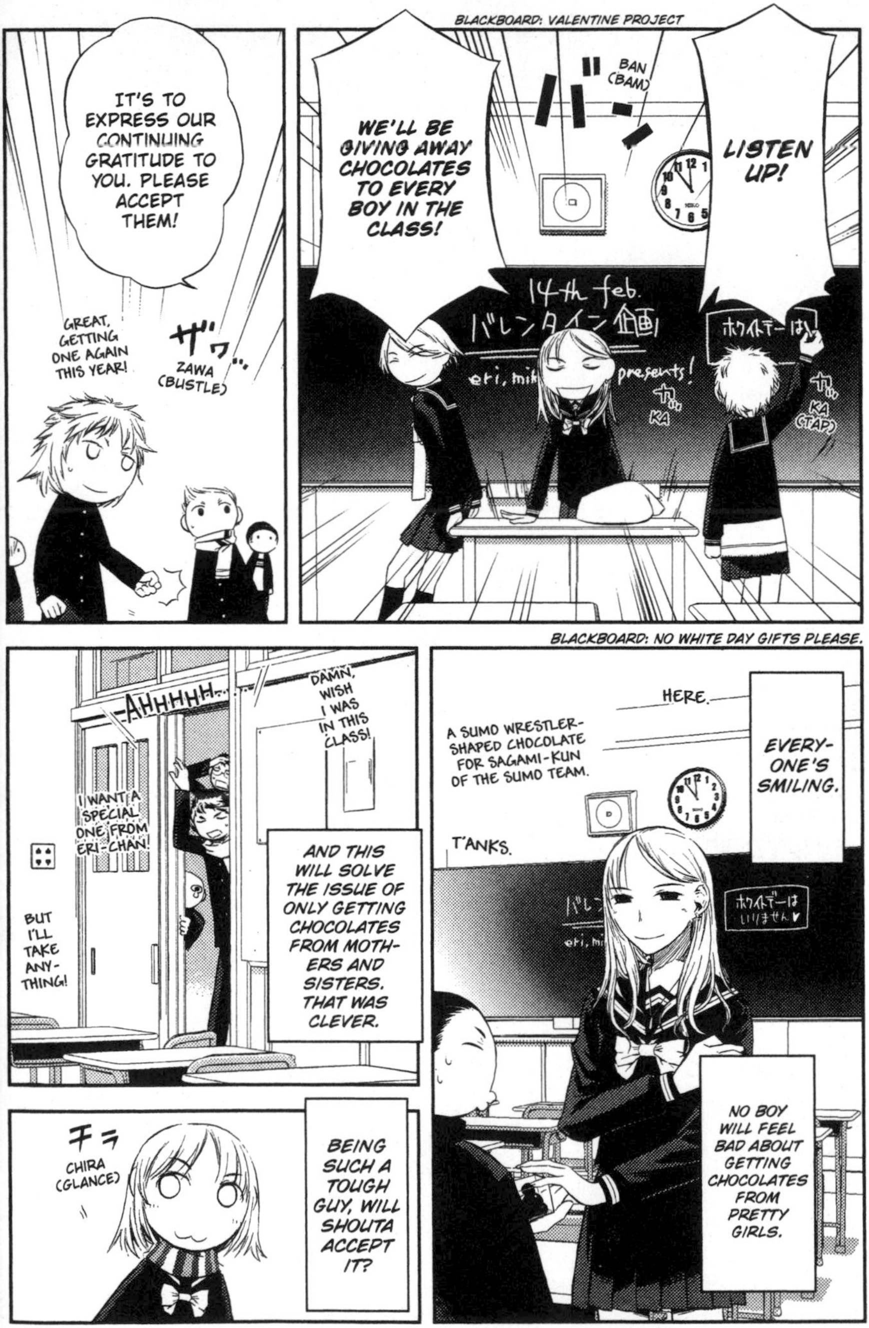
BLACKBOARD: VALENTINE PROJECT
LISTEN UP!
バーン
BAN (BAM)
WE'LL BE GIVING AWAY CHOCOLATES TO EVERY BOY IN THE CLASS!
14th feb. バレンタイン企画
eri, mik presents!
ホワイトデーは
カッ
KA (TAP)
カッ
KA
IT'S TO EXPRESS OUR CONTINUING GRATITUDE TO YOU. PLEASE ACCEPT THEM!
ザワ…
ZAWA (BUSTLE)
GREAT, GETTING ONE AGAIN THIS YEAR!
BLACKBOARD: NO WHITE DAY GIFTS PLEASE.
EVERYONE'S SMILING.
HERE.
A SUMO WRESTLER-SHAPED CHOCOLATE FOR SAGAMI-KUN OF THE SUMO TEAM.
T'ANKS.
ホワイトデーは いりません♥
NO BOY WILL FEEL BAD ABOUT GETTING CHOCOLATES FROM PRETTY GIRLS.
AND THIS WILL SOLVE THE ISSUE OF ONLY GETTING CHOCOLATES FROM MOTHERS AND SISTERS. THAT WAS CLEVER.
DAMN, WISH I WAS IN THIS CLASS!
AHHHHH...
I WANT A SPECIAL ONE FROM ERI-CHAN!
BUT I'LL TAKE ANYTHING!
BEING SUCH A TOUGH GUY, WILL SHOUTA ACCEPT IT?
チラ
CHIRA (GLANCE)

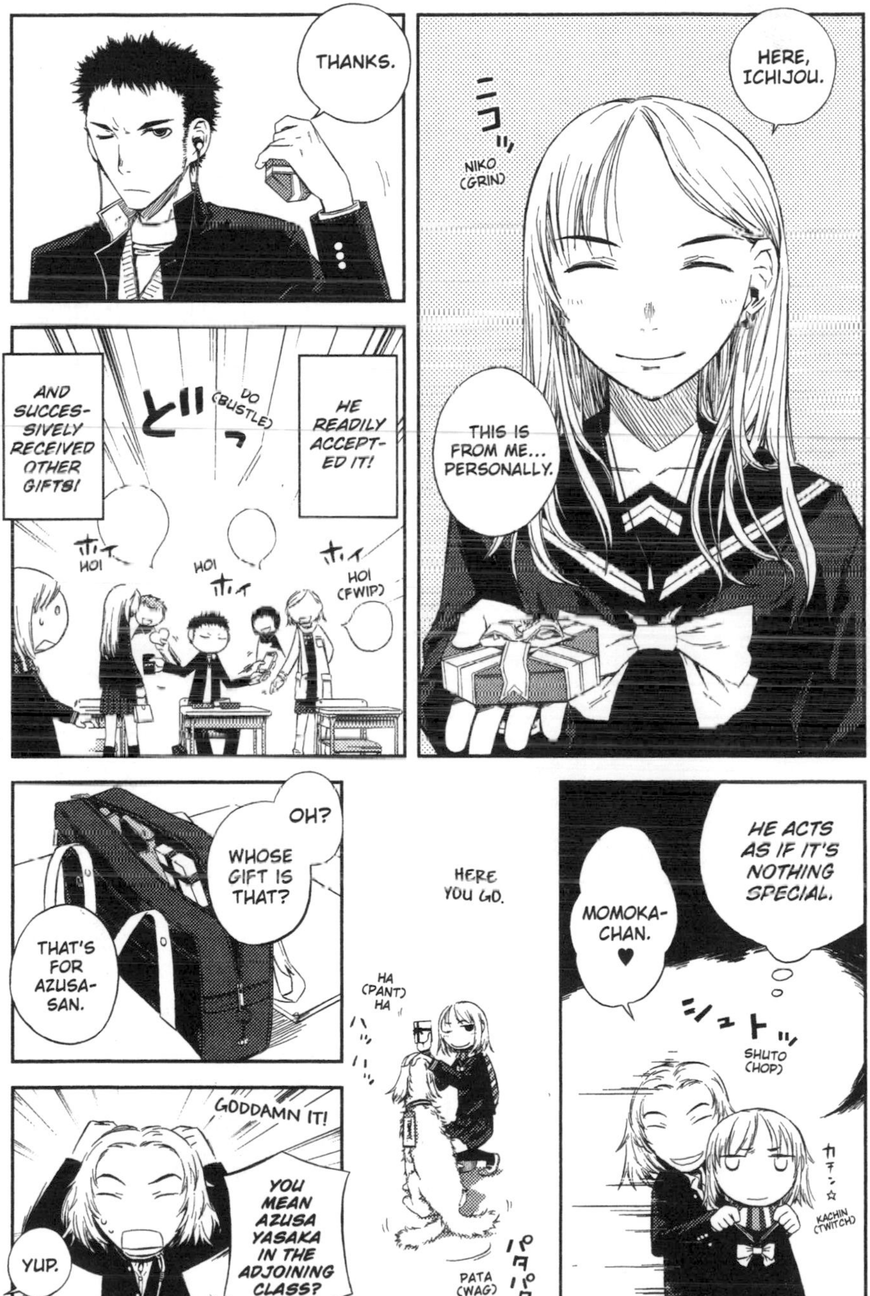
HERE, ICHIJOU.
ニコッ
NIKO (GRIN)
THIS IS FROM ME... PERSONALLY.
THANKS.
HE READILY ACCEPTED IT!
DO (BUSTLE)
AND SUCCESSIVELY RECEIVED OTHER GIFTS!
HOI (FWIP)
HOI
HOI
HE ACTS AS IF IT'S NOTHING SPECIAL.
MOMOKA-CHAN. ♥
SHUTO (CHOP)
KACHIN (TWITCH)
HERE YOU GO.
HA (PANT) HA
PATA (WAG) PATA
OH?
WHOSE GIFT IS THAT?
THAT'S FOR AZUSA-SAN.
GODDAMN IT!
YOU MEAN AZUSA YASAKA IN THE ADJOINING CLASS?
YUP.

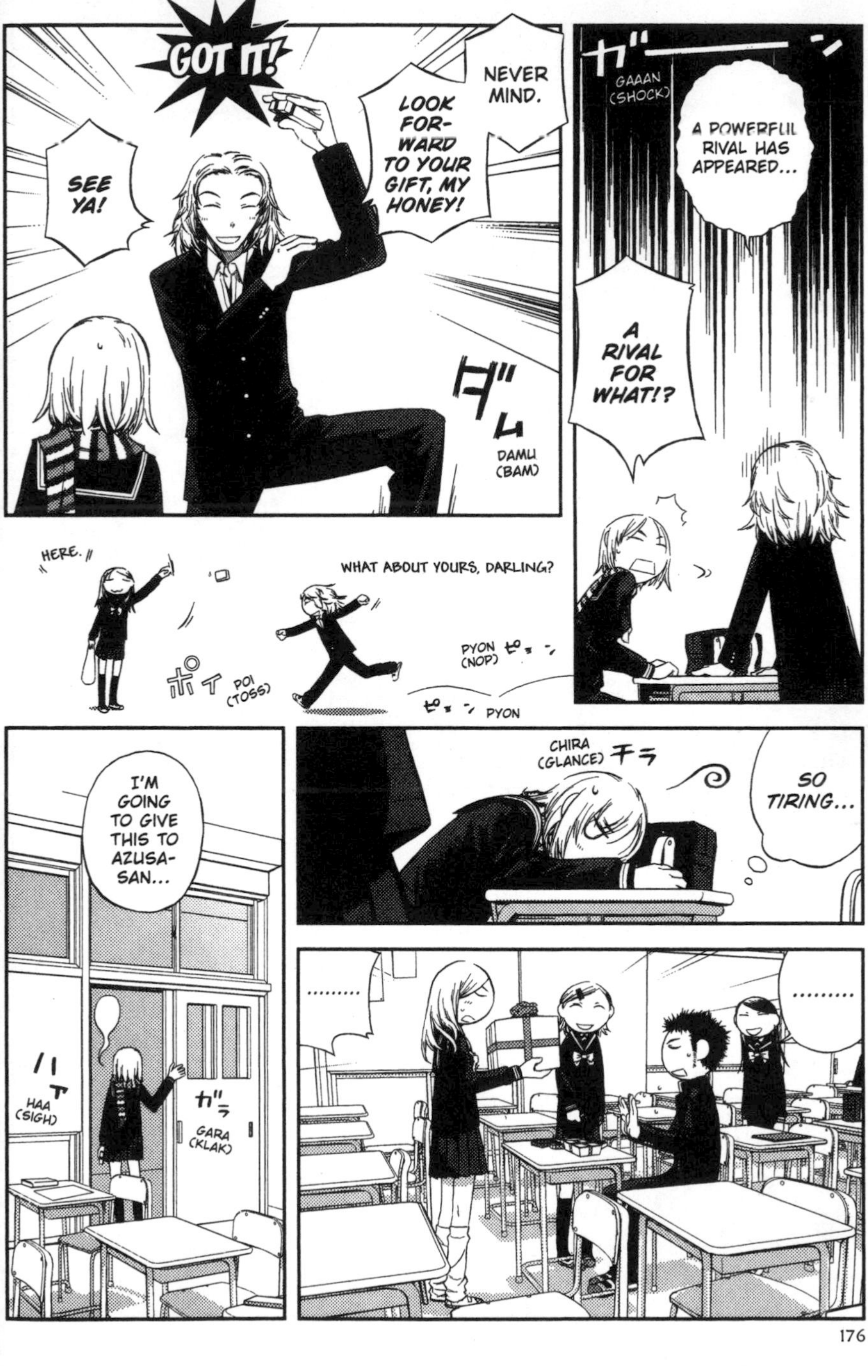
ガーーーン
GAAAN (SHOCK)
A POWERFUL RIVAL HAS APPEARED...
A RIVAL FOR WHAT!?
GOT IT!
NEVER MIND.
LOOK FOR-WARD TO YOUR GIFT, MY HONEY!
SEE YA!
ダム
DAMU (BAM)
WHAT ABOUT YOURS, DARLING?
PYON ぴょーん (NOP)
ぴょーん PYON
ポイ POI (TOSS)
HERE.
SO TIRING...
CHIRA (GLANCE) チラ
....
....
I'M GOING TO GIVE THIS TO AZUSA-SAN...
ガラ
GARA (KLAK)
ハァ
HAA (SIGH)

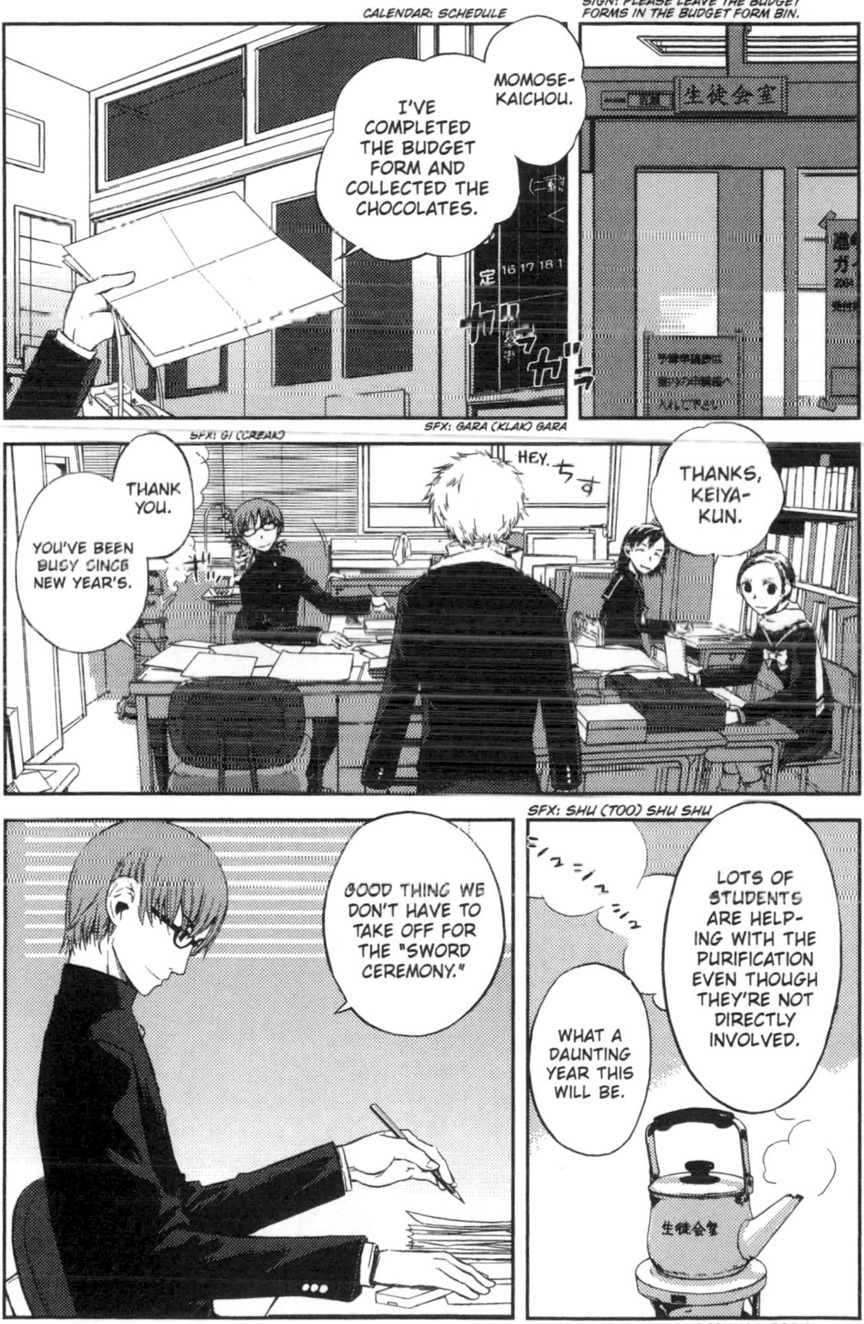
SIGN: STUDENT COUNCIL ROOM
SIGN: PLEASE LEAVE THE BUDGET FORMS IN THE BUDGET FORM BIN.
MOMOSE-KAICHOU.
I'VE COMPLETED THE BUDGET FORM AND COLLECTED THE CHOCOLATES.
CALENDAR: SCHEDULE
SFX: GARA (KLAK) GARA
THANKS, KEIYA-KUN.
HEY.
THANK YOU.
YOU'VE BEEN BUSY SINCE NEW YEAR'S.
SFX: GI (CREAK)
LOTS OF STUDENTS ARE HELPING WITH THE PURIFICATION EVEN THOUGH THEY'RE NOT DIRECTLY INVOLVED.
WHAT A DAUNTING YEAR THIS WILL BE.
SFX: SHU (TOO) SHU SHU
POT: STUDENT COUNCIL ROOM
GOOD THING WE DON'T HAVE TO TAKE OFF FOR THE "SWORD CEREMONY."

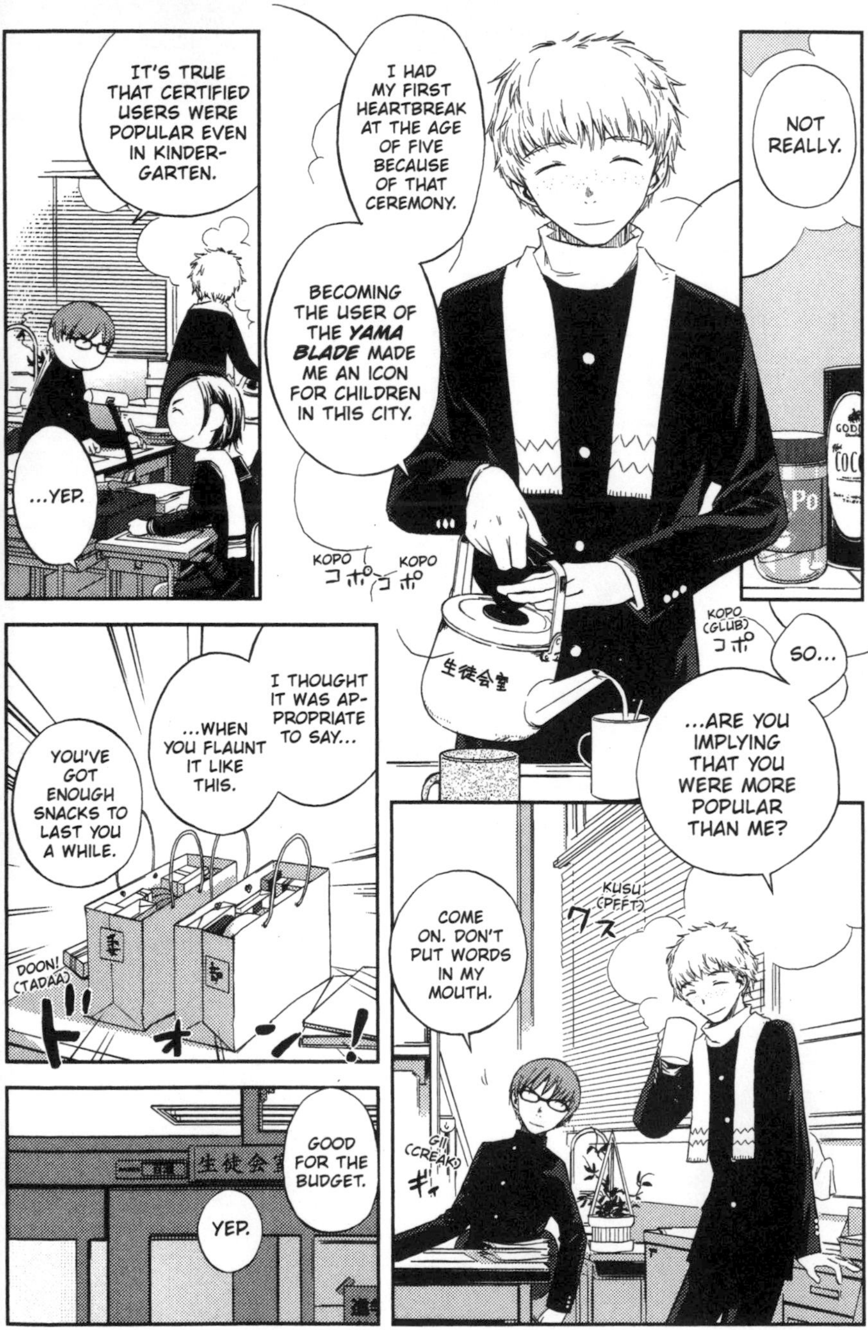
NOT REALLY.
I HAD MY FIRST HEARTBREAK AT THE AGE OF FIVE BECAUSE OF THAT CEREMONY.
BECOMING THE USER OF THE *YAMA BLADE* MADE ME AN ICON FOR CHILDREN IN THIS CITY.
IT'S TRUE THAT CERTIFIED USERS WERE POPULAR EVEN IN KINDER-GARTEN.
...YEP.
KOPO
KOPO
コポコポ
生徒会室
KOPO (GLUB)
コポ
SO...
...ARE YOU IMPLYING THAT YOU WERE MORE POPULAR THAN ME?
KUSU (PFFT)
クス
COME ON. DON'T PUT WORDS IN MY MOUTH.
GII (CREAK)
ギィ
I THOUGHT IT WAS AP-PROPRIATE TO SAY...
...WHEN YOU FLAUNT IT LIKE THIS.
YOU'VE GOT ENOUGH SNACKS TO LAST YOU A WHILE.
DOON! (TADAA)
ドォーン!
生徒会室
GOOD FOR THE BUDGET.
YEP.

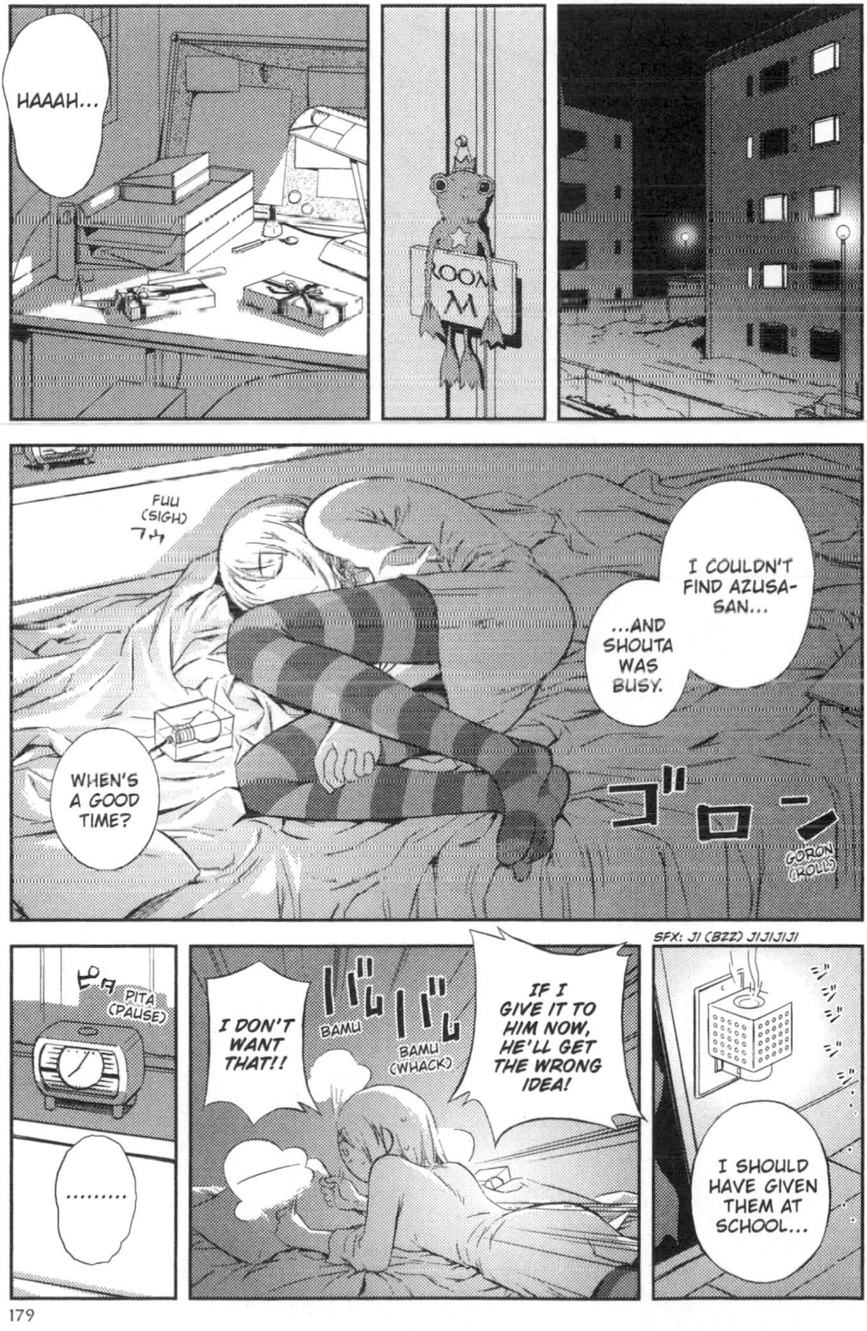
ROOM M
HAAAH...
I COULDN'T FIND AZUSA-SAN...
...AND SHOUTA WAS BUSY.
ゴローン
GORON (ROLL)
FUU (SIGH) フゥ
WHEN'S A GOOD TIME?
SFX: JI (BZZ) JIJIJIJI
ジジジジ
I SHOULD HAVE GIVEN THEM AT SCHOOL...
IF I GIVE IT TO HIM NOW, HE'LL GET THE WRONG IDEA!
バムバム
BAMU BAMU (WHACK)
I DON'T WANT THAT!!
ピタ PITA (PAUSE)
....

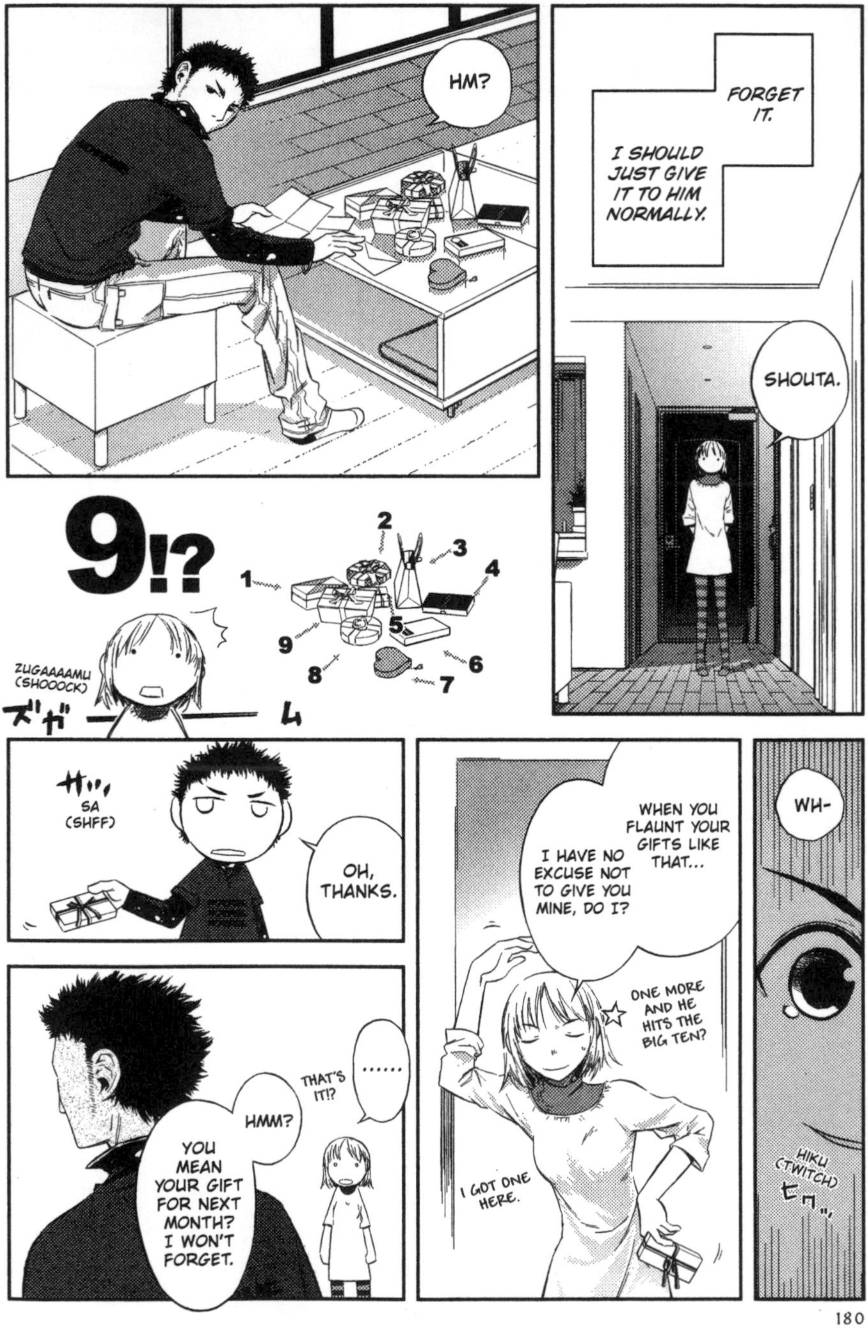
FORGET IT.
I SHOULD JUST GIVE IT TO HIM NORMALLY.
SHOUTA.
HM?
9!?
1
2
3
4
5
6
7
8
9
ZUGAAAAMU (SHOOOCK)
ズガーーーム
WH-
HIKU (TWITCH)
ヒクッ
WHEN YOU FLAUNT YOUR GIFTS LIKE THAT...
I HAVE NO EXCUSE NOT TO GIVE YOU MINE, DO I?
ONE MORE AND HE HITS THE BIG TEN?
I GOT ONE HERE.
サッ
SA (SHFF)
OH, THANKS.
......
THAT'S IT!?
HMM?
YOU MEAN YOUR GIFT FOR NEXT MONTH? I WON'T FORGET.

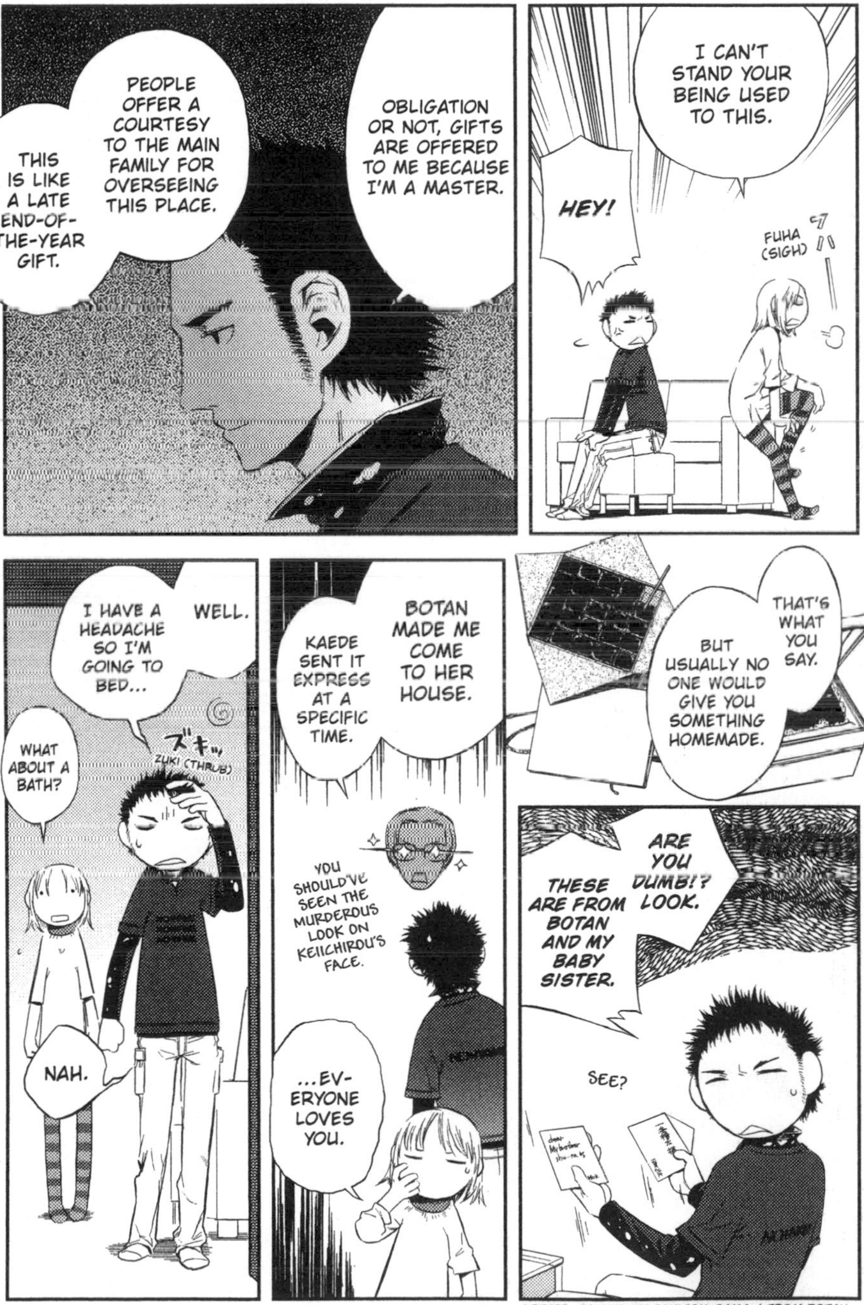
I CAN'T STAND YOUR BEING USED TO THIS.
HEY!
FUHA (SIGH)
OBLIGATION OR NOT, GIFTS ARE OFFERED TO ME BECAUSE I'M A MASTER.
PEOPLE OFFER A COURTESY TO THE MAIN FAMILY FOR OVERSEEING THIS PLACE.
THIS IS LIKE A LATE END-OF-THE-YEAR GIFT.
THAT'S WHAT YOU SAY.
BUT USUALLY NO ONE WOULD GIVE YOU SOMETHING HOMEMADE.
ARE YOU DUMB!? LOOK.
THESE ARE FROM BOTAN AND MY BABY SISTER.
SEE?
BOTAN MADE ME COME TO HER HOUSE.
KAEDE SENT IT EXPRESS AT A SPECIFIC TIME.
YOU SHOULD'VE SEEN THE MURDEROUS LOOK ON KEIICHIROU'S FACE.
...EV-ERYONE LOVES YOU.
WELL.
I HAVE A HEADACHE SO I'M GOING TO BED...
ズキッ
ZUKI (THROB)
WHAT ABOUT A BATH?
NAH.

LETTER: TO SHOUTA ICHIJOU-SAMA / FROM BOTAN

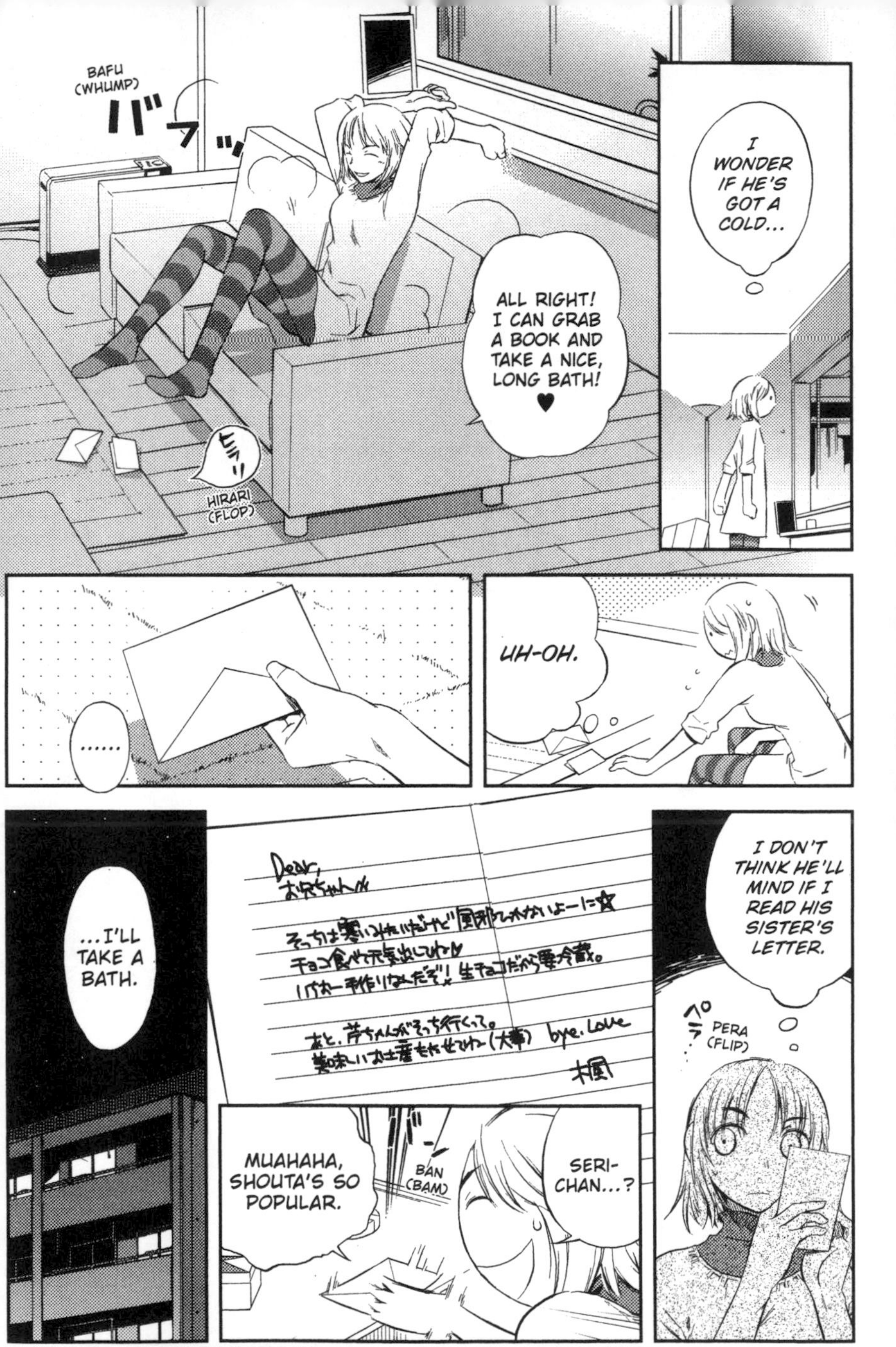
I WONDER IF HE'S GOT A COLD...
BAFU (WHUMP)
バフッ
ALL RIGHT! I CAN GRAB A BOOK AND TAKE A NICE, LONG BATH! ♥
ヒラリ
HIRARI (FLOP)
UH-OH.
......
I DON'T THINK HE'LL MIND IF I READ HIS SISTER'S LETTER.
ペラ
PERA (FLIP)
Dear,
お兄ちゃんへ
そっちは寒いみたいだけど風邪ひかないよーに☆
チョコ食べて元気出してね♥
いちおー手作りなんだぞ！生チョコだから要冷蔵。
あと、芹ちゃんがそっち行くって。
美味しいお土産もたせてねー(大事) bye. Love
楓
SERI-CHAN...?
BAN (BAM)
MUAHAHA, SHOUTA'S SO POPULAR.
...I'LL TAKE A BATH.

LETTER: DEAR ONIICHAN, I HEARD IT'S FREEZING OVER THERE SO TAKE CARE OF YOURSELF. [STAR] I HOPE THIS CHOCOLATE WILL CHEER YOU UP. [HEART] IT'S HOMEMADE! KEEP THIS FRESH CREAM CHOCOLATE REFRIGERATED. SERI-CHAN SAID SHE'S GOING TO VISIT YOU. GIVE HER A TASTY SOUVENIR (IMPORTANT!). BYE. LOVE, KAEDE

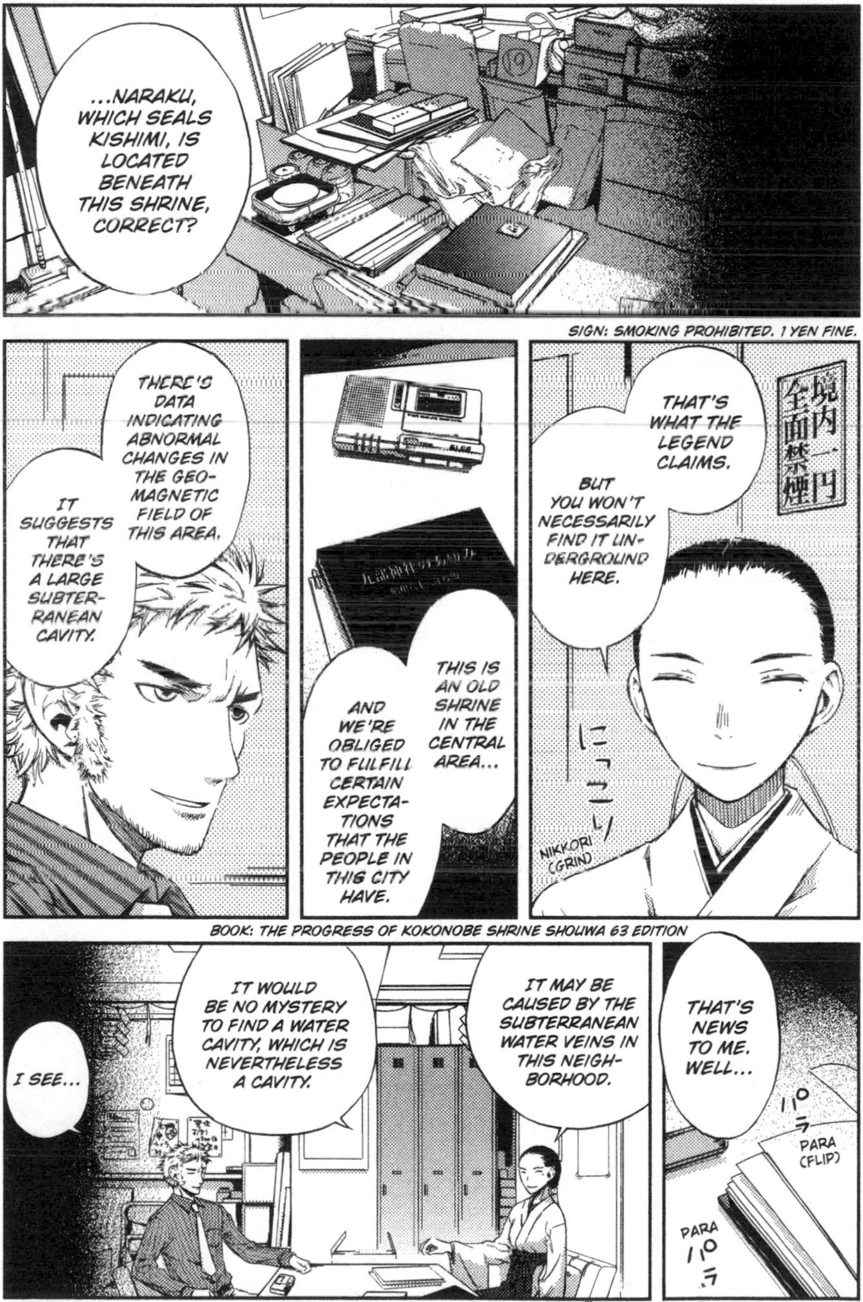
...NARAKU, WHICH SEALS KISHIMI, IS LOCATED BENEATH THIS SHRINE, CORRECT?
境内一円
全面禁煙
THAT'S WHAT THE LEGEND CLAIMS.
BUT YOU WON'T NECESSARILY FIND IT UNDERGROUND HERE.
NIKKORI (GRIN)
THIS IS AN OLD SHRINE IN THE CENTRAL AREA...
AND WE'RE OBLIGED TO FULFILL CERTAIN EXPECTATIONS THAT THE PEOPLE IN THIS CITY HAVE.
THERE'S DATA INDICATING ABNORMAL CHANGES IN THE GEO-MAGNETIC FIELD OF THIS AREA.
IT SUGGESTS THAT THERE'S A LARGE SUBTER-RANEAN CAVITY.
THAT'S NEWS TO ME. WELL...
PARA (FLIP)
PARA
IT MAY BE CAUSED BY THE SUBTERRANEAN WATER VEINS IN THIS NEIGH-BORHOOD.
IT WOULD BE NO MYSTERY TO FIND A WATER CAVITY, WHICH IS NEVERTHELESS A CAVITY.
I SEE...

SIGN: SMOKING PROHIBITED. 1 YEN FINE.

BOOK: THE PROGRESS OF KOKONOBE SHRINE SHOUWA 63 EDITION

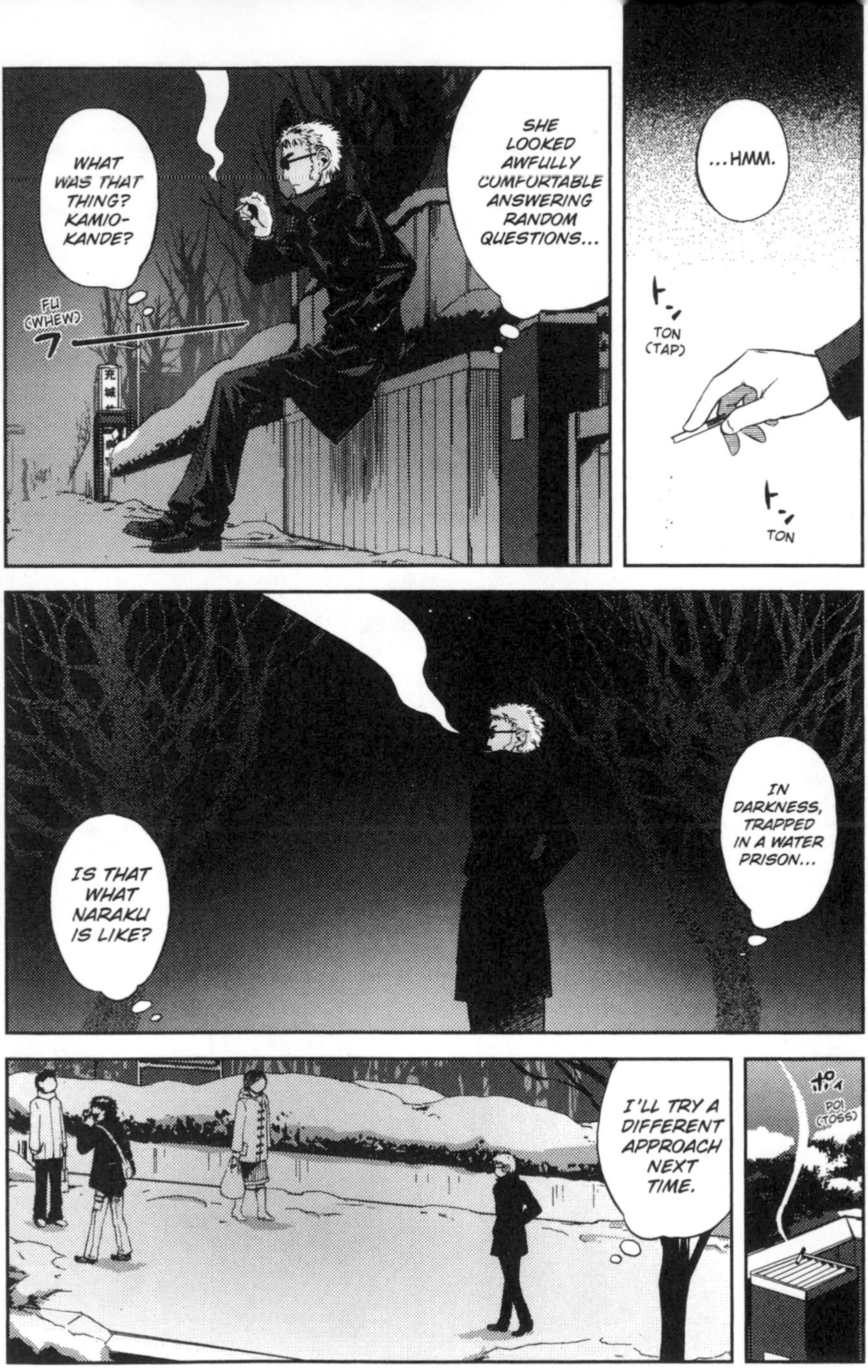
...HMM.
TON (TAP)
TON
SHE LOOKED AWFULLY COMFORTABLE ANSWERING RANDOM QUESTIONS...
WHAT WAS THAT THING? KAMIO-KANDE?
FU (WHEW)
IN DARKNESS, TRAPPED IN A WATER PRISON...
IS THAT WHAT NARAKU IS LIKE?
POI (TOSS)
I'LL TRY A DIFFERENT APPROACH NEXT TIME.

SIGN: MITSURUGI MUTUAL HOSPITAL

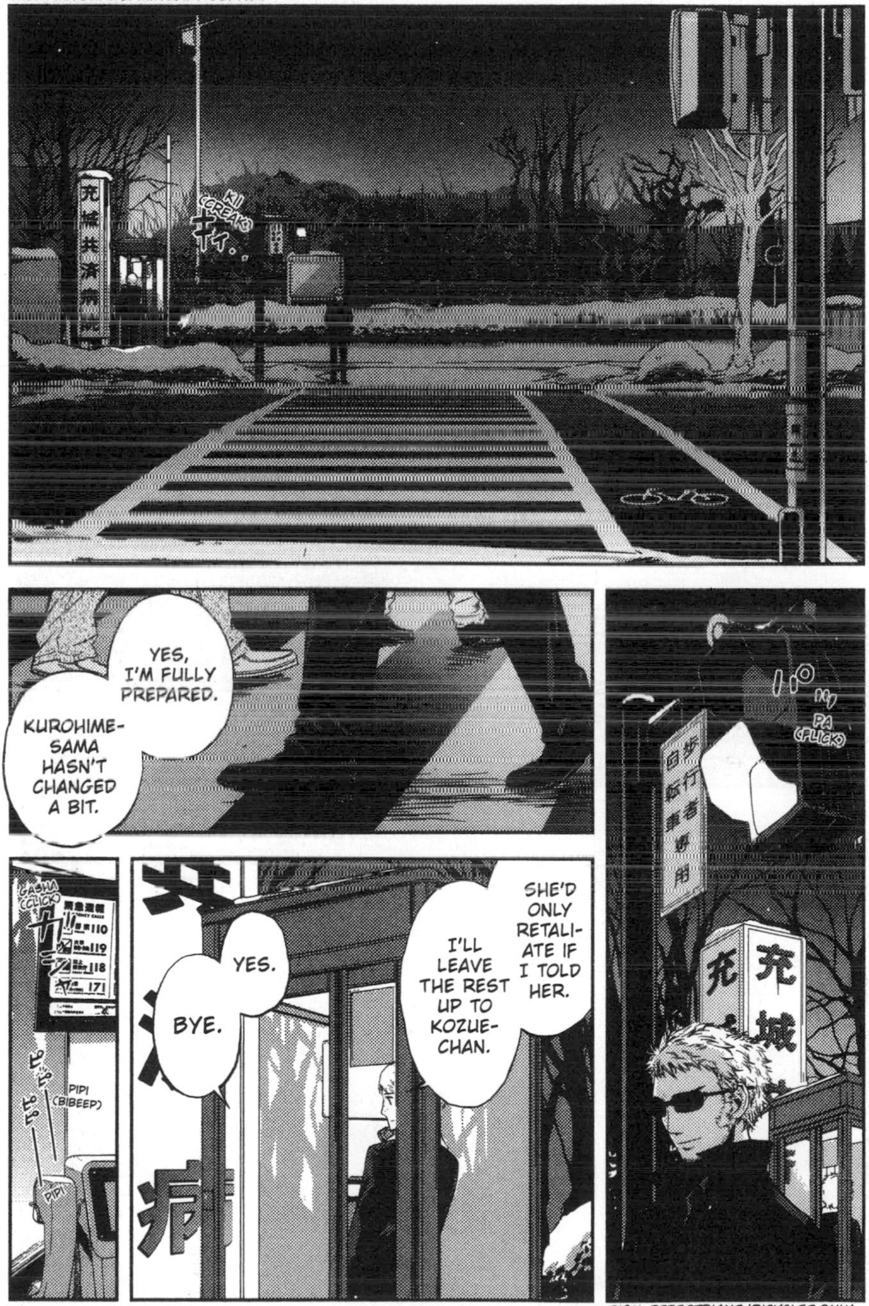
KI (CREAK)
PA (FLICK)
YES, I'M FULLY PREPARED.
KUROHIME-SAMA HASN'T CHANGED A BIT.
SHE'D ONLY RETALIATE IF I TOLD HER.
I'LL LEAVE THE REST UP TO KOZUE-CHAN.
YES.
BYE.
GASHA (CLICK)
PIPI (BIBEEP)
PIPI

SIGN: PEDESTRIANS/BICYCLES ONLY

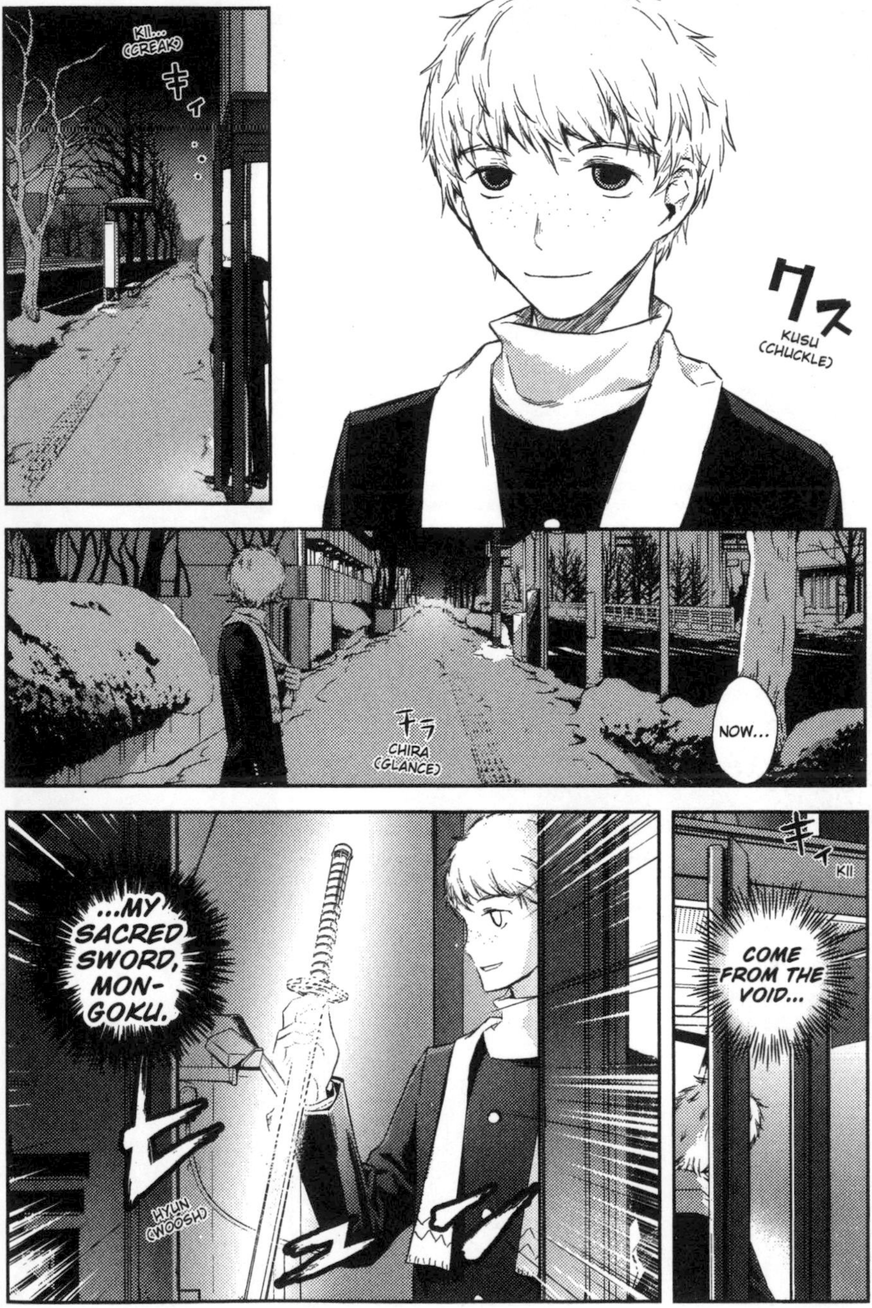
クス
KUSU (CHUCKLE)
KII... (CREAK)
キィ
NOW...
チラ
CHIRA (GLANCE)
ギィ
KII
COME FROM THE VOID...
...MY SACRED SWORD, MON-GOKU.
HYUN (WOOSH)

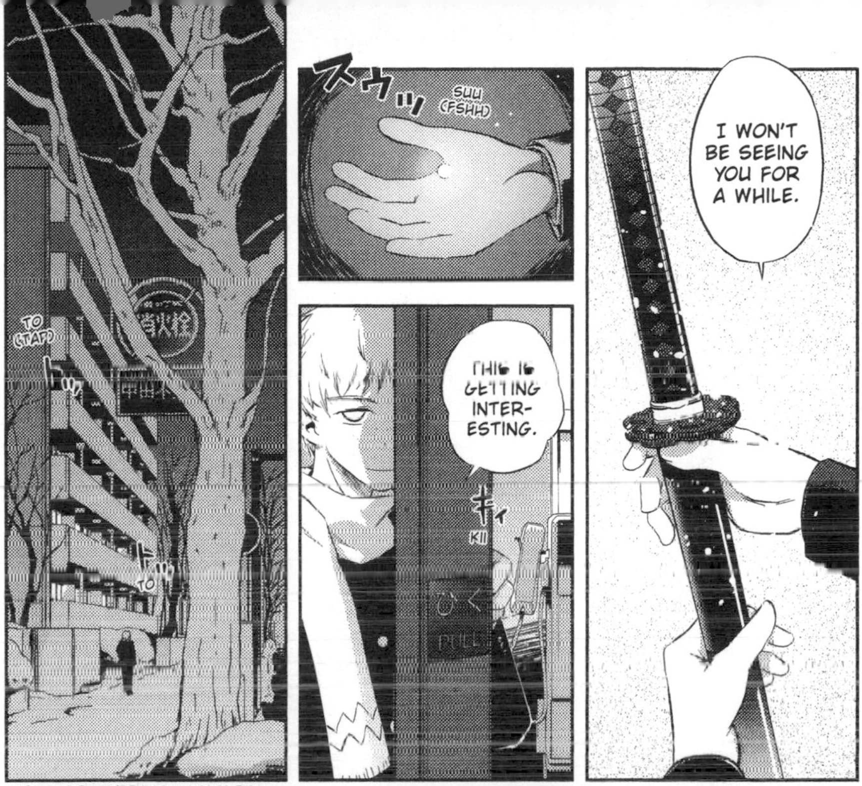
I WON'T BE SEEING YOU FOR A WHILE.
SUU (FSHH)
THIS IS GETTING INTERESTING.
KII
TO (TAP)
TO
SIGNS: FIRE HYDRANT, NAKATA REAL

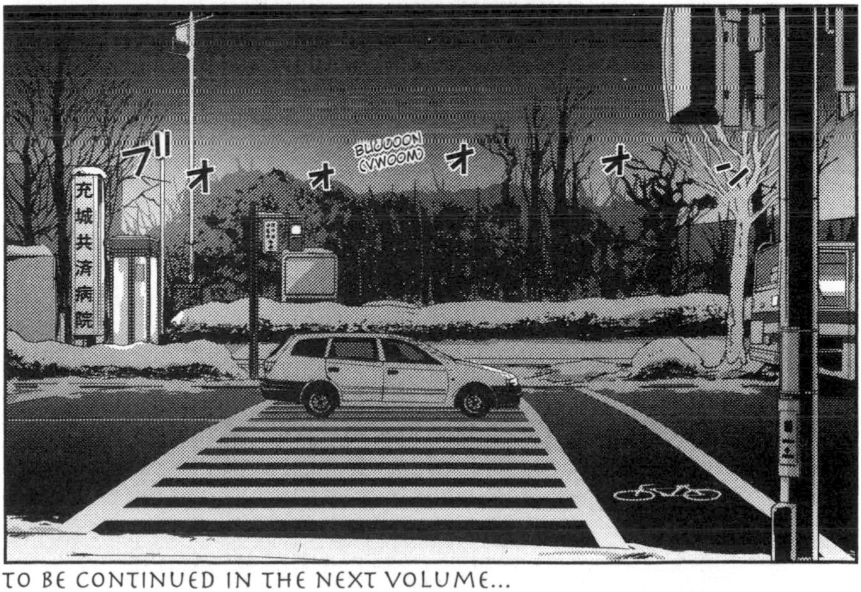
BUOOOON (VWOOM)

TO BE CONTINUED IN THE NEXT VOLUME...

YUMMY
CHOCOLATE.

KAZE NO HANA [1]
STAFF LIST

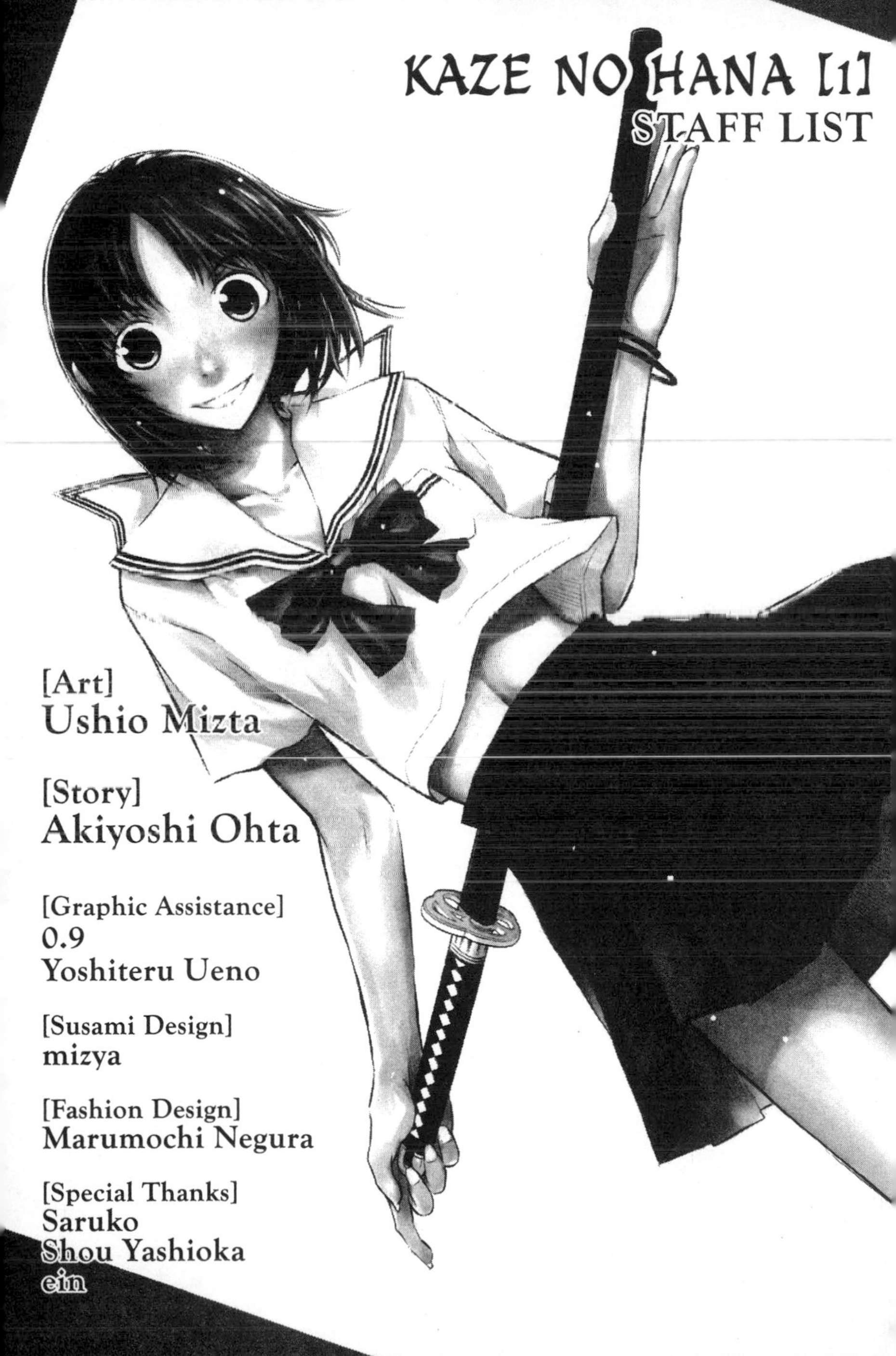

[Art]
Ushio Mizta

[Story]
Akiyoshi Ohta

[Graphic Assistance]
0.9
Yoshiteru Ueno

[Susami Design]
mizya

[Fashion Design]
Marumochi Negura

[Special Thanks]
Saruko
Shou Yashioka
ein

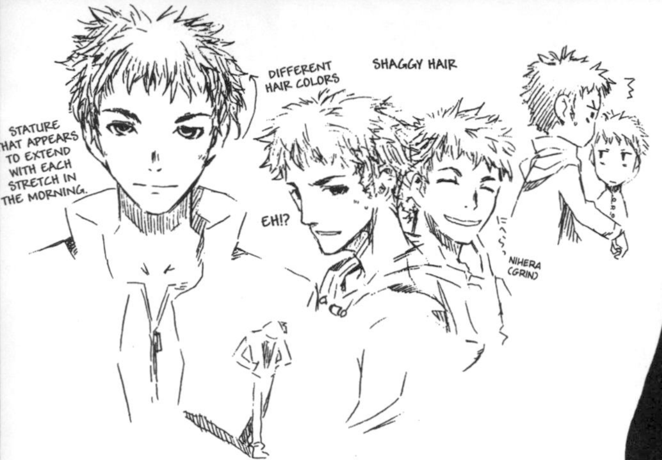
STATURE HAT APPEARS TO EXTEND WITH EACH STRETCH IN THE MORNING.
DIFFERENT HAIR COLORS
SHAGGY HAIR
EH!?
NIHERA (GRIN)

SHOUTA ICHIJOU

MALE • AGE 16 • 5'9" TALL • SON OF ICHIJOU FAMILY • RESIDES IN TOKYO • SWORD: HAYATE (TACHI) / URA SHIMON (HIMEKARI) • WIND DRAGON • FATHER (DECEASED), MOTHER (DECEASED), OLDER BROTHER: SOUMA (23), YOUNGER SISTER: KAEDE (15)

SHOUTA ALWAYS SEEMS MOODY AND ACTS IRRITATED. HOWEVER, HE IS A HARD WORKER BENEATH HIS CANTANKEROUS EXTERIOR. HE HATES BULLYING. TRAINED AS THE HIMEKARI TO SLAY SUSAMI ESCAPING FROM MITSURUGI CITY SINCE HIS EARLY CHILDHOOD, SHOUTA INHERITED HIS SWORD AT THE AGE OF TWELVE. THOUGH HE PERFORMS HIS DUTY WITHOUT HESITATION, HE SEEMS TO RELIEVE HIS FRUSTRATION WITH HIS FAMILIAL OBLIGATION DURING BATTLE. HE IS ALWAYS AGGRAVATED AT NOT KNOWING HOW TO CHANGE HIS CURRENT SITUATION.

Fashion Design

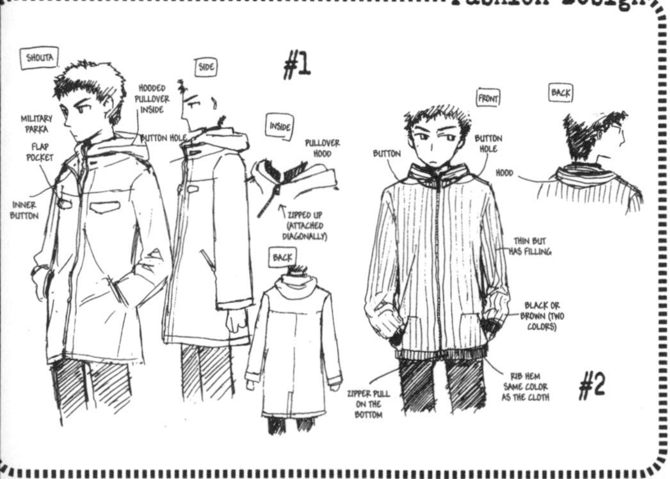
SHOUTA
SIDE
#1
HOODED PULLOVER INSIDE
MILITARY PARKA
FLAP POCKET
BUTTON HOLE
INSIDE
PULLOVER HOOD
INNER BUTTON
ZIPPED UP (ATTACHED DIAGONALLY)
BACK
FRONT
BACK
BUTTON
BUTTON HOLE
HOOD
THIN BUT HAS FILLING
BLACK OR BROWN (TWO COLORS)
RIB HEM SAME COLOR AS THE CLOTH
ZIPPER PULL ON THE BOTTOM
#2

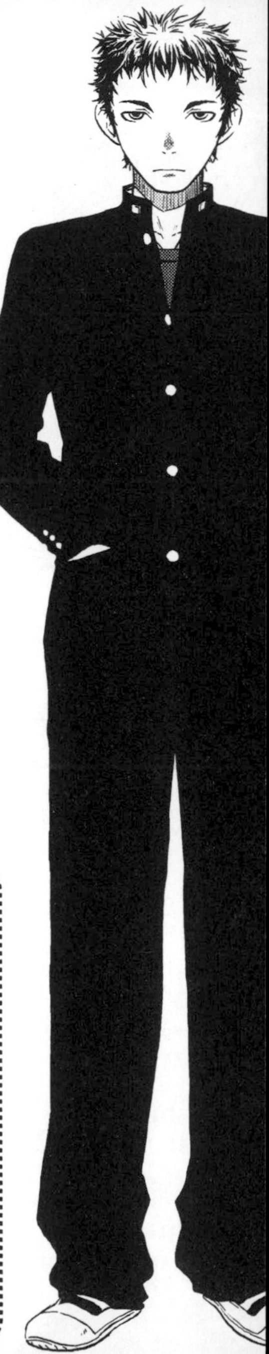

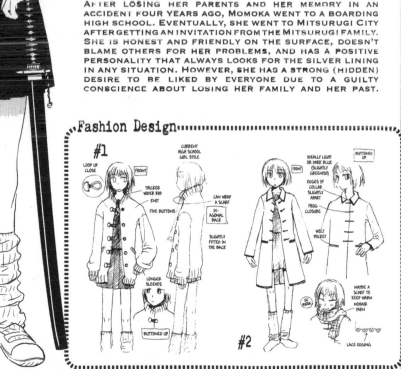

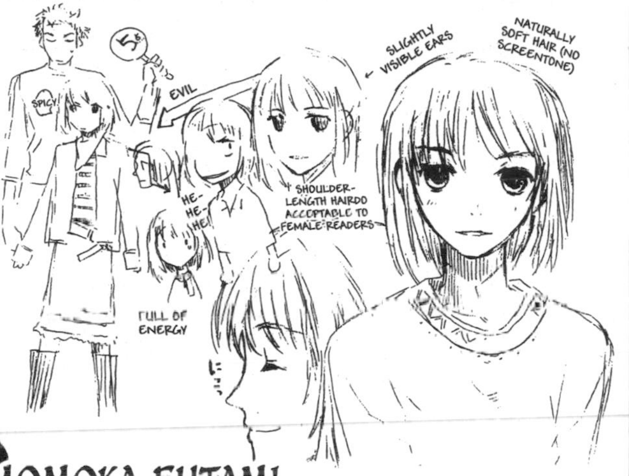
SPICY
EVIL
HE-HE-HE!
FULL OF ENERGY
SLIGHTLY VISIBLE EARS
NATURALLY SOFT HAIR (NO SCREENTONE)
SHOULDER-LENGTH HAIRDO ACCEPTABLE TO FEMALE READERS

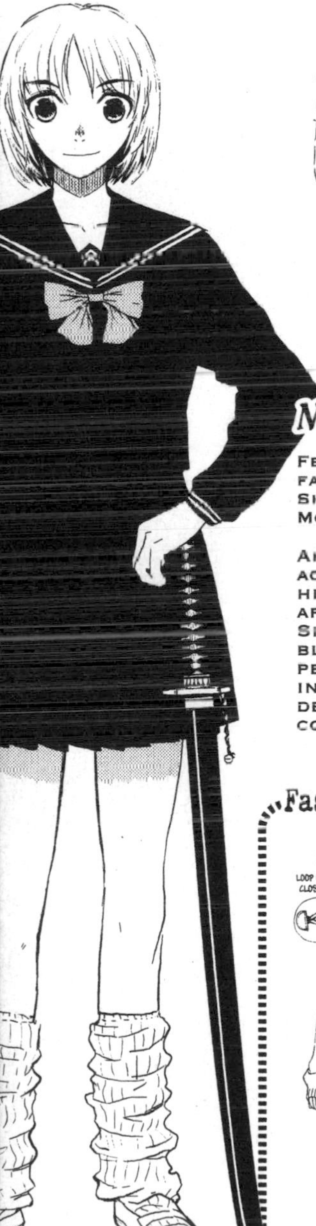

MOMOKA FUTAMI

FEMALE • AGE 16 • 5'4" TALL • DAUGHTER OF FUTAMI FAMILY • RESIDES IN TOKYO • SWORD: SUZUKAZE (TACHI) / SHIMON (TONOMORI) • WIND DRAGON • FATHER (DECEASED), MOTHER, KYOUKA (DECEASED)

AFTER LOSING HER PARENTS AND HER MEMORY IN AN ACCIDENT FOUR YEARS AGO, MOMOKA WENT TO A BOARDING HIGH SCHOOL. EVENTUALLY, SHE WENT TO MITSURUGI CITY AFTER GETTING AN INVITATION FROM THE MITSURUGI FAMILY. SHE IS HONEST AND FRIENDLY ON THE SURFACE, DOESN'T BLAME OTHERS FOR HER PROBLEMS, AND HAS A POSITIVE PERSONALITY THAT ALWAYS LOOKS FOR THE SILVER LINING IN ANY SITUATION. HOWEVER, SHE HAS A STRONG (HIDDEN) DESIRE TO BE LIKED BY EVERYONE DUE TO A GUILTY CONSCIENCE ABOUT LOSING HER FAMILY AND HER PAST.

Fashion Design

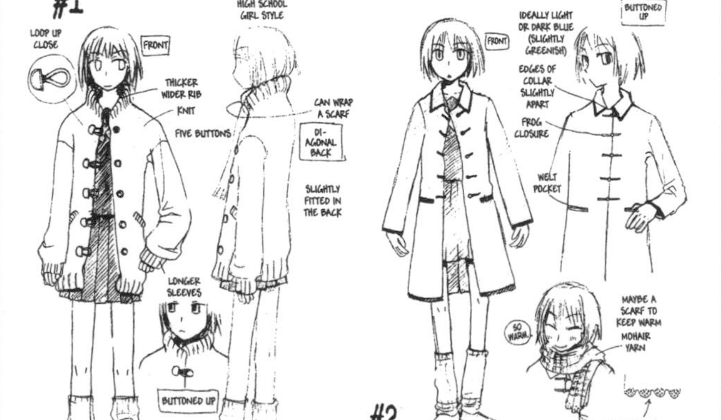
#1
LOOP UP CLOSE
FRONT
CURRENT HIGH SCHOOL GIRL STYLE
THICKER WIDER RIB
KNIT
FIVE BUTTONS
CAN WRAP A SCARF
DI-AGONAL BACK
SLIGHTLY FITTED IN THE BACK
LONGER SLEEVES
BUTTONED UP
IDEALLY LIGHT OR DARK BLUE (SLIGHTLY GREENISH)
FRONT
BUTTONED UP
EDGES OF COLLAR SLIGHTLY APART
FROG CLOSURE
WELT POCKET
SO WARM.
MAYBE A SCARF TO KEEP WARM
MOHAIR YARN
LACE EDGING
#2

NARAKU
THIS IS THE NAME OF THE BARRIER WHERE KISHIMI IS SEALED.

[P]

PATROL
WHEN A SPIRITUAL SWORD BEARER OR A GROUP OF THREE OR FOUR YAMA BLADE BEARERS GO OUT TO THE HOLLOW WORLD TO BATTLE THE SUSAMI. SOME OCCASIONALLY LOSE THEIR LIVES.

[R]

RIKUGOU FAMILY
THEY ARE ONE OF THE MASTER FAMILIES AND THE URA SHIMON MEMBER FAMILY REPRESENTING THE WATER DRAGON.

[S]

SACRED SWORD
THE SWORDS PASSED ON THROUGH THE SHICHIJOU GROUP. THEY WERE PROVIDED BY KISHIMI AND ARE USUALLY KEPT IN THE HOLLOW WORLD, READILY AVAILABLE AT THE MASTER'S CALL.

SEIROU ASSOCATION
THIS IS THE MAIN SUPPORT ORGANIZATION FOR THE SHICHIJOU GROUP.

SHICHIJOU GROUP
THE COUNTERPART OF THE MITSURUGI HOUSE, THE SHICHIJOU GROUP PASSES ON THE SACRED SWORDS RECEIVED FROM KISHIMI FOR GENERATIONS. THEIR INDIVIDUAL POWER IS SAID TO EXCEED THAT OF MITSURUGI HOUSE. THEY MANIPULATE SUBORDINATE SUSAMI AND HAVE A SPECIAL POWER EQUIVALENT TO THAT OF SUPERORDINATE SUSAMI, DESPITE THE FACT THAT THEY'RE HUMAN. IN ADDITION, THEIR MEMBERSHIP IS BASED ON THEIR ABILITIES, NOT KINSHIP.

SHIGA FAMILY
THEY ARE ONE OF THE MASTER FAMILIES AND THE SHIMON MEMBER FAMILY REPRESENTING THE FIRE DRAGON. THEY INHERIT THE SPIRITUAL SWORD, SHIRANUI.

SHIMON
THEY ARE THE FOUR MAIN FAMILIES—FUTAMI, MITSURUGI, SHIGA, AND YASAKA—WHO REMAINED IN MITSURUGI CITY. THEIR ALIAS IS TONOMORI.

SHIRANUI
THE SPIRITUAL SWORD PASSED DOWN IN THE SHIGA FAMILY. ITS CURRENT BEARER IS BOTAN.

SHIRATSUYU
THE SPIRITUAL SWORD PASSED DOWN IN THE YASAMA FAMILY. ITS CURRENT BEARER IS AZUSA.

SPIRITUAL SWORDS
ALSO KNOWN AS THE DRAGON SPIRIT SWORDS, THESE ARE THE EIGHT SWORDS KUZURYUU ENTRUSTED TO THE MITSURUGI HOUSE. THEY RESPOND TO THE FAMILY BLOOD AND CHOOSE THEIR OWN MASTERS. THEY CAN'T BE DRAWN BY ANYONE ELSE.

SUSAMI
IT IS AN ALTER EGO AND A SUBORDINATE BODY OF KISHIMI. THOUGH THEY APPEAR FROM THE CRACK IN KISHIMI'S SEAL INTO THE HOLLOW WORLD, THEY'RE CONTAINED WITHIN MITSURUGI CITY BY THE OUTER BARRIER, SENGOKU.

SUZUKAZE
THE SPIRITUAL SWORD PASSED DOWN IN THE FUTAMI FAMILY. ITS CURRENT BEARER IS MOMOKA.

SWORD CEREMONY
A CEREMONY THE CHILDREN IN MITSURUGI CITY CAN VOLUNTARILY PARTICIPATE IN WHEN THEY TURN FIVE. ITS OBJECTIVE IS TO DETERMINE THE POTENTIAL USERS OF THE YAMA BLADE. AS RIN MOMOSE AND KEIYA MANO MENTIONED IN THE MANGA, A CHILD'S ABILITY TO DRAW THE SWORD IS TESTED.

[Y]

YAMA BLADE
SUBSTITUTES FOR THE SPIRITUAL SWORDS PEOPLE CREATED FOR THE BATTLE AGAINST SUSAMI. SINCE IT IS FAR LESS COMPETENT THAN THE REAL SPIRITUAL SWORDS, IT IS USED FOR A GROUP ATTACK. BECAUSE IT HAS NO DESIGNATED USER, IT CAN BE USED BY ANY POTENTIAL SWORDSPERSON AND IS TAKEN INTO POSSESSION IN ROTATION.

YASAKA FAMILY
THEY ARE ONE OF THE MASTER FAMILIES AND THE SHIMON MEMBER FAMILY REPRESENTING THE WATER DRAGON. THEY INHERIT THE SPIRITUAL SWORD, SHIRATSUYU.

GLOSSARY

[E]

EIGHT MASTERS
A GENERAL NAME FOR THE MAIN FAMI-
LIES WITHIN MITSURUGI HOUSE WHO
HAND DOWN THE EIGHT SWORDS FOR
GENERATIONS.

[F]

FUTAMI FAMILY
THEY ARE ONE OF THE MASTER FAMI-
LIES AND THE SHIMON MEMBER FAMI
LY REPRESENTING THE WIND DRAGON.
THEY INHERIT SUZUKAZE.

[G]

GORYUU FAMILY
THEY ARE ONE OF THE MASTER FAM-
ILIES AND THE URA SHIMON MEM-
BER FAMILY REPRESENTING THE FIRE
DRAGON.

[H]

HAYATE
THE SPIRITUAL SWORD PASSED DOWN
IN THE ICHIJOU FAMILY. ITS CURRENT
BEARER IS SHOUTA.

HOLLOW WORLD
A MIDDLE BARRIER CREATED BETWEEN
THE NARAKU, WHERE KISHIMI IS
SEALED, AND THE REAL WORLD BY THE
SUSAMI THAT ESCAPED. TIME PASSES
FASTER WITHIN THE HOLLOW WORLD.

[I]

ICHIJOU FAMILY
THEY ARE ONE OF THE MASTER FAMI-
LIES AND THE URA SHIMON MEMBER
FAMILY REPRESENTING THE WIND
DRAGON. THEY INHERIT THE SPIRITU-
AL SWORD, HAYATE.

INCANTATION MEETING
A MEETING HELD EVERY MORNING
AT KOKONOBE SHRINE. THEY MAKE
A DAILY PROGNOSTICATION FOR THE
CURRENT LOCATION OF THE HOLLOW
WORLD. A PRIESTESS PARTICIPAT-
ING IN THIS MEETING IS CALLED THE
PRIESTESS OF INCANTATION AND RAN
IS THEIR LEADER.

[K]

KAGEROU
THE SPIRITUAL SWORD PASSED ON
THROUGH THE MITSURUGI FAMILY. ITS
CURRENT BEARER IS KEIICHIROU.

KISHIMI
ORIGINALLY CALLED "KISHIMI" WRIT-
TEN WITH ANOTHER KANJI, IT WAS
WORSHIPPED AS A SACRED GOD THAT
PROMISED GOOD HARVEST TO THE
PEOPLE OF KISHIMI VILLAGE THAT IS
NOW PRESENT-DAY MITSURUGI CITY.
HOWEVER, IT EVENTUALLY DEMANDED
A SACRIFICE, WHICH ENRAGED THE
DRAGON GOD, KUZURYUU, CAUSING IT
TO BE SEALED AWAY.

KOKONOBE FAMILY
A MEMBER FAMILY OF THE MITSURUGI
HOUSE, THE KOKONOBES ARE COMMIT-
TED TO GUARDING THE NARAKU, WHICH
SEALS KISHIMI. THEY DON'T POSSESS
A SPIRITUAL SWORD.

KOKONOBE SHRINE
A SHRINE BUILT DIRECTLY ABOVE THE
NARAKU.

KUROHIME
SHE IS THE LEADER OF THE SHICHIJOU
GROUP AND IS THE BEARER OF THE SA-
CRED SWORD, HAGUN.

KUZURYUU
THE DRAGON GOD THAT LIVED BY THE
LAKE AWAY FROM KISHIMI VILLAGE.
ENRAGED AT THE SACRIFICE OF ONE OF
ITS YOUNG WORSHIPPERS, IT SEALED
KISHIMI AND DIED AFTER BURNING
DOWN THE VILLAGE.

[M]

MITSURUGI CITY
THE LAND UNDER WHICH KISHIMI IS
SEALED, MITSURUGI CITY IS PROTECT-
ED BY ITS PEOPLE. THE CITY GOVERN-
MENT SUBSIDIZES THE SEALING EX-
PENSES.

MITSURUGI FAMILY
THEY ARE ONE OF THE MASTER FAMI-
LIES AND THE SHIMON MEMBER FAMILY
REPRESENTING THE EARTH DRAGON.
THEY INHERIT THE SPIRITUAL SWORD,
KAGEROU.

MITSURUGI HOUSE
THIS IS THE NAME OF THE EIGHT MAIN
FAMILIES LED BY THE MITSURUGI FAM-
ILY. THEY CONTROL THE POLITICAL
AND ECONOMIC POWER OF MITSURUGI
CITY.

MIZUCHI GROUP
THEY WERE ORIGINALLY PART OF THE
SHICHIJOU GROUP, BUT SECEDED TO
SIDE WITH THE MITSURUGI HOUSE.
THEY POSSESS THE SACRED SWORDS,
YATENKOU AND TSUKITENSHIN.

[N]

NANASE FAMILY
THEY ARE ONE OF THE MASTER FAMI-
LIES AND THE URA SHIMON MEMBER
FAMILY REPRESENTING THE EARTH
DRAGON.

page 81, *Shinshuu*
Shinshuu is another name for *Shinano*, which in present-day is the Nagano Prefecture.

page 81, *Kuzuryuu*
Literally, "nine-headed dragon."

page 88, *Shichijou Group*
Shichi and *jou* literally means "seven" and "stars" respectively.

page 93, *Hiyoko*
Hiyoko manjuu is a cake in the shape of a chick with a sweet bean filling.

page 93, *First bath of the year*
The Japanese have the custom of getting a fresh start to the New Year by clearing any impurities such as a dirty house and debts incurred during the year.

page 105, *Choume*
Synonymous with "street" in Japanese.

page 109, *Tonomori*
Literally, "a protector of the lord."

page 117, *Kagerou*
Literally, "heat haze."

page 126, *Spica's Spanker*
A small constellation named for its sail-like shape (specifically, a "spanker" sail) which leads to Spica, a very bright star often used for navigation. It appears to be used as a codename here.

page 126, *Laconian Key*
Though used here as a sort of codename, this was once the Greek name for the constellation Cassiopeia.

page 155, *Shiratsuyu*
Literally, "white dew."

page 156, *Kiri Fubuki*
Literally, "blizzard mist."

page 166, *Valentine's Day*
On Valentine's Day, it is traditional for women to give chocolates to men in Japan. While women can give it away out of obligation (*giri choco*), some use it to express their love (*honmei choco*) to a potential boyfriend. A month later on March 14th, known as White Day, men are expected to give a gift in return.

page 177, *Kaichou*
"Chairperson" in Japanese.

page 181, *End-of-the year gift*
There is a major gift-giving season that occurs at the end of the year called *oseibo*. People give gifts to family, friends, co-workers, or anyone who has helped them during the year.

page 184, *Kamiokande*
Kamiokande was a detector of proton decay used in the Kamioka Nucleon Decay Experiment. It was later found effective in observing solar neutrinos. Okuda is making a reference to its underground location which is in Kamioka Mining and Smelting Co. in Gifu Prefecture.

page 185, *Kurohime*
Literally, "dark princess."

page 192, *Seirou Association*
Sei and *rou* mean "celestial" and "old age" respectively.

page 192, *Yatenkou and Tsukitenshin*
Yatenkou is a natural light in a clear night sky that has no moon. *Tsukitenshin* means a full moon in a clear sky.

page 193, *Shiranui*
"Sea fire" in Japanese.

TRANSLATION NOTES

Names
The eight masters in the Mitsurugi house have family names based on numbers. For example,
Ichijou for *ichi* (one); Futami for *ni* (two), Mitsurugi for *san* (three); Shiga for *shi* (four); Goryuu
for *go* (five); Rikugou for *roku* (six); Nanase for *nana* (seven); and Yasaka for *hachi* (eight).

page 3, *Shinano*
An old province of Japan that is now present-day Nagano Prefecture.

page 8, *Gift*
The Japanese have a custom of offering food as a gift to someone who will be taking care of them.

page 9, *Oba-san*
A respectful term for an older woman who is unrelated to the speaker.

page 10, *First class ticket*
Momoka is referring to Green Car seating, which is first class on the Japanese *shinkansen*, or bullet train.

page 16, *-niichan, aniki* (page 94), *-niisan* (page 145), *oniichan* (page 182)
Terms (verying in degree of formality) used to refer to an older brother or an unrelated young man
who is senior to the speaker.

page 16, *Shimon*
Literally, "four families."

page 16, *Shinkansen*
A high-speed Japanese railway line; the train itself is sometimes referred to as a "bullet train"
because of its shape and speed.

page 17, *Ura Shimon*
Literally, "another four families."

page 30, *Hayate*
Literally, "gale."

page 53, *Ryuusui Senpuu*
Ryuu, *sui*, and *senpuu* mean "dragon," "to blow," and "whirlwind," respectively.

page 57, *Huge apartment*
Ran actually mentions the size of an apartment is *3LDK*. *LDK* stands for living room, dining room,
and kitchen, and the number preceding it indicates the number of additional rooms it has.

page 61, *House layout and room size*
A typical Japanese house has Western-style rooms with hardwood floors, a traditional Japanese room with
tatami (traditional Japanese flooring made of woven straw), a bathroom with a bathtub only, a powder
room, a kitchen, and a combination of living room and dining room. Room sizes are determined by the
number of tatami floor mats (always a uniform size) that can fit in a room.

page 61, *Oyaji*
An impolite term for a middle-aged man who is unrelated to the speaker

page 62, *HP*
"Hit Points" or "Health Points" in videogaming. 0 HP equals a game over for the player character.

page 69, *Naraku*
Literally, "abyss."

page 73, *Bentou*
A takeout or home-packed meal, typically for one person.

page 79, *Suzukaze*
Literally, "cool wind."

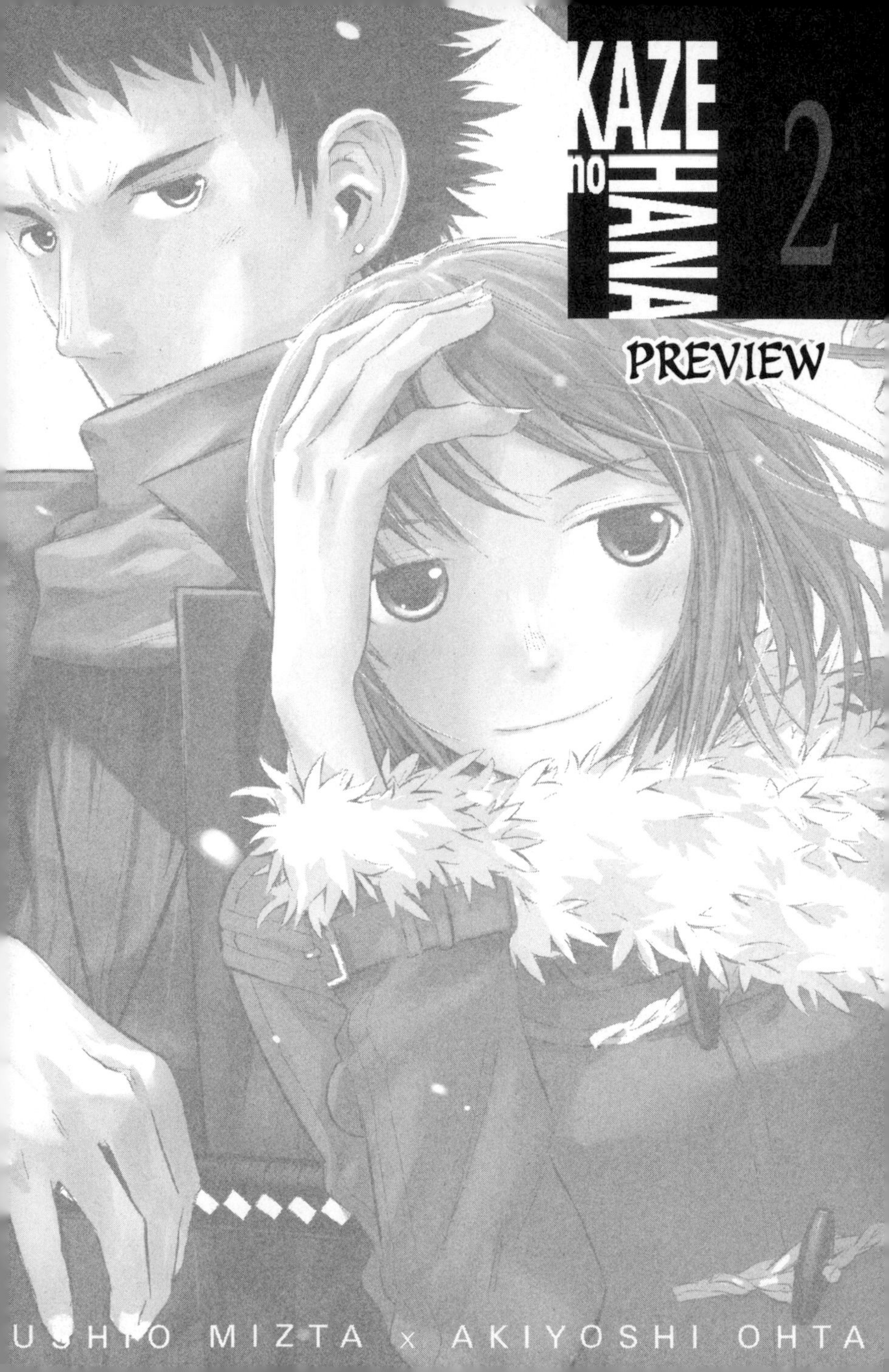
KAZE no HANA
2
PREVIEW
USHIO MIZTA x AKIYOSHI OHTA

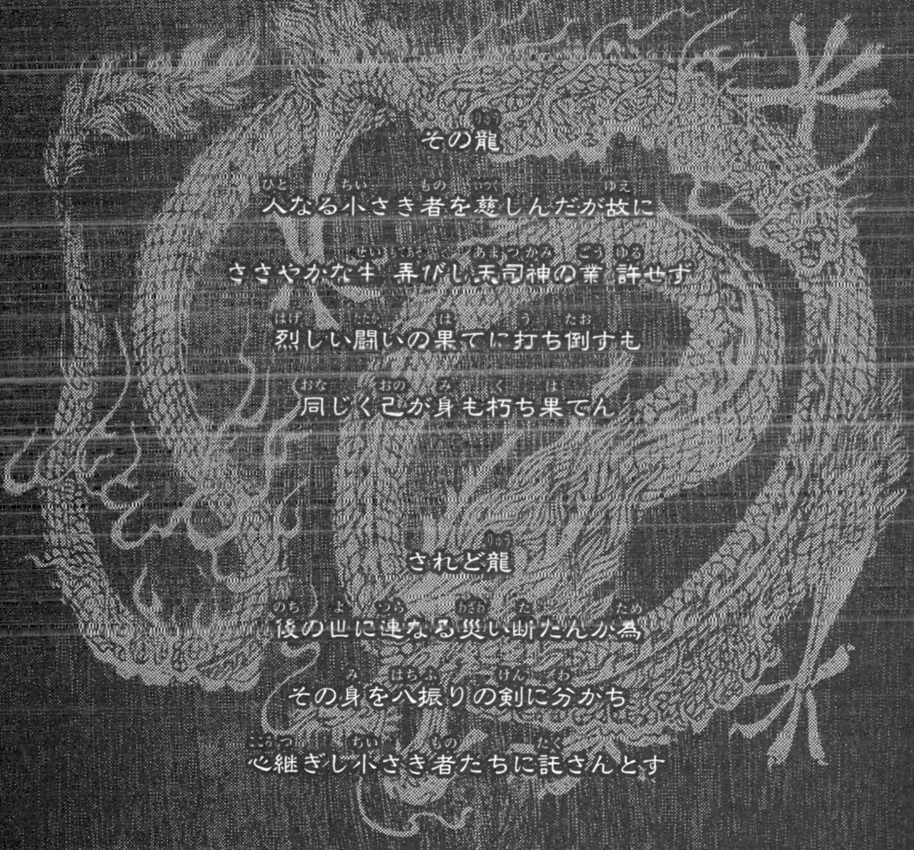

今は昔

信濃の國の峰深き地に

猛き龍ありけり

その龍

人なる小さき者を慈しんだが故に

ささやかな生 弄びし天司神の業 許せず

烈しい闘いの果てに打ち倒すも

同じく己が身も朽ち果てん

されど龍

後の世に連なる災い断たんが為

その身を八振りの剣に分かち

心継ぎし小さき者たちに託さんとす

充城市教育委員会 編

「充城市に伝わる昔話・民話」より

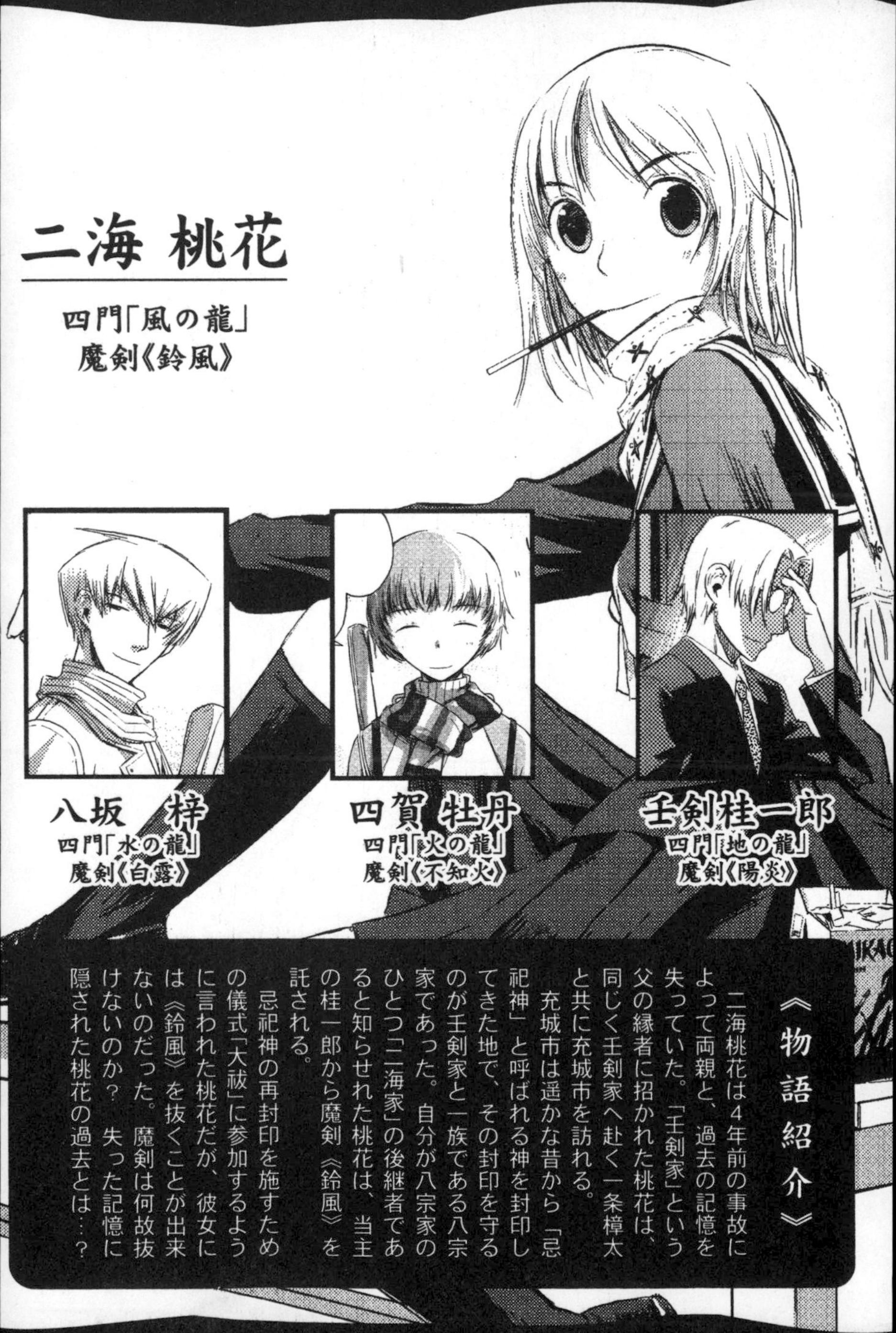
二海 桃花
四門「風の龍」
魔剣《鈴風》
八坂 梓
四門「水の龍」
魔剣《白露》
四賀 牡丹
四門「火の龍」
魔剣《不知火》
壬剣桂一郎
四門「地の龍」
魔剣《陽炎》

《物語紹介》

二海桃花は4年前の事故によって両親と、過去の記憶を失っていた。「壬剣家」という父の縁者に招かれた桃花は、同じく壬剣家へ赴く一条樟太と共に充城市を訪れる。

充城市は遥かな昔から「忌祀神」と呼ばれる神を封印してきた地で、その封印を守るのが壬剣家と一族である八宗家であった。自分が八宗家のひとつ「二海家」の後継者であると知らせれた桃花は、当主の桂一郎から魔剣《鈴風》を託される。

忌祀神の再封印を施すための儀式「大祓」に参加するように言われた桃花だが、彼女には《鈴風》を抜くことが出来ないのだった。魔剣は何故抜けないのか？ 失った記憶に隠された桃花の過去とは…？

登場人物紹介

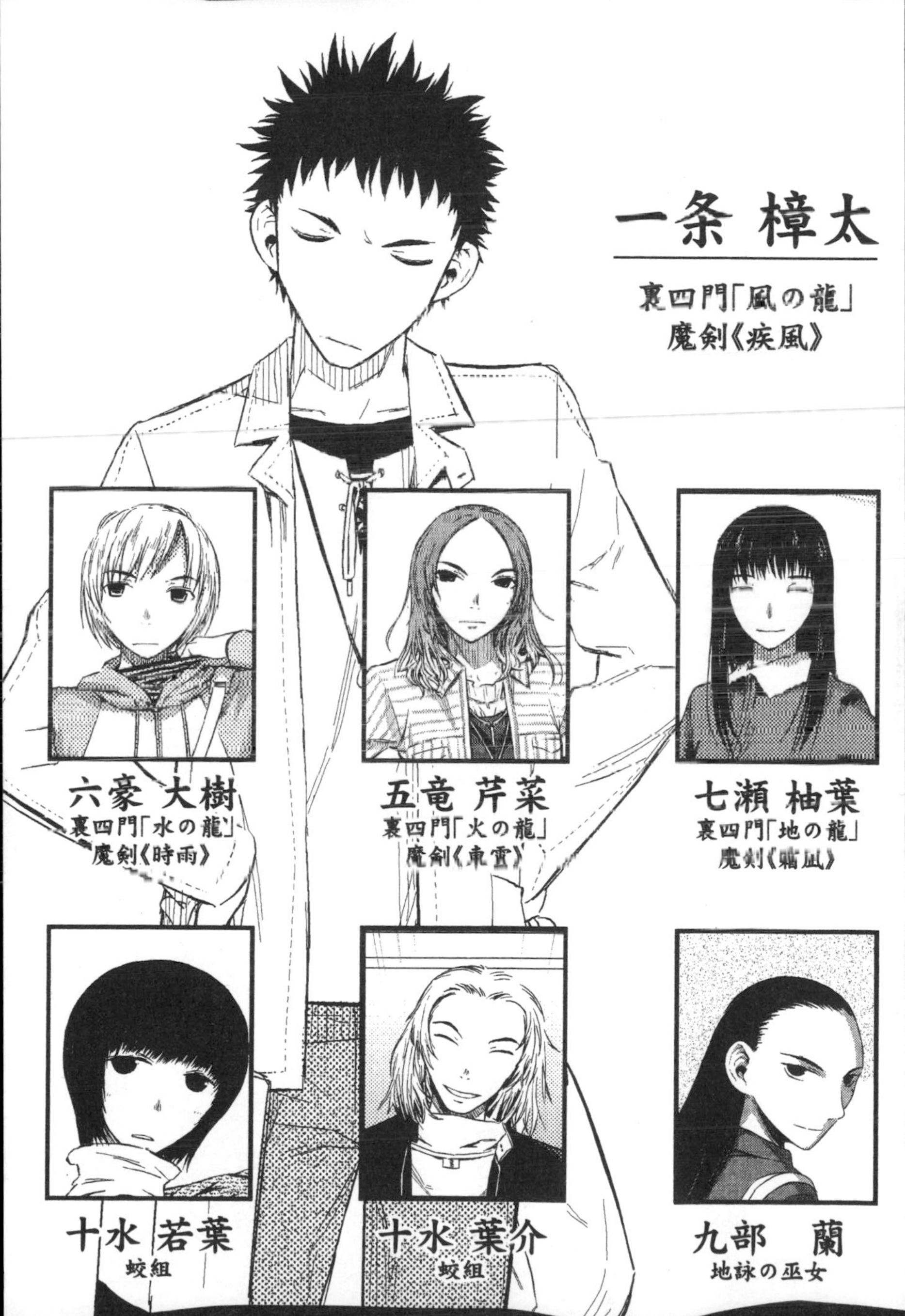
一条 樟太
裏四門「風の龍」
魔剣《疾風》
六豪 大樹
裏四門「水の龍」
魔剣《時雨》
五竜 芹菜
裏四門「火の龍」
魔剣《東雷》
七瀬 柚葉
裏四門「地の龍」
魔剣《蜩凪》
十水 若葉
蛟組
十水 葉介
蛟組
九部 蘭
地詠の巫女

登場人物紹介

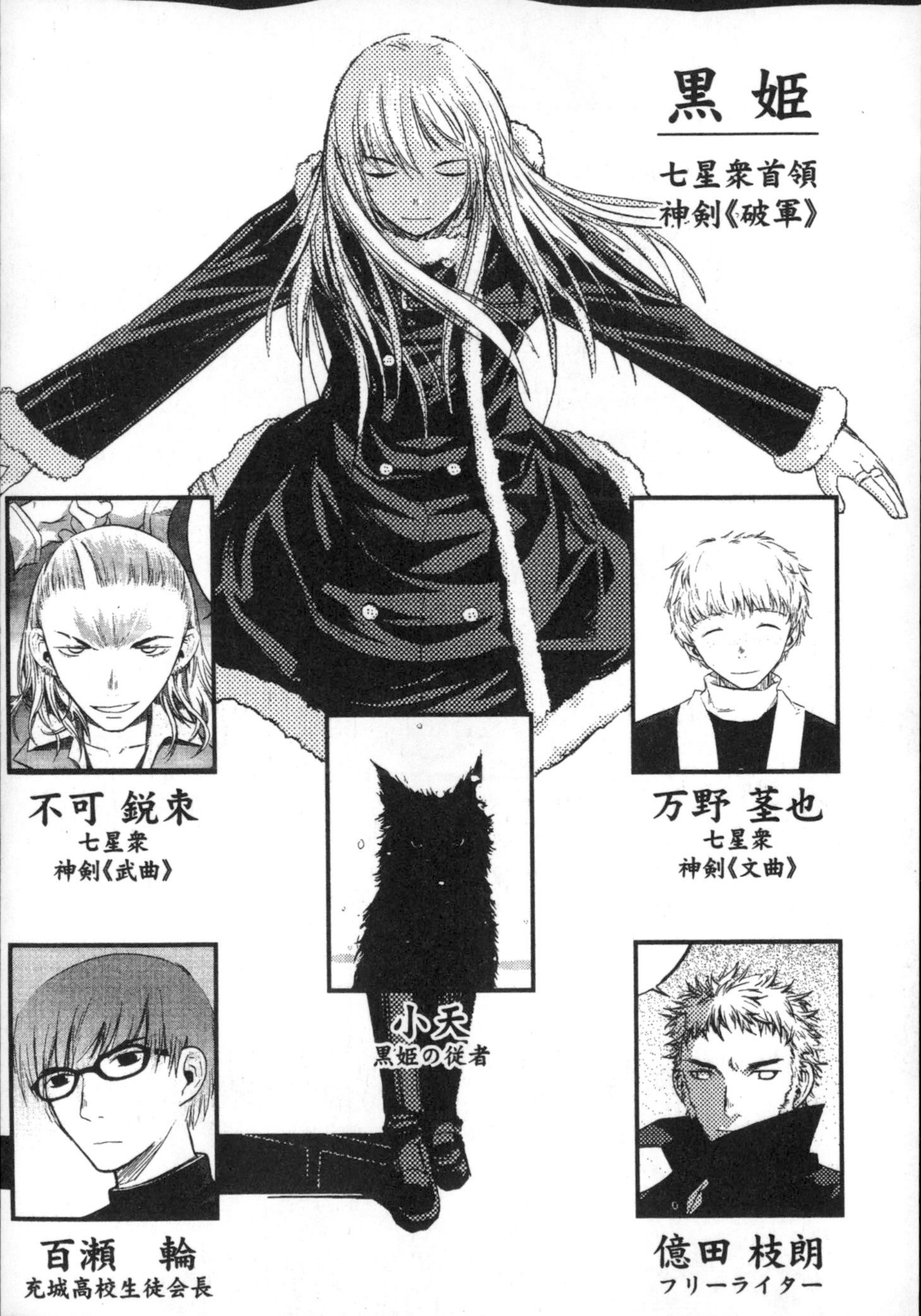
黒姫
七星衆首領
神剣《破軍》
万野 茎也
七星衆
神剣《文曲》
小天
黒姫の従者
不可 鋭東
七星衆
神剣《武曲》
億田 枝朗
フリーライター
百瀬 輪
充城高校生徒会長

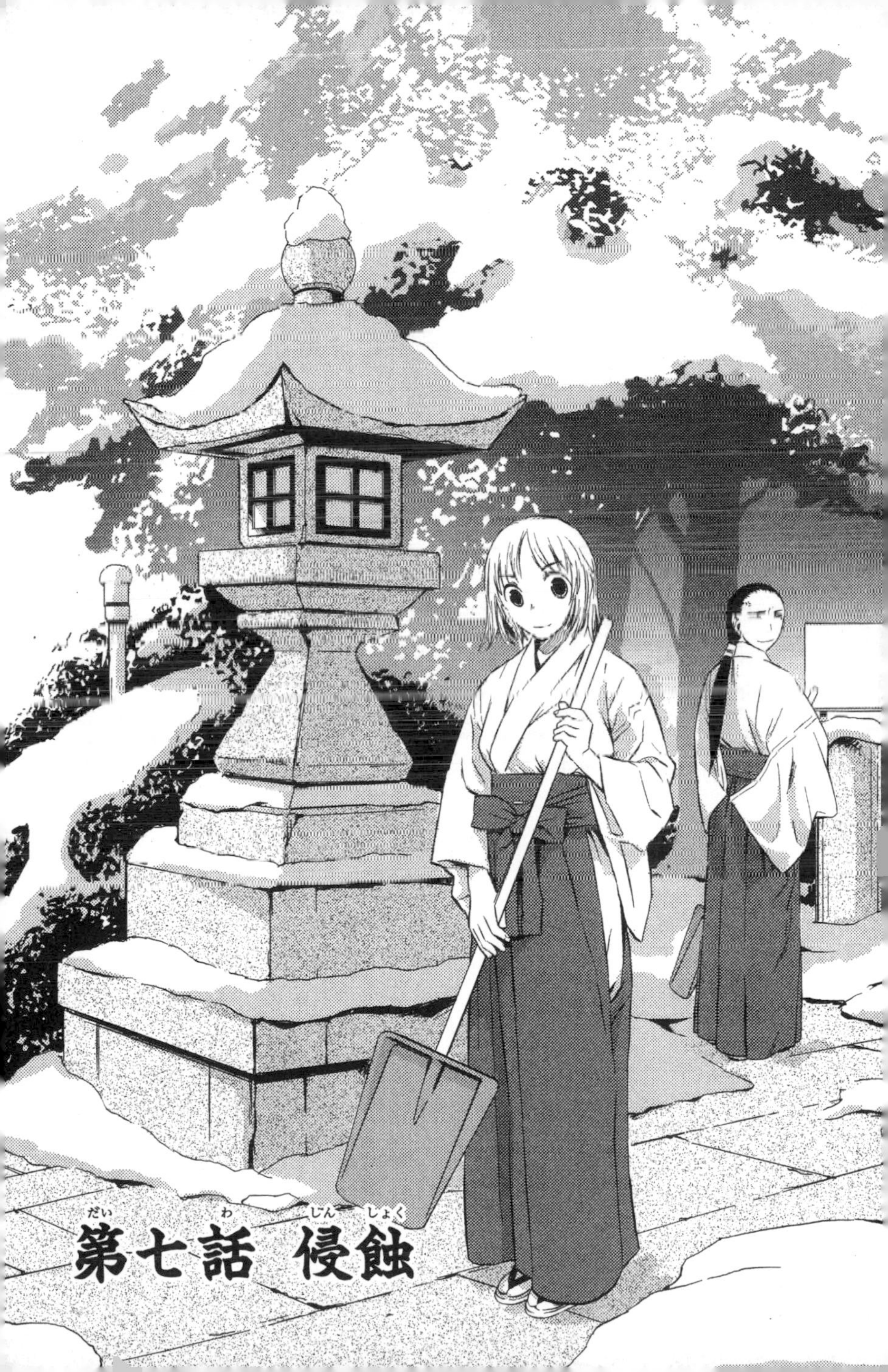
第七話　侵蝕

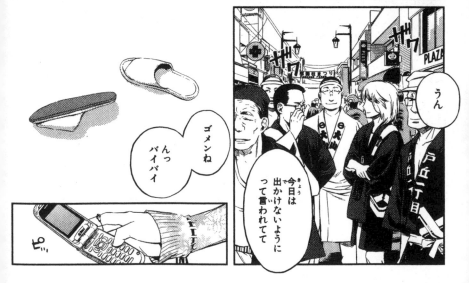

うん

ゴメンね
んっ
バイバイ

今日は
出かけないように
って言われてて

ピッ

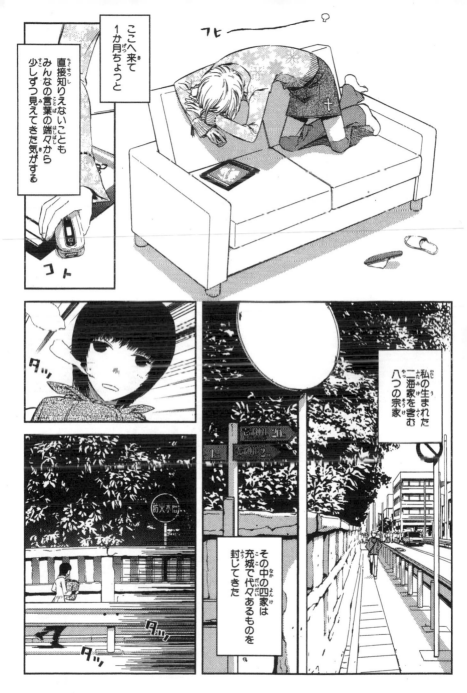

ここへ来て
1か月ちょっと

直接知りえないことも
みんなの言葉の端々から
少しずつ見えてきた気がする

フヒ————

コト

タッ

防火水槽

光神町 2
光神町 1
光神町 20

私の生まれた
二海家を宗む
八つの宗家

その中の四家は
充城で代々あるものを
封じてきた

タッ
タッ

9

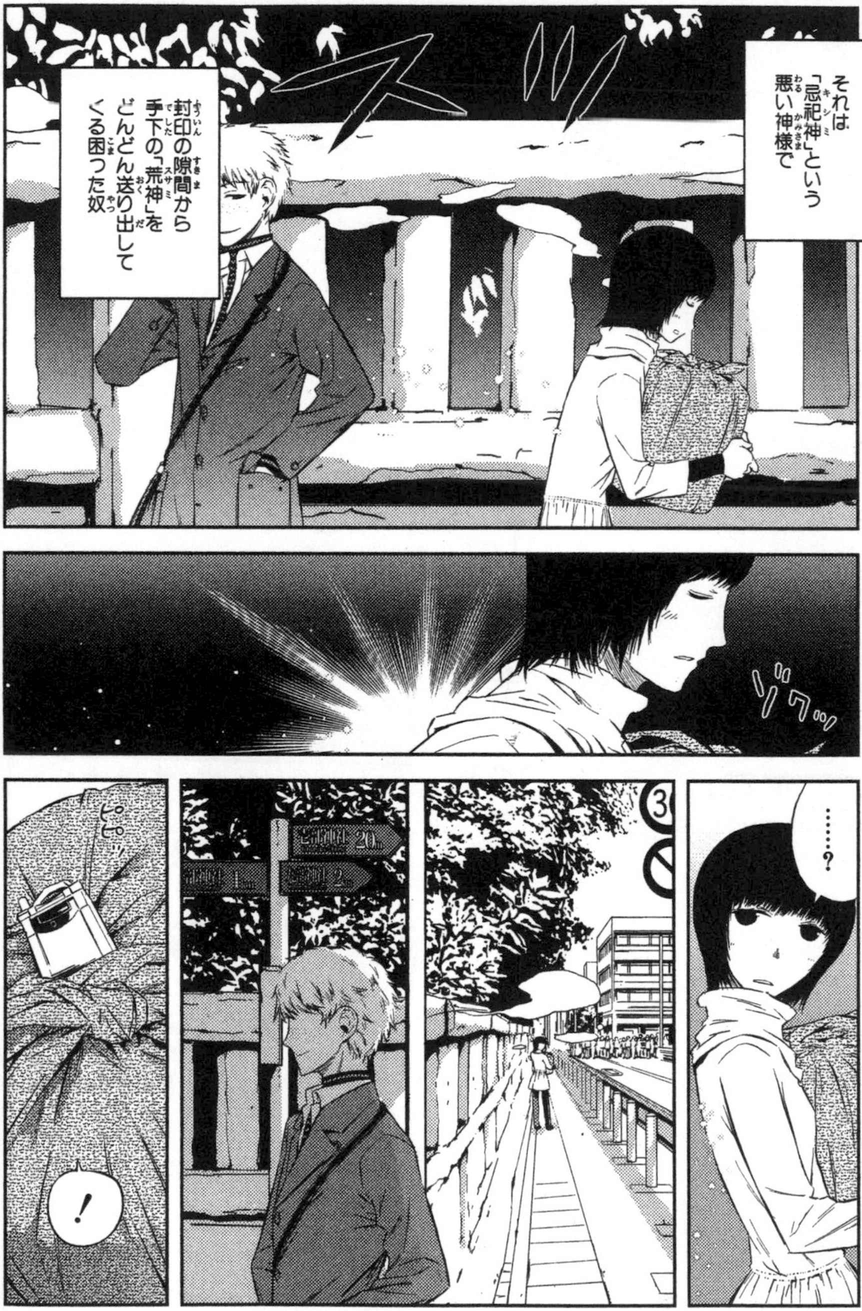
それは「忌祀神」という悪い神様で
スッ
封印の隙間から手下の「荒神」をどんどん送り出してくる困った奴
ゾクッ
……？
ピピッ
！

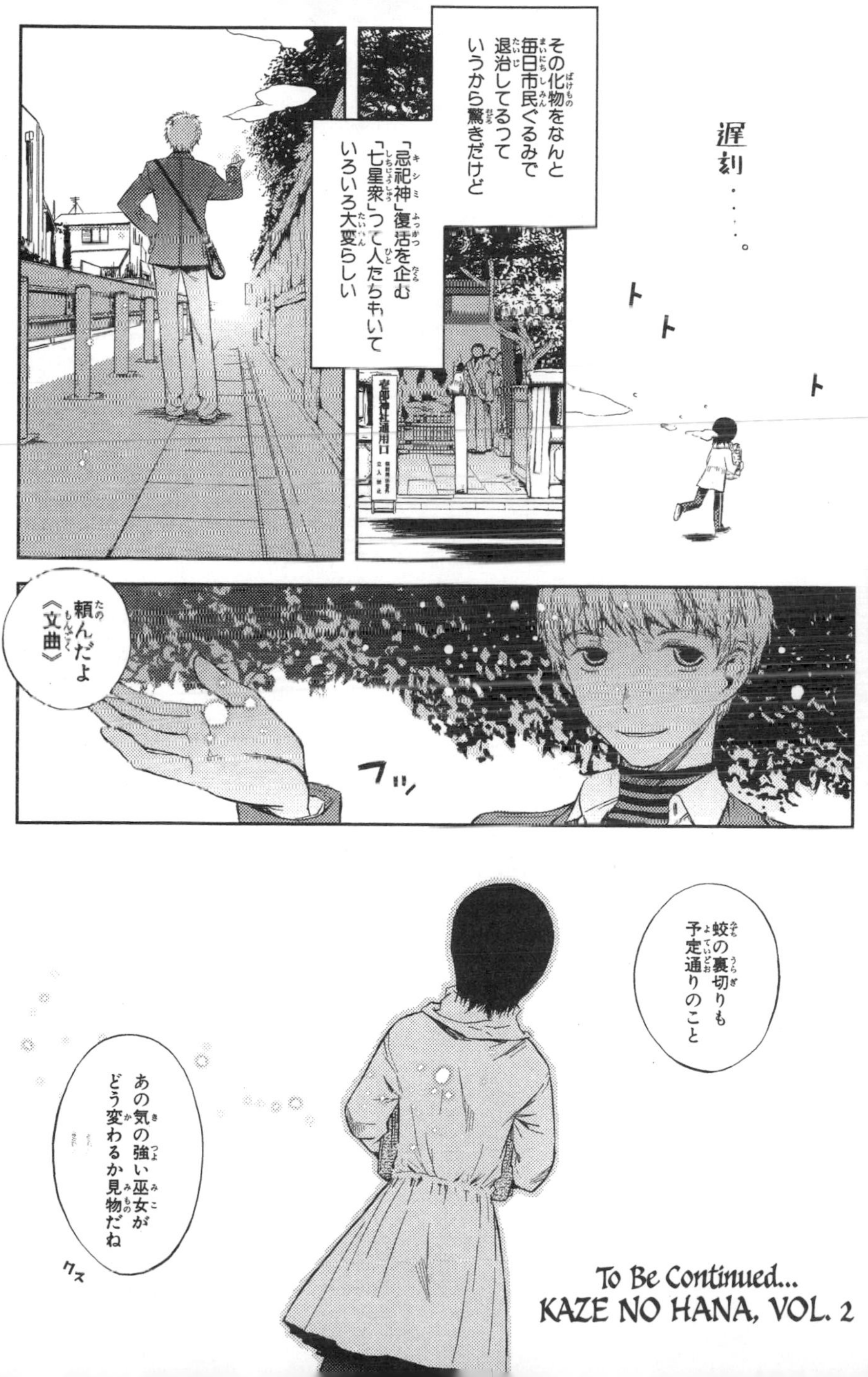
遅刻・・・・。
ト
ト
ト
その化物をなんと毎日市民ぐるみで退治してるっていうから驚きだけど
「忌祀神」復活を企む「七星衆」って人たちもいていろいろ大変らしい
頼んだよ《文曲》
フッ
蛟の裏切りも予定通りのこと
あの気の強い巫女がどう変わるか見物だね
クス
To Be Continued...
KAZE NO HANA, VOL. 2

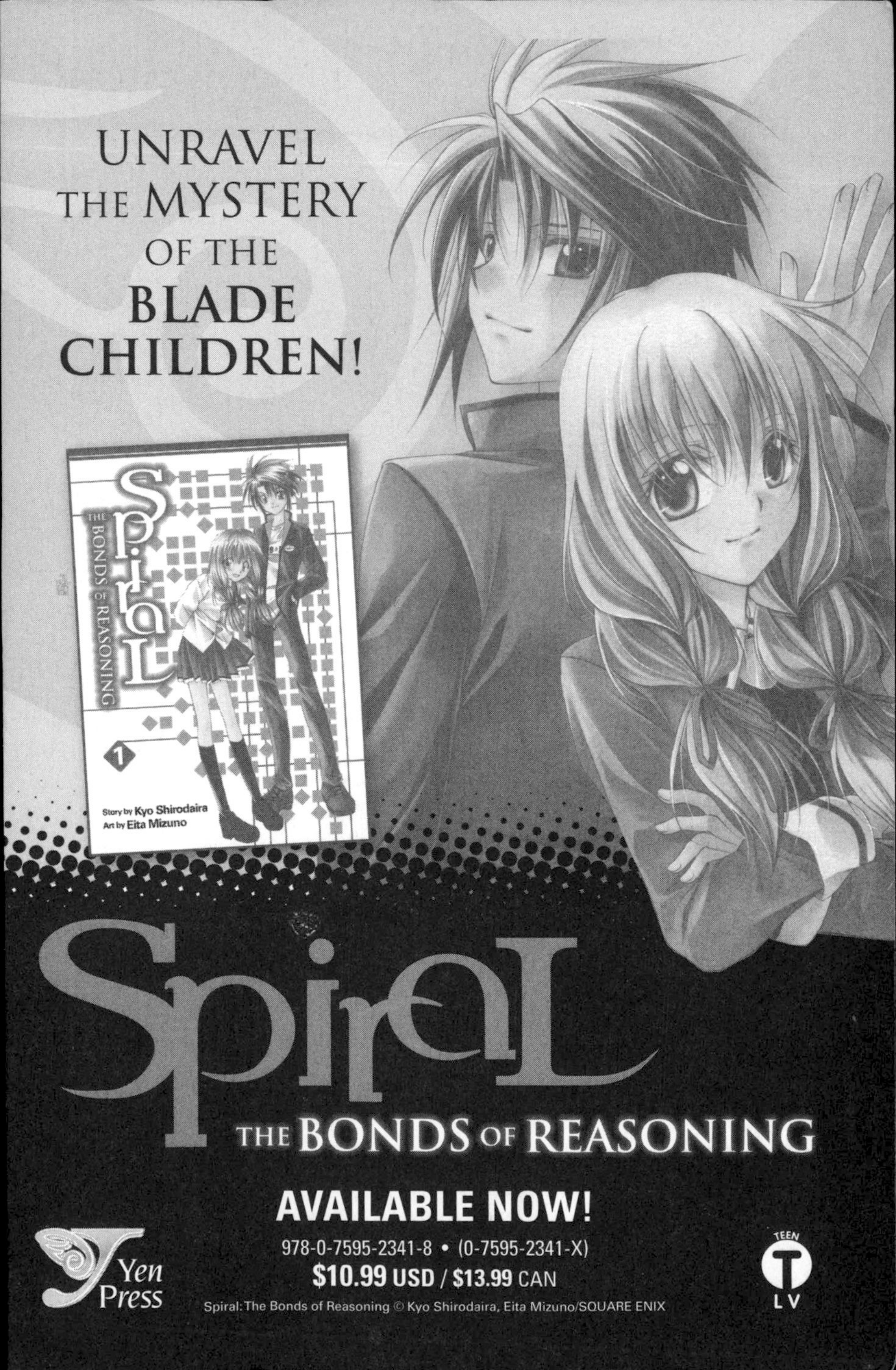
UNRAVEL THE MYSTERY OF THE BLADE CHILDREN!
Spiral THE BONDS OF REASONING 1
Story by Kyo Shirodaira
Art by Eita Mizuno
SpiraL
THE BONDS OF REASONING
AVAILABLE NOW!
978-0-7595-2341-8 • (0-7595-2341-X)
$10.99 USD / $13.99 CAN
Yen Press
Spiral: The Bonds of Reasoning © Kyo Shirodaira, Eita Mizuno/SQUARE ENIX
TEEN T LV

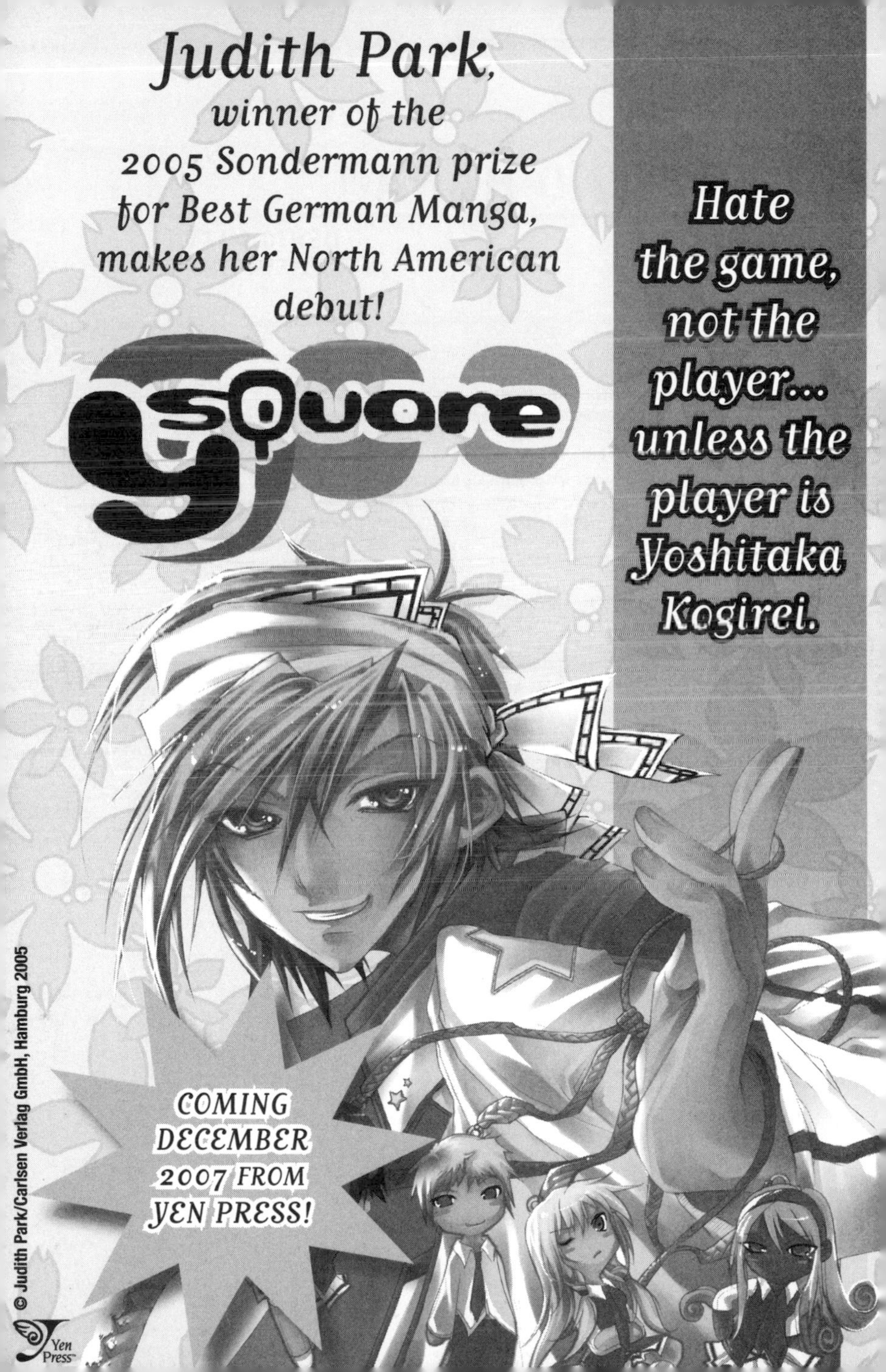
Judith Park,
winner of the
2005 Sondermann prize
for Best German Manga,
makes her North American
debut!
y square
Hate
the game,
not the
player...
unless the
player is
Yoshitaka
Kogirei.
COMING
DECEMBER
2007 FROM
YEN PRESS!
© Judith Park/Carlsen Verlag GmbH, Hamburg 2005
Yen Press

KAZE NO HANA ①

USHIO MIZTA
AKIYOSHI OHTA

Translation: Elina Ishikawa

Lettering: Alexis Eckerman

KAZE NO HANA ~MARYU HAKKEN-DEN~ Vol. 1 © USHIO MIZTA / AKIYOSHI OHTA 2004. All rights reserved. First published in Japan in 2004 by MEDIA WORKS INC., Tokyo. English translation rights in USA, Canada, and UK arranged with MEDIA WORKS INC. through Tuttle-Mori Agency, Inc., Tokyo.

Translation © 2008 by Hachette Book Group USA, Inc.

Yen Press
Hachette Book Group USA
237 Park Avenue, New York, NY 10017

Visit our Web sites at www.HachetteBookGroupUSA.com and www.YenPress.com.

Yen Press is an imprint of Hachette Book Group USA, Inc. The Yen Press name and logo is a trademark of Hachette Book Group USA, Inc.

First Yen Press Edition: April 2008

ISBN-10: 0-7595-2856-X
ISBN-13: 978-0-7595-2856-7

10 9 8 7 6 5 4 3 2 1

BVG

Printed in the United States of America